Home Again Home Again

A Vienna LaFontaine Novel

JULIANA ANDREW

ISBN 978-1-959895-43-5 (paperback)
ISBN 978-1-959895-42-8 (eBook)

Dedicated to Roy,
The man who made my
Fairy Tale Love Story
Real

Thanks to my Great Granddaughter
Vienna Ferguson {age 10}
For her Fairy Story

Also by Juliana Andrew
Vienna 2013
The Curse if the Infinity Bracelets 2014
Seventh Crossing 2015
The Ladies of Avanloch 2016
The Arcadia Project 2017
Beyond the Yellow Doors 2020
November Queen 2020 Author Photo
Karren Almstrom Dixon

PROLOGUE

On June 11th nineteen hundred and sixty, Vienna LaFontaine met Rainey Quinn. She fell hopelessly in love with him. She and her family had moved to the township of Bridge Falls six months earlier. She was sixteen. Rainey was twenty-one and from Hawthorne, a small hamlet twenty five miles away. He was in the final years of fulfilling his dreams of becoming an architect. The Labor Day weekend saw Vienna confessing her love for him. He was not ready for such a commitment and told her that he wasn't good enough for her and that she must forget him and to find someone worthy of her love. Half- heartedly she started a new relationship with Jack Jennings. Their plans for New Year's Eve were interrupted when Rainey called her and asked if she would go to the dance with him in Hawthorne. Against her better judgement, she went. Life was never the same for her and Rainey after that fabled evening. He continued to break her heart several times over while away at university. She always forgave him, and in the summer of nineteen sixty one they became lovers. Rainey never once told her that he loved her. He went off to Italy to further his education in the fall as an architecture exchange student promising her that he would write her every day.

Miscommunication sent Vienna off to Scotland to live with her aunt in Scotland when she discovered that she was pregnant with Rainey's child. Her location was to remain a secret from everyone except her family who vowed not to disclose it. Rainey returned and was broken hearted to find her gone. He did search for her in Wales as that is where she had always talked about going to live, but was unsuccessful in finding her. His grief was overwhelming, and he took to the bottle. He returned to Italy and had a meaningless relationship with a woman whose name was Zeta. His dream of owning his own architectural business materialized when he returned to Vancouver and met Louise whose father had influence in the business. He married her knowing full well that the marriage would not last as he was not in love with her. He sired two boys with her, Morgan and Mason. He moved out when he believed that the boys were old enough to get along without him. He entered into a lustful relationship with Jorja, a woman that came close to destroying him.

Vienna never stopped loving Rainey, but went on to have a loveless and sexless marriage with Lord Jeremy McAllister, and became the Mistress of Avanloch Castle. She adopted Jeremy's daughter Rosalyn, and gave birth to Rainey's child whom she named Ava. The castle was a wondrous place and held many secrets. Vienna embraced them all and was a magnet for the departed souls that roamed the corridors. Ten years later on a trip to Vancouver, she came close to contacting Rainey, but could not go through with it. She suffered through many bouts of depression. The full extent of the consequences would not be fully realized for many years.

Vienna returned to Bridge Falls several times over the years as her family and forever friends Lara and Jimmy were still there. Still, she was secretive as to where her home was. A chance encounter at a winter carnival in Hawthorne brought her face to face with Rainey. Twenty one years had not diminished their feelings for one another. Rainey divorced Louise and Vienna and he married and made Avanloch their home.

Rainey had bought three antique bracelets in 1961 intending on giving them to Vienna for Christmas only to find her gone when he returned from Italy. He kept them and gave them to her when they were united. These bracelets were called the Infinity Bracelets and had a legacy all their own. They had been made for Anton Christoval, a valued member of Queen Isabella's legion in the 1800's, for his wife Katarina. He had met her in Andorra while recuperating at a monastery for wounds that he had acquired fighting in the war against the Carlists. It was rumored that Katarina and her daughter had been murdered, and the bracelets which were of great wealth had been stolen off her lifeless body. Vienna knew of these bracelets and wanted to find an ancestor of Katarina's so she could return them where she felt they belonged. Vienna's passion to do so led her and Rainey to Spain with friend Roberge, and then to Andorra where the unthinkable happened. Vienna disappeared during a freak earthquake and was lost for almost two years. She had been taken unconscious to Verde El Mar Spain by helicopter by a powerful and secretive man Anton DeMarco who was searching for the missing hundred year old bracelets.

Vienna was in a coma for several months and when she awoke had no idea who she was. Anton claimed her as his wife Katarina and the father of her unborn child. In his delusional mind he believed that he and Kat were reincarnations of the fabled Anton and Kat.

Rainey and Vienna's family never gave up hope that she would be found, and she was, thanks to Stu, a long- time friend of Rainey's. Now, a year later with adopted daughters, Zoe and Tanny, and Lilianna, {the child of Rainey's that Vienna gave birth to in Spain} and newly born twins, Novia and Zander they are leaving Scotland to return to where they first met in Bridge Falls, British Columbia, Canada. They leave behind Rosalyn and her husband Evan to reign over Avanloch Castle, dear friends Amma and Johnny, who manage the estate, Mary and Duffy, and Vienna's special friend Meggie Magan.

References throughout novel:

Maveryn is Rosalyn's mother. She lies in the family crypt and is the resident ghost of the castle.

Miss Mary or Miss Mary's closet: Miss Mary was Rosalyn's great grandmother; her father Jeremy McAllister's grandmother. Her room was left intact when she died including a wardrobe of timeless designer clothes which Vienna wears from time to time.

Avaleena: Mistress of Avanloch circa 1850's. She has appeared to Vienna and Rainey and led them to her diary in a clandestine room in the cellars. Vienna translated this diary and the history and lineage of Avanloch was brought to light.

Tatylyanna {Taty} was once engaged to Rosalyn's father Jeremy. Mary McDuff dubbed her "The Black Russian." Their engagement was dissolved when he learned that she was only marrying him for his money and planning on using it to regain wealth to her family in Russia. She refused to leave Avanloch and mysteriously lost her life on the grand stairway. However, her evil soul remained and took up residence in room 6 until her daughter came to retrieve it.

Meggie Magan Friend, Mystic, Sage, spiritualist. Known for Tarot card reading, therapeutic potions, and salves.

Somner Vienna's friend from Verde El Ma; Anton DeMarco's right hand man.

Part 1

 **aircademia**

yeah libraries are cool but have you ever found a library with a secret doorway disguised as a bookshelf that leads to a smaller, hidden library filled with ancient books full of mysteries and forgotten knowledge? me neither and i'm sad about it

CHAPTER 1

AVANLOCH CASTLE

August 17th, 1984

Atlantia came to a halt as I gently tugged on the reins a few feet before the drop-off at Widow's Hummock. I leaned forward and caressed her silky mane. "I'm going to miss you ole girl. You've been my friend and taken me to places on this majestic estate that I could never have reached without you. I'm hoping Rosalyn will exercise you once in a while." I slid down off her back, threw the reins over her shoulders and told her to go indulge in the lush green meadow. I plunked myself down onto a bed of dense clover and surveyed the valley that stretched all the way to Widow's Peak. It was only August and yet the tip of the mountain was snow laden. I had never been beyond the range as it was a great distance away and covered some very rugged ground. Millerfloss River dipped and wound its' way around the lowlands until it found its' way to McClaren Inlet which would eventually reach its' destination which was the North Atlantic Sea. Tomorrow I would cross that same ocean with Rainey and our family to start life anew in Bridge Falls, the town where he and I had met so many years ago. I picked up a handful of clover and rustled through them hoping to find a four leafed one.

I knew he was behind me even before he put his hands on my shoulders. He always thought he could sneak up on me, but he never could. I suppose it came from years of always being alert to the vibrations and the voices that echoed throughout the silences of the castle which no one else heard but me.

"Am I intruding Vienna?" He asked in his usual courteous voice.

I placed my hands on his. "Of course not; I knew you would come. I just wanted a head start."

"Well, you left me enough clues but I still had to guess as to where you were actually going."

"Didn't Liliana tell you?"

"I haven't seen her since breakfast. Amma took all the girls for a final walk around the village. What was she supposed to tell me?"

"She was supposed to meet you with the picnic basket and give you a note. Who's looking after the twins, or did Amma take them in their prams on the walk?"

"Rosy has the twins. I didn't get any note, but found my riding boots by the back door when Mary handed me the picnic basket. I asked her where I was supposed to meet you, but she hadn't a clue. Lucky guess that I figured that you might be here. What did the note say?"

"Why did you think I would be here?"

"I don't actually know…maybe because it's the first place you brought me three years ago, and I know it is a favorite of yours. I'm pretty attuned to you, you know."

"I know; I'll let you guess about the note until Lili gives it to you."

"What makes you so sure that she still has it?"

"I saw her put it in her pocket. Shall we have lunch?"

Rainey opened the basket and commented that there wasn't much in it except apples.

"The horses have to eat too. Who are you entrusting Arabesque to in your absence?"

"Evan as he would want to keep him and Atlantia together. Has Rosy agreed to become her mistress?" He asked as he passed me a sandwich. "Whose idea was it that we should dine on peanut butter and jam?"

I laughed. "Your daughter's"

"I have several so you will have to be more specific than that." He said smiling cheekily.

"Your favorite, of course."

"I don't have a favorite."

"Please pour me a cup of milk so I might wash away this sticky stuff. You know Liliana is your favorite. She had you wrapped around her little fingers from the moment you laid eyes on her, and nothing has changed."

"I can't deny that, but she's not the only one who has me wrapped around her finger."

"Pray tell who the other damsel is?" I asked demurely.

"You know perfectly well that it's you. Do you want to make out… you know we won't be back this way for quite some time?"

I pushed him away playfully. "In front of the horses; don't be silly! Finish your sandwich as we have many stops to make and the day is already half over."

"May I inquire where we are off to My Lady?"

"I want to go to Gypsy Hollow and pay my respects to Mollie Magan, and then to the cabin as I have something to give Meggie."

"What is that?"

"You will see my dear."

"You are such a tease." Rainey exclaimed as he gave me a heave-ho onto Atlantia.

We stopped in an open field where heather and thistle bloomed abundantly. Rainey dismounted and picked a large bouquet of heather and a few sprigs of thistle. We deposited them on Mollie's burial plot after I had cleaned the dead vegetation off. I blew her a kiss.

"Rainey and I, along with our brood are off on a new adventure back to our homeland my dear friend. You taught me much about life and customs here in this majestic land and I will carry you and its memories close to my heart forever. Someday I will return and visit your realm again."

I was a little misty eyed as we walked our horses down the trodden path to Mollie's old cottage which was now inhabited by her granddaughter Meggie. We found her tending to the herb and medicinal plants in the back garden. Rainey said he would give us some privacy as I visited with her.

"Nonsense," I said, "you are just as big of part of this as I am. I hope you will agree that this is the right thing to do."

I coaxed Meggie to take a break and sit with us for a few minutes on an old wooden bench. She wanted to make us coffee but I declined saying that we had much to do before we left for Bridge Falls tomorrow. I reached into my jodhpurs and pulled out an envelope.

"What's this then?" She asked as I handed it to her.

"Read it and you shall see." I directed.

She squinted as she read, and then looked at me wide-eyed. "Is this true My Lady; you are deeding this property to me? What have I done to deserve this?"

"This should have been deeded to your family a long time ago. You and Mollie, and her parents before her have cared for this unique piece of land for over a century. You have shared the fairylike brook, the enchanting Gypsy Hollow, and the wonderful healing plants with everyone who comes calling. It is high time that this property be known by its rightful title, that being Magan's Meadows. You shall always be protected by Avanloch overseers and need only to call should you ever have any problems. Johnny O'Shea will be only too happy to assist you."

"But I shall not live forever, and my children would not be interested, so what will happen then, or even when I am too old and feeble to care for the land?" Meggie questioned.

"Oh, silly ole goose, you are way ahead of yourself and worrying for nothing. Is not Millie a distant relative? I know the two of you argue about everything just as Mollie and she did, but I think she, or one of her children would be delighted to be named as your heir. It would be nice to keep it in the family don't you think? If that is not to your liking, or proves impossible then it can revert back to Avanloch...are you all right with that?"

"Yes, yes I am, but what does it all mean?"

"It means that this cabin and all the land that surrounds it... approximately six acres wouldn't you say Rainey?"

"Yes, I believe that it is depicted in the archives as "the six acre field"; the lands that border Miller Creek northwest of Avanloch, surrounded by old growth forests of Black Alder, Aspen, Oak and Gean. I must admit I do not know what the latter looks like."

"Aah," Meggie sighed, "the gean". It is a white spring flowering wild sweet cherry. Sweet Cherry is its' more common name. I grow dizzy recalling its delicate scent."

"A cherry tree...did you know that Vienna?" Rainey asked inquisitively.

"Of course I did, and I have pointed them out to you when we have ridden through the glen in the spring. The blossoms from those trees are what Mollie helped me concoct a fragrance from in my early days at Avanloch."

"Why have you not asked my help in reviving the perfume Vienna?" Meggie asked.

"I gave up wearing it many years ago." I said smiling sadly at Rainey. "Anyhow, enough; we must take our leave. Remember Meggie, Rosalyn now takes my place as Mistress of Avanloch, and is available to you for anything you might need or want."

She held me at arms- length after we had embraced each other. "Come close Rainey…I need to see the two of you together as I fear it will be many days before you pass by this way again. Yes, just as I suspected, your energy fields radiate the colors of love and happiness. Together your auras are a virtual rainbow of colors."

"Rainey laughed. "I have an aura now do I?"

Meggie shuddered, and mumbled in my ear. "Something wicked this way comes. Be ever vigilant my dear; be very wary of a she wolf at your doorstep."

I wasn't sure I had heard her right so I asked her to say it again.

"Nothing, nothing…be off with you now. I will keep you ever in my prayers."

Rainey asked me what that was all about. I told him I had no idea, and that it was just Meggie being Meggie. We rode back to the stables and let the groom deal with our horses. We usually enjoyed rubbing them down and combing them, but we were a little pressed for time, so we surrendered them somewhat guiltily. We were halfway up the path that led to Avanloch when Rainey put his hand on my arm and stopped me.

"Where do you think Tanny is off to?"

I followed his gaze. Sure enough there was Tanny toting what looked like a suitcase at the bottom of the driveway. Three more steps and she would be through the gate.

I called out to her. "Tanny, where are you going?"

She ignored me so I called out again a little louder. She kept walking.

"TANNY!" Rainey yelled, "Did you not hear your mother?"

He had left the path and was hurriedly walking down the drive. I had to run to catch up to him. Once again he asked her in a stern voice where she was going.

She turned around to confront us and said that she was going to the Village.

"Haven't you just been there with Amma? Why are you going back, and why are you toting a suitcase, and why didn't you answer your mother?" Rainey asked harshly.

"Well, Vienna is not really my mother, but she wants to take me away from my real mother so I am not going with you to Canada. I am going to stay here. You won't miss me because you have lots of your own children." She spoke without batting an eyelash, but didn't look at us directly. She asked if she could go now and picked up her suitcase.

I could tell that Rainey was about to explode so I interjected quickly.

"Actually Darling, I am your mother and Rainey is your father. We adopted you because we wanted to because we loved you and we wanted you to be part of our family, and if you stay behind, we will all be very sad. You know all that Tanny, but if you don't want to be a part of our family any longer than I will understand. Who are you going to live with in the village?"

Rainey looked at me as if I had lost my marbles. "Are you serious Vienna? You can't just let our daughter make her own decision as to where she is going to live. March right back to the house young lady… that's an order…get a move on."

"Mommy said I can stay if I want." Tanny said defiantly.

"Oh, now she's your mother is she? I minute ago you said she wasn't." Rainey fumed. "Make up your mind, is she your mother or not, and just who am I?"

Tanny had moved close to me. She looked up at me. "You are my mother too Vienna, but I can't leave my other mother behind. There is no one here to look after her."

I bent down to her level. "Your mother isn't here anymore Tanny. She does not lie beneath that cold stone. She went to heaven a few years ago, but she is still with you." I touched her heart. "She is here within you, and you can take her with you wherever you go. You know what, I think she would very much like to go to Canada with you, and Rainey and I very much want you to go too. You are our very special little girl because we chose you specifically to be ours. You would break our hearts if you didn't come with us and Liliana…oh, what would she do without you?

You are the only one she listens to half the time. I don't think we can manage her without you."

"Oh Vienna," Tanny laughed, "she's not that bad!"

Rainey had caught on that the way to handle Tanny was with kid gloves. He reached down and scooped her up in his arms. "Oh yes, she is **that** bad!"

"She always listens to you too Rainey. I would be really lonely without her."

"Wouldn't you miss me and Vienna too?"

"I think I would, but I am a little scared to go on that big airplane."

"I am a little scared of that plane too so I guess we'll both just have to sit on Rainey's knee so he can protect us, what do you say?"

"You might be too big Vienna."

"Oh, I think I can handle the both of you. Now how about you and me go up to Vienna's rose garden and pick a few dozen roses and take them to your Mum?"

Tanny's eyes lit up. "Can we Vienna?"

"Of course you can. Flowers are to be picked and enjoyed. Will you pick her a white one for me? How about if we asked Rosy to pick her flowers after we go?"

"I will Mommy. Come on Daddy; let's go before it starts to rain."

There wasn't a cloud in the sky. Rainey smiled at me and nodded towards the mausoleum as he knew I had planned on visiting Maveryn before we left. I told him that there was no need as I was taking her with me. I patted my heart and walked with them up the drive until they took their leave for the gardens. I walked up the front steps and surveyed the view beyond the gates. Oh, how I was going to miss it all! I turned and stroked the heads of the stone lions that guarded the entrance to Avanloch. "I trust you to look after Rosalyn and all else who dwell in this castle while I am gone. I will come home again as often as I can and one day this will be my final resting place." I patted Zeus and Zoar again smiling as I remembered Rosy telling me that it was she who had named them so many years ago. I entered the four digits into the key pad under the lion head knocker on the front door and let myself in hoping no one would be in the hallway. Rainey and Johnny had installed this security feature on all the doors after I had been rescued from Anton in Verde El

Mar. The back door was the only one that was always unlocked during the day. I had never thought it was necessary, but of course I was out voted.

I closed the heavy oak door as quietly as I could and made an attempt to kick my riding boots off. I was not successful, so I wiped them off as best I could. I needed a few minutes of solitude and headed to the parlour. I walked over to the French doors and pulled the lacy panels open so I had an unrestricted view of Brackenshire Manor, the stables and workshops. Had it really been twenty four years since I had fled Bridge Falls? I was seventeen at the time and had no intention of informing Rainey that I was pregnant with his child because I believed he didn't love me, and I didn't want to sabotage his career dreams. I planned on telling him someday, but time went by and I fell in love with Avanloch and my life here. I put Rainey on the back burner until it was too late. But, twenty years later we had finally been reunited, and now we were returning to the place where we had met and leaving Avanloch behind. It had been my idea to return to Canada. I had pooh-poohed all of Rainey's reasons why it wasn't a good idea. I had been pampered and treated like a queen at Avanloch. He was afraid that I wouldn't be able to hold up under the pressure of running a household and raising five children on my own. He would be right beside me every step of the way, but it still wouldn't be the same. There would not be a houseful of hand-maidens to do the laundry, make the beds, clean the house or help with the children. There would be no Amma to run the household, to do the banking and keep the books, and do the grocery shopping, and there certainly wasn't going to be a Mary McDuff to run the kitchen. There also was not going to be anyone like Johnny. My reasoning was that I could do all of that with his help, and surely there would be many ladies in Bridge who were looking for employment by an aristocratic family. Rainey had laughed at that saying that we would not be regarded as such outside of Scotland. I had told him that I planned on taking my title with me. I would become Mistress of the Palace just as I had long been Mistress of Avanloch.

We had had many discussions of the same over the last six months. Rainey always threw a new wrench into the plan, but I was persistent, and even more so when he admitted that it had always been his dream that we would return "home" one day to raise our children, and build me the house he had promised me. Yes, I was positive that I wanted to go. I wanted to go yesterday…but this was today; one day before the last, and I wasn't so sure. I wasn't sure at all.

I slid the curtains back into place and walked around the room lovingly touching each piece of furniture, figurine and art work. I settled myself in my colossal yellow armchair, and picked up one of my favorite books of poetry from the end table. I held it close to my breast and closed my eyes... so many memories…so many memories.

I watched as the last twenty three years unfolded quickly before me like a movie on a projection screen. The day I met Rainey, our first kiss, how we had both smelled cherry blossoms, the first time we made love, the day he waved good- bye as I boarded the bus home from spending a weekend with him in Vancouver before he shipped out to Italy for four months of study. It never entered my mind that it would be the last time I would see him for many years. The images before me had started out in color, but gradually shifted to grey as my life went from happiness and hope to one of uncertainty and sadness as I made plans to go to Scotland. I saw myself warning my parents not to reveal where I was going or my pregnancy to anyone, especially Rainey, or they would never see me again. I saw tears of relief running down my face when I slipped into the arms of Aunt Jannie as I got off the train at Waverly, being welcomed by Mrs. Sharp, Millie and Emma at Brackenshire Manor. I smiled as Rosalyn, the little red haired lass who told me that I was her new Mama and assumed herself into my life turning it into a rainbow of colors again. She was the daughter of my dear deceased friend Maveryn whom I had met when I was twelve years old on one of my visits to Scotland with my mother. Rosalyn was three years old and lived at Avanloch Castle with an absentee father, Lord Jeremy McAllister. A stern nanny was her caretaker. I soon saw to her firing and took Rosalyn to Brackenshire to live with me. Rainey's and my daughter, Ava Lane was born in May. I agreed to marry Lord Jeremy in July and made a home for the girls at the castle. Ours was not a marriage of love, but of convenience. We never shared the marriage bed. Jeremy was still in love with Maveryn, and I, Rainey. Having a secure future for my girls was all that mattered, but I was soon made aware that as Mistress of Avanloch, I had responsibilities. I wanted nothing to do with the financial aspects of the estate. Jannie's husband, Uncle John was Jeremy's solicitor and accountant, so most of the holdings of the estate and McAllister Holdings were handled by him, but I was to have a say in anything pertinent. I learned to accept my role, but abstained from the business end as much as I could and delegated wherever and whenever. I was glad to be leaving that part behind. Rainey had promised me that he would be in charge of finances in Bridge Falls which suited me just fine.

Nothing would ever compare with the first time Maveryn made her appearance. I had thought I had felt her presence the night Ava was born at Brackenshire Manor, and once as a fleeting vision at the bottom of the castle stairs one stormy evening not long after I had married Jeremy. She appeared to Rosy, Ava and me many times throughout the years. Rainey still doubts that he also saw her, but is more a believer since Evan, our son-in-law, swears that Maveryn had alerted him to save me from certain death as I lie haemorrhaging on the path to the crypt. The twins and I would not be alive today if it wasn't for Maveryn and Evan.

What was that? Something jarred me out of my dream-like state. Someone was calling me, but the voices were far away. It was probably one of the children…I closed my eyes again and watched the screen as the years sped quickly by marked with remembrances of the people who had enhanced my life throughout the years. In the early years there was Aunt Jannie and Uncle John, and the staff at Brackenshire. After I married Lord Jeremy, Amma and Johnny O'Shea became my best friends. Amma was the administrative of Avanloch, and her husband Johnny was the manager of the estate. They and the McDuffs were the heart and soul of the whole domain. Mary McDuff ran the kitchen and anything else delegated her way. Her hubby, known as Duffy wore many hats around the estate. Oh, there standing at the front entrance was my dear friend, Mollie Magan. Prophet, soothsayer, clairvoyant, physic, fortune-teller…all these descriptions had been used by many to describe her. She was the one who helped me accept my mystic capabilities that sometimes got me into trouble with Rainey.

And then I met this annoying man, Roberge Farradan. His wife Lauren, a Lady herself, had bestowed the title of The Duke of Shaunessey upon him. He was full of himself and liked to flirt with me. I was not amused and I was not impressed by his ice queen of a wife's grandiose. How they wormed their way into my heart is a story all on its own.

All of a sudden, the years sped by. I saw myself in Bridge Falls meeting up with old friends, Lara, Jimmy and Jack…oh Jack, the only other man in my life. Hastily, I was transfixed on an image before me. It was a fleeting moment in time when I had caught a glimpse of Rainey as he stood outside his place of business. I don't know why but I tried to hold on to that instant, but it disappeared to a picture of me fleeing before he could see me. I was heartbroken all over again.

I saw myself as Vela in my early days at Avanloch. Maveryn had given me that name. No one knew except Jannie and John who I really was or what I had left back in Canada. Jeremy passed away in 1977. His sister Ash left her theater troupe to co-operate McAllister Holdings with Uncle John and his son, Gray. He and Ash became engaged years ago but have never married. Rosalyn had taken her rightful place at the helm of the company, but now she was to be Mistress of Avanloch. Would it all be too much for her?

The picture show had turned dark and ominous…where was I? Who was this man telling me he was my husband? How could I be married to a man I had never seen before…how could I be carrying his child… why didn't I know who I was? Somethings wrong. Liliana, there you are, my precious baby. Why are your eyes so blue…I know that azure blue… where, how, who am I…why is this man calling me Katarina. My name is not Katarina.

Flashes of this tall, dark, handsome man who called himself Anton insisting that he was my husband kept coming into view along with a young girl named Zoe and a man named Somner. Who was that woman dressed in white…was she a nun? She says the Black Russian is her mother…I'm lost. No, it's not me… it's Ava. Her plane is plummeting down; down into a blanket of white…help me Maveryn, Avaleena… Rainey where are you…the babies, the babies. I screamed.

"Vienna! Wake up Love; you're dreaming."

"Where are they, where are they?" I strained to find my voice.

"Who are you talking about Vienna?"

Rainey was kneeling beside me with his arms around me telling me that I must have had a bad dream, and that everything was all right and I should wake up.

"I'm not asleep, I've been watching a movie, but I don't know where I left the children."

"Okay," Rainey sighed, "you were watching a movie in your sleep. It's not unusual to be a little disorientated when you wake up, but the children are all fine."

"Where are they Rainey?" I demanded.

"They are all in the playroom with Amma. Everything is good Hon."

I slouched back into my big yellow chair. "I thought I left the babies on the path to the crypt."

"You didn't Honey. Come on, I will take you to them."

I patted the arms of the chair. "I used to read to Rosy and Ava in this chair every night when they were young. It is where I sit with Tanny and Liliana and tell them stories. I nurse the twins here…I want to tell them stories too Rainey."

"Well then, let's have the chair shipped to Bridge and you can make lots more memories in it with them there."

"I don't think I can go Rainey."

"Where can't you go?"

"I can't leave Avanloch…I can't move to Bridge Falls."

He let go of me and stood up. "Well, that's a little crazy. Are you forgetting that it was *your* idea to move back to Canada? I argued against it, but you shot me down saying it was what you wanted and what we all needed…a new start. As long as you and I and the children were together we could manage anything. Now, on the eve of our departure you say you can't go. I have catered to your every whim and desire Vienna just as has every other being in this house has. Whatever Vienna wants; Vienna gets…well, not this time!"

He started towards the door throwing his arms in the air. "If that's what you want, then stay; stay here and tell Rosy that you want to be Mistress of Avanloch again, that you want to be Lady Vienna again and that you want to rule over the kingdom again. Remain here with all your ghostly friends, and your secret rooms, and mysterious encounters. So be it; I'm done! I'm leaving tomorrow and taking the children with me. That's it, plain and simple."

"Rainey!" I cried as the door slammed. I waited knowing he'd come back, but he didn't. I pulled myself up and ran after him. I glanced up the great hallway towards the kitchen. He was nowhere to be seen. A movement towards the front door caught my eye. Did I just see the door to the Grand Drawing Room close…no, he wouldn't go in there, would he? I hesitantly crossed the hall and stood at the door expecting that it would open. It did not so I cautiously turned the knob and entered my least favorite room in the castle. I had dubbed it the Harem Room twenty some years ago because of its' gaudiness.

"Where are you Rainey…why did you come in here? Are you trying to make some sort of point? You know this room gives me the heebie-jeebies…"

I walked through several of the little privacy draped rooms until I came to the Grandfather clock. "Are you in there Rainey? Have you finally figured out how to get inside from out here?"

I doubted it, but perhaps he had and was keeping it from me. It would be an easier entrance into Avaleena's room so he definitely wouldn't want me to know about it. I had given up all that searching after the twins were born. I figured I knew enough about the castle to last a lifetime. I must have imagined the door closing because surely Rainey wouldn't taunt me by luring me into the room I hated. He was upset with me, but he wouldn't scare me.

"That's odd." I said out loud as I picked up a large black key that was sitting in a small silver tray atop a round wooden table that Duffy had built many years ago. There was usually a picture of Avanloch, circa the eighteen hundreds sitting on it. I looked around; the photo was nowhere to be seen. "Hmmm…" I mused wondering who had placed the key there. I brushed my right shoulder off feeling as if I had run into a cobweb. No, that wasn't it…someone was breathing down my neck. "Rainey, that's not funny!"

I turned quickly and felt myself falling. I reached out and grabbed the big tassel on the twelve foot long call bell. It didn't break my fall and I saw the edge of the divan and the floor coming up to meet me.

"What are you doing down there Vienna?" Rainey asked as he untangled my hands from around the call bell. "You certainly know how to get our attention don't you? If your intention was to deafen us, then you succeeded."

"I've got a headache." I moaned.

"I wouldn't doubt it." Johnny said pulling me to my feet.

"What is everyone doing here?" I asked as my eyes darted back and forth to Rosalyn, Evan, and Johnny. I turned to Rainey and asked him why he had pushed me.

"Pushed you; what are you talking about?" He asked annoyingly.

"Are you denying that you snuck up behind me, breathed down my neck and pushed me?"

"I most assuredly am. I would never do such a thing."

"Mama, Rainey was with us in the kitchen when the call bell rang. We knew it had to come from here even before we checked because no other room has the same blaring ring, so you can quit thinking that it was him, or anyone for the matter." Rosy said pointing to a disheveled scatter rug. "Is it possible that you tripped?"

"I suppose so, but it doesn't account for the creepy feeling that something was breathing down my neck does it? Never mind, I want to see the children and I'm hungry."

"Amma and Zoe are getting them ready for dinner, so come along." Rainey said taking hold of my arm.

I shot him a dirty look still believing that he had pushed me and shook his hand off. I walked on ahead of everyone else whom I guess were all wondering what was up between him and me. The twins were in their high chairs in the family dining room between Rainey's and my seats. Liliana was on the left side of him. She asked me where he was.

"Right here Sweetie." He said picking her up and kissing her on her ear making her laugh.

Tanny usually sat across the table from me between Amma and Mrs. D. She got up.

"You sit here Mommy because Amma and Mary are going to miss you."

I was about to thank her for the thought, but Rainey interjected.

"Not to worry Tanny because your mother has decided that she's not moving with us. She's decided to stay here… haven't you Vienna?" He said sweetly.

I supposed that he was baiting me. I said nothing.

"What's he saying Mama?" Rosy demanded.

"Oh dear…" Mary moaned.

"It's okay Mary, Rainey's just joking." Tanny promised patting Mary's hand.

Rainey rose and placed Lili back down in her chair. "Be right back Sweetie; I need a few minutes to talk to your mother. Will you all excuse us please?"

He held his hand out to me. "Vienna…"

I took it hesitantly because I couldn't see another way out of my predicament. I let him lead me out the door, through the kitchen, into the hallway and to the back stairway. He grabbed on to my waist and turned me around and physically sat me down on the third step. Without saying a word he bent down, placed one of my legs on his knee and pulled my boot off and threw it across the hall where all the other boots and shoes rested. He did the same with the other boot.

He looked up at me smugly. "Who's going to take your boots off for you when I'm gone?"

"Tanny."

"I'm afraid not my dear because she will be with me. And," he said reaching up and pulling on my necklace, "who's going to deck you out in pearls when you go riding?"

"Liliana."

"Nope, she will be with me too. And, who is going to wake you up in the middle of the night because they are hungry and need a warm breast to nestle in?"

"The twins."

"Sorry, but they will be, as will I, enfolded in the arms of a yet unknown well- endowed bosomed young lady." He brazenly winked at me.

I raised my hand fully intending to wallop him. "You're a heartless bastard Rainey Quinn!"

He caught my hand. "You got that right Sweetheart. I'm the bastard who never told you he loved you so you had to run away and have Ava all on your own which kept us separated for twenty years. I'm the bastard who let you out of his sight in Andorra and let another man claim you and Liliana as his, and I'm the bastard who didn't keep you out of harm's way and put you in the hospital clinging to life and almost losing our babies. I'm to blame for every misfortune in your life so it's no wonder that you are afraid to start a new life away from here with me." He backed away. "But, you know damn well that I would never take the children away from you, so you win again Vienna. The only question that remains is whether you want me to stay or go on alone without you?"

He had me. "None of those things were your fault Rainey, and you know it. I'm the one who put all the events in motion. I'm pig-headed, defiant, and spoiled. The one thing I am above all is that I am still hopelessly in love with you, so if you think for one second that I am going to let you run off into the arms of another woman you had better think again if you want to see another birthday!"

"Is that a threat?"

"You damn right it is!"

"Then I suggest you get off your high horse and get down into the arms of the man who loves you more than life itself."

I smiled smugly. "Well, you put me up here."

He lifted me down. "Are you sure you want to give up your title as Mistress of Avanloch and become simply Mrs. Quinn, wife of a commoner?"

"I do, but first I want you to tell me why you pushed me."

"Well, I had to do something to get your attention." He teased.

I knew he was kidding. "Well, someone or something pushed me!"

"All the more reason to get you out of here Hon. Now I think our two minutes are up so what say we make our way back to the family?"

"Do you have the key?" I asked suddenly remembering it.

"The key to what…your heart?"

"No silly, the black key from the Harem room."

"Sorry, but I know nothing about a key. What does it unlock?"

"I have no idea because I just found it. I had it in my hand just before I fell. It was sitting on the little table that Duffy made. I must have dropped it. I'll go back and look."

"I think not. How important could a key be anyway?"

"Please humor me Rainey, just this one last time."

"As if this will be the last time…"

We walked into an array of glum looking faces. Tanny ran up to me and wrapped her arms around my torso. "Are you okay Mommy?"

"I am *Sweetie*." I replied hugging her.

"Are you okay Daddy?"

He answered smiling that he was.

"See, I told you everything was going to be all right didn't I?" Tanny gloated.

"Yes, you did Tanny." Rosy agreed. "So, what's the verdict?"

"What do you think?" Rainey asked rolling his eyes.

"I'm not sure; is Mom going, or are you staying? It's one or the other as if I am sure about anything it's that you can't live without each other."

"You are right about that Red." He said grinning. "Now, get on with your dinner. Vienna lost something in the Harem room so I'm going to see if I can find it. Be right back."

"Sit ye down Mister Rainey…please. You can do that later. Right now I want us all to hold hands and have a little prayer. Can you do that for me one last time?" Mary beseeched.

"Yes Mary dear, I can, but quit acting as if this is going to be the last time you are going to see us. We will be back many times I promise, and especially now it will be a lot easier since Rosy and Evan have that new plane at their command."

"I will take that as an affirmative that the move is on?" Rosy asked looking at me.

"Yes my dear, we'll be out of here, Canada bound at the crack of dawn." I answered positively. "You all know that I am not happy about leaving you all behind don't you?"

"We do." Johnny assured me. "As Rainey says having a plane at our disposal will make it easy for us to visit back and forth without all the hassle of the big airports. Who knows, I may just get Amma to relent and fly." He laughed as she cringed.

Everyone had their hand in the prayers with more than a few tears being shed. At the end of another delicious meal Rainey got up to go and look for the key.

"This wouldn't be what you lost is it Vienna?" Evan said producing the mysterious key from his pocket. "I found it under the divan and wondered what it was doing there." He passed it across the table.

"Yes, that's it." I explained how I had come across it.

Amma said that it wasn't there yesterday when she had taken one of the new girls in to dust.

Tanny asked if she could look at it. "It's heavy. There is a number on it I think, but it is in that other language."

I asked her what other language. She said the one with all the letters. She knew one and five but couldn't remember the others.

"Well, your eyesight is definitely better than mine because I can't see a number on it. I think you are talking about Roman numerals. What do they look like?"

"There are two exes and two ones. Look here," she said putting my hand on the embossing, "can you feel them? They are kind of hidden under the flowers."

"Yes, I do now, but I can't make out any flowers. Two exes and two ones make it number twenty two."

"May I see it?" Rainey asked. "Looks like a Fleur- de- Lis to me."

"Why would a key with France's emblem be on a key in a Scottish house?" Rosy asked.

"The Fleur-de-Lis isn't just an insignia from France you know Rose, and the relationship between Scotland and France goes back a long way." Evan said.

"I guess I have never thought about it. Why would I; it has nothing to do with Avanloch."

"Don't tell me that you have never noticed that the collars around your lions at the front door are decorated with the Fleur-de-Lis?"

"I think you are mistaken Evan as I would have noticed." Rosalyn said accusingly.

"He's right Red." Rainey said agreeing with Evan. He passed the key to her.

She studied it for a minute with the help of Mary's magnifying glass. "It's small, but I guess it is the flower though it is rather odd shaped."

"Yes, flower of the lily, but it is also a symbol of the Holy Trinity as well as an emblem of the Virgin Mary. It looks odd because I believe another image is hiding behind it." Evan said.

"I don't know what you saw because I can hardly make out the number. What do you think its covering up and why?" I asked.

"I have no idea Vienna, but it looks like the cross of the Knights Templar."

Rainey raised his eyebrows. "How do you know all of this Evan being from Australia and all? Show me what you see."

Evan laughed. "We do have history books down under you know. I may be wrong…here, have a look."

None of us had noticed that Rosalyn had left the room until she approached us from behind out of breath. I asked her where she had been. She said she had to check on something.

"And, what did you find on the lions?" Evan asked smugly.

"You know darn well what I found!"

"So, what is the significance of the cross Evan and why do you say that it's a Templar cross? Oh, I just remembered something…Quinn's uncle was a Knight. Maybe he brought it here." I laughed at my own revelation.

"What the hell are you talking about Vienna?" My husband asked rather rudely.

"Do you not remember Avaleena's man- servant Quinn? He was banished from the castle by Edward, but he and Gracie Darling were protected because his uncle was a soldier with the Knights Templar?"

"I remember no such thing."

"Well, there's a possibility that I didn't elaborate, but it's in Avaleena's diary I assure you."

"I don't remember you mentioning it neither Mama. Perhaps it's time to revisit the diary."

"Do it on your own time Red because we are out of here!" Rainey picked Lili up in one arm and Zander in the other. "Get your half Vienna; time for bed."

"Just a minute Rainey," I picked up the key instead of Novia, "I'm not positive, but pretty sure that I have seen this key before. It should be on the round key ring in my upstairs parlour...would you mind fetching it for me Zoe?"

She looked at Rainey wanting his approval I suspected.

He sat back down with the kids on his lap. "Go ahead Zoe. She won't rest until she knows for sure, so let's get it over with."

Tanny asked how many rooms were in the castle.

I answered that there were somewhere around forty plus the tower rooms. She asked how many were down stairs. I told her twenty two if we counted pantries and lavatories.

"Then this key is for room twenty two, right?"

"There are no numbers on the rooms down here Honey, but you could be right if they were once numbered."

"That would have been a long time ago Tanny as all the locks have been changed once or twice with remodeling. I myself have installed new doors over the years." Johnny stated.

"This one looks like it might be for an out building being so large… the mausoleum perhaps. What do you think Johnny?" I asked.

He smiled amusingly. "Anything is possible Vienna, but me thinks it is just a key that doesn't open a damn thing, and probably never did."

Rainey said he agreed.

"Tell me then, how did it get into the Harem Room, and where is the photo of Avanloch that it replaced? Keys just don't get up and walk."

"That's funny Mommy, a walking key." Tanny giggled.

We all laughed with her. Zoe returned with the oversized key ring and placed it in front of me. It wasn't hard to find several keys that matched the one I had found. With the use of the magnifying glass I was able to detect the same insignia on them. There was an array of different sizes, but not one was the same size as the one from the Grand Drawing Room. The ones that appeared to match the large key were also engraved with Roman numerals and some sort of decoration. Evan and Johnny both thought it was a cross.

I passed the ring of keys to Rosy. "Not my riddle to figure out. Do as you wish with them Lady Rosalyn."

"It's just like you Vienna to leave us with another mystery." Johnny teased.

"I will be doing nothing with them as I have a castle to run." Rosy stated. "As far as I am concerned they are, as you said, the keys that open nothing."

"That's my girl." Rainey applauded.

I gathered a sleeping Novia up into my arms. "Give us half an hour to get our babes into bed, and then we will join you all for a farewell evening."

CHAPTER 2

DEPARTURE

We left Avanloch at six the next morning after a tearful goodbye to the McDuffs. We needed two cars to make the trip to Waverly where Jin the pilot was waiting for us. Evan was to be the co-pilot. Rosy was coming on the trip with us and she and Evan had plans to visit Ava and Nash in Akemantack after delivering us to Bridge Falls. Rainey, Liliana and Zander were in the lead car with Evan and Rosy. Johnny was driving the second car with Tanny, Novia and me. Amma had come along postponing the farewell for as long as possible. I closed my eyes and covered them with my hands as we drove out the gate. Tanny asked me why I was doing that.

Amma laughed. "Because she's afraid that she'll see a black cat."

"Why would you be afraid of that Vienna?" Tanny asked reverting back to calling me Vienna.

I told her that it was just a silly superstition. She said she didn't really understand superstitions, but she remembered that her grandmother had a lot and so did Mrs.D. I asked her to tell me what ones she remembered.

"Well, Grandmother would scold me if I put my shoes on the table because she said that was bad luck, and she said that 13 was an unlucky number so I should stay in bed on that day, and especially if was a Friday I think. Are those superstitions?"

"Yes, I think they are. A lot of people believe that Friday the thirteenth is unlucky for one reason or the other."

Tanny asked me if I was afraid of that day and why was everyone. I didn't want to get into the religious, Templar Knights, or witch suppositions regarding the day as she was too young to be thinking about such things. I told her I was not afraid of the number thirteen or Friday if it fell on that day. She asked me again why I was afraid of black cats.

"I like cats of all colors, but if I am in a vehicle and a black one crosses in front of me I feel uneasy. It's silly I know and kind of funny don't you think? Anyway, if I don't see one then I am okay so I just close my eyes if I remember to."

"Suppose if you don't remember and you see one, what happens then?"

I didn't want to scare her and tell her that I had seen one cross in front of me at the gate on Rainey's and my trip to Andorra. How could a black cat have caused the earthquake that had taken me away from Rainey and my family for almost two years? I shuddered.

"I don't think anything will happen that wasn't going to in the first place. People believe in some funny things and a lot they have inherited from their relatives. One of the funniest I have ever heard is that if you break a mirror you will have seven years of bad luck."

"That is funny. What other things are you afraid of Vienna?" Tanny wasn't through yet.

"I don't walk under ladders, and when I spill salt I always throw some over my left shoulder."

She laughed. "That is funny. Why do you do that?"

"We all do that because apparently the devil is standing behind us and if we throw the salt at him he will disappear. Originally, salt was a rarity so if one spilled any they scooped it up right away to save it. I don't know how the devil got into it." Amma added.

"Do you have any superstitions Auntie?" Tanny asked.

"Pretty much the same as your mother's, but the ones I don't like is that bad luck comes in threes and seeing one magpie brings bad luck to a stranger that crosses your path. There are some good luck beliefs also like planting a Rowan Tree for protection, and by putting a poker and tongs in the fire because they will protect the house in an electric storm."

Johnny laughed. "Yeah, that'll work. If you want to hear what the Irish believe then I have a good one for you."

"Pray tell what it is Johnny." I dared.

He tilted the mirror so he could see Tanny and asked her if she knew what a fairy fort was.

"Is it like a fairy ring Uncle Johnny?"

"Sort of, and if you ever come upon one you must never disturb it because if you do the little people won't be happy with you, and they might put a hex on you."

"What does that mean?"

"It's like a jinx. You might not be able to sleep at night, or all your food might taste salty, something like that, or you might feel like dancing all night long. Farmers are very careful that they don't till up one of those forts when they are plowing and especially in May as that is when Fairies are at their worst."

"At their worst for what Uncle Johnny?"

"That is when they are the most mischievous, but also very bad tempered." Johnny explained flashing us a wink and grinning.

Tanny said she'd be sure not to do that and asked me if there were Fairies in Canada. I told her that there certainly were. Amma said she had one more and asked me if I knew why Mary MacDuff always nicked her bread with a cross before cooking.

I laughed and said I did as it was to let the devil out. Tanny asked how the devil got into the bread in the first place. I hugged her and told her not to pay attention to any of these customs. She asked me if Rainey had any.

"If you mean superstitions, then no I don't think so. He thinks he's too smart for any hocus-pocus, and even if he encounters something unusual he will try and explain it away with science or logic."

"That sounds like Rainey all right." Johnny quipped.

God, I was going to miss him. In half an hour we would be at the airport and I was going to have to say goodbye to him and Amma. I didn't know how I would be able to.

Rainey met us at the hangar. I took Zander from him as he said his farewells to Amma and Johnny. He then took all the kids into the airplane to settle while I said my farewells. I pulled them into my embrace and held them close to me not saying anything. Amma broke down and uttered something about life being so cruel. She kissed me, told me she loved me and that Avanloch would never be the same without me. I consoled her as best as I could and reminded her that I wasn't going away forever and we'd talk all the time. She left crying uncontrollably as she made her way back to the car leaving me alone with Johnny.

"How am I ever going to manage without you Johnny? You have been my right arm and my very best friend for so very long." I lamented.

"You won't have an estate to manage anymore Vienna, so you won't need me anymore and your old friend Jimmy can take up the reins helping Rainey keep you in check."

"No one can replace you Johnny! You and I have a connection that is unquestionably unique and it was there from the first day we met."

"And unexplainable at times like that night in room six and afterwards…"

I stopped him from saying anything else. "It's all good Johnny. You saved me from the Black Russian, and whatever else may or may not have happened will remain a secret forever."

"We've never really talked about it Vienna."

"No, and it has to stay that way, you know that."

"I do, but sometimes I look at you and I get the feeling that you are wondering too."

"If anything, it was just a dream."

"Yeah, one that we both had."

"Sometimes it's best to leave the unknown alone, and in our case it has worked."

"It's going to be hard not seeing you every day, but that's my problem. You made me what I am today, and I will always be indebted to you. You know I love Avanloch and the lands, and as long as I live and breathe I'll keep it just the way you left it. The next chapter of your life is just beginning and I won't worry about you because Rainey will see that you stay on the straight and narrow, or he'll try." He laughed then added that he loved me.

"I love you too Johnny." I kissed him and walked away with tears running down my face.

Evan was waiting for me by the plane with a short dark skinned man. I assumed he was the pilot, and indeed he was. Evan put his arm around my shoulders and introduced me to him.

"I would like you to meet the second most important woman in my life, my mother-in-law Lady Vienna Quinn. This is our renowned pilot Vienna, the highly decorated Jnina Lahloy."

"I am ever so pleased to make your acquaintance My Lady. Your son-in-law is ever so generous. I am nothing but a bush pilot such as he was. Please to call me Jin."

"And, I am just Vienna. Your name sounds vaguely familiar; Laszlo was it? Is it possible that you knew my first husband Jeremy McAllister?"

"Sadly, I had not the privilege of meeting him, but have come to know him through Evan. You would not be the first American to confuse the name Lahloy with that of Victor Laszlo of Casablanca fame." He replied laughing. "The character was Algerian however, not Moroccan."

Evan corrected him saying that I was Canadian and not American. He bowed and asked that I excuse his blunder and suggested we board the plane. Rosy met me with a handful of Kleenex.

"How about a quick tour of the cabin Mom and you can freshen up before we take off?"

I followed her down the aisle. She opened the door into a very fashionable lavatory. I remarked that it was more like a swanky hotel's powder room and that the men must find it a little too feminine. She laughed and said that was too bad then wasn't it. I turned the fancy faucet on at the porcelain sink remarking that it was fancier than anything at the castle. I washed my tear-stained face, wet my fly-away hair, and applied a pinkish lipstick that Rosy passed to me. I asked her if I was presentable now.

"Oh Mommy, you are always presentable and you are always beautiful. I just wanted you to have a little pick-up after the emotional day you are having saying farewell to Avanloch and Amma and Johnny and the McDuffs, but it's not as if it's forever is it?"

I hugged her and said, "Can you make me a cup of tea in that fancy galley?"

Evan found us having a good chortle. He said he didn't mean to intrude, but did we still plan on leaving today or what. Rosy said we would take our seats as soon as she made me tea. He asked what I was going to do with it. Everyone knew of my distaste for tea, so the question was commonplace. I answered that I hadn't the foggiest idea. He put his arm around me and asked if he could escort me to my seat, and that the stewardess would bring me a cup of coffee as soon as we were in the air. I remarked that this was some big honkin plane. He said it was and that I had my daughter to thank for it. He sat me down in a plush leather chair across from the three girls. The twins shared a seat between Rainey and me. He asked me if I was okay. I said I was, but he knew me too well and knew very well that I had mixed feelings about leaving Avanloch.

The flight was smooth. Small white clouds followed us. Tanny was mesmerised by them. She asked me if her mother lived among them. I told her that I was pretty sure she did. She seemed content with that, and after a few hours joined Lili and Zoe who were playing board games and cards with Rosalyn until they seemed to all decide at once to close their eyes. Zander slept most of the way. Novia was her usual curious and content self. I was flipping through a picture book with her when Rainey picked her up and sat down beside me. He had been taking the flight in sitting behind Evan and Jin.

"There was a time I thought that I'd like to become a pilot you know."

I asked him when that was as this was the first I was hearing about it.

"I guess it was before I met you."

"I suppose there are a lot of things that you did before and after me that I know nothing about."

He laughed. "Yeah, believe it or not, I did have a life before love took me down."

"In other words, it was me who dragged you down."

"I've never thought about it as such. If you hadn't come into my life I might be sitting on a bar stool in some dimly lit dive at the ripe old age of forty five waiting for some bimbo."

"One like Jorja you mean? Did you know a lot of her sort when you were young?"

That was the wrong thing to say and he let me know. His eyes were full of disdain. I wasn't sure if it was for me or her. He kept his voice low, but the inflection of revulsion was clear.

"Thank you very much for reminding me of the most deplorable time in my life! I trusted you to never mention it again, but for some ungodly reason you've chosen a most bizarre time to throw it in my face."

"I didn't mean to Rainey. Her name just popped out."

"I don't think it was an accident. Excuse me, I need a drink."

He stood up, looked down at me and shook his head. "Sometimes I think that it is me who doesn't know you, and that you have no idea at all of just how much I love and need you, and that my past means nothing to me."

He was gone before I could reply. I didn't call after him because I had the sense not to call attention to an ugly conversation which was clearly my fault. It didn't appear as if anyone had heard or had seen the way he had looked at me. He was back almost immediately with two cups of coffee and a cookie for Novia.

"I'm sorry." He said. "May I sit with you?"

It took all I had to keep from bursting into tears. "You're sorry; you have nothing to be sorry about. It's me who owes you an apology. I promised you I'd never mention her name and…"

He put his fingers on my lips. "Hush; it's said and done, so let's just leave it at that. We can air my dirty laundry another day okay? I know this has been a very emotional day for you and I haven't made it any easier for you by accusing you of betraying my trust, so I apologise for that."

I kissed his fingertips. "I do know how much you love me as that is the same way I love you, and always will, no matter what."

"Amen to nothing ever coming between us."

We touched down in Halifax for refueling. Evan had said it wasn't necessary, but this way they would be sure to have enough fuel for their trip to Akemantack, and it would be cheaper… as if that was a concern. We were greeted in Bridge Falls by Lara and Coop. They were waiting for us at the airport with two vehicles. It was seven p.m. It had been a long day.

The Palace was most welcoming. It was brightly lit up. The first one in the house was Lili. She ran down the hallway and back again where we had all stood watching her amazed at her exuberance. Rainey picked her up and asked her if she wanted to see her bedroom. He asked Tanny and Zoe to join them, passed Zander to Lara and up the stairs they went. Coop relieved me of Novia and I followed them into the living room where a crib was waiting for the sleepy babies. Lara asked me if I liked the new look. Rainey had wanted to spruce up the inside and outside of the house with new paint jobs. He had consulted me for the choice of colors and had gone ahead and hired painters whom Lara had lined up for him. I hadn't paid much attention to the walls and ceilings so far as I was much too tired to even take notice.

Rainey made an appearance and asked Coop for help with the luggage. He asked me if I approved of the new kitchen. New kitchen… what was wrong with the old one? Lord, what had he done? With great apprehension I went with Lara to have a look.

I had given him permission to do whatever he wanted to, but had been hesitant that he could accomplish it all by telephone and the fax machine. He had shown me the blueprint he'd made, but he had caught me at a bad time so I just told him that it looked great, not really understanding the plans anyhow. I wasn't sure what to expect.

"Oh my God," I exclaimed, "my husband is a genius!"

"I guess you like it. Didn't you see the plans?"

"I didn't pay much attention to them Lara, so it's a surprise, a most delightful one. Oh, just a moment…the pantry; please tell me it's still intact?" I cringed as I walked around the newly constructed island noticing a little seating nook across from it. I swung open the half-door into the pantry, entered and returned beaming. "Is this all Coop's work? It's amazing, just amazing!"

"He did most of it, and hoped it would meet with Rain's approval. Did you not see the photo?"

"I did not, so obviously he was happy with it. I suppose he wanted to surprise me and indeed he did. I love it and your husband is also a genius."

A few minutes later Rainey and Coop joined us. I hugged them both and complimented Coop on his carpentry, and Rainey on his ability to keep the remarkable new kitchen under his hat. The girls were happy with their rooms and came down to have a light snack of Lara's fixings before bed. Tomorrow would be soon enough for me to explore the rest of the revamped house. I said goodnight and thanked my old friend and her husband for all that they had done and wearily let Tanny and Lili escort me to my room. Rainey said he'd meet me upstairs with the twins. Had I been so tired that I had forgotten them?

Two days later I took stock of the remodeled and improved Palace. It hadn't had a new coat of paint since 1960, the year my father and mother had bought it. That was the same year I met Rainey and fell in love. The years between then and now had many more heartaches than rainbows. I could only hope that with our move here where it had all started would keep the past in the rear view mirror.

Tanny started school on September the 4th. She was six and a half years old.

Nash and a very pregnant Ava arrived on the 18th. They would be with us until April. Rainey and I were in a very good place. I was very happy.

CHAPTER 3

RAINEY'S PAST COMES KNOCKING

The Palace

It was two in the afternoon on a beautiful, warm late September afternoon. I had just managed to get the twins down for a much needed nap in the living room where we kept a crib for daytime use. Novia had already figured how to get out of it, but I never worried about her as she was not overly adventurous and was content just to play with what was right in front of her. She was able to walk holding on to furniture whereas Zander wasn't even interested in crawling. Liliana was a little antsy waiting for Tanny to come home from school. Rainey had opened an office downtown and was meeting with his first client so he was off tending to that which meant that I was on my own with Lili and her little tantrums for another hour. She made do with me, but she was definitely her father's girl. Ava and Nash were at the doctor's office so I didn't even have them for back-up. Every bone in my body cried out in agony from lugging Zander around. I needed a relaxing warm bath and a soft pillow to lay my head on. It was not to be as Lili wanted a tea party. I relinquished believing that I could rest just as well in a comfy chair on the veranda, and anything to keep her pacified. She had just poured me a cup of iced tea in one of her little cups when the doorbell rang. She screamed in delight that daddy was home. She went tearing down the porch before I could stop her. She was back in a few seconds pouting because it wasn't him. I asked her who was at the door. She said someone with yellow hair. I walked down the veranda and peered around the corner of the house to see who was still ringing the bell. Sure enough it was a woman with long blond hair. A vision flashed before me, but was gone before I could embrace it. I called to the woman asking if I could help her. She said she was looking for Rainey Quinn. A moment of unease engulfed me. I told her he wasn't home and asked her if she would like to leave him a message. Silly me, I thought she might be seeking an architect. She started to walk towards me and stopped at the bottom of the steps. She asked me if I was Rainey's wife and could she wait for him. I wanted to say that yes, I would mind, but I knew I would be wondering the rest of the day who she was and what she wanted with my husband, so I asked her if she was a new client of his. She laughed ever so slightly, and said that she wasn't, but that he might mistakenly consider himself one of hers. I never thought that I would meet any of my husband's ex- lovers, but I was pretty sure that I just had. He had assured me that lover was the wrong word because he had never loved anyone but me. If lovers weren't what they were then I had no idea what he thought their titles were. The women that I knew about were his ex-wife Louise, whom I had come face to face with, and Zeta, the model from Italy. This woman was neither of them, so that left Jorja; the woman I had promised never to speak of again. I blamed my answer on fatigue. "You may as well come and wait for him then."

She followed me and sat down in a chair next to Lili. "Thank-you Vienna; and what is your name?" She asked my daughter.

"Lili. Do you want some tea?

"Yes, I would love some. I have a little girl just like you. Her name is Patricia Ann. I named her after her father's mother." She smiled at me knowingly.

"What do you want Jorja?" I asked although I was afraid of the answer.

"How do you know my name?"

"I know who you are because Rainey and I have no secrets. It appears as if you have always been the one who is the keeper of secrets though isn't it?"

"It was all a horrible misunderstanding. I could have explained everything if he would have just given me the chance. We were very much in love, but I'm afraid I hurt him deeply. I can make that all up to him when I tell him that he has another daughter."

Was I ready for this? "Rainey already has enough daughters. He will not be at all pleased to see you or to hear you claim that Patricia is his child. Where is the proof that she is his?"

"When he sees her, he will know."

"Does she have his deep blue eyes like Lili does?"

"Her eyes are brown like mine. What do you mean when you say he already has enough daughters? Are there more?"

"Rainey and I have nine children; six of them are girls." I said proudly.

"Oh my God, now I know why he was so secretive about where he lived! Nine children, that is very hard to believe."

"You don't know Rainey's and my story do you?"

"I have heard via the grapevine at work that you just moved here from Scotland. I would have gone there to find him when I saved up enough money, but luckily I found out that he was here in the town where he grew up. It took me three years to track him down."

"Scotland is a very large country, so chances of you finding him there are doubtful. By the way, Rainey did not grow up here. Are you living here in Bridge Falls?"

"Wasn't I lucky to have gotten a job so quickly? Everything is finally falling into place."

"You shouldn't congratulate yourself so fast because Rainey won't want anything to do with you and your supposition that he is the father of your daughter."

"Who are you to speak for him?"

"I am the woman whom he has loved all his life. You were just a blemish in a most troubling time in his life; the time when we were not together. Your sordid lifestyle could have damaged him for life, but as fate would have it we were reunited and I banished all those feelings of shame that you had inflicted on him. Now, let's talk about your daughter. Where is she and how are you going to convince Rainey that he is her father?"

"She is living in a foster home in Vancouver. As soon as I find a nice place to live I will bring her here. You are wrong about Rainey's and my relationship. He loved me and we were going to get married."

I took a deep breath. She was starting to annoy me. "He didn't love you, and the proof of that will be when he sees you."

The opening of the front door alerted me that he was home. He called out. "Where are all my beautiful ladies hiding?"

"Daddy, Daddy…" Lili screamed.

"Don't wake the twins Lili, and don't slam the screen door." I cautioned. Too late; Zander was already awake and crying. I flashed Jorja a smile. "Daddy's home."

We could hear him talking all the way into the kitchen. He pushed the screen door open with his foot as he had one arm around Lili and the other was holding Zander.

"Little help here Sweetheart…" His tone changed from affectionate to one of outrage. "What in the hell is *she* doing here?" He demanded.

"She is here to see you Rainey. She has something to tell you." I said calmly.

"Like hell she does!" He glared at her. "Get off my porch, get away from my wife, and don't ever come back here again!"

"But Rainey…" She begged.

"Get in the house Vienna!" he ordered as he threatened Jorja. "You have one minute to vacate the premises before I call the police and report you as a trespasser!"

"Take the kids inside Rainey. I just need a few seconds to get some information from her."

"Information; what the hell for?"

"She claims you are the father of her child…"

He laughed vulgarly. "This from a lying piece of trash that screwed every man in a hundred mile radius; don't make me laugh. One minute and I'm calling the cops." He warned as he slammed the screen door shut.

I had to talk quickly. "There's going to have to be a paternity test done Jorja. Give me your daughters address." I passed her one of Lili's crayons and opened up a page in her coloring book. "Here, write it down, and yours too …hurry."

She scribbled something and then opened her purse and passed me an envelope. It was addressed to her and had a return address on it. She said that there was a picture of Patricia inside. She said that Rainey didn't need to get a paternity test because he would know as soon as he saw the photo. I ushered her off the porch. She asked me if I was going to help her. I said I didn't know.

Lili was sitting on the counter eating marshmallows. Novia was in her high chair and Zander was still in Rainey's arms.

"Look Mommy, flowers. Can I have the red one?" Lili asked.

"Of course you can. Do you think you can go and wait for Tanny in the living room while I talk to Daddy?"

"I want to play with Daddy."

"She doesn't have to go anywhere because I have nothing to say to you except to ask what were you thinking letting that tramp in our house?" Rainey demanded angrily.

"She was not in the house, only the veranda, and what makes you think I knew who she was?"

"Oh, you knew all right!"

"Sure I did because every blonde woman I see I think is your former slutty lover." I snapped.

"She was not my lover! Don't ever call her that again!"

I had never seen Rainey so angry, but I wasn't about to concede to him. "Well, she wasn't your wife or fiancé or even your girlfriend according to you, so what do you call the woman you were screwing every night? I think it is way past time that you stop pretending that she meant nothing to you and admit that you may have sired a child with her."

"She meant nothing to me and she's an f-in liar."

"And that's what precisely got you into this predicament isn't it; all the f---ing!"

I could tell he was appalled by the look in his eyes. He passed me Zander and said he needed changing. He pulled Lili into his arms. "How stupid do you think I am? We will not speak of this again! Do you understand? And, I don't care much for your language!" He turned his back on me, and stomped out of the kitchen with Lili.

Tanny and Zoe arrived home from school just then. Zoe asked me if something was wrong with Rainey because he didn't even say hello to them. I told her that he had a bee in his bonnet and I needed to tend to him. She said she'd keep an eye on the twins and get Tanny a snack. I hugged her and pulled my weary body up the stairs.

He was sitting on the floor in our bedroom with Lili and her hat box that contained my jewels, both paste and genuine. She was pretty much weighted down with necklaces and bracelets. I sat on the edge of the bed facing them. I asked Rainey if we could talk.

"You can talk, but I probably won't listen as I don't have anything to say. As you can see I am a little busy at the moment."

"Yes, I can see that. You need to take a paternity test Rainey so we can put this all to rest."

"I don't have to do anything of the sort."

"Please Rainey; we can't leave a child out there that might be yours."

"A few years ago I discovered that I had a child that had been kept from me for twenty years. I lived very well never knowing she existed, so I've been there, already done that, so can do it again without ever knowing, but the possibility doesn't even exist, so no need to."

"The situation is entirely different Rainey. Jorja has been looking for you for years whereas I always knew where you were. Her daughter shouldn't be punished because of my mistake, and you love Ava, so if her daughter is yours, you'll love her too."

"You promised me that you would never speak her name, and now you are acting as if you are best friends." His voice was accusatory.

"I am not her friend. How do you think I felt sitting next to her in my shapeless housedress and apron with baby spittle all over me, and my unkempt short mousy brown hair next to her while she sat with perfectly styled golden locks in a sexy summer dress that revealed every curve of her young body?"

"She's not that young, and perhaps if you didn't wear granny dresses and torture your hair with finger nail scissors you wouldn't feel so inadequate."

"I've never felt inadequate until right now, so thank-you very much for your depiction."

"Well, now you know how I felt when I stood next to your Adonis husband."

"What did you say?" I stood up not believing what I'd heard.

He bent down and picked Lili and her jewels up and headed for the door.

"Are you going to walk out on me without explaining your remark?"

"Liliana doesn't need to hear any more of your foul tongue which I know is about to explode even more."

I heard him walk down the hall and call Zoe to come and get Lili. It gave me a minute to try and calm down. I was aghast that he had referred to Anton as my husband. He came in and sat back down on the floor and started to put the rest of the jewellery into Lili's oversized purse. He didn't look at me but snarled and said that he supposed he was going to have to put up with Jack fawning all over me too.

I ignored the Jack comment. "You called Anton my husband. All this time you have been lying to me haven't you? You never believed that I had amnesia, and that means that you think I made Katarina up, and that it was really me with Anton? How could you, how could you do that to me?"

"Yeah, and it wasn't a pretty picture me envisioning my sweet little wife lying in bed in another mans' arms doing God knows what."

"Don't stop there. What about your best friend Jimmy's arms, and how about Roberge, and let's not forget Johnny...maybe I had affairs with all of them. Maybe I'm no better than Jorja...yes Jorja, Jorja, Jorja! You like them wild and seductive, well hell, I'll do my best to make you lust after me just as you did after her, but then I'm still carrying twenty pounds of extra weight from having *your* babies, so I can't fit into any sexy clothes right now, and my hair looks as if Lili chopped it off with a dull knife, so you might have to wait a year or two for sex with your desire for a femme fatale, but wait, you don't have to... here, I have her address, so go have fun!" I spat throwing the envelope that she had given me at him. "Oh, and there's a picture of the daughter that you sired with her in there too!"

"You're going a little overboard with this aren't you? You're taking everything out of context. Where do you think you're going?"

I had started to walk away. "Anywhere away from you! The man I love has just accused me of faking my amnesia, and keeping Ava away from him once again. His promises mean nothing. He has kept all of this from me until today…today, the day his whore lover shows up on my doorstep and stirs up his hidden desires for her. How often have you thought about her slithering body peeling off her clothes as she caresses the greasy pole while you're making love to me? Be sure to thank her for me for bringing out the real you and freeing me from living with a lie. I hate this house and I hate it here! I want to go home!" I cried as I ran out of the room.

"Vienna, get back here…Vienna!"

I ran down the hall, down the stairs, out the door, across the street and into the alley. I just kept running and running and running. Rainey's voice was getting fainter and fainter. A huge dog tried jumping a fence to get to me. I fell to the ground landing hard on jagged rocks. I picked myself up and started running again. Where was I going? I had no secret rooms or the mausoleum like I had at Avanloch to hide in. I had taken so many back alleys that I had no idea where I was or how long I had been running, and it was hard to see beyond the tears. Suddenly, there were horns honking and people yelling. I weaved my way through the passing cars because up ahead I saw the bridge, and I knew where I was. I swear I heard someone yell "V!" as I clambered down the bank to the path. It couldn't have been because no one had called me "V" for years. I fell three more times before the forty steps to the river were before me. I stumbled down them and made my way to the waterfall wondering why my feet were stinging. I collapsed in the sand and let the tears fall. Why had I come here? This was the place that Jimmy had brought Lara and me to on June eleventh nineteen sixty, twenty four years ago. It was the day I met Rainey; the only man I had ever loved. Now he was the last person I wanted to see. How had it all come undone so fast?

"Vienna, my God, what are you doing here? What has happened… look at me?"

"Jack, oh Jack." I cried as he folded me into his arms. "What are you doing here?"

"Did you forget that Sissy and I were arriving today?"

"Where is she; where's Sissy?" I asked looking around him.

"You ran right in front of us. Didn't you hear us calling you? She dropped me off here and went to get Rainey."

"No, no I don't want to see him! Don't make me see him Jack."

"Okay, but first you have to tell me what's going on. Why were you running like the devil was chasing you?"

"The past is chasing me Jack; Rainey's past, and now she's come back to claim him and I don't stand a chance. He's going to leave me…"

"That's the most ridiculous thing I have ever heard. Rainey would never leave you, not for anyone or anything. He loves you more than life itself; you know that Vienna. You're upset with whatever you think happened and that's up to the two of you to fix, but right now I have to see what you've done to yourself…your feet are cut and bleeding and that gash in your leg will probably require stitches." He undid my apron. "I'm going to wet it and try to clean you up a little. You are going to have to go to the hospital."

"I'm not hurt. I don't need to go to the hospital." I sniffled.

He dabbed at my face and my hands and arms shaking his head. "Tell me you had a fight with someone in a back alley because you couldn't have possibly hurt yourself like this on purpose?"

"My body isn't hurting; just my heart."

"That's because you're in shock. I need to get you out of here."

I saw him over Jack's shoulder. "Thanks Jack; I'll take over from here."

"No, don't leave me with him!" I cried clinging to Jack.

"You need to listen to your husband Vienna." He said untangling my arms from around him.

"She needs to go to the hospital Rain. Her feet and legs are cut pretty badly. You may require help getting her up the steps. I can wait if you like."

"Sissy is waiting for you. She wants to get back to the kids because they are all pretty upset. How about you check back with me in half an hour and if we're still here then you'll know we need help. Thanks; I'm glad it was you who found her."

"Right; see you back at the Palace." Jack said backing away.

"Don't go, please Jack, don't leave…" I pleaded lowering my head.

Rainey lifted my chin up so I had to look at him. I brushed his hand away. "Go away; I don't want to see you!"

"Well, I want to see you, and I'm not going to leave you here. I'm the reason you're here in the first place, so how about we get you looked after and then we can talk about the misunderstanding later."

"Misunderstanding; you think I misunderstood what you accused me of?"

"I'm sorry; it was a moment of mania. Was what you accused me of any different?"

"You never denied anything; that's the difference."

"I denied being a father to that she-bitch's child, and you know she disgusts me, so there's the difference." He pulled something out of his pocket and tore it to sheds. "This is what I want to do to her, and you giving me her address because you think that I want to go and see her is just as disgusting. I said we would talk about this later, so get up."

"Is that an order?"

"You bet it is Lady Vienna! You're not in your castle right now, so no one is going to come and rescue you. I'm all you've got at the moment. You've had your little rave, so be done and come back home to your children who heard you screaming as you ran out of the house."

"Jack will be back."

He didn't say another word but grabbed me and threw me over his shoulder. I protested by pounding on him and screaming to let me down.

"Settle down Vienna! You're acting like a goddamn child!"

I sobbed that I wasn't a child and he should stop treating me like one. He said nothing until we reached the steps. He sat me down on the third one and kissed me. I showed my disapproval by wiping it off. He smiled at me and said that I'd have to beg for the next one. I snarled at him and told him that hell would freeze over first.

I braced myself, took a deep breath and pushed myself up to the next step. It hurt, but I was determined to get myself to the top.

"Hold on Hon; I've got an idea. Wait here, don't exert yourself anymore." He instructed as he ran up the steps.

What was wrong with him? He can't kiss me and call me hon when we're fighting. I pulled myself up another step.

He returned with a handful of diapers. "Feisty little broad aren't you? Here, I'll lay these down and they will cushion your feet. You're going to have to let me help you stand."

He didn't wait for me to answer, but took my hands and pulled me up and turned me around so I was facing the top. I hung unto the rail and tried taking a step by myself. He caught me just before I fell.

"Let me help you please."

The diapers helped to cushion the sting in my feet but they still hurt. I was thankful that Rainey had come up with the idea and that I hadn't taken the twin's knapsack into the house. Fifteen minutes later we made it to the top. Rainey helped me to get into the car. He shut the door and asked if I needed help buckling up. I said I didn't and there was no need for me to go the hospital. He didn't answer me but drove the few blocks there anyhow. He parked in the visitor's lot and gave me a bottle of water and told me to drink it all.

"Before I take you in I have a few things I need to say. I know you don't consider the Palace as home, and you want to go back to Scotland and your castle. I will not get in the way of you going and taking the kids, but I hope you will give me one concession and leave one of the girls with me."

I was aghast. "You want me to leave Liliana behind?"

"No, she's too much for me to handle on my own. I was hoping you'd talk Ava into staying."

"Oh, because I took her away from you once you think I'd do it again? I guess you need reminding that she is fully grown and has a husband and is about to make us grandparents and has no desire to return to Scotland."

"No, I haven't forgotten. I'm a lot of things, but I'm not absentminded. She saved me from going crazy when you were lost for almost two years, so I am going to need her to keep me sane when you leave again."

"You make it sound as if I had a choice when I was abducted from Nazeth."

"I didn't mean it like that, but this time it would be your choice wouldn't it?"

"I won't worry because you will have company won't you? It wouldn't surprise me one bit to find out that you were cavorting with her all the time I was…"

"Don't you dare!"

He was angry and for the first time in my life I was afraid of him. The fire in his eyes scared me. I managed to escape his hands, opened the door, stepped out, tripped, and fell hard to the pavement landing on my derriere. I tried not to cry, but the waterworks came fast and hysterically. He was at my side immediately. He sat down beside me and pulled me into his arms. He rocked me silently until I calmed. A passerby asked if we needed help. Rainey shook his head and said we were okay. He managed to get me up and back into the car.

"This backbiting has got completely out of hand and I'm afraid of the consequences, so I'll deliver you to emerge and leave. You can call Jack to pick you up. I won't be at the house when you get back. That way I won't see the look of disgust in your eyes anymore. I don't think you have any idea of how very much I love you, but I hope that while you are getting patched up you will have some compassion for me, and try to understand what this accusation has done to me. The rage you had to witness was not directed at you, but at myself. Seeing *her* brought back all the self-loathing that you had vanquished, but it's back staring me in the face. If I even thought for one second that she'd come looking for me, or…well, it's too late, the die has been cast. I'm sorry I took my frustration and anger out on you. They say that once the stone has been thrown you can never get it back again. I hope that you will let me retrieve it in time."

He was out the door before I could say anything. He returned with a nurse. He helped her get me into a wheelchair, patted the back of it and said they'd look after me.

"Aren't you coming with me?" I asked sorrowfully.

"I thought we decided it was best if I leave?"

"I didn't have a say, but I want you to stay." I held my hand out to him and he took it. We were both shaking.

The nurse whose name was Donna, led us to a curtained cubicle and she and Rainey got me onto the narrow bed. She took my temperature and blood pressure. She had a quick look at my injuries and asked what type of accident I had been in. Rainey said that I had fallen off my bicycle. She looked at us rather dubiously, but didn't comment. She excused herself saying that she would be right back with a gown and the doctor.

I wanted to laugh at Rainey's ridiculous answer, but the waterworks were on again and my backside hurt. He pulled the stool up beside the bed and leaned into me. Our faces were two inches apart. "What have we done to each other?" I sobbed.

"Nothing that can't be fixed. Do you trust that we can put us back together again?"

"I do. Someone should have put a muzzle on me."

"On me too Honey. How about we table this until we get home because I have a lot of apologizing to do and I prefer to do it in private. What do you say Mrs. Quinn?"

A tapping made us both look towards the moving curtain. She was drumming her pen on the surface of a clip board scrutinizing us. "So, you *are* the Quinns?"

Rainey stood up. "Yes Ma'am. I'm Rainey, and this is my wife Vienna."

She did a quick visual scan of my wounds "What has happened here? Donna says you fell off your bike. These injuries, especially the cuts on the feet are most unusual. They are not what I would expect to see from a bicycle accident."

"Rainey was just being funny. We had an argument and I ran away and fell down a lot."

"So, I don't have to call the police then. Should I be recommending a marriage councillor?"

Rainey and I both cringed. We looked at each other, smiled into each other's eyes, and told her "no." I said that we preferred to keep our craziness private.

"Your life is anything but private though isn't it? I did not think that I would be meeting the infamous Vienna and Rainey so soon." She commented before informing us that she was Dr. Nelson. "I don't mean any disrespect, but I'm afraid your sagas have preceded you."

"Have you been talking to my friend Lara Cooper?" I asked inquisitively.

"I am fairly new to the area, but I already knew some of your history before I even moved here. You were a very big national news story my dear. Lara did mention that you were moving back to Bridge, and I hoped that I would have the privilege of meeting you some day. I hardly thought it would come right on the heels of my visit with your daughter.

She has given me a bird's eye view into life in a gothic castle, and into the lives of her adventurous parents."

"Is she all right? Is she and the baby all right? Are there complications?" I pleaded.

"Let the good doctor speak Honey."

"She is in excellent condition although exhausted from the long trip. Baby is doing just fine. Everything is progressing just as it should be, so nothing to worry about. You will be grandparents to a healthy baby in two or three days. Now, let's get back to this *accident*."

"I'm to blame Dr. Nelson. We had an unexpected unwelcome visitor and I lost my cool. I'm afraid I took it out on Vienna. She ran away and as she said, fell down a lot."

I interrupted him. "He is not to blame Doctor. I'm compulsive and I take everything to heart. I reacted badly and childish to the heat of the moment and I'm embarrassed sitting here taking up your valuable time. I wanted to go home but Rainey insisted I come here. I'm sorry."

"Your husband was right to bring you here. Donna and Geraldine will get you all cleaned up and then I will assess your wounds. They all look shallow, but it's the feet I am concerned about. Your blood pressure is a little high. I'm going to give you something so you can relax, and you may need an anti-biotic."

"Oh, I can't take anything because I'm still nursing the twins."

"Vienna, you need to think about yourself for once. They do very well with a bottle and it's time you gave your body a rest. Let's deal with your injuries okay?" Rainey suggested.

"I won't give you anything that will harm you or the twins Vienna. I'll send the girls in to clean your abrasions, and we'll need to soak those feet in a nice warm water bath, and then apply an anesthetic to block the pain while removing any particles left. I will look at the wounds on your legs then. Try to relax Mrs. Quinn."

"Dr. Nelson, may I speak to you privately for a minute?" Rainey asked.

"Call me Barbara. I think I'm going to be seeing a lot of your family, so we may as well be on a first name basis. Follow me and tell me what I can do for you."

"Rainey, what's wrong?"

"Nothing Honey; I just need to ask the doctor about a test. Rest easy; I'll be right back."

What kind of a test did he think I needed? My thoughts were interrupted when Donna and Geraldine arrived with a cart loaded with utensils, towels and a deep basin. First I had to drink a bottle of some sort of liquid. I had a choice of coconut, watermelon or orange juice. I asked if I was dehydrated because I didn't feel like it and I'd already had a bottle of water. Apparently, the drink was to help replenish my body's electrolytes. While I was drinking they started to clean up my lacerations on my face, arms and legs. I told them they could throw my dress in the trash.

"What's this?" Donna said as she retrieved something from the bodice. She laughed holding it up for me to see. "I don't think this is where you normally keep your treasures is it?"

I took it from her examining it. "Rainey gave it to me this morning. I must have broken the chain when I fell. I would have been heartbroken if I had of lost it."

"It's the loveliest family necklace I have ever seen. There must be a stone for every month."

"Well, we have nine children between us."

"Nine; wow, how old are they all?" Geraldine asked.

"They range from twenty-four to eight months. Rainey wanted me to have something to celebrate us all so he had this made. It was supposed to be here on the Labor Day weekend because nothing good had ever happened to him on that weekend, and he said it was finally…" I couldn't continue.

"What is it Mrs. Quinn?" Donna asked concerned.

"I'm sorry," I sobbed, "because I wrecked the occasion by starting a fight with him."

"I saw the way he looked at you, so whatever sparked the argument he has forgotten it. We've all been there and blamed ourselves, but remember it takes two to tangle."

"Thanks, but if you knew me you'd know I'm usually the one at fault."

"How about you tell us about life in a castle while your feet are soaking? Gerry is excellent at removing foreign objects as she has a sturdy hand."

My feet objected strenuously to the water bath. I grated my teeth and braved it. "I could bore you with anecdotes of the obligatory teas and duties the lady of the house has to cope with, or perhaps you would be more interested in the lively spirts of those souls who once occupied the premises and now wander the hallways at midnight in search of what only they know."

"Oh, by all means the latter! Gerry's aunt Lucille lives in an estate known as The Towers. She and all visitors say that it is haunted, but the aunt says it isn't."

"What makes you think so Gerry?" I asked.

"Strange noises and the feeling that I am being watched. Someday if you are willing I would like you to visit with me. Lara told me that you have psyche powers."

I laughed lightly. "Psyche impulses perhaps, but yes I do seem to attract departed souls. Yes, I would very much like to meet your aunt at the Towers and see if I can detect any spirits. We will have to keep it a secret from my husband though because I promised him that I wouldn't get into any more mischief with the departed."

My feet were dried and left to absorb the anesthetic for a few minutes before they prodded the soles of my feet with tweezers and needles removing grime and embedded gravel. I distracted myself as best I could from the discomfort and my fight with Rainey by relating tales about my beloved Avanloch.

Twenty minutes later they rewashed and dried my feet and applied a little more of the Lidocaine and wrapped them in thick layers of cloth bandages and secured them with an elastic. The girls placed a pillow behind me and one under my feet and told me to relax as Dr. Barb would be in shortly. A wave of dizziness hit me just as my head touched the pillow. I sat up quickly and saw Rainey and a woman come through the curtain. They were laughing. I pointed a trembling finger in their direction. They were fading fast from my sight. Where were they going? I could hear voices, but they were muted and garbled. I opened my mouth to speak, but my mouth felt like it was coated in peanut butter and the words were all stuck to the roof of my mouth. I could hear what I was saying, but it was in another tongue. Did someone just jab me in my leg? My ears were ringing, my heart was racing…

"Vienna, thank God you're back! You scared the living daylights out of us. Don't try to talk; just breathe. You've had a shot of epinephrine. The doctor thinks you had an allergic reaction to the antiseptic. Can you hear me Honey?" Rainey was holding my hand begging me to acknowledge him.

All I could do was nod. The doctor was standing on the other side of me. She was shining a light into my eyes. Her hands were cold as she felt for my pulse.

"You gave us quite a fright Vienna. Allergic reactions to Lidocaine are rare, but you have obviously had one. I know you were all set to go home, but now we need to monitor you for a while and replace the feet wraps."

It seemed to take forever before I could speak. The words came out slow and apologetic. "I thought you were her. Meggie told me to be wary of the she-wolf at my door, but you're not her are you?"

"Is that what you were trying to say when you pointed at us Honey? We heard you say Meggie, but then you went limp and we couldn't understand you. Did you think Dr. Barb was Jorja? Please tell me you didn't?" Rainey asked dismayed.

"Who's Jorja?" I asked smiling.

He bent down and kissed me and whispered that he loved me.

"Meggie warned me and I did not heed, just as I didn't listen to Mollie when she warned me, and you know what happened. I don't want to go back there Rainey."

"You're not going anywhere except home with me Honey."

"Who are Mollie and Meggie?" Dr. Barbara asked.

"They are dear friends from back home in Scotland. Mollie has passed, but her granddaughter has taken over for her."

"Taken over for what?"

"They are visionaries."

Rainey felt that he had to clarify. "Scotland is a land steeped in centuries of mystical beliefs and superstitions. I have seen things that I cannot comprehend, but I choose to take it all with a grain of salt, but Vienna is a believer in all things questionable."

"Really Mr. Quinn; how do you explain Vienna's spectral rescue as she lay hemorrhaging on the path to the crypt then? Was her rescue not convincing enough for you? " Donna asked.

"You know about that?" Rainey asked dumbfounded.

"We have had a delightful time listening to your wife's stories of Avanloch while we tended to her injuries, but the crypt one came from your cousin Lara."

Rainey laughed. "I should have known. Nothing gets by my cousin does it Vienna?"

"I had to have someone to confide in all those years I was in isolation."

"You weren't alone or imprisoned, so what do you mean?" Donna asked.

"I suppose isolation is the wrong word. I could go and do anything that I wanted to, but I kept myself from doing what I wanted most, so it was self-penance of a sort. Rainey, you should go as it looks like I have to stay here for a little while longer and everyone will be wondering what's going on."

"I've already called home so all is well. I'll wait until you are given the green light."

"I've already taken up enough of your day, so you should go."

"You still owe me a quarter of a lifetime, so I'll just wait with you please, and thank-you."

An hour later I was given the green light to leave. My feet had been rewrapped sans the Lidocaine. I was being sent home with a wheelchair as I was to stay off my feet for several days. I didn't see how that was going to be possible. Rainey said he would make sure that I followed instructions. Dr. Barbara asked if she could drop by tomorrow evening as she would like to see how I was faring and that way she could check on Ava also. It would save us both an exhausting visit to the hospital. I wanted to object, but Rainey said we would look forward to her visit.

In the car I told him that he shouldn't have been so quick to accept her self-invitation.

"It's not a social call Vienna. She just wants to check on you and Ava. It's unheard of these days for a doctor to make house calls, so you should be grateful." He said tartly.

"Maybe Ava and I are her excuse for her just wanting to see you." I retorted.

He shut the car off and turned to me. "Why the hell would you say that?"

"Did you not go off with her and return almost an hour later chortling like you had made some sort of a pact? Did you not stand at my side acting like the concerned husband all the while keeping eye contact with her?"

"Damn it, you're good! I figured that Jorja might not be enough for me anymore so Babs looks like she would fit into my harem quite nicely. I just didn't think you'd catch on so soon."

He started the car again and sped out of the parking lot. Neither of us spoke until he pulled into the driveway at the Palace. He told me to stay put while he retrieved the wheelchair. I asked him if we were going to stick with the story of me having a bicycle accident.

"Sure, anything you want Vienna."

Jack and Nash were the first to arrive followed by Tanny and Lili. Sissy stayed on the front porch with Ava who was in tears. I told them that I was just fine. Lili wanted up on me.

Rainey took hold of her and spoke very sternly. "No, you may not sit on your mother's lap.

Can you not see that she has bandages all over her and is hurting? Tanny, please take your sister in the house."

Lili kicked her dad and said "NO!"

Rainey and I looked at each other. For a brief second it broke the tension between us. I knew he wanted to scold her again, but it was just all too funny seeing her standing there arms crossed, defying her dad. I smiled and said she couldn't hurt me because she was so tiny.

He relented. "Well, like mother, like daughter." He placed her gently on my lap and told her she had to sit still.

"What do you mean by that remark?"

"You both always get your own way don't you, so just stating a fact."

I had a quick comeback. "Well, you're to blame for that aren't you?"

Tanny walked beside me holding my hand as Jack and Nash helped Rainey lug the chair with me and Lili up the front steps and into the house. I waited until Sissy and Ava finished hugging and assuring them that I was all right before letting Rainey deposit me on the love seat. He told me to sit quietly as he was going to do the talking now. First he explained to everyone why my feet were bandaged so heavily, my reaction to the antiseptic, and what my care would entail. Tanny asked what happened to the bicycle. Rainey answered her a little agitatedly.

"I need to speak with the adults right now Tanny, so can we talk about that later. Zoe, would you mind taking the girls upstairs for half an hour or so? Vienna will fill you in afterward okay?"

The room was silent except for Lili who clung to me and said she wasn't going. I could tell that Rainey had about all he could take from his women folk for one day, so I'd better try to reason with her without hurting his ego. I knew that he and I could talk through anything eventually, but how do you reason with a child who isn't even three yet? I didn't want Rainey to scold her again, so bribery was the next best thing. As if on cue both the twins woke up. Sissy went to tend to them, Jack went to check on dinner and Nash walked over to the liquor cabinet and asked the girls what they would like. He passed Rainey a generous glass of whiskey on the rocks. Tanny and Lili both said they wanted crème soda. Nash told them it was in the kitchen so they were going to have to go and ask Uncle Jack for that, and then they would have to stay in there to drink it.

"Can Lili and me have ice cream with ours Nash?" Tanny asked.

"What do your mom and dad say about that?"

"They say it's all right if they stay with Zoe until called to come out. There might just be a few new books in the pantry when their hands are clean. Are you all right with that Vienna?"

"We just broke our own rules Rainey."

"Yeah, desperate times, desperate measures. You ready for this?"

"I'm supposed to be quiet remember, so I can't object can I?"

He laughed. "As if that has ever stopped you before."

He waited until everyone had returned and had a drink in their hands. "I wish I could say that this was my happy hour, but it isn't, and I'm pretty sure it isn't Vienna's either." He relieved Sissy of the twins and asked me which one I wanted. I said neither and to put them on the floor in front of us and let them entertain each other. He sat down beside me. Ava who had been quiet so far said she couldn't imagine what trouble we had gotten into this time.

"Why do you think we're in trouble Honey?" Rainey asked.

"Oh, just a feeling, and how does a bicycle fit into this exactly?"

"I had to come up with an explanation for the nurses and your doctor as to your mom's injuries and that is what popped into my head."

"My doctor; did you see Dr. Barbara?"

"Yes, we did. Your father is on a first name basis with her already." I tried to free my hand from his, but he had a firm hold on me. I guessed that I was stuck here next to him while he gave his remorseful rendition of his affair with Jorja whether I wanted to be or not.

CHAPTER 4

RAINEY'S CONFESSION

> *"And those who were seen dancing were thought to be insane by those who could not hear the music."*
> -Friedrich Nietzsche

I squeezed my wife's hand a little too hard and winked at her. Hell, I was already up the so called creek so what were a few more shovelfuls? "Yes, and a very lovely lady she is. She's coming by to check on you and your mother tomorrow evening Ava. Now I best get on with things before Liliana returns and we have to put up with her insolence again." I cleared my throat. "I came home today to find my daughter and my wife having tea with someone I once had a tainted relationship with. I was not pleased to see her at all."

"Was it Zeta Daddy?"

"How do you know about her Ava?" Vienna demanded looking at us both frostily.

Oh Christ, had I forgotten to tell Vienna that Zeta had contacted me while I was in Vancouver while she had been in Spain?

"Daddy told me about her when you were missing, that's all. I never met her or anything."

"And why would you have met her?"

Ava was very uncomfortable. "I'm sorry Daddy; I thought she knew."

Vienna jerked her hand away from mine. "Oh, I knew about her all right. I just didn't know your dad was seeing her while I was *AWAY* as you people like to refer to the time I was held prisoner in Spain!"

"I wasn't seeing her Vienna. She phoned and that's all there was to it. I talked to her that once. I'm sorry I never told you, but it wasn't important enough to even mention."

"Did she know I was missing? Did she ask you to marry her again?"

I got up and looked down at her. "I'm not discussing this with you now. If you can't let me get on with the reason we are here then perhaps you should go and keep the girls company."

Ava was visibly upset. "It's my fault; me and my big mouth. I'm sorry Mama. I want to sit with you and hug you, but I'm afraid I'll sink and never be able to get up again."

"The boys will get you up my darling. Nash, help her sit please so we can let her father get on with his confession. I promise not to interrupt you anymore Rainey."

"You don't have to promise me anything Honey. I just need you to understand."

"I'm trying, but you keep throwing road blocks in my way."

Ava and I traded places. I reached my hand out to Vienna. "I'm sorry I forgot to mention that Zeta had phoned, but as I said, it was inconsequential."

She took my hand and said that she wished it had of been Zeta at the door today instead of Jorja. What could I do but smile and say that I wished that Jorja never existed and that today had never happened. I looked around the room at the faces that were waiting for my explanation as to what I had done that had resulted in their beloved Vienna's so-called bicycle accident. Sissy had always looked up to me. She was the one who had struggled the most keeping Vienna's whereabouts from me all those years ago. Ava would be disappointed with me. Nash was new to the family, so I had no idea what he would think of me. Jack was another story.

"So, it was another Labor Day weekend; the weekend where everything goes wrong. It was 1980, and my two best buddies, Jimmy and Yates had come down to Vancouver to celebrate with me. Nash, you'll be meeting the two of them soon. Jimmy and his wife Ruth are in Halifax awaiting the birth of their first grandchild just as we are awaiting ours here. Yates is working in some gold mine in the Yukon and is expected home any day. They were all instrumental in our relationship in the sixties weren't they Honey?"

She squeezed my hand, agreed, smiled and corrected me saying that the mine was in The North West Territories and was a diamond mine. "Not that it matters though." She added.

"You have always been better at remembering things so I stand corrected. It seems like a lifetime has passed since that weekend four years ago. The three of us spent the day with Mason and Morgan at the PNE. After we dropped them off at home we went bar hopping. It was Jimmy and Yate's holiday so I elected myself as the designated driver. We ended up in an area known as the Yard which is full of specialty bars; you know the ones that cater to exotic dancers and strippers, and gambling in the back rooms. I've never been one for strip joints as watching young women bear themselves to a room full of strangers is not a turn on for me. Jimmy and Yates were game, so we ventured into the Prohibition Club. Unfortunately, I didn't have the foreknowledge of things to come, and today I'm paying for those decisions I made back then. Anyhow, an hour or so later it was time to get the boys out of there. Any longer and I'd have to carry them both out. It was about then that this dancer who called herself Tequila came on stage. She centered her act around us, and for some reason she chose me as her target. I wasn't thrilled, but the guys thought it was great when she left the stage and came over to our table. She flirted with them, but kept her eyes on me. She somehow managed to sit on my lap and asked me if I would come back and see her. I think I might have told her I was married. The guys told her that they'd make sure I came back. They were going home tomorrow so I never thought any more about it, and I didn't. So what happened? It was probably three weeks later that I found myself in the vicinity of the Yard once more. I had this client who was buying up unoccupied old buildings throughout the city, remodeling them and turning them into offices, restaurants, housing or whatever. So, I had a two hour meet with him on Justin Street. I gave him my output on the cost of remodelling and my fee and a deal was struck if I agreed to supervise the job. We sealed the deal with a drink. I thought I had recognised the name of the bar where we went, but paid it no mind until I realised that it was the joint that I'd been in with Jimmy and Yates. The memories came back as we were asked to give a big welcome for Tequila. We were sitting at the bar so I didn't bother in turning around and left shortly afterwards. That should have been the last I would ever hear the name Tequila, but sadly, it wasn't. As it turned out she lived just three blocks away and I was to run into her every day for a week as I was supervising the remodel. The first time was when I was leaving the site one late afternoon. She came by carrying a shopping bag full of groceries. She smiled and said hi. I guess I said hi back. She asked if we had met before. She knew damn well we had, but I played her game and said no. She said her name was Jorja Elliot, and if I was going to be working here then we would be running into each other now and then. A week later I was walking her home. She told me what she did for a living two or three times a week which was dancing, as she called it. It paid really well and because of it she was able to put herself through business school. She had only three or four months to go and then she could quit dancing and hopefully get a better more respectable job. She invited me up to her apartment for dinner one night, but I declined and took her out to a nice restaurant instead, and that's how it began."

I walked over to the fireplace mantel where we kept the bar supplies so little fingers couldn't reach anything. No one else wanted a refill so I poured myself another stiff one, took a swig and sat down. Ava had questions.

"Daddy, why are you so down on yourself? So you had a tryst with an exotic dancer, so what?"

"Did you miss the part where I said she was here today, and that she is claiming that I am her daughter's father? Oh, and did I forget to mention that she's a prostitute?"

Ava grabbed her stomach and yelped. Vienna yelled for Nash. I got up and dropped to the floor at my daughter's feet afraid that my revelation had brought on labor pains. She laughed and told us all to quit panicking as it was just Samie kicking up a storm.

"Are you sure it wasn't what I said?" I asked guiltily.

"No Daddy, it was not. I'm sorry if I scared you all." She said stroking my head. "It was a little shocking to hear what you said, but it makes no difference in the way I feel about you. It was a time when you were most vulnerable. I imagine you have your reasons for seeking out her kind because there must have been many women out there for you to choose from that were a little more respectable. I suppose she had other attributes…"

"Ava," Vienna interjected, "you need to let your father continue as there is more to the story."

"You knew?"

"Yes," I answered, "I couldn't have asked your mother to marry me with that albatross hanging around my neck." I smiled at my wife. "She understood and said that we never had to speak of it again, and we didn't, and then I come home this morning to find *her* having tea with my wife and daughter. I'm afraid I went off the deep end, but your mother, being the saint that she is took command. I reacted badly and now she is the one suffering for my indiscretions."

Nash settled in beside Ava asking her if she was sure she was okay. She assured him it was just Samie. He asked me as to how and why this woman came to signal me out as her child's father as seeing what her profession was she couldn't possibly know for sure who the father was.

"He was having what she thought was a romance with her, and she thinks he still loves her. Are you going to finish your story Rain, or do you want me to?" Vienna offered sardonically.

I attempted to get up off the floor, but a spasm stopped me and sat me back down. I swore.

"Oh Daddy, what is it?" Ava said reaching for me.

"He hurt his back while carrying his hefty wife for half a mile through sinking sands." Vienna stated. "Can you give him a hand up Jack?"

I didn't refuse Jack's help, but felt that I had to correct my wife. "You aren't the reason Vienna, and you are not as heavy as you seem to think you are, and it certainly wasn't anywhere near half a mile. I tweaked my back weeks ago lifting furniture and it has been acting up now and then. It's nothing I can't manage."

"Says the man who couldn't get up off the floor." Ava quipped.

"Maybe it was just Samie broadening his kick." I joked. "And," I said looking at Vienna, "I would never have told her that I loved her. Her thinking that I did doesn't make it so."

I looked around the room at the five pair of eyes waiting for the rest of my sleazy nightmare. "I guess one might refer to me as the original middle aged fool wearing those famous rose tinted glasses." I snorted obscenely. "If it was a mid-life crisis then I had it in spades. I was under the misconception that I was the only one sharing her bed. We went to dinners and the movies. We went sightseeing and for long walks. In all honesty it was a normal relationship despite her occupation as an exotic dancer. I never watched her performances. I waited outside chatting with the bouncer on the nights that I picked her up which were usually Saturdays and an occasional Tuesday. She worked Tuesdays to Fridays. All the other nights she was attending classes." I laughed rudely again. "One day she left me a message on my home phone and said she had Friday off, but had to work Saturday so could I change my night with my sons? I couldn't because they both had a hockey tournament, so I said I'd still see her after work on Saturday. I had never taken her to my suite. I can't explain why, something always stopped me if I thought about doing so. It was just going to complicate things with the boys so I hadn't been able to talk myself into it. So, that night I go to pick up the boys and they are down with the flu. Their useless mother didn't bother to let me know, so I thought I would surprise Jorja as she would just be at home studying. I stop at one of those corner stores that have displays of flowers outside and picked up a bouquet of flowers. Her apartment was up three stories so I'm slightly winded when I get to her door. I knock and she opens the door dressed in a sheer open negligee and skimpy undies and holding a twenty dollar bill. I wondered why she was dressed so scantily as she wasn't aware that I was coming. She is horror-struck to see me and tries to pull herself together saying that I shouldn't be there and that it is not a good time for her. I hear a male voice call out to her to bring the bloody pizza as he doesn't have all night. I ask her who he is. She says it is just an old friend and that I should go and she'd explain later. She is very anxious. I push past her and encounter a man of about fifty sitting naked on her bed. He asks me who the hell I am and I ask him the same thing. Jorja pulls a blanket around her and is crying that it's not what I think. This guy pulls his pants on, grabs his shirt and shoes, and a hundred dollar bill off the nightstand. He laughs vulgarly and tells her that she hadn't come anywhere near earning his hard working money, and if this is what she meant by a three-way then he was out and that she better check her schedule for double booking a little better. He wished me luck and left. She's still sobbing and denying that it wasn't what it looked like. I asked her what I owed her, told her she disgusted me, emptied my wallet and pockets of every bill and coin and threw it on the floor at her feet. I met the pizza delivery boy at the door and told him she was all his. I went home and showered for an hour. I had never given her my business number or told her the name of it, or told her where I lived for some reason. She thought I was a construction supervisor. I had been contemplating asking her to quit her job and concentrate on her schooling, and I'd pay for her expenses, but something always stopped me from doing so…thank God. As it turned out, I was just another "John", who was given freebees for some reason. I unplugged the phone at the suite and got a new unlisted number. I was not stupid and can never remember a time when I didn't use protection, but my wife has informed me that isn't a guarantee that an accident didn't happen. I was given a clean bill of health after a number of testing for STDS. That was it for me and women. Then in January I went to Hawthorne and changed my mind." I smiled at my wife.

She smiled back and said. "Good God, I never thought you'd quit talking. Get me out of this sofa and into my chair. No, not you Rainey; we can't afford to both be crippled. I don't know about anybody else, but I am starving and Sissy's fried chicken is calling my name."

I bowed to Jack and let him help her into the wheelchair and then help Nash get Ava up. I felt useless. "Before you ask little girl, paternity testing is already in motion so it's just a wait and see game right now. And, when did you find out you were having a boy?"

"I was wondering the same thing." Vienna said. "I like Samie for a name, but wouldn't Sam or Samuel be more masculine?"

Ava laughed. "We'll explain over dinner. Nash, can you take Mom into the kitchen? I want to have a minute with my Dad."

"Don't be too hard on him Ava. It was before me, so I'm not the one he cheated on. That was Louise, but I guess he didn't think of it as cheating because he had already left her. It was difficult for your father to tell me about her, but he didn't want any secrets between us. I didn't, and I don't love him any less because of it. Let this be a warning to you boys;

tell your women all your past discretions, no matter how trivial they were so they can't come back to haunt you."

Nash and Jack both laughed and said it was already taken care of. I bent down and kissed my wife thanking her yet knowing full well that I wasn't out of the woods with her yet. Ava just wanted me to know that she still respected me and that nothing I had done or would ever do would change her feelings for me, but I best make amends with my wife because the "flower thing" hadn't gone over very well with her. Damn, why had I mentioned that I'd bought Jorja flowers? That was my thing with Vienna. Damn, I was stupid. The women in my life had just reversed one of the most deplorable days of my life, and I'd have to do some more damage control, but right now I had to deal with Liliana. Hopefully, she wasn't still mad at me.

I found her sitting on her mother's lap squirming around and banging her utensils on the table.

I picked her up. "What did I tell you about sitting quietly with your mother? Did you forget that she is hurting? You'll come and sit with me or in your own chair and behave yourself, understand?"

She wiggled her way out of my arms and stomped out of the room.

"Oh Rainey," Vienna bemoaned, "she wasn't hurting me. You need to go and bring her back. You might have to eat crow, but whatever… please."

I squeezed her shoulder and said I'd see what I could do. I figured I would have to get down on my hands and knees and beg Lili to forgive me, but she wasn't to be outdone. She came around the kitchen door toting two very large cushions. She put them down, pulled a chair alongside of Vienna and tried to pile the pillows on it. We were all stifling our giggles. Nash was closest and asked her if he could help her. He looked at me for approval. I nodded. He helped her with the pillows, put an apron on her and tied her to the chair with its strings. She thanked him, didn't look in my direction and told her mother that she was ready for a bun with butter. I was going to offer to do it, but thought better of it when I got the look from Vienna. I had been rebuffed by the child that could melt me like hot butter.

I waited until everyone had their plates full before I spoke directing my question at Ava and Nash. "It was our understanding that you didn't know the sex of the baby, so when did you find out it was a boy? Was it today with Dr. Nelson?"

Ava giggled a little. "We still don't know Daddy. Sami is a unisex name. If its's a boy, he will be Samuel Quinn Nash, and if it's a girl, she will be Samantha E Vienna Nash. We plan on calling them Samie or Sam, so we have started calling the baby Samie."

"There is a reason for the name." Nash explained. "We wanted to honour our friends that we spent two months with in the wilds of the north, so we, actually it was Ava who came up with the name. S is for Sally, A is for Ace and of course Ava, M is for Monty and the E is for Evie."

"Oh, what a tribute! They will love it, and I do too!" Vienna exclaimed.

I raised my water glass and winked at my daughter. "To Samie; can't wait to meet you whether you are a grandson or a granddaughter."

Nash laughed. "To be perfectly honest we don't care if it's a girl or boy, as long as he/she is healthy." He looked lovingly at Lili. "Was Ava as robust as her little sister Vienna?"

"Ava was born a lady. She never had any of Liliana's temperament just as Novia hasn't. Lili was also well behaved for the first year and a half of her life, and then she met her father. Her behavior is on him, and you are going to have one heck of a time keeping him from pampering Samie. Good luck with that." Vienna said smiling at me.

I was on the verge of making a big mistake commenting that I hadn't had the chance to pamper my first daughter so was making up for twenty lost years with Ava, but I caught myself just in time and just smiled back at my wife. "Looks like I'll have to set my eyes on Novia then because it's obvious that Lili prefers you over me. Oh course I still have you don't I Tanny?"

"You're so funny Rainey. We all know Vienna's your favorite girl." Tanny stated.

"I can have more than one can't I?" I asked teasingly.

"You want to have more than one wife?"

"I don't think that's what he meant Tanny." Ava said laughing.

Vienna rubbed her neck. "I think about now I could use a sister-wife."

"I'm your sister and I'm going to be a wife soon, so will I do Sis?" Sissy asked caringly.

"Oh Sweetie, I'm already indebted to you and Jack for looking after the twins today. I'm probably going to need your help for a few more days as I can't expect Zoe to do everything."

"I don't mind Mum, and I can skip a few days of school." Zoe offered.

"No need Zoe; it seems as though *Mum* has forgotten about me." I said getting up and rubbing my wife's shoulders. "How's that Mommy?"

"She's *my* Mommy." Lili informed me

"Yes I am Lili. Daddy is just being playful when he calls me Mommy. The massage feels good Rain, but I'm afraid the day has caught up to me and I'm going to have to lie down. Will you help me make up the sofa bed?"

"Don't you want to sleep in your own bed Mama?" Ava asked.

"Of course I do, but umm, did you forget that I'm not supposed to walk? I think I could make it up the stairs though with a little help, but I will forgo it for today."

Nash was on his feet before I could object. "No need to subject yourself to any more pain Vienna. I think Jack and I can get you up the stairs quite nicely. I'll come back for your chair so that you can get into the washroom by yourself, okay."

"Hey, what am I, chopped liver?" I questioned.

"Your back might be, so take the help Dad." Nash said.

"Just a minute guys; I don't want anyone else to get hurt carrying me. Nash you're going to be a father any day and Jack you have a wedding to be healthy for...when's the big day anyhow?"

"As soon as the kids can get their acts together and manage to get the same time off. It'll be just a simple ceremony with a justice of the peace, so no big plans." Jack said.

"Is that what you want Sissy?" Vienna asked.

I didn't let my sister-in-law answer. "I hardy think so, and we won't hear of it, will we Hon? There will be a ceremony and a party right here at the Palace! Oh yeah also, Novia and Zander don't have godparents yet, so we'd be honored if you two would take the job...what'd you say?"

Sissy started into crying. "I was alone for so long and then Jack came along and rescued me, and now I have my sister home and all of her family..."

Now Vienna and Ava and Zoe were crying. It was up to us men to console the women, and we did the best we could. I asked if the answer was yes. Jack said it was, and he and Sissy would be honored to be the twins Godparents.

"Okay, you big strong men, come and give me a heave-ho. Tanny will you please bring Lili upstairs and help her get ready for bed, and then the two of you can come and snuggle with me in the big bed and read me some stories." Vienna relented.

Zoe and Sissy said they would see to the twins and bring them in to say good night. As soon as the boys had Vienna in their arms I grabbed the chair and headed up the stairs with it. We all heard Ava lamenting that she had nothing to do. Nash said he'd be right back. I told her to sit tight and that she had the most important job of all looking after herself and Samie.

I thanked the guys as they deposited Vienna in her chair at the top of the stairs. She said she loved them. I wheeled her into the bathroom, helped her get out of the hospital garb, and gave her a bath towel to cover up with. She asked me to take her "sock-feet" off so she could have a bath. I filled the sink up with warm water, passed her a wet facecloth and told her that was her bath for the next few days.

"I see you are going to use my impairment to take advantage of me. Don't get too overconfident because I can still get away from you if I want to."

"Do you want to?"

"We'll see what happens in the next few days. I don't like being told what I can or cannot do."

"No one is more aware of that than me my lady."

"Can you find me a nice soft gown and turn the bed down, please and thank you?"

"I can, You are more than welcome my dear." I found her a pale blue silky gown and went to turn the bed down. Liliana was hiding under the covers. She pulled them back over her when she saw me.

"Still not talking to me eh? Okay, guess I'll find me another little girl."

"She's just being a brat Rainey." Tanny said from the doorway.

"Come on, you may as well climb in too."

"No, I will wait and help Mommy."

"Okay, good idea. You'll make sure Lili behaves herself won't you?"

"Rainey, what is taking you so long?" Vienna yelled.

"Oh-oh Dad, you're in trouble again." Tanny mocked.

I shook my head. Apparently it wasn't my day for the fairer sex. I found Vienna trying to rearrange her hair. She had wet it and was using her fingers to pull it in little tendrils around her face. I told her I liked the look.

"Well it will dry and look dreadful again in a few minutes so don't get used to it."

"I don't love you for your hair-dos you know?"

"You did once."

"I doubt it."

"I was sixteen and had black curls plastered to my face."

"I remember the black hair, but it wasn't the only reason I was attracted to you."

"Yes, attracted…that's the word of the day isn't it?"

She pulled the gown down and wheeled away from me. I knew she was intent on getting herself into bed so I thought I'd let her try. She attempted to stand. Pain was written all over her face as soon as her feet hit the floor. I grabbed her around the waist and pivoted her into bed. There were tears in her eyes. Tanny asked me why I let her do that. What could I say?

"It's not his fault Tanny. I wanted to see if I could stand by myself, but I couldn't. It was too hard and painful. I'll be better tomorrow."

"Yes, you will. Shall I come back for the girls in half an hour?" I asked.

"Maybe just a little bit longer so that Lili will be asleep."

"I no sleep Mama." A little voice answered from under the blankets.

I rejoined the family downstairs. No one looked at me with disgust or commented anymore on my shameful disclosure. Instead they were working on a plan that Vienna would be happy with regarding the problem of getting her up and down the stairs. Jack and Sissy would be available day and night, and of course Nash would be here. I was not above having a lift of sorts installed, but by the time it was installed she'd probably be on the mend, and would object to it anyhow. I wanted to be the one doing everything for her and definitely felt inadequate. Ava told me to get over myself and accept the help. I acknowledged the support all the while believing that they all blamed me for her condition. They weren't wrong. Half an hour later I thanked Sissy for the coffee, said good night and said I'd better go rescue Vienna from Liliana.

"I don't think that I would go in empty handed Rainey. Let me get you a cup of coffee for her."

I kissed my sister-in-law telling her she may have just saved my life.

Tanny met me at the bedroom door. "Shh, they're sleeping."

I thanked her and told her that I would be in to tuck her into bed in a minute. I set the coffee on the nightstand and managed to gather Lili up in my arms without waking her or Vienna. I settled her in bed and turned to say goodnight to Tanny. She sat up and threw her arms around me.

"I'm so glad you're my dad Rainey."

"And, I am so very happy that you are my daughter."

"You don't have to worry about Lili because I am going to take care of her until Mommy gets better. I can help with the twins too."

"You are the best sister anyone ever had. I think with your help and Auntie Sissy's and Zoe's, we'll be able to manage just fine."

"I like Uncle Jack. Doesn't he have any children of his own?"

"I know he has a son, but I am not sure if there are any more."

"Does Auntie Sissy have any?"

"I don't think so, but how about if we ask your mother tomorrow?"

"Okay. I love you Rainey."

I kissed her on the forehead and told her I loved her too.

I didn't want to wake Vienna, but I needed a shower so thought I could sneak in, grab some clothes and use the main bathroom. I needn't have worried as she was sitting up drinking the coffee. She asked what had taken me so long. I told her about my little chat with Tanny, and that she had questions about Sissy and Jack, and their families, and that we'd talk about it tomorrow because I wasn't too sure myself of all the details.

"I'm a little ashamed that I don't more about your sister's lives." I said guiltily.

"That's not all that you're ashamed of is it?"

I was expecting some form of admonition regarding the way I had presented my fall from grace to the family, but her question of me being shameful stung. I told her we would talk after I showered, but if she preferred I could use the other bathroom and sleep downstairs, or in the cot in the twins' room. Her next words hit below the belt.

"Don't worry; I am through slut-shaming you, but if you want to sleep somewhere else I will understand why." She uttered as she turned her back on me.

I thought it best if I give myself a few minutes to plot how I was going to fix things. I'd hurt her enough for a lifetime already so whatever I had to do, or say, or promise, I would because she was my world, and I couldn't take another minute of her condemnation. I walked away hoping that a cold shower would numb my tongue. When I returned she was sitting up on the side of the bed with her feet hanging awkwardly over the edge. Without hesitation I found the hassock and placed her feet on it. She rubbed the back of my head when I bent down. I looked at her fighting back a tear. She smiled at me.

"I'm glad she was a shady lady."

Well that was a shitty thing to say. "You're glad I had relations with a prostitute…not just once, but for six weeks?" I hoped my bewilderment was evident.

"Yes, because you were falling in love with her, and if you hadn't discovered what she was you would have asked her to move in with you, and then you would have married her and had a family with her, and I wouldn't have Lili, or Novia, Zander, or you because you would never have come to Hawthorne, and…"

She was crying so hard that she couldn't get any more words out. I fell to the floor, took her hands and looked up at her. "I was always going to go to Hawthorne."

"You don't know that."

"It was my destiny, and my destiny *was*, and *is* you. I am so sorry that I took so many back roads to find my way to you."

"I'm afraid Rainey."

I lifted her feet up and told her to scoot over because I needed to hold her. I crawled into bed and pulled her into my arms. "You have nothing to be afraid of Honey. I will never let evil touch you again."

"I see you with her and if that is the image you have of me and Anton… I don't know how to deal with it." She lamented.

"I should never have said what I did earlier about you and him. I have never doubted that you had amnesia. It was very uncouth of me, and saying that it was just a remark in the heat of the moment is no excuse. I am so sorry for hurting you. I wasn't in love with her Vienna. I don't want to say it but I have to…it was just sex, plain, ugly sex. Yes, I am ashamed of that relationship, but I wasn't at the time. I was forty years old and lonely. She was just a port in the dark storm that I had made of my life. I beg you to put her out of your mind as I have. The day I looked into your eyes at Hawthorn all the darkness left me. Only love can do that, and you know I love you and only you; always have and always will."

"You took her flowers."

"Is that what is bothering you? They weren't anything I planned on. I stopped at a corner store to pick up a newspaper and the proprietor practically threw them at me. He was closing and wanted to get rid of them. I think I paid two dollars for them. I never took her flowers before."

"What happened to them?"

"That I can't answer. Now can we put this to rest for tonight and the rest of our lives?"

"I've read the diary that Katarina kept. There are passages in it that I remember faintly, but they are few and far between. My biggest fear is that one day I will remember being with Anton, and I don't think I will be able to handle it, and I am so afraid you won't be able to either."

"First, let me put your fears to rest because nothing is going to come between us, and definitely not Jorja or Anton. There is a big difference in the relationship that we had with them though. Mine was short lived and with a deceitful tawdry woman, but yours as Katarina was with a kind and caring man for almost two years. He loved you, and if you remember anything I hope it will be that. Yes, he was conniving and a liar, but he was mesmerized by you, just as I am, so I can understand his obsession with you, but I cannot forgive him for keeping you away from me. That said, I am wondering if you are looking for something in that diary that will bring you closure, or are you hoping to find something that may spark your memory?"

"I really don't know." She admitted.

"Then you should put it far out of your reach because you don't need to know anything else. Now let's put an end to all the negativity, get you into the bathroom, and get some sleep."

She found a tube of muscle relaxant and brought it back to the bedroom. I asked her where she was hurting. She said it was for me and told me to turn over. I said I didn't want her exerting herself, but she insisted. I found myself relaxing completely as my pain was fading into the gentleness of her hands which had turned into caressing, and then she spoke.

"I think it all started out innocently on your part. She just happened to walk by one day when you were leaving the construction site. Was it a coincidence? You know how I believe that everything happens for a reason?"

I turned over. "I thought we were through with this Hon, and what could the reason be?"

"That I am not sure of, but after three or four chance meetings, she comes by one day with several large bags of groceries. You do not realise that she has been stalking you and knows when you come and go. She bides her time watching, waiting and then that day she plays the damsel in distress card, and you being the gentleman that you are offer to carry them for her, and of course she gracefully lets you. You talk, she asks you up for dinner one day and you suggest that you go out for dinner, and you do. How long this goes on for I do not know, but the day comes when you accept her invitation to join her for dinner or drinks in her apartment. Maybe you just talk and get to know one another; I know not that neither. Then comes the day, the passion erupts and you are blinded by her charms as I am sure she is by yours. You may tell yourself that it is just a one-time thing, but your man parts want what they want; any maybe your heart does also until that ill-fated night...is that about right?"

I moved away from her. I hope my voice depicted my ire. "Christ; it's like you were there! You missed the part where she opened up a drawer and passed me an unopened box of condoms. The rest you were spot on." I moved to the edge of the bed.

"Where are you going? Don't you want to hear what else I think?"

I stood up. "No Vienna, I do not." I reached for my pillow.

"You'll be sorry then because I understand exactly what was going on in your head. I wanted so badly to find someone to love, and to be loved, but it never happened, so I lived for twenty years without a man's arms around me. I never intend to do that ever again. I would have eventually become a bitter old woman when the girls married and left me, but the fates were kind and felt that I had suffered enough and they spun the silver threads to the path that led me back to you. I will not let some little two-bit tramp interfere with what you and I have built together. I know you love me as I love you. I will fight tooth and nail for you, and I will stay with you to the ends of time if you will still have me." She professed

"I must be the stupidest man on earth for I am married to the most loving and forgiving woman on earth. She has forgiven me time after time, and still I doubt her. I should know that just because she says that she's through discussing something, she is not, and will keep putting the pieces all together until they meet with her approval. She will come up with some way to romance a difficult situation. I so want this thing that arrived at our door this morning to be over and done with, but I will have to take a page out of your handbook and show some patience. What happened, happened, and what will be, will be. Can I come back to bed now? I'm afraid to ask, but have you anything more to say on the subject?"

"No, I think I am done on that toxic subject, but what do you think about us buying a house for Ava and Nash and Samie?"

I climbed in next to her. "You really are in my head aren't you? I have been thinking the exact same thing and was going to discuss it with you this morning, but then all hell broke out, so it was not at the top of my list anymore. I'm a little worried that they might think we are trying to get rid of them, and I am unsure what Nash's reaction would be. What do you think?"

"They have only been here for a week, so I don't believe they will think that we don't want them here. I love that they are here and I don't care how crowded it is. It makes me feel more like I am back at Avanloch. But, I think they are the ones who are going to feel like they are in a fish bowl. They have been living in partial isolation for six months, so this must feel like a three ring circus to them. Well, not Ava, but Nash for sure. For all we know they are looking for a place of their own anyhow. I don't think that he is too proud to utilize Ava's trust fund if it benefits their way of living, and I don't think accepting a house as a gift from us will cause any ill feelings. I mean their plan is to spend the winter months down here every year so it makes sense that they have their own place to come back to. I don't want them moving way across town though so we are going to have to do a thorough search of available properties close to us."

"How close are you talking about? Would across the street be too close?"

"Wishing for something doesn't make it come true Rain. No one knows that more clearly than me. I have no idea how many times I sat on the front steps of Avanloch next to the stone lions wishing that a bright shiny red 1956 Oldsmobile would come driving through the gates and this blue eyed sandy haired man would be behind the wheel."

"Oh Sweetie, you know I would have been there if only I had known where you were."

"And that is on me. Sorry, I didn't mean to go there. What were you saying about a house?"

"I noticed a for sale sign on Mrs. Podmaroff's house when we got back from the hospital. Did you know she was selling?"

"I did not. I haven't seen her since we got back so just figured that she was visiting her daughter at the coast. I'll have to ask one of the other neighbors what's going on with her. That house would be perfect for them Rainey, and us." She laughed. "You need to phone the realtor right away before someone else snaps it up."

"First thing in the morning, and didn't we decide that we need to talk to them first?"

"Yes, but I want it to be so. I can't imagine anything better than having my daughter right across the street from me for six months every year."

"Does that mean that you have put your plans to go "home" on the back burner for now?"

"I will always miss Avanloch, but you and the kids are here, so this is home. Oh, by the way, you have to buy us all bicycles."

"I do? Why is that?"

"Well, you're the one with the bicycle story. I did not know that you had informed the household of my hypothetical accident when you had phoned home from the hospital. Tanny asked me where I had gotten the bike. Without even thinking I told her that you had bought it for me and that you were buying bikes for the whole family, but it was a secret as you wanted to surprise us all. Apparently, I found you out and took mine for a spin. She wanted to know where the rest of them were. I told her she would find out soon enough, but not to spoil your surprise."

"Thanks for fixing my blunder; four bicycles coming right up."

"You miscounted; there are five of us capable of riding."

"You don't think you're getting another one after you ditched yours today do you?"

"Very funny. If you don't trust that I can handle my own bicycle then you are going to have to buy us a tandem. Now do you want to kiss me or what?"

I laughed. "A tandem might be fun. Do I want to kiss the cherry lips of the teenage girl who enraptured me forty years ago…yeah, I think I just might."

CHAPTER 5

FAMILY

I awoke to Rainey's soft, gentle voice; the one that was reserved for the twins. "I smell baby." I murmured.

"Yeah, I got me one. There's another one across the hall if you want one."

"No, I want that one."

"Sorry Babe, but she wants her daddy."

I pulled my nightgown down. "No, I think she wants her mama."

He passed her to me. "You and those damn boobs win again."

"They always do, in one way or the other, but this cow is almost empty so you are going to have to warm up a bottle for Zander."

"On my way to do just that."

"Check on the girls please, and don't be too long because I am going to need to get into the bathroom pretty soon, and Zander should be waking any minute.

"Yes Ma'am; anything else?"

"No; just that I want to thank you for taking me back to 1961 last night."

"Yeah, I felt it too. What say we renew some of that old, yet new love again up at the line shack or in the back seat of the Oldsmobile?"

"Rainey Quinn! I'll have you know that I am not a frolicking teenager anymore, but a respectable married woman with half a dozen kids."

"And just how did you come by those kids my fair Lassie?"

"I asked for them and they magically appeared."

He laughed. "I guess you have forgotten the nightmare you had last night then?"

"What nightmare?"

"Something about some demon-like hooded figures sacrificing some damsel."

"That's not funny Rainey."

"No, it was pretty scary. We'll talk later, gotta go before the little fellow wakes up."

"Rainey…" I cried but he was gone.

Zoe poked her head in the door and asked me if I needed her. She was a second mother to the twins. She had been my saviour in Spain and now she was looking after me again. It's strange that I have so few memories of my time in Verde El Mar when I was living life as Katarina DeMarco, but I remember the day I met her. She was an orphan and had been hired by Anton to be my guardian, but she was so much more than that. Rainey's and my efforts of finding any lost family of hers had been unsuccessful, but we hadn't given up yet. I always considered her as family because I loved her like a daughter. Rainey and I had adopted her last spring. We had three adopted daughters and we never considered them as anything but ours.

Zander woke up, so she was off to tend to him. Rainey returned with a bottle, checked on them and came and helped me up. He was going to put Novia back in her crib, but I told him to put her down on the floor. He was afraid she'd go out in the hall so he had better go and put the gate up on the stairwell. I suggested he just shut the bedroom door.

He laughed. "I guess that would work, but I'm not comfortable with her out here and us in the bathroom."

I suggested he leave the bathroom door open so he could keep an eye on her.

"I guess I have left my razor-sharp brain downstairs." He quipped.

"I guess you have. Don't worry about her. She'll just crawl or try to walk over to the window seat and pull herself up so she can see out the window."

"She's done that before?"

"Yes Dear, she has. Now tell me about my dream."

"I don't think that it was a dream because you were trembling when I awoke you, so it was obvious that it was a nightmare."

"You said there were cloaked figures. Were there 13, and was the girl blonde?"

"Well Honey, it wasn't my dream so I only know what you told me."

"I've had this vision before. There were 13 figures in black robes. They were chanting "Alleluia, the witch is dead." The girl had long blonde hair and she was lying in a pool of water. Meggie warned me about her. She said I should be wary of a she-wolf at my door. The damsel on the floor is Jorja. I think I am going to kill her."

"Oh God Vienna; why would you say such a thing?!"

"Sorry; oh look, Novia is right behind you. Find her something to do while I finish dressing."

He picked her up, popped her down on our bed and opened the hatbox and gave her all the bracelets. He showed her what to do with them. She had six or so on each arm by the time I wheeled myself over to them. He placed her on my lap where she gave me one of her new trinkets. I thanked her and glumly wished that it was the infinity ones that Rainey had bought me. He read my mind, and said he knew what I was thinking because I had never worn another bracelet since I had handed the treasures over to James and Althea in Andorra. They had found Sister Anita, a relative of the doomed Katarina. We were still awaiting word from her.

I quickly broke out of the remembrance and told Rain that we should wake the girls. He said they were already up and enjoying Nash's blueberry pancakes.

"Nash is cooking? We really lucked out with him didn't we?"

"I think Ava did Hon, but we are equally blessed."

"Yes, we are and now Sissy and Jack are here for good. Are you okay with that?"

"I am because she's your sister and he's your best friend, and that makes them family."

"I think Jimmy is going to fight Jack for that title, but you know you are my very best friend don't you?" I affirmed.

He bent down and kissed me. "I do, but it's my other titles that I relate more to."

Jack and Nash were waiting at the bottom of the stairs to assist me. A few minutes later I was sitting in the nook with the girls. Liliana was banging on the table with her spoons. I put my hand on hers and asked her not to do that. She defied me of course. Rainey slid in beside Tanny still holding Novia. Lily yelled "Daddy" and trampled over Tanny to get to him.

He smiled at me welcoming her and told her to be careful with Novia. "I guess the Quinn women just can't stay mad at the ole man for long."

Nash poured us coffee and said that Jack was taking over for him at the grill as he had to go and help Sissy with Ava. I called out asking her how she was. She answered back that she knew what a whale felt like. I commiserated. Tanny wanted to know why Uncle Nash had the same first and last names. I told her as soon as breakfast was over with we would find out and she could also ask Aunt Sissy and Uncle Jack all the questions that she wanted to, and she did just that when we all joined Ava and the rest at the big dining table. Nash grinned when she asked him why he didn't have a first name. He said he did; it was Colton.

"I like it, can we call you Colton?"

"No, you may not. Well, you can, but I won't acknowledge you." He teased.

"Why?"

Rainey suggested she let it go, but Nash asked her a question continuing on.

"Do you know the saying, curiosity killed the cat, but satisfaction brought it back?"

Tanny said she did not.

"Well, we can't have you going around wondering for the rest of your life, so questions need to be answered. When I was about your age I went to the movies with some of my buddies. It was a western and there were a lot of bad guys in it. One was named Colton. He was a very bad fellow and shot anyone who got in his way. After that my friends pretended to be afraid of me and ran away whenever I showed up, and called me "Colton, the scary meany". I guess you might say they bullied me. They were all bigger than me so what else could I do. I was pretty scrawny back then, so I just put up with the teasing, but I was angry all the time. Then one day this new kid moved next door to us. His name was Frank Crank. He was 15 years old and had been teased when he was younger because of his name. He was tall and thin as a beanpole back then. Everyone called him "Cranky Lanky Frankie". He had put up with it just as I had, but not anymore. He had put on weight and learned how to box when he was 12, so no one messed with him ever again. He became my mentor, taught me how to defend myself and control my anger. He always called me Nash, and so I adopted it as the name I wanted to be called, and that is it. Technically, I am not your uncle Tanny as being married to your sister makes me your brother-in-law, but you can call me uncle or just Nash, whatever you like."

"I like just Nash. They were bullies weren't they? I'm glad you had a nice friend who helped you. Thank-you for telling me your story."

"You are welcome Tanny. Just remember, bullying at any age is unacceptable. I never told my parents because I thought I could handle it, but I couldn't and I cried myself to sleep many nights. If you ever see or hear of someone being bullied remember it is all right to report it."

"Can I tell you?"

"You betcha."

I asked Ava in a whisper if it was a true story. She said she had no idea as she had never heard it before. He'd told her he was Nash and that was all there was to it. Rainey asked her if she had any more questions.

"I want to know about Sissy's and Jack's kids." She said looking at them.

"I do too. You mentioned kids last night Jack. I thought you only had one son?" I questioned.

Jack had his arm around my sister. She smiled and nodded to him.

"I have a twenty year old son, and Sissy has a seventeen year old daughter, so that makes two."

I almost dropped my coffee cup. I looked at my sister in bewilderment. She smiled timidly. Rainey noticed my astonishment and tried to cover it up by asking Tanny if she was through.

"What are their names?"

Jack answered again. "My son's name is Jake and Sissy's daughter is Joannie."

"Okay then. How about you take your sister and vamoose for a little while?" Rainey suggested.

"What are you doing Liliana?" Tanny exclaimed as she made her way over to Lili who was relieving Novia of her bracelets one at a time saying, "Mine" every time she took one off. I was about to scold her again when Rainey shook his head. What…I'd scold her if I wanted to, but Tanny beat me to it.

"Lili, Lili, Lili, what am I going to do with you? Can I please have a bracelet? Thank-you; how about one for the other arm…thank-you. Let's go play with the new puzzle okay?"

The two took off for the living room, but not before Tanny turned and dropped the two bracelets unto Novia's tray. I thanked her. She said to think nothing of it.

We were all trying hard not to laugh, and as soon as the girls were out of sight the laughter started. Jack asked where on earth had we found her, and was she really only six.

"Actually, she's almost seven and she came to live with us when her mother was ill. She passed away when I was "away". Tanny loved Rainey and he started working on adopting her. I'm sure she filled a void in everyone's life back then. I was very happy to come home and find that she was to be a part of our family forever. As for what just happened, I have no answer. You'll have to ask Rainey as they had a father-daughter talk last night."

"All she told me was that mommy and me didn't have to worry about Liliana because she was going to look after her. I'm quite happy to have the help, but as soon as Vienna is back on her feet we'll lift the burden of Lili off her."

"Oh Daddy, Lili isn't that bad. I just love the interaction between the two of them." Ava said.

"We love them both just as they are. I am sure Tanny is going to want to be a big sister to Samie too. Now, I really need to talk with *my* sister if you'll excuse us." I started to pull away from the table but Rainey asked me if it could wait another five minutes because we should discuss our proposal with Ava and Nash first.

"Yes of course. Have you made the phone call yet?"

"I have, and the viewing is scheduled for ten if the parties are agreeable to that?"

"What's going on here you two?" Ava asked.

"Your mother and I want to buy you and Nash a house."

"You want to get rid of us?" Ava pretended to pout.

"I told you she'd say that." I interjected.

"I'm kidding. Nash and I have been thinking of renting a house ourselves. We love staying with you, but once the baby comes…I mean you have babies of your own, so I think we would be in the way. I won't be up to looking for a while, and I want to be close to you after Samie's birth so we haven't done anything about it yet."

"You'll never be in our way, so never think that, but you've only been married seven months and living all by yourselves, so this house must feel like your living in a three ring circus. If I had my way I'd keep you all here forever, but that's just me being selfish. You won't be far away if you like the house your father has found."

"How close is it?"

"Would across the street be close enough?" I enticed.

"Mrs. Podmaroff's house; is it for sale? I love that house; really Mama?"

"Yes Dear, your dad says so."

Rainey told her it was just put on the market yesterday, and he had called the realtor and that was what the ten o'clock appointment was about. They were both very excited and couldn't wait to view it. Nash suggested that Ava should lie down and rest until then, but she said she'd never be able to get up again, so he could just help her into a comfy chair in the living room because she knew he was itching to go check the house out on his own. He agreed that he was.

"You all do what you have to do because Sissy and I have an appointment of our own in the library. Rainey, can you please see what the kids are all up to and relieve Zoe?"

He said he would. Jack asked him if he could have his advice of a remodel to his Dad's shoe repair shop and a refashion of the old house's kitchen. Rainey said he'd be delighted. Ava complained that she'd be alone again. Nash promised her he'd only be ten minutes. I blew her a kiss and told Sissy that she could drive me to the library. We settled in the antique overstuffed chesterfield that mother had found at an estate sale many, many years ago. I took my sister's hands and told her I couldn't imagine what her story was.

"I probably wouldn't have ever old you, and I certainly couldn't tell mom and dad when it happened, but things have changed now. Jack and Erin are the only ones who know. It was a long time ago. You know that after graduating Erin and I worked for Mom at the café. We saved every penny and bought a small older car together and went to Banff where we were hired as chambermaids at a fancy resort. I don't expect that you would remember that because you were very busy with the girls and Avanloch."

"I know we only talked once or twice a month, but I do remember you going to Banff, and then a year or so later you and Erin went to Edmonton right?"

"Yes, and the fall of sixty seven Daddy had a minor heart attack and I decided to go home. Mom had enough on her hands with the restaurant and a rebellious Addy. I left Edmonton in mid- afternoon planning on driving straight through to Bridge Falls. I took a short cut through a less traveled back road. I stopped at a rest stop to use the facilities which of course was an outdoor toilet. There was a man there leaning over the hood of his car reading a map. I had to pass by him on my way up the path. He asked me if I was from around here and did I know the way back to the main Hiway. I said I did and I'd show him in a minute. That minute never came because he was waiting for me when I came out of the bathroom barring my way. He suggested that we go for a walk. I told him I didn't want to go for a walk and tried to get by him. We struggled. I probably screamed but there was no one around to hear anyhow. I think you know what happened next. Fortunately, it only lasted a minute."

I held back the tears for as long as I could. She put her arms around me.

"It's okay V, you can cry."

I was struggling with my emotions because my sister had been the victim of an unspeakable act by some fiend while she was on the way home to help my parents, and where was I...safe and sound in my fortress across the ocean. No one had asked for help because they were all too worried about upsetting dear Vienna. Well, I was pretty damn upset now. She was so calm speaking of the violation as if it had happened to someone else.

She sat back. "Breathe V; it's okay. It happened a long time ago, and it's not like nothing bad has ever happened to you."

"I was never raped."

"You were in a way because Anton abused you for almost two years."

"He never physically hurt me." I hated that she had brought up his name, and that I had basically defended him.

"Maybe not, but he left you with emotional scars and two years of your life that you can never get back."

"Are you telling me that you weren't and aren't emotionally scarred?"

"I was angry at myself for choosing such a remote location. If I'd had a gun I would have followed him and shot him, but I didn't, so I came home because Daddy was sick."

"And, where was I when everyone needed me? Oh, I know in the bloody castle in Scotland because I couldn't tell Rainey I was pregnant and I made my family keep my selfish secret."

"And, that is why I never told you and I never would have except I guess a miracle came out of it all anyway, and she'll be here soon." Sissy beamed.

"I get the part that you had a daughter, but why have you kept her a secret? Please reiterate a little more please. Did he hurt you…oh God, were you a virgin?"

"No, I had a boyfriend for a few months in Banff, so I knew what it was all about. He slapped me around a little because I fought him, but it was to no avail and when he flipped open a pocket knife and held it to my throat I quit fighting. As I told you, it was quick. I locked myself in the bathroom, threw my panties down the toilet and tried to wipe his filth from me. I heard a car and looked out and he was driving out so I ran to my car, locked the door and took off. I didn't stop until I reached a service station. I went into the washroom and washed with hot water, got back in the car and drove all the way home."

"And then you reported it?" I was finding it very hard to keep my emotions at bay.

"I did not. I stayed here until Dad was given the ok, and then I went back to Edmonton. Erin talked me into making an anonymous phone call to the police. I did from a phone booth half way across town. The next month I found out I was pregnant. Erin thought that I should have an abortion, but I couldn't go that route, so I carried her to term and gave her up for adoption. I never even glanced at her when she was born. Those nine months were just a sordid page out of that nauseating chapter of my life, and I never wanted to speak of it again. Four years later I married Harv, didn't want to have children, so stayed on the pill. We fought constantly over it and he became verbally abusive, so we divorced, and you let me live here until I got my life back on track. I knew one thing and that was that I never wanted to get involved with a man ever again, and then I met Jack." She smiled.

"I am so glad you did because he is a wonderful and caring man."

"I struggled with the knowledge that he had loved you, and maybe still did for a while, but I got over it. Did you know that Rainey was the one who introduced me to him?"

"If I knew, I don't remember. I was given so many details about what had taken place while I was away on that unplanned sojourn that I am still putting pieces together. Sometimes I just put a halt to what I remember because I am afraid of reviving Katarina, and apparently I have a selective memory and can control it. Go on please."

"Sorry V; I didn't mean to remind you of that. It was sometime around Christmas of '81. Rainey and Ava, Mason and Morgan came to spend the holiday with Rainey's parents and Jack was home for a few days also. You had been missing for over three months. Rainey knew from Lara that I was back living here, so he came to check up on me and see if I needed anything. We commiserated for a bit, so I was rather sullen when Jack arrived. He heard I was living here and came by to see if there was any news regarding you. Rainey filled him in with what we knew which was nothing and said the coffee was still hot if he wanted to get a little more update from me. I guess he took it for granted that Jack and I knew each other because of you. I barely remembered him. After Rainey left I asked him if he would like to stay and chat and he said he would. Throughout the year we became friends. He'd phone me every other week to check up on me, but I'm sure it was you that he really wanted to know about. Our divorces were both finalized early in 1982 and you were still missing. He started coming home every few months, and pretty soon we were more than just friends. He wanted me to come and live with him in Edmonton and I did for almost a year. First his mother became ill and then his father so he took an extended leave from his job and we came back here to Bridge to look after them. I was closer to Mom and Dad too so it was all good. Jack's mom passed away first and his dad seven months later. Jack didn't want to go back to the oil fields so he put his house in Edmonton up for sale, and here we are."

"I am so very glad you are, and I can't wait to meet Joannie. Why haven't you told us that you found her?"

"I never thought about looking for her, and I probably would have had a very hard time if I had tried, but she found me. It was the same time last year when Ava's plane was missing. I certainly wasn't going to bother you with something you never knew about, so I just kept it to myself. Well, that is not true because Jack was right by my side. He was with me when I got the call. I was shocked to say the least. I had just found out about Ava so I couldn't even talk to her sensibly. I told her I was going to have to call her back. Jack sensed something was up and asked who was on the phone. My exact words were, "She says she's my daughter." He took the phone from me and talked to her for ten minutes. I wasn't really listening to what he was saying to her. The only thing I had grasped was when he told her that no, he wasn't her biological father. He explained that I had just received some very upsetting news, got all her pertinent information and told her we would phone her in a day or two. He told me that her name was Joannie. I wasn't sure that I wanted to meet her, but Jack convinced me that I should, and so I did. Five days later on a Saturday, her adopted father arrived with her. I was a mess and wouldn't even go out to greet her so Jack did. When he walked in with her, I nearly passed out."

"Oh Sissy, that must have been traumatic for you."

"No, I had dealt with the fact that I was about to meet my teenage daughter, but I was unprepared to see this girl who was practically the splitting image of me when I was a teenager."

"Oh my; what happened then?"

"I think I held my hands out and she came to me and took them. We looked at each other for a while not saying anything, just smiling and sizing each other up I guess. Jack suggested we sit down and he would get some refreshments. He asked her if she would like a soda or tea. She asked me what I was going to have. I said just water or maybe coffee. She asked if she could please have coffee because she wasn't allowed to drink it at home. Jack said, "Sure, we aren't above breaking the rules." That seemed to break the tension and we had a wonderful visit. Jack did most of the talking explaining to her why I had been so cool on the phone. I got a daughter that day, but I also knew that I had landed one hell of a man, and it was time that I take his proposal seriously."

"I am so glad that you did. Why have you waited until now to take the vows?" I asked.

"We wanted our children to be at the wedding, and so we needed to let them get to know each other, plus Joannie and I had many things to sort through. I guess we did everything right because they adore each other. Jake doesn't have any siblings but Joannie's parents adopted two more children, a boy and a girl, so she has. They are much younger than her so she identified with Jake as he is closer to her age, and believe me he has the role of big brother down pat."

"You didn't tell her the truth about her biological father did you?"

"Apparently, I wasn't the only one to be attacked at an isolated rest stop. I remembered the last digits of the car he was driving and another victim knew the first ones, so he was caught and charged and went to prison even before Joannie was born. His name was Brad Duncan and he was shanked in prison and died, so he is dead and gone. I explained as delicately as I could what had happened. I didn't want her to have any regrets of never knowing her father. It was hard for her to hear how she was conceived but she understands why I couldn't keep her. All is well now, and maybe someday we will see if we can track down a relative or two of his. Right now she is only interested in my family. She would be here with us now, but it's her last year of school so she needs to stay where she is. She's a grade A student so uprooting her would be a mistake, plus she is just 16 so her parents have the final say I guess."

"You are one remarkable young lady Sissy! I am so very proud of you and all that you have accomplished. I just wish I had of been here for you."

"I'm proud of you too V. I guess I will get used to calling you Vienna someday as everyone else does. You have accomplished so much as the Mistress of Avanloch, and you have never taken on the persona of an uncaring aristocrat just sitting pretty in her kingdom. Your children will never want for anything."

"And, neither will you or Addy as you are my kin and share the same rights to the name."

"None of that hierarchy business interests me or Addy. You have been more than generous to all of us even before you knew about the legacy or the McAllister fortunes."

"You are my real family, not those who lived hundreds of years ago. The castle which was originally called something like Kings Keep had been uninhabited for many years before Jeremy's great, great grandfather decided to revive it somewhere around 1700. Wait a minute; that must be wrong because Avaleena was mistress there in the 1800's. Oh well, it doesn't matter. Anyhow, the wars had taken a toll on it, but it needed a complete overhaul. I guess the inside was pretty much left intact because if it hadn't been then all the secreted rooms and tunnels would have been destroyed. From what little Jeremy told me it was mostly the outside that had suffered. The place had been fully modernized when I arrived on the scene. I was given cate blanch to spend whatever I wanted, and as you know, I did. All I wanted was to make a home for the girls when I married Jeremy. I am ever so thankful that he didn't want anything more from me than to be a mother to his daughter. But, was it worth the sacrifice I made to keep Ava away from her father? Why did I do it Sissy? I asked myself that question every day, and then I quit asking because the decision was taken out of my hands when Rainey married. I used to tell myself that I was living in a fairy tale, and that someday my prince would find me. I waited and I waited, but he never came, and so I lived twenty years without love because I was too afraid to step outside the castle walls."

"That's all over now V, so your story has a happy ending. I know it was your decision to move back here, but will you be totally happy here?"

"I love Avanloch and I will miss it every day because it wasn't just a magnificent castle, it was my home for twenty years, and everyone associated with it will always have my heart. This is my home now and

I plan on making the best of it. You know Rainey never wanted the title of Lord or anything to do with the riches of Avanloch, and especially those of the McAllister businesses, but as my husband he didn't have any choice. He did take his place and everyone respected him, but there was a longing in him to come back home. He wants us to live entirely on his money and wants to build us a house on his parent's property. Do you like the changes that he made to the Palace? He did it all by phone and faxed his blueprints to Coop who is the carpenter who did most of the work. I think it turned out beautifully."

"Yes I love it. Was it a surprise for you?"

"I knew he was having it all cleaned and painted as he asked me to choose the colors. I agreed to opening up the kitchen into the dining room and I didn't care what he did with mom's conservatory because I knew we needed a room for Ava and Nash and baby. I did not know that there would still be room for a smaller dining room, so that was a surprise and the remodel of the bathrooms, but the biggest one was the ensuite in our bedroom with a jetted tub. Now his eyes are on the basement."

"How did you feel about losing the conservatory? You had such a huge one at Avanloch."

"I have no time for one anymore. If I change my mind Rainey will build me one. I told him he could do anything he wanted as long as he didn't alter the pantry."

Sissy laughed. "Ah yes, the pantry; your favorite hiding place."

"Hey, I wasn't hiding; I was baking."

"Does that mean that a chocolate cake is on the horizon?"

"You bet it does!"

The door opened a crack. "You girls all right in here?" Rainey asked.

"Yes Dear, coming out right now."

"No need; kids are all wrapped up and we're going for a walk."

"You and who, and where are you going?"

"Jack and me; twins are in the pram and Lili and Tanny are walking with us over to Jacks'."

I looked at my sister. "Jack and Rainey; who would have thunked?"

She asked me if I'd like to go for a walk.

"I'd love to, but I'm afraid I'm housebound for a few more days."

"There is only one step out the back door so I'm thinking we could get you out that way if you can manage one step. You can sit on a chair while I get your wheels out, but if it is going to hurt you we can just forget it."

"I can manage that as I can take a few steps quite easily, so let's go."

"We can take the foot path along the river over to the house if you don't mind a bit of a rough terrain. It is a nice view of the river and what's left of the woods."

She got my coat and five minutes later we were on our way. She laughed and said that she was probably going to catch hell from Rainey. I laughed with her saying that she had better pray that we didn't get stuck. The timing was perfect because we came out one block ahead of the troupe.

Tanny saw us first, yelled, and ran to meet us as we crossed over to the sidewalk. "Why didn't you tell us you were coming Mommy?"

"We wanted to surprise you." I answered.

We waited for the entourage to join us. Rainey asked whose idea it was. Sissy and I both answered in unison. "Mine."

"We'll continue on to the house while you guys check out the shop. I don't think it's a safe place for the kids to be." Sissy said.

"You're right; it isn't safe for little hands. We'll see you in about half an hour." Jack agreed.

Rainey wasn't appeased. He relieved Jack of Lili and said we couldn't handle the wheelchair and the pram so he had better walk us over to the house.

"It's only two blocks Rainey and its easy going. Lili can sit on my lap and Tanny can help me wheel while Sissy pushes the pram."

"I'd rather you didn't use your hands on the wheels Vienna as they aren't healed yet." He countered as he placed Lili on my lap. "I worry about you, you know."

I held up my hands. "Look, all bandaged, and it's too late to worry about me. Let's go Tanny."

Sissy gave us a tour of the downstairs of the Jennings homestead. She asked me if I had been in the house before. I said that I hadn't and I didn't remember if I'd even known where Jack had lived. I thought I had better clarify Jack's and my involvement. "We had a very brief relationship. It did not become physical Sissy. He was my Rainey rebound and he knew it. I am a ashamed of the way I may have led him on. I hope he has forgiven me now that he has found love and happiness with the sister who was meant for him."

"Thanks Sis; I knew that, but it is nice to hear it affirmed."

Zander was sleeping as usual, but Novia wanted out of the buggy so I picked her up and placed her on the carpet in the living room. Lili had spotted a chess set on a table and made a bee-line for it. Sissy assured me that she couldn't hurt it because it was made of pewter. I asked Lili if she could let Novia play too. She said maybe. Tanny followed Sissy and I into the kitchen where we still had a view of the living room.

"I like it just the way it is but Jack wants to modernize it, new cupboards and everything. I would like the window seat made into a booth-like sitting area around the table, and the pantry modernized, but that's all. The stove and dishwasher are only four years old. Jack bought them for his mother a year before she became ill."

"He was a good son, and I am sure they were much appreciated." I said candidly.

"He turned the dining room into a downstairs bedroom for his parents because they couldn't handle the stairs anymore. It's just as they left it. Jack wants to revert it back to a dining room."

"It's strange that they both became ill at the same time don't you think?"

"Jackson had a multitude of health problems and had been dealing with them for years. His heart just gave out trying to cope with them all. Elvira had an aggressive metastatic cancer. She wouldn't have lived much longer, but Jackson's passing hastened her departure. She was basically living, if you can call it that, on morphine. She was going to die anyhow so she just closed her eyes and willed herself to join him. Jack was with her. He said she passed away with a smile on her face and told him to look after me and Jake. I think we have timed it just right for lunch. Do you want to help me Tanny because your mom has to keep an eye on the girls?"

"Sure; what are we going to have?"

"Just sandwiches; I have lots of cold cuts and cheeses and condiments."

"Do you have peanut butter? Me and Lili like peanut butter and blackberry jam."

"I do, both kinds, but no blackberry jam. But I have strawberry and raspberry."

"Lili doesn't like nuts so she will have plain. I think I will have the one with nuts. I can make them Auntie. Mommy, can Novia have peanut butter?"

I told her no and to make sure she cut the crusts off Lili's bread. I sat down where I could keep watch over the girls. Zander woke up, cranky as usual. Thankfully Rainey had packed a bottle and treats for him. I wasn't having any luck getting him to drink out of a cup. Sometimes he exasperated me as he was so much slower than his twin sister. It was to be expected as he'd had the rough start to life. I pawned him off on his father as much as I could.

The guys arrived and we had a nice lunch around the kitchen table. I told Jack that I agreed with Sissy about the kitchen. He said he thought I would and excused himself as he wanted to pick up a drawing for Rainey to take home and ponder over that he'd left upstairs. Tanny asked him if she could go with him as she hadn't been upstairs yet. He said sure and to come along.

"How many bedrooms do you have Uncle Jack?" She asked as they climbed the stairs.

"We have five." He answered.

"Five? Wow, we have five too but there is seven of us and only two of you. We need more bedrooms don't you think? Did you know that my mother owns a castle? There are a zillion bedrooms in that house."

"Yeah, I think I heard something like that." Jack laughed.

"She says you're a good boy."

"Why would she say that?"

"Because you bought your sick mother a dishwasher."

Rainey and I just shook our heads. Sissy asked me if we'd consider farming Tanny out. Jack was grinning from ear to ear as they returned. I asked him what other secrets she had told him. He said that was just between her and him. I was glad that she had found a replacement for Johnny. Maybe I had found one too.

Rainey insisted that we take Jack up on the offer to drive us home. Sissy volunteered as she wanted to hear what Dr. Barbara had to say about my feet. Jack and Rainey loaded up the truck and we crowded in. I put Novia on my lap and wrapped the seat belt around us. Of course I had passed the whiny Zander to Rain. He gave me a look that said he wasn't pleased with me.

Sissy asked if she could bathe the twins when we got back to the Palace. I told her she was an angel. Zander wasn't all that fond of being submerged so he was still having his bath in the baby tub in the kitchen sink. Novia liked to share the big bath with Lili. I asked Lili if she would like to have a bath with her sister. She said, "No." She sat down in front of the TV and said she wanted Petey Paney. Rainey plunked the video in and came to deal with me. I asked him why he was giving me the cold shoulder. He said it was because I disobeyed him.

"Excuse me…I disobeyed you?"

"I asked you not to go out on your own and you did."

"I wasn't alone and just what did you think would happen to me?"

"You no longer have round the clock protection. Anyone can accost you any time they want."

"So, you want to keep me a prisoner? I was basically that at Avanloch and I refuse to be kept in captivity again just because you are paranoid!"

"I'm not paranoid; I'm realistic. Did you forget that there is a crazed woman out there and what about the threat from the Spanish connection?"

"I never found Jorja crazed and Anton has no interest in me. Did you forget he remarried?"

"If I was him I'd be looking for you."

"Rainey, what has got into you?" I beseeched.

"We'll talk about it later. Jack is here so I have to go."

"Jack…why is he here? We just left him and he didn't say anything about coming over."

I didn't get an answer. He had deposited me in the living room and just left me there sitting in the wheelchair. Sissy and Tanny were busy with the twins. Where were Ava and Nash? I heard the back door shut and then open. Laughter, banging…I called out but no one answered. I was just about to go and find out what was happening when Sissy came in with a wet Zander and placed him on my lap. I asked her what was going on. She said the guys were taking the back door and screen off. I said that my husband was crazy and he was taking Jack down with him. She laughed. Ten minutes later I was in tears as they placed my big yellow chair in front of me. Rainey asked where I wanted it.

"There…there to the left of the fireplace in front of the window." I sobbed. "Ava can sit in it with Samie. Why didn't you tell me it was coming?"

"Wouldn't have been a surprise then would it? Bad news though Hon; the roundabout is taking a roundabout journey. It's currently missing in action."

"It's okay, it's okay." I whimpered.

"If you quit crying I might just sit you in it."

"If this is your idea of a bargaining chip to keep me home I am not conceding."

"Would I resort to such chicanery?"

"It's right up your alley."

"I don't know what is going on with you two…should I be worried?" Sissy asked.

"Yes," I laughed, "be very worried. My husband has reverted to bribery to keep me under his thumb and control my every move."

"Why would he do that V?"

"He thinks I am in grave danger."

"Why?"

"Because Meggie told me to be aware of a she-wolf at my door."

"Then you should do as he requests."

"Well, she has already shown herself and I'm not afraid of her or Rainey's suppositions. It's not *me* she is after anyhow."

"No, but you might be in her way." Jack chimed in.

"Exactly;" Rainey agreed. "I don't want to be caught flat footed again and until the paternity test comes back we have to be ever vigilant. Knowing that you are all on my side will help me to rest a little easier."

That evening while we were getting ready for bed my husband told me that he was going to close up his shop and stay at home and help me.

"You just hung your shingle up two weeks ago and now you want to take it down…why?"

"I am almost done with the draughts for the two clients so I can put the finishing touches on them right here on the dining room table. I want to do my share with the house and the kids."

"So, you think you are going to boss me and be under foot from day to night… I think not. If this is just another ploy to keep watch over me you can just forget it. You are going to keep your office downtown or else become a full time house husband and I will get a job."

"I'd be a good boss, but just for fun, what do you think you would do?"

"I'm sure there are plenty opportunities out there for a former royal of the House of McAllister."

He smirked. "Yes perhaps, but your duties were countless, so you would be over qualified for any mundane job around this town, so I think not."

"Well, somebody has to bring in the bread. If it isn't going to be you it'll just have to be me."

He laughed heartily "I guess it's time to introduce you to my Cayman accounts."

"You have money?"

"I do, and if you're a good girl I just might share with you."

"Sometimes you want me to be good and sometimes you want me to be bad…make up your mind, what do you want me to be?"

"And, sometimes I love you wild and sometimes I love you tame. How do you want me to love you tonight?"

"I don't care just as long as you love me. Now take these bloody rags off so my feet can breathe again!"

Dr. Barbara had been pleased with how well my feet had healed in one day. I was allowed to take the wraps off for two nights and then assess them in the mornings. She thought I could get along with soft slippers for a while before trying shoes. Rainey and Ava had both laughed and informed her that shoes were not in my dress code. She said that she had gathered that but that I should be a little more conscientious about wearing footwear, at least outdoors. She didn't know me very well.

Our grandson Samie Quinn Nash made his arrival on Tuesday October 2nd. He was a strapping eight pound wonder. Two days later he and Ava arrived home. Rainey kept the girls busy in the kitchen until Nash and I settled Ava and Sammie in the big yellow chair in the living room.

Tanny and Lili were introduced to their nephew a few minutes later. Tanny kissed him and said he was beautiful. She asked me if his eyes would stay blue because Zander's hadn't. I told her maybe and maybe not, and that we would just have to wait and see. Lili asked what he was.

"He's a baby Honey; just like Zander and Novia."

"Can he walk and talk?" She asked.

"No, not yet. The twins are older and they can barely talk and Zander isn't even walking yet.

"Zanie talks."

"It's called babbling. You can't understand what he is trying to say can you?"

"Sometimes, but not Novie."

"Oh, why do you think that is?"

"She talks gibberish."

I explained that was the same as babbling, but she was having none of it.

"Is not and Tanny knows."

With that she left us and went to find her father.

Ava and I laughed a little. I wondered where Lili had learned the word "gibberish". I asked Tanny if she knew what Lili meant.

"Novia doesn't speak English, that's all."

"Well, she doesn't really talk much, but what language do you think she talks in?"

"The one from Scotland."

"You mean Scottish or Gaelic?"

"No, not that one."

"Only English and Scottish are spoken at Avanloch Tanny."

"The other one; you know the one on the key."

"On the key? You've lost me; what key?"

"The one you found in the big room, that language."

"I think she means the big black key that you told me about in the harem room Mom, so Italian I guess. Is that right Tanny?" Ava asked.

"No, not that one, the other one. The one Evan said was on the flower."

I was starting to get a headache. "The flower…the Fleur De Lis; do you mean French?"

"Yes."

"So you think Novia babbles in French?"

"She does." Tanny said as if it was fact.

That was the end of that as Rainey and Nash arrived with snacks for everyone. I took the plate prepared for the twins, sat on the floor, and called them over to sit with me. They had been playing quietly arranging blocks chatting in their own special tongue… French, I presumed.

Rainey sat down beside me letting the little ones crawl all over him. "I guess if Novia speaks French then Zander must too because he understands her." I mumbled.

He asked me what I was talking about. I told him about the strange exchange that I'd had with Lili and Tanny. He laughed and said that he guessed Novia had picked it up from me. I asked him what he meant.

"You are aware that you curse and say "I love you" in French quite often aren't you?"

"I don't curse."

"Honey, you have been saying "sacre bleu" ever since I met you."

"I got that from my dad, and it isn't swearing."

"If you say so. It's just a matter of time before the kids will start speaking Spanish too."

"Oh, now you are saying I speak Spanish?"

"Si, te quiero."

"I love you too. I'll leave you to keep the peace here while I go and arrange that sink full of flowers that you left me to deal with."

Jake and Joannie arrived on the eve of October 11th two days before the wedding. They had come together. They were both delightful and we welcomed them into our family. Joannie and Zoe hit it off so well that Joannie didn't want to go back to Edmonton. Rainey had a surprise for me. He had talked my parents and Addy and her daughter Sylvia, and new beau to come for Sissy's and Jack's wedding which had been perfectly executed by my husband. We celebrated for three days. I missed my Avanloch family a little less that weekend. We had something else to celebrate; Rainey's paternity test had come back negative. He had been so busy with preparations for the wedding that he hadn't had time to fret about the delay in the paternity results for a few days. Jorja had refused for her daughter to have the paternity test, so it was court appointed. Clive Owens, the lawyer at Quinn and Associates in Vancouver was handling Rainey's legalities. Jorja had been appointed a lawyer. She never contacted us and as far as we knew had left town. Her house had been vacated and she had quit her job at the bank. I suspected that she may have been dismissed as Rainey had promised the bank manager that we would take our business elsewhere if she caused us anymore grief. Her reason for objecting to the test was simply that there was no need as Rainey was the father. She did not win that argument.

Rainey had arrived home that day to find Lili attempting to feed Zander while I was trying to get Novia to eat. Neither of them liked mashed peas and carrots. He placed the two bags of groceries on the counter, and took over for Lili. She asked him what he had bought her. He pulled a treat for her out of one of his pockets and an envelope out of the other. He passed it to me. It was a registered letter from a lab in Vancouver. I knew what it was and asked him why he hadn't opened it yet.

"Because if it is positive I don't think I will be able to deal with it if you are not by my side. You open it. I will be able to tell by your expression if I should kiss you or run out of the house cursing like a mad man."

"Well Darling, you may kiss me either way because you know I'm with you all the way."

I opened the envelope and smiled. I got a long sweet kiss. He let out a hoot and a holler and left me to deal with the kids again as he went off to give the news to Ava and Nash without me reading the rest of the report. He said there was no need. I read it to myself just for my own satisfaction. I was sure that he would read it later.

"**Rainey Quinn** is **EXCLUDED** as the biological father of one Patricia Ann Elliot. Data does not support a paternity relationship. Combined paternity index is 0. Probability of paternity is 0." Well, that was that, thank God.

Ava and Nash took possession of their house at the end of October. Rainey took them shopping for all the necessities and a new crib and other furnishings. We had equipped the spare bedroom with everything a new born could need. It all went to the house across the street with the exception of the crib which was kept at the Palace for when Samie came over which would be often.

Zoe was taking driving lessons. We were going to buy her a car in the spring for what we had once thought was her birthday. In late August she told us that she had never been sure of the actual day of her birth and so she would like it changed to September 29th as that was the day her life had really begun. That was the day she had come to be my companion. Now she was Rainey's and my daughter. It had been a barrage of tears.

Sometime in November I accepted an invitation delivered by Donna from her grandmother to have tea at the Towers; the supposedly haunted house. It was a delightful visit. I did not have any ominous vibes so I agreed with Grandmother Lucille that her house wasn't haunted. I think Donna was a little disappointed. I promised a return visit in the spring.

Suddenly, it was late December and only four days before Christmas. Rainey and I had spent the early hours lying in bed with the twins crawling all over us. Tanny and Lili had heard the ruckus and came in to join us. This was going to be a Christmas of celebrations as it would be the first one for Rainey and me. We had been together last year, but Ava was missing and feared dead, so that was not a time we wanted to remember.

Four hours later I was in the kitchen with the children. Tanny and Lili were assembling nutty treats for the birds. Novia was watching them attentively; Zander was clinging to me whining. Rainey phoned and said he had finished with the client, had one more stop to make and would be home in fifteen minutes. The doorbell chimed. Lili cried out "Daddy, Daddy..." and took off running down the hall. I yelled at her saying it wasn't her father. I followed her clutching Zander to my hip. I pulled the blind on the side window open and saw a little girl standing there with a basket in her hands. I told Lili that she must be selling chocolates. She pouted saying it wasn't daddy, stomped her feet and ran off down the hall. Zander managed to maneuver himself down my leg just as I opened the door.

CHAPTER 6

THE SHE-WOLF

I got to the door of the Nosegay Floral Boutique with my five bouquets of posies, turned and asked Iris, the proprietor, if she had access to cherry blossoms at this time of year. She asked me when I wanted them.

"Christmas day would be nice, but I will take them whenever I can get them. I know it's a formidable task so don't worry too much about it."

"I can't guarantee that I can find any, but I will do my best for my best customer. Are they for a special occasion?"

"Sort of; you know, I think any white or pink branches with blossoms would suffice."

"That may be more attainable. Merry Christmas to you and Vienna and your family Rainey."

I wished her the same and glanced at my watch. Good thing Liliana couldn't tell time as I was already late. I turned down River Road and wondered why there was a police car in my neighborhood. When I got closer I realised that it was outside the Palace. I parked crosswise in the middle of the street and ran into the house. The door was wide open. Everyone was standing in the hallway. Ava saw me and threw her arms around me crying that she was gone.

"Who's gone Ava…what's going on here? Where's Vienna?"

Nash pulled Ava away from me. "We think Jorja took her Rain; her and Zander."

I ignored him and pushed past him and Jack not paying any attention to the RCMP officer who was asking me if I knew where my wife was. "Vienna… Vienna, where are you Honey?"

I stopped at the living room door. Sissy was sitting in the big yellow chair holding Novia and looking very distraught. Tanny and Lili were sitting on each side of her. I asked them where their mother was. Lili ran to meet me. She pointed to the door as I picked her up. I asked Tanny what her sister was saying.

"She doesn't know much Rainey. Tell him what you told us Tanny." Sissy prodded.

The rest of the family plus the officer had followed me. I asked Tanny where her mother went.

"We were making the bird treats when the doorbell rang. Lili ran to answer it thinking it was you. Mommy told me to keep an eye on Novia and went after Lili. She had Zander with her. Lili came back, but Mommy didn't. I just thought she was busy with Zander until I felt it getting cold in the kitchen. I checked and the door was open wide. I shut it and thought that Mom must have gone to Ava's. I asked Lili and she just shook her head. I asked her who was at the door and she said a little girl and the lady with the yellow hair. I called Ava. I didn't see her Daddy. Was it that bad lady…Mommy didn't even tell us she was going…" Tanny stammered.

"It's okay Baby; we'll find them." I sat Lili back in the big chair with Sissy. "Do you remember when a lady with yellow hair had tea on the back porch with you last summer?"

She nodded. I asked her if it was the same lady that came to the door. She nodded again.

"Did she have a little girl like you with her Sweetie?"

"Like Tanny." She said.

I thanked her. "Doesn't sound like Jorja's daughter then does it?" I said to no one in particular.

The officer said that the word of a two year old was not very reliable. Tanny informed him that her sister was almost three and very smart. I hugged her again and asked Sissy if she could stay.

"Of course Rainey; you don't have to ask." She answered. "Go find Vienna."

"We'll take my truck Rain. I know every road in and out of town and every backroad. It's been snowing for half an hour so there'll be fresh tracks down all the side roads." Jack said.

Ava said that she was coming with us. I told her she wasn't as she was needed here with Samie. Nash said that he'd keep vigil over everyone. I asked the RCMP officer what was being done to find my wife and child. He said that Mrs. Quinn was an adult and had only been gone for less than an hour, and there was no evidence to suggest that she was in any danger. I remarked sarcastically that he didn't know her history or what the hell was going on, and that it would be a good idea to get his commanding officer over here. He was still disputing his position when Jack and I walked out the door.

We got half way up the block when Jack thought it might be a good idea if we asked the neighbours if they had seen anything out of the ordinary. I agreed and we walked back towards the Palace. He took one side of the street and I took the other. Only Mrs. McNamara, our next door neighbour had seen any vehicle that she didn't recognise. It was a dark older four door car and she thought there was a woman in the passenger seat and that she was holding either a child or a dog. She couldn't be sure of the hair color. That was enough for me. I called to Jack and we walked back to the truck.

"Fifteen minutes…fifteen minutes…why am I always late Jack?"

"Don't beat yourself up Rain. At this point we don't know what happened. Maybe she came looking for help; maybe something was wrong with the little girl and she was looking for help. Maybe Vienna went with her willingly."

"Without telling anyone and taking Zander with her…I hardly doubt that." I disagreed.

"Yeah I agree. There are a hundred scenarios and we don't have enough facts to even speculate on what really happened. We don't even know for sure that it was Jorja. Do you know anything about her or where she went to after she left here? Is it possible that she didn't even leave town?"

"It was her. I can feel it in my bones. The only time we ever saw her was that day she showed up unannounced in September. I was advised not to seek her out and believe me I didn't want to. Our lawyers handled the testing. We never heard from her before or after. The house she was renting was vacated and her job was terminated; there was no reason for her to stay."

"Unless she had plans of revenge…"

I didn't answer, but in my gut I knew. I knew and it wasn't anything good.

After two hours of futile searching we returned to the Palace to see if there was any news. Two more police cars were parked at the curb. An officer was stationed at the door. I'm sure he had intentions of barring us but Jack suggested strongly that he should step aside as we were family. Nash, Ava and Sissy were in the living room with two officers. One, whose name was Tony was on the phone with his commanding office, Sergeant Rolph. Zoe had taken the children into the kitchen and shut the door. Constable Tony hung up the phone and informed us that the Sergeant had deemed that Vienna's disappearance was serious enough to warrant an investigation. Roadblocks had been set up at the three main roads that led into and out of Bridge Falls. Special attention would be given to the roadways in and out of Hawthorne to the west, and Potsdam to the east. A door to door search was also in progress. He thanked Nash and Ava for their insight. A few minutes later Sergeant Rolph arrived.

The town's population was five thousand or so which didn't include the outlying area, so it was a formidable task to go door to door. I listened to the plans without paying much attention as to what was being said. I was accomplishing absolutely nothing by standing around so walked out as the Sergeant was explaining the strategy. I said that I had to get something out of the car. I grabbed the frost bitten flowers, walked back to the house and deposited them on the floor in the doorway. I shut the door quietly and resumed my search for my wife and son. An hour later realising that I had been down the same road three times I returned home. Vienna had been missing for almost four hours. I opened the front door to see her near the top of the stairs.

"Vienna! Thank God you're home! Are you okay Sweetheart?" I started up the stairs barely able to control my elation.

She turned and put her hand out to stop me. Her eyes and voice were not those of my wife. **"Don't take another step! Get out of my house; get away from my children!"**

"Honey, what are you saying? What's happened…I need to see you, I need…"

"I know what you need, and it's sure as hell isn't me! I never want to see you AGAIN! You know damn well what happened because you planned it all. Now, take your lying cheating body out of here before I have you arrested!"

"You're upset Honey, you don't know what you're saying. I'm coming up and we can talk."

"Mr. Quinn Sir, your wife has made her request of you, and I'll ask you to comply please."

I stopped half way up the stairs and addressed Officer Stark with disdain. "Don't presume that you can order me not to talk to my wife in my own home!" I looked down at Ava and Nash and Jack. "What's happened; what did she say, where's Zander? How did she get home? She's wearing my coat…was that blood on it?"

"Constable Stark found her wandering down the Hiway. He wanted to take her to the hospital but she insisted she had to bring Zander home. She didn't tell us anything Daddy. She just handed Zander to Sissy and told her to warm him up and she started up the stairs and then you came in." Ava sobbed.

"Is he okay?"

"Yes, he seems to be. What happened Daddy; why did she say you know?"

"I know nothing, but I'm damn well going to find out. Jack, can you find out where she's been and what's going on?"

"I'm on it Rain. Go look after Vienna."

"I'm coming with you." Ava started towards me.

Nash suggested that she give me a few minutes. She said she would, but only five minutes.

Vienna was about to enter the bathroom when I caught up to her. I called to her calmly. She turned clutching my blood-spattered coat to her body.

"What was it that you didn't understand when I said that I never wanted to see you again?" She spurned.

"You didn't mean it Vienna. Something terrible has happened to you, and I am worried that you're in shock. Please let me help you Darling. Is that blood on my coat...Oh God, are you hurt?" I started towards her.

Again she stopped me with her hand. She laughed maliciously running her hand down my coat along the dark ominous streak. "How fitting that I have your mistress's blood all over your coat. Give me a minute and it's all yours. You can sleep with her one last time."

"What the hell are you saying Vienna? What lies has she filled your head with? It was Jorja wasn't it; what did she do to you?"

More laughing. "So, she is not your only mistress? I will take your silence for a "no". I am still standing and that is more than I can say for that crazy bitch. Now get the hell out of here!" She spat as she entered the bathroom. She locked the door.

"I'm not going anywhere until you calm down and tell me why you are accusing me of things you know aren't true." I couldn't hear if she answered me as the water was on full volume.

Ava was at the door asking if her mother was all right.

"I don't know as she hasn't told me anything yet. I am pretty sure that something terrible happened for her to say that I know what it is and that she wants me gone. There was blood on my coat, and why she was wearing it is another mystery. Her feet are quite red...tell me she had something on her feet."

"She had your old slippers on. There's not much left of them."

"Okay; give me a few more minutes with her. The water is still running full force so I have no idea how long she is going to be in there. If she won't talk to me I guess I'll have to give her time to come to terms with whatever happened. Has Jack found out anything yet?"

"The only thing I know is that according to Constable Stark, Sergeant Rolph is on his way back here. Hopefully he will have some answers for us. Should I call Barbara and see if she can come over to check Mom out?"

"At this point I have no idea Ava. If it will ease your mind, then by all means call her. One way or the other I'll be down after she has given me some answers. If she refuses to come out of the bathroom I'm afraid I am going to have to break the door down because she may be injured."

I hugged my daughter, saw her to the door, and sat down on the window seat to wait. Just as I was about to call Jack to help me with the door, the water stopped running. Ten minutes later my wife emerged with dripping wet hair clutching her white terrycloth robe to her.

She was not smiling. "Why are you still here? Do you not understand that I never want to see your lying, cheating face ever again? If there is any decency left in you at all you'll get out."

"I have not lied, or cheated Vienna, and you know that. Whatever happened with Jorja has somehow distorted your mind. You are emotionally distressed, and I understand that something terrible happened, but we can fix it, so let's sit down and talk calmly."

"Something terrible happened; you got that right darling, but you're not going to like it. She's gone…so sorry dearie, but you're going to have to find yourself another whore because I killed your old one. I killed her with my bare hands, over and over again, and I would do it again in a heartbeat." She spewed.

She had spoken so precisely and almost tranquilly that I thought she had calmed down, but her eyes said otherwise. She turned and opened a drawer on her dresser. She spun around quickly holding a large pair of scissors in her hands. She spread them open and held up one hand with them aimed at me.

"Put them down Vienna before you hurt yourself." I ordered.

She laughed. "It's not me I'm going to hurt, but if you don't get out of here this very minute I am going to take your perverted blood and put it next to her decaying black fluid that is lying on the bathroom floor. You want to be with her for eternity…well, I can send you there!"

She took a step towards me holding the scissors high. I wasn't worried about my safety, but was afraid that she'd slice her own hand by the way she was wielding them.

"I see that you are not ready to talk sensibly so I'll leave before you do something you'll regret. You are obviously traumatised by whatever happened and need some time to calm down, but there is no way that I believe that you killed Jorja."

"Jorja, Jorja, Jorja… the she vixen at the door." She hissed as she started to walk towards me.

I made my way to the doorway. "You win for now, but I'll be back. I love you Vienna."

"Liar, liar, liar…" Her voice echoed as I walked down the hall.

Jack had been unable to get any confirmation regarding Jorja or her whereabouts. I related what had transpired with Vienna to the family and asked them to give her a few minutes as I headed for the front door. Ava asked me where I was going.

"Not far Honey. Maybe I will track down Sergeant Rolph and get some answers from him. I just need to clear my head for a bit. Don't worry; I'll be back."

How had this day that had started out so promising turn into a nightmare in such a short time? Without even thinking I parked the car across the street from the liquor store. I crossed over, entered, picked up two bottles of Crown Royal and deposited them on the counter. I had not replenished the liquor cabinet at the Palace because I had decided that I no longer needed a pick-up every evening, and I had promised my wife that I would leave the hard stuff alone. A glass of wine at dinner, or a beer with Jack and Nash was ample enough, but then today happened and I needed something a little more substantial. Sorry Vienna, but your accusatory remarks about me being unfaithful has caused me to waiver. Les Arnold, an old school friend rang up my purchase. We shot the breeze for a few minutes. He walked with me to the door commenting on what a wild day it had been. I concurred not mentioning what had gone down at my house. He opened the door and we were met with the howling of sirens. We stood and watched a police cruiser take the corner and speed past us. Les said that he guessed that nothing had calmed down yet.

"Hey, isn't that an ambulance parked in front of your place?"

I cursed and thrust the paper bag at Les and took off running. It never occurred to me to cross over and get the car. Two blocks and my chest was throbbing wildly. My feet felt like lead as they slipped and slid in the mushy snow. I managed to tear my coat off and throw it to the ground. Damn it, damn it, why had I left her? Vienna, please, please be all right. My mind was racing with ominous scenarios. Four more blocks, three, two…I wasn't going to make it; the ambulance was pulling away. Ava, Nash and Jack were standing in the street watching it as it drove off, siren blaring. Jack caught me just before I collapsed.

"She's hurt isn't she?" I gasped as I took a long breath.

"I found her bleeding to death." Ava's voice was flat.

I choked. "What?"

Jack had the doors to his truck open. "Get in you guys; Vienna needs you."

Nash and Ava climbed in the back and I jumped in the front. "Someone better tell me right now what happened." I demanded.

Ava said through tears that she went upstairs a few minutes after I had left. She had found her mother lying on the floor in a pool of blood. She had yelled for Nash as she applied pressure to the wound. I asked her what wound. Her answer was full of venom.

"From the knife wound that your girlfriend inflicted on her."

"That was uncalled for Ava. You know damn well she was not your father's girlfriend." Nash said. "You need to take a step back."

"I know nothing except what I heard Mama accuse him of, but you're right, she wasn't his girlfriend; she was his slutty mistress."

I didn't look at my daughter or correct her as this was not the time for me to deny anything. Jack pulled up aside the emergency entrance. Nash and Ava got out. I didn't move. Nash asked me if I was coming. I said I'd be in a moment. I turned to Jack as I needed some reassurance that Vienna wasn't as bad off as Ava had said she was.

"I won't lie to you Rain; the wound was deep. I think she was stabbed. There was a hell of a lot of blood, a hell of a lot of blood. Didn't you see any blood?"

"Just on the coat. She said it was Jorja's. She said she killed her."

"Hell! Okay, I'm on my way to the cop shop, and I'm not leaving until I get some answers. You get in there and be with your wife. Don't worry because Sissy and I have the kids covered."

"She doesn't want me Jack. She said she hates me."

"Yeah, she hates you all right, and that's why your name was on her lips as she opened her eyes just before she slipped into unconsciousness."

I opened the doors to the emergency ward and was met by a nurse who told me that I couldn't be in there. I said that I had to be as my wife was just brought in. Dr. Nelson emerged from behind a closed curtain. I asked her if Vienna was in there. She said she was and was still being assessed and stabilized. I asked her what that meant. She took my arm and suggested that we join Nash and Ava in the waiting room. I told her I wasn't going anywhere until I saw my wife.

"Please Rainey; your daughter needs you. The best thing you can do for Vienna and yourself right now is to wait until Steven arrives and evaluates her situation. She most assuredly is going to require surgery, but let's wait and see what he has to say."

"Why isn't he here?"

"He didn't have any scheduled surgeries for the day so had no need to come in."

"Surely there is another doctor already here who can operate and do you even know for sure that she needs surgery? This is Vienna we're talking about Barbara."

"And, that is precisely why I want Stephen attending her. You know she is one of my favorite people and Stephen is the very best surgeon, and I am not saying that just because he's my husband. I assure you. Dr. Amnad is fully qualified, but he is in surgery as we speak and frankly Rainey, I'm not sure if Vienna can wait that long."

"What are you not telling me Barbara?" I asked worriedly.

"Nothing I promise, but she has lost a significant amount of blood and that is troublesome because at this point we do not know how deep the wound is, or if it has nicked any vital organ. Let's join the kids. Stephen will be here any second and as soon as he has completed his assessment he will come and inform us."

"Did you see Mama; is she okay?" Ava sobbed meeting us at the door.

"I haven't been allowed to see her yet." I answered dolefully.

"You can be assured Ava that she is in very good hands, and as soon as Stephen is finished with his assessment he will inform us of her condition. The loss of blood is a major concern and she will require several transfusions. She will most assuredly require surgery, but let's wait and see what Stephen has to say."

"She just had major surgery last February and had to have transfusions then. It can't be happening again. If I hadn't found her when I did she would have…"

I pulled my daughter into my arms. "That's my fault that I told you to give her a few minutes. I am at a loss as to what could have happened so fast after I left."

"She must have been hiding it from you though I don't know how or why. I went up as soon as you left and found her on the floor soaked in blood; it was barely three minutes."

"Thank God you did as you probably saved her life by applying pressure and calling the ambulance as quick as you did." Barbara commended her.

"Nash and Jack helped as they both have first aid certificates. I would have panicked if I had of been alone." Ava said still shaking in my arms. She looked up at me with tearful eyes. "I'm so sorry Daddy that I accused you. I know you would never cheat on her."

"Never thought anything of it Honey."

"Will you be assisting Dr. Fraser, Barbara?" Nash asked.

"I will be observing, but I won't be assisting. We have excellent surgical nurses for that.

Right now we just need to be patient. First thing is to get you and Nash out of those clothes."

Ava looked down at her bloody clothes and asked me if she had gotten blood all over me. I shook my head saying it was dry and not to worry. The door opened and Lara and Coop walked in. They had been in Potsdam and unaware of anything happening back here. They had returned to get a startling message from Sissy on the answering machine. Barbara excused herself saying she would be right back after checking on Vienna's condition. I tried to go with her, but was told that I would just be in the way. She apologised and said that as soon as she found out what the prognosis was she'd return. I felt useless. Lara sent Coop for coffees and made me sit down while Ava and Nash went into the bathroom to change into the scrubs a nurse had brought in.

I leaned forward, head in my hands. "How did it all come undone in such a short time Lara? This morning we were lying in bed with the twins and the girls planning Christmas day. We were so happy. Last year was our first Christmas together. Can you believe it, twenty five years and we had never spent the holiday together, but Ava was missing, so it was no celebration was it? This was the year, this was finally the year, and because of me my wife is in the hospital again, and she may very well die."

"She's not going to die Rain. She's a fighter and she has a lot to live for." Lara comforted.

"That doesn't include me anymore. She thinks I cheated on her and she wants a divorce. It's all over. I blamed those cursed bracelets for everything that happened to her, but it wasn't them; it was me. I'm the curse, and she is better off without me."

"Don't say that Rainey; she loves you, and she is going to need you..."

I brushed her hand away. "No, she doesn't. She wants me dead. Why in hell were we reunited if it was all going to end like this? Karma truly is a bitch. Look after Ava; I need some air."

Jack found me sitting on an icy bench outside. He sat down beside me and asked if there was any news. I bummed a cigarette from him. He asked what I was going to do with it. I managed a chortle saying that I had no idea just like I had no idea what I was going to do without Vienna. He said that I would do the same thing as I had been doing all my life and that was that I'd keep loving her. I told him everything that she had said, and that she had even threatened to kill me. He had the audacity to laugh.

"Yeah, if that was ever going to happen."

"You didn't see her Jack. She was wielding an open scissor and she had fire in her eyes."

"What else would you expect from a woman who had just been held hostage by a crazy person and for all we know had threatened to kill Zander? We can only imagine what lies Jorja told her, or was threatening to do to her and Zander. Come on, you're smarter than that. Now get your ass up and back where you belong."

I crushed the unlit cigarette in my hand envisioning that it was Jorja's neck.

Ava was waiting for me. "Where have you been?" She demanded. "They've already taken Mama into OR. Dr. Fraser says there is no time to wait. You have to go and sign the papers for consent at the main office."

"I'm sorry; I just needed to clear my head. Sissy says Sammie is up and needs his mommy. Jack will take you and Nash back to the house. Take your time and don't worry, Lara and Coop will keep me company."

"It is not you I'm worried about." Ava said snarkily and walked away.

Nash gave my shoulder a little squeeze and a nod as he sped to catch up to his wife.

Lara gave me the synopsis of what Dr. Fraser had told them. He was concerned for the blood loss and until they could determine the source there was a danger that she could suffer a blood clot or worse. He had left without further comment to join his team in the OR. All righty then. There was nothing to do but sit and wait. Lara asked me if I wanted to accompany her to the chapel. I told her that I wasn't recognized by the deity.

"I don't know how you can say that Rainey. I know you prayed over and over again for her return for twenty years and again after the earthquake. Your prayers were answered weren't they, and what about last year when she almost died giving birth to the twins?"

"Who says prayer had anything to do with any of that? You go do your thing; I'll just sit here and discuss the price of tea with Coop."

She gave me a disgusting look as she left. "Sometimes I don't even know who you are."

I didn't know who I was myself. The woman who meant more to me than anything else in the world was fighting for her life once again, thanks to me, and I was being glib about it. This was the last straw, and I was going to make sure nothing could ever harm Vienna again, and the only way I could do that was to do what she wanted. I would give her a divorce and it would be done. Yeah, that was what I would do.

Ava and Nash returned at the same time Lara did. She filled them in on what the doctor had said, and then she told my daughter that I needed a hug.

Ava started to apologise again. I stopped her as I held her. "Things are going to be said, tempers are going to flare, accusations are going to be made, and I will be in the centre of it all, but it doesn't matter. Nothing matters except your mother surviving yet another crisis. No apologies necessary. We've been through this too many times Ava, so let's just be supportive of each other, and I don't mind at all if you beat on me. I'm numb so I won't even feel it."

"That wouldn't solve anything would it, but it might relieve my angst. Shall we just worry and pace together instead?"

And, we did. The clock clicked ever so slowly. People came and went. Sissy and Zoe arrived. Lara and Coop left to help Jack with the kids. Sergeant Rolph popped in saying he hoped he wasn't imposing. He had understood that Mrs. Quinn was undergoing surgery and he needed to be informed of her progress as the sooner he could get her account of the alleged attack the sooner they could get on with the investigation.

I was incensed. "My wife could very well be dying from an obvious knife wound inflicted by a mad woman, and you have the audacity to call it alleged! You need to get your priorities straight and be searching for her before she wrecks anymore havoc on our family!"

"I am sorry if I came off as insensitive Mr. Quinn as that was not my intention. However, it is imperative that I get a statement from her as soon as possible. Please accept my apology."

Nash stepped in before I could reply. "Not to be disrespectable Sir, but Mrs. Quinn will not be answering any questions until she is fully stable. Her prognosis is still very much in question. The best thing that you can do for the family is to locate Jorja Elliot, put her in jail, and charge her with kidnapping, attempted murder, and any other abhorrent violation that she has committed against the Quinns'!"

"Then I am pleased to inform you all that we have located Ms. Elliot, and she is in police lock-up and being questioned by Staff Sergeant Mitchell as we speak."

Nash asked if he could inquire as to where she had been found and was there evidence of Vienna's stabbing; the knife so to speak.

"It is an on-going investigation Mr. Nash, and until we have some answers from both Mrs. Quinn and Ms. Elliot, I am not at liberty to disclose anymore. I hope you can appreciate that."

"So, fundamentally you are saying that Jorja is not talking?"

"Not at the moment. While I am waiting for Mrs. Quinn's statement it would be helpful if any of you had anything to add to what we already know."

"And, why would we do that Sergeant? Sharing goes both ways you know. Now if you will excuse me I need to check in with Dr. Nelson." I answered briskly walking away.

I met Barbara outside the door. She asked me where I was going. I said that I was pace-walking. She told me that I could quit because Vienna had come through the surgery with flying colors and she was in the recovery room. I asked her where it was as I wanted to sit with her. She told me that I couldn't. I told her that she had better call security then because I was going to knock on every door until I found my wife. She asked me why I was being so cantankerous and said that Vienna needed to wake up on her own.

"It's you who doesn't understand Barbara. This is the last time I am going to be able to hold her hand. She is divorcing me because she believes I slept with the woman who stabbed her."

"Oh Rainey, that can't be so!"

"It is. I promise I won't talk to her. I just need to see her and hold her hand one last time."

"Come with me."

She led me to the recovery room and talked with the startled two nurses. She told them that I wouldn't pose a threat to their patient and that I wouldn't interfere with their monitoring. I thanked her and sat down beside the love of my life.

I fumbled under the warm blankets for her hand. It was ice cold. I wanted to remove the coverings and take her in my arms because I knew I could warm her better than any old blankets could. I hadn't quite gone over the edge yet, so I resisted. Another clock on the wall to watch…how long had it taken her to wake up in the hospital in Scotland…an hour or so I thought. An hour, and then what?

I felt her stirring after what seemed like an eternity. Her eyes fluttered open and then closed again. She seemed to be struggling to keep them open. I was sure she knew I was there as I felt a little squeeze on my hand. Dare I to hope? She attempted a smile as her eyes opened and she saw me. The smile disappeared quickly, and her body tensed. She appeared to be panicking. One of the nurses told her everything was all right and to try and relax. I let go of her hand and stood up.

"It's me." I said. "She doesn't want me here."

I walked to the door, opened it, and didn't look back. Ava and Nash had taken up my vigil in the hall. I told them that Vienna was awake and they could probably see her after they got her settled in the ICU. I forced a smile and said I'd see them later.

"Where are you going Daddy? Is she talking; did she say anything to you?"

"Yup, her eyes told me to get out and never come back."

"Daddy, she just came out of surgery so she doesn't know what she's saying.'

"It's all right; it's what I expected. See you back at the Palace."

"You can't walk without a coat, so take mine and our car." Nash insisted.

"My car is just a couple of blocks away so I'm good."

I thanked him for the jacket and made my way back to where I had left my car hours ago. It was still there and the keys were still in the ignition. I walked into the silence of an empty house. What did I expect; it was 10 o'clock at night. I found Sissy and Jack in the kitchen. Jack was ready with a glass of whiskey for me. I told him that I had promised Vienna that I would lay off the hard stuff. He laughed and said I could start again tomorrow because if anyone needed a drink it was me. I gave them a quick recap of the last few hours and sent them home. Sissy said the kids were all in bed and hopefully asleep, supper was in the fridge and just needed a warm-up, and that Sammie's bottle was in the warming pan. She had brought clean clothes down for me as she didn't want me to go into the bedroom. I asked her why. She said she didn't want me to be any more upset than I already was, so I needn't see where Vienna had almost died. I hugged her and told her I loved her. I walked them to the door thanking them again. I picked up my grandson from the bassinette, grabbed his bottle and settled into the big yellow chair. He wasn't interested in eating so we had a heart to heart. I told him that he wouldn't be here if it wasn't for me and his grandmother, that he was very lucky because she would be here to see him grow up, and I hoped I would also be lucky and that she would be in my life to see me grow old.

"What are you two talking about so seriously?" Ava asked surprising me.

"Oh, just life in general. Where's Nash, and how is your mother?"

"Nash went to turn the heat up. Mom was so groggy that she couldn't keep her eyes open, so we just stayed for a few minutes. She knew we were there and told us to get home to our baby. I'll go back first thing in the morning. Are you going to be all right alone?"

"I'm hardly alone Ava. The kids will all be up before you know it, and Sissy and Jack will be back at the crack of dawn. I honestly don't know what we would do without those two."

"I know Daddy; we are so fortunate that they are here." She agreed lifting Sammie up off my lap and wrapping him in a big blanket. "Try and get some sleep okay?"

"I will, and you too. See you in the morning."

She bent down and kissed me. "I love you Daddy, and I know Mama does too. I know she will come around as soon as the shock wears off and she is back in her right mind."

"I love you too Sweetie. The only thing important here is her recovery, and if she chooses to do so without my help then so be it, but I will never give up without a fight."

"Good, here's Nash. Good night Daddy."

I did a quick walk through the house turning the lights off and locking the doors that no longer needed locking now that Jorja was in jail. I settled into my recliner hoping that I would be able to get a few hours' sleep before the twins woke me up. The monitor and cordless phone were on the table beside me. I closed my eyes. The sharp squeal of the phone brought me back to life.

"Hello." I answered warily.

"Mr. Quinn?"

"Yes."

"Mr. Quinn I am Yvonne Whynters. I am here with your wife…"

"Oh God, what's wrong?"

"She is in a heightened state of anxiety of sorts Sir. She has pulled her IV out and is trying her best to get out of bed all the while calling out your name crying that you have to save Zander."

I was out of my chair. "I'm on my way."

"Come to the second floor, ICU ward."

I had the sense to put a coat and boots on. Zoe was at the top of the stairs asking if it was Vienna. I told her it wasn't anything to worry about. She told me to go as she had the kids.

Thankfully the hospital was less than ten minutes away. I'm sure I made it in two. I skipped the elevator and ran up the stairs. Ms. Whynters was waiting for me. I followed her into a scene I will not soon forget. My wife was being held down by two nurses. They were having one hell of a time doing so. Vienna was yelling, "She's here, she's here, let me go." over and over again.

I walked over to her and placed my hands on her shoulders. "Vienna, stop!"

Her pupils were dilated to twice their normal size. Her hands, face and gown were all coated in blood. The IV was dangling from the pole half way across the room. She was thrashing about but stopped when she saw me. I put my hand on the top of her chest and asked her if she would try and relax. I told her the nurses were worried that she may have pulled her stitches out.

"I don't care, I don't care; you have to get Zander before she does."

I spoke as soothingly as I could. "I have Zander Vienna. No one is going to get him."

"She's here, she's here. Don't you understand, she's going to escape and she's going after him! You have to stop her, you have to stop her! If you ever loved me, you have to save him. She is supposed to be dead, I killed her, I killed her; why isn't she dead?"

"She's locked up in jail Honey. She is never going to get out and hurt anyone ever again."

"She's not, she's here, she's here, they know, they know!" Vienna's eyes were glowering as she accused the nurses.

I looked away and caught a strange look on all their faces. Nurse Whynters nodded and told me that I needed to go with her. She told me to tell Vienna that I was going to check it out. I did and she whimpered, "Hurry Rainey, hurry."

As soon as we were out in the hall I asked what the hell was going on. Why did Vienna think that her assailant was in the hospital? She said because she was. I told her that didn't make any sense as Sergeant Rolph told us she was in jail.

We took the stairs to the basement where Yvonne Whynters halted me. "There is a lock-up down here where injured detainees are held. The woman in question is being monitored for a concussion."

"That mad woman is Jorja Elliot, and she is the one who tried to kill my wife! How does Vienna even know that she is here?"

"There was a problem with the thermostats on the ICU floor, and maintenance was trying to locate the glitch. Unfortunately, a newly hired worker was in your wife's room and asked Karla, one of Vienna's nurses, if it was customary to house prisoners in the basement. She asked him what he was talking about, and he said that some maniac had kidnapped and tried to kill a woman and her baby and that she was being held here. Karla told him to leave and not say another word. It was too late because Vienna had heard and started to scream. Karla and her co-worker Deanna could not calm her, and called me up from the first floor. You know the rest. I will be reporting him to management you can count on that. It was unfortunate that it happened Mr. Quinn, but you can rest assured that there is no possible way that woman can escape. She is behind two steel doors and a police officer guards the doors."

"I am not yet appeased Ms. Whynters."

"Follow me, and you will be."

We passed by offices, the cafeteria, maintenance headquarters and storage areas on our way to the lock-up. We stopped at a steel door with a barred and wired window. Yvonne pushed a button on the wall announcing who she was and that she was here to check on Ms. Elliot. The door opened by a constable I recognised as one that I had met at the house. He was surprised to see me. Before he could speak Yvonne explained about Vienna's anxiety upon learning that her assailant was being retained here was detrimental to her recovery and it was vital to her state of mind that me, her husband, be allowed to see Ms. Elliot so he could assure his wife that she was safely imprisoned.

Constable Tony said it was highly irregular, but having had first-hand knowledge of the case could see no harm. He would give me one minute to verify that the internee was satisfactorily confined. I could not approach or touch her. I agreed. He unlocked the second door. I was met by an elated, wild looking woman.

"Oh Rainey, you're here! I knew you would come. I have such a headache. You won't believe what that bitch wife of yours did to me. She tried to kill me, but I was too strong for her and I got rid of her so we can finally be together again. Get these shackles off…hurry, hurry before they come back!"

I heard someone laughing maniacally. It was me. "You think I'm going to free you and that I want you? You are crazier than I even imagined. You are the sorriest excuse for a human being I have ever seen. Death is too good for you. If I had my way you would be buried alive with nothing but ravenous worms to keep you company. You will never see the light of day again while I live on with the woman who defeated death. Yes, Vienna lives and you will rot in hell." I spewed. I wanted to spit at her, but that would have brought me down to her level.

I turned. She called out to me again. "Rainey, Rainey, come back, I love you."

Yvonne followed me out. Constable Tony locked the door behind us. I thanked him. He said it was no problem and it was best if we keep this visit between us. We agreed. He asked Yvonne if he should document her visit as an official check-in of Ms. Elliot's condition.

She smiled at him. "I didn't examine her did I, and I am not her nurse, so perhaps not."

He nodded and told us to have a good night. Yvonne said she'd walk back to the ICU with me. It was then that I learned that she was not a nurse on that floor, but was the night supervisor and was stationed on the first floor. She had been called to the ICU when Vienna had her outburst. When we arrived back at Vienna's room we found one of the nurses sitting outside her room at the monitoring mainframe and the other behind the desk manually doing the paperwork. Yvonne asked about Vienna's condition. They had managed to get her bathed and changed without resistance, and the IV replaced. Her blood pressure had come down, but was still a concern. She had been given a sedative and appeared to be at rest.

I approached her bedside hesitantly not wanting to wake her if she had fallen asleep. Her eyes opened wide. I was reminded of her always telling me that no matter how quiet I thought I was when I was trying to sneak up on her, she always knew I was there.

"You can sleep peacefully Vienna as she is securely locked up behind two steel doors. She is handcuffed to the rails and a police man is on guard."

"You can say her name you know. The damage is already done. I said her name once too often. You summoned her, and she appeared to wreak havoc with my life."

I was somewhat relieved that she was cognisant enough to compare what had happened to a movie from the eighties. "I did not summon her Vienna. I will rue the day I ever met her for the rest of my life for what she has done, not just for you, but for me also as she has cost me your trust and love. I have loved you forever, and I will love you even unto death."

A small tear slid down her face. I had upset her. Her body stiffened and she muttered, "Liar."

I held up my hands and backed away. "I have never lied to you, but there is no convincing you. I know when I am licked. I see the disgust in your eyes so I will not distress you anymore. You won't ever have to see me again. I will give you the divorce and ask for nothing. Everything is yours. Good night Vienna, and one last time I will say, I love you." I'm sure it fell on deaf ears.

Yvonne was waiting for me. "Come on; I'll walk out with you. She's still traumatised Mr. Quinn. Give her time to come to terms with what has happened. I'm on duty for the next few nights so I am going to keep an eye on her. I know in my heart that love will win out."

"You don't know us, so you can't really say that."

"Oh, but I do. Everyone here knows the story of Vienna and Rainey Quinn. Your love story is what legends are made of, and it is not going to end with some mad woman's irrational manipulations. Have a little faith Mr. Quinn; love will be the victor."

I gave her a hug, thanked her for the pep talk, and her assistance. I walked out depressed and fearful into the cold nights' air. I sat in the car and let the defroster to do its job. I was so numb that I barely noticed the cold. I put my head on the steering wheel and let the desolation wash over me. I needed a drink.

Outside the Palace I remembered the first time Vienna had invited me in to meet her father. I had been in the house many times before as the one and only dentist had his offices there when I was young. It was a cold and unfeeling building back then, but now it was home to a family and I had felt the love pouring through the walls. I wondered what sensation I would encounter when I opened the door tonight. The warmth of the house sent a calming sensation through my body as I closed my eyes and heard the sound of laughter, little feet on the steps, and Lili calling, "Daddy, Daddy." I glanced into the living room and envisioned Vienna smiling at me with the twins sitting beside her in the big yellow chair. I walked into the kitchen, opened the fridge and poured myself a big glass of milk. I picked up the portable phone from out of the charger, went into the living room, sat down in *the* chair, and dialed a number that I had called every day when I had been living in Vancouver when Vienna was missing. She answered on the second ring.

"Hi Red, how are you and Evan and the kids?"

"Daddy, what are you doing up so early? Is everything all right? Where's Mama?"

"I hope she is sleeping by now."

"Why; has she been wandering the Palace at midnight again, or is she not feeling well?"

"Sorry Honey, but she's in the hospital recovering from surgery."

"Oh my God; what now? Is she all right?"

"The doctors say she will make a full recovery. She may have had her spleen removed. It has been so hectic that I am not sure of anything at the moment."

"Why, why would she need to have her spleen removed?"

"I guess it was damaged when she was stabbed. Like I said, I am not sure."

"Stabbed? Are you saying that she was assaulted? By whom, where, why?"

"It was Jorja."

"Who the hell is Jorja?"

"Did your mother not tell you about her?"

"This is the first time I am hearing the name. Who is she to Mama?"

"She is no one to Vienna. She is someone from my sordid past."

"I need more information than that so you had better start explaining."

And so, for the next five minutes I told Rosy as much as she needed to know for the time being. I ended by saying that her mother believed I had cheated on her and that she was going to divorce me. She said that was the most ludicrous thing she had ever heard and that no way would I have cheated, and that her and Evan would be here as quick as they could. I told her that I didn't want them flying in the middle of winter, and Vienna would kill me if she knew I had called. She said planes fly every day regardless of the weather, and by the sounds of it I was already dead, so that didn't wash. There was no talking her down, so I asked her to at least fly commercially and not on her little jet. She told me she loved me, not to worry, and she'd call me as soon as Evan had made the arrangements.

I returned the sentiment, went upstairs and checked on the twins. There cribs were side by side. They were usually separated enough so that we could get between them. This was the third time that I had found them together. I had a sneaking suspicion how they had got that way. I resisted opening up Vienna's and my bedroom door. I took a peak in the girl's room. Lili was in bed with Tanny. I thought, what the hell, and climbed into Lili's bed and drifted off.

I felt as though I was being jabbed with a stick. I opened one eye and peered out at Liliana standing beside the bed holding a pencil in her hand smiling at me.

"Daddy's awake Tanny!"

"Yeah, I'm awake. Why did you poke me with that pencil?"

She turned it over and showed me the eraser. "It don't hurt. Why you in my bed?"

Tanny sat up and rubbed her eyes. "She thought you were dead. What time is it anyway?"

I guessed it was time to get up. I reached out and pulled Lili into bed with me. "It did hurt a little and I want you to promise never to wake someone up or jab anyone with anything sharp again, okay? You wouldn't do that to the twins or Tanny would you?"

She pursed her lips and said she wouldn't.

"Speaking of the twins… I don't suppose either of you know how their cribs get so close together in the night do you?" I asked not expecting the answer I got.

"Lili and me do it. They like to hold hands when they fall asleep, and they can't the way you guys leave them. Novie looks after Zaney you know, so we just help them." Tanny confessed.

"That is very caring of you. I'm sorry that Mommy and I didn't think to do that."

"Well, you don't speak their language do you Rainey? Vienna says it is gibberish, but they understand each other you know."

"Yes, I am sure they do just as you understand Lili when no one else does. Someday soon the twins will be speaking perfect English, and we'll all understand them. Right now they are still babies, so we best enjoy their lovable babble while we can."

"You mean French?"

"Are you still on that kick that Novia is speaking French?"

"She calls Vienna Maman. I asked Zoe if she knew what it meant and she said that it was mommy in French. Papa is daddy. Has she called you that?"

"No, and I'm pretty sure she says mama. Enough about that as I am hungry. What say we go down and open up a fresh box of corn flakes? Go wash up and I'll see you down stairs after I check on the twins."

I undid the child-proof gate in their room. I had installed it as soon as we had discovered that Novia was climbing out of her crib. Sure enough she was standing up in bed and by the mischievous look on her face was planning on breaking out. I scooped her up and checked her for wetness. She was dry, but Zander was another story. I loved these two just as I loved all of our kids, but they needed their mother more than they did me. I was resigned to the fact that I wouldn't be in their lives once Vienna was well, so I had better cherish every moment with them.

Sissy relieved me of Zander when I sauntered into the kitchen. "You know you carry him around like a sack of potatoes?"

"Yeah well he's always squirming, so I have no choice." I sat Novia in her high chair. "You guys are here early."

"We were awake and nothing is going on at our house so we thought we may as well mosey over here where the action is." Jack said.

"It is very much appreciated as who knows what the day will bring."

"Ava's here." Tanny announced as she and Lili arrived two steps ahead of their older sister.

I asked Ava where Nash and Sammie were. She said that Sammie was still asleep so Nash was waiting on him. She was going to the hospital to check on her mother. Sissy said she'd go with her if she liked.

"I would rather you come with me later when her team does her assessments. It is scheduled for around ten. I might miss something important and seeing Dad can't be with me…"

I didn't feel like it required a response so just smiled and nodded.

Half an hour later Ava returned looking flustered. She poured herself a cup of coffee. Sissy asked her if Vienna was all right.

"I think she's got anesthesia brain."

"What in the world is that?" Sissy asked the question that we all wanted an answer to.

"I don't think her brain has fully awakened from the anesthesia yet. She is very confused. She looked okay, said she wasn't in any pain, but then she goes and says that you were there last night Dad, and that you went downstairs to see your girlfriend, and then you came back and said that you would gladly give her a divorce. Then she told me to go home and look after my man."

"She thinks Jorja is downstairs…how horrible." Sissy lamented.

I asked Tanny if she would take Lili upstairs and help her get dressed. I didn't think they needed to hear any more negative talk about their mother.

"Vienna is not confused. I was there last night, and I did see Jorja."

There were a lot of "Whats?"

"Why didn't you tell me you went to see her?" Ava demanded.

"Did you want me waking you up at midnight? That was when a nurse by the name of Yvonne said that my wife was in a heightened state of anxiety. She said she was trying to get out of bed, had pulled her IV out, and kept yelling for me saying that I had to save Zander. I was not quite prepared for what I saw. Vienna was fighting the two nurses who were trying to keep her from getting out of bed. Her IV pole was laying half way across the room. I approached her cautiously, placed my hands on her shoulders and sternly told her to calm down. Believe it or not, she listened to me. She was a mess though. Her gown, face and hands were awash with fresh blood from her pulling the IV out. Her eyes were frightfully wide open. She kept saying, "She's here, she's here, she's come for Zander." I tried to reassure her that Zander was safe and that *she* was in jail, but Vienna was having none of it saying again that **she** was here and that they knew. I followed her eyes as they were glaring at the nurses and realized that they knew something. Yvonne nodded to me. I followed her to the door and she told me that there was indeed a woman in custody down stairs and that it might be Vienna's alleged attacker. Yvonne accompanied me to the basement and together we talked Constable Tony into letting me in the room to see her."

Ava was on her feet. "So, she's really there? I'm calling Sergeant Rolph; this is unacceptable!"

Nash suggested that she sit down and let me finish. She sat back down reluctantly.

"The reason Jorja is there is because she is being monitored for a concussion. I got the distinct impression that her lawyer ordered her to be monitored. You all know that Vienna claimed that she had killed Jorja, don't you? I imagine there was quite a struggle between the two of them, and hopefully she will relate the details to one of you today. I'm thankful that Vienna's rantings about killing her were false as we wouldn't want Vienna to have to live with that."

"It would have been self defense and I for one wish she was dead. Did you talk to the bitch?"

I needed to calm my daughter down so I spoke softly. "I wouldn't call it talking Ava. I told her what I thought of her and left. I was only there to appease your mother. She wasn't worth the breath I used to curse her to damnation."

Sissy asked if she showed any signs of remorse.

I laughed with a rude snort. "She did not. She thought I was there to rescue her. I went back to relay my findings to Vienna who had settled down, been cleaned up and had a new IV in. I assured her that *she* was secure behind two steel doors as well as being handcuffed to the bed, that an officer was on guard, and no one could get passed him. I told Vienna that I had never lied to her and that I would love her forever. She said I was a liar. At no time did I tell her that I would happily divorce her. I told her she never had to see me again and that I would do whatever she wanted."

I had explained sufficiently I thought, so I picked up Novia in one arm, swung Zander under my other arm and retreated saying that they needed a bath. "Oh yeah," I added. "She said I could say *her* name because I had already said it once too often and the damage was done… something along those lines. By the way Ava, I called your sister. She will be phoning when travel plans are confirmed. I would appreciate it if you would take the call as I'll be busy with the kids." I proceeded into the guest bathroom and closed the door. I would have taken them to the upstairs tub if I'd had the energy to do so.

Ten minutes later the door opened. "I brought clean outfits for the twins. Oh my, what is that horrible stench?"

I turned and pointed to the garbage can. "No amount of soap and water would ever get those clean. What has Sissy been feeding them? Thanks for the clothes. I was just going to let them run naked through the house."

"Squash I think." Ava said opening the door and calling for Nash. "Be a dear and take this to the curb please." She came back, put her arms around me, kissed me on the cheek, and sat down on the floor beside me. "Sorry that I was so snarky Daddy."

"No harm done." I assured her.

"What are we going to have to do to convince Mom that you never cheated on her?"

"Nothing; this is not about me. I'm not the one who was abducted after an earthquake, or barely existed for months in a coma, had amnesia, or almost bled to death on the mausoleum path. I was not kidnapped by a crazed woman, stabbed and almost died again, or had surgery and lost my spleen. How much more can one woman take? For twenty years she lived a fearless and sheltered life, and then I show up and all hell breaks loose within months. I can't, and I won't be responsible for any more tragedies in your mother's life."

"Are you saying that you're not going to fight for her? It definitely will be the end for her if you agree to a divorce. You are everything she has ever wanted; she just needs time."

"Exactly; it has only been one day. We'll see how things play out, but don't get your hopes up for there may very well be no repairing the damage that's been done. It will all come to a conclusion one way or the other. I want to make it perfectly clear that you will not try and sway your mother by singing my praises. It is best if you don't talk about me, or even say my name. I am leaving it in your hands to relay the message… actually, call it a directive to the rest of the family. Are we clear on all of that?"

"I'll try."

"You have to do more than try. Let's get these munchkins out before they shrivel up."

"Sorry to interrupt, but Rosalyn is on the phone asking for you Rainey."

"Thanks Sissy, but Ava is going to talk to her. Why don't you help me dry these two off?"

Novia was quite happy paddling around in the tub. Zander was not. Sissy lifted him out, laid him on the bath mat, and wrestled with him talking his language all the time.

"You're very good with him. Is that gibberish or French you're talking?"

"Very funny Rainey. I worry though that I may be overstepping the boundaries of an aunt by doting on him and Novia too much. It may be because I gave Joannie away so never got to know her in her early years."

"Maybe so, but they love you just as much as you love them, so quit fretting. You and Jack have been a great help to us, and Vienna is going to need you more than ever when she comes home. I'm afraid my days are numbered Sissy."

"Don't say that Rainey! I will not let that happen. She'll come to understand that everything that woman said was all a lie. She knows in her heart that you would never deceive her."

Sunday December 23rd

Vienna was still refusing to talk to Sergeant Rolph. Dr. Barbara had a word or two with him telling him that she was not mentally prepared to deal with the ordeal and forcing her to talk would be considered harassment. He reluctantly agreed to wait until he had her consent. There was also no change in Vienna's behavior towards me. If anyone mentioned my name she would turn away quickly so they knew they had better change the subject. Jimmy was sure that he could change her mind by reminding her of our history. He was wrong. He was still stinging from her tongue-lashing when he arrived at the Palace after his short visit with her.

"I warned you and everyone else to keep your thoughts to yourself, but did anyone listen to me…obviously not." I lectured.

"We're not done yet Rain. If she throws us out she throws us out. She'll be in the hospital for a week or more, so we'll be used to it by then, right Jack?" Nash joked.

"Did it ever occur to you guys that you're attempt to sway her is just distressing her?" I asked.

Nash apologised and said I was right and they'd leave the pleading up to Evan.

"What makes you think he has more influence over her than any of us?" Jimmy asked.

"He saved her life; him and Johnny? They have a special relationship. Believe me, Vienna will listen to him." Nash insisted.

"I think it's time you guys got up off your asses and help the girls with the decorating. And speaking of Johnny… does anyone know if he has called her?"

Evan said he'd go and ask Ava.

"This Johnny, he's her best friend in Scotland isn't he? In other words, he's a substitute for me, right?" Jimmy queried.

"Don't fret it Jimbo. Vienna and Johnny go back almost twenty five years. They are so much more than just best friends."

"What do you mean by that Rain?"

"Hell if I know. Come on, I'll walk you to the door. You don't want to be late for dinner do you? Give Ruth a kiss for me. What are you grinning about Jack?"

"Nothin; just minding my own business."

"Yeah Jack, just where do you fit into this string of V's admirers being an old boyfriend and all?" Jimmy jested.

"Just happy to be her brother-in-law and friend." Jack answered honestly.

"All kidding aside guys, she's going to need her friends more than ever after the divorce."

"Way to end the day Rain. You know damn well there ain't gonna be any divorce!"

I reached into a box by the front door and thrust a Christmassy wrapped box at Jimmy.

"Nuts, I didn't get you anything."

"I didn't get you anything neither Buddy. This is for you and Ruth from Vienna."

"The card says it's from you and her."

"Yeah, that was before catastrophe Friday."

Ava rescued me from uttering anymore doomsday prophecies by calling me. I gave my best friend a hug and a boot out and retreated to the living room.

"What can I do for you Honey? The tree looks magnificent."

"It's missing something." She said as she handed me the angel that was to adorn the tree top. "This is Mama's crowning glory. I'm glad she brought it with her as it is a family heirloom. She's not here so you have to take her place and complete the tradition."

"I don't think I can do that." I answered humbly.

"Of course you can, and these two are going to help you." She said as Nash and Jack gave Tanny a heave-ho, and Lili held out her arms for me to pick her up.

Together we crowned the tree. I excused myself right afterwards. Ava followed me into the kitchen and closed the door behind her. I broke down. "This isn't right, this isn't right Ava. She should be here… she should be here not lying broken and alone in some goddamn infirmary! This was going to be our first real Christmas together. Just the other morning, hell it was last Friday, the day to end all days that we were in bed with the girls and the twins laughing and making plans for the big day…"

"I know Daddy, I know. We are all here for you, and we'll get through it just like we always have. It's not like before; we know where she is, and she will heal and then you will be together again. Please tell me that you believe that?"

I lifted my head, smiled and nodded. There was no need for her to know anymore right now.

Ava sat up with me to wait for Rosy and Evan to arrive. They couldn't land the Gulfstream in Bridge as the airport was not yet equipped with landing lights or a de-icing system. I wasn't pleased that they had chosen not to fly commercially, but I was confident in Jin's and Evan's expertise. They would land in Potsdam and then rent a car and travel to Bridge. Jin was carrying on via the Greyhound to Vancouver to spend Christmas with relatives.

It had been a slow drive for Rosy and Evan as snow was falling once again. They had followed behind a snow-plow most of the way. Ava and I welcomed them at 1:33 a.m. Monday, Christmas Eve morning. We caught them up on Vienna's progress while they sat down to a late supper that Sissy had made for them. I let Ava take the lead as she knew more about Vienna's prognosis than I did.

"The spleen plays a crucial role in the ability to fight off bacteria, so without it you are more likely to develop infections such as streptococcus and anemia. However, other parts of the immune system like the liver and lymph nodes take over for it. She will require yearly vaccines and probably antibiotics. It is advised that she always check in with her doctor before travelling anywhere, and always have antibiotics with her. She will be receiving a meningococcal vaccine in a week or so. Dr. Nelson said she will remain in the hospital for another 4 to 5 days, and that her recovery will take 4 to 6 weeks. Her appetite will probably not be the same and she may feel fuller faster. She is to take iron supplements and lots of fluids. She will probably do best on low fat foods. Rice, yogurt, toast and broiled proteins like chicken and fish are recommended. If I know Mom she might adhere to this diet for a while, but when she feels better she will go back to eating whatever she wants. That's about it."

We had a little laugh because we all knew that was exactly what Vienna would do. She would say that it was quality over quantity of life. Someone else was going to have to enforce the guidelines because I wouldn't be here to do so.

I shooed them out just before three. Ava and Nash had moved Sammie's crib into their room across the street making room for Rosy and Evan. Our downstairs bedroom was made up for my parents. We could have remade the bed in the morning, but Ava wanted time alone with her sister anyhow, so it was all fine. They would all be here most of the time anyway. I trundled up the stairs wondering how I was going to break the unabridged news to my parents.

I never needed a clock to wake me even when I was living on my own, and now I had two little alarm clocks right across the hall from me. I woke up feeling quite lethargic, rolled over and seen that it was almost 8 o'clock. I shot out of bed and crossed the hall to find the babies gone. That would have been alarming if Sissy wasn't here. I went back to the bedroom, washed my face, brushed my teeth and tossed a clean shirt and khakis on and rushed downstairs.

I glanced around the animated kitchen counting heads as I did so. Everyone was accounted for. Jack handed me a cup of coffee. I thanked him and said two more and I might just make it. Rosalyn had Tanny and Lili in her embrace. Tanny was pleading with her to let them go all the while laughing and telling her she was silly.

"Oh, my little girls, I will never let you go." Rosy crooned hugging them tighter.

"You should get some girls of your own Rosy." Tanny suggested.

"You are right, I should. Maybe you should talk to Uncle Evan." Rosy laughed.

Tanny squirmed her way out of Rosy's clutches. "He's not my uncle you know."

Evan asked her from across the table if she missed him. She walked over to him and said that she'd been so busy with school and looking after Lili that she only missed him a little. Then she added that she had Nash and Uncle Jack, and sometimes Uncle Jimmy came to visit, but he wasn't a real uncle and he was a little crazy. Then she asked a question that only a Tanny could.

"Hey, did you guys ever find the door that the big black key opens? You know the one with all the numbers and flowers on it. You said it was from France didn't you Evan? Can you speak that language? Because if you can you can tell us what Novie is saying."

"We've been a little busy too Tanny so we haven't had time to even think about that key. Now what's this about Novia?"

"Well, when you have the time you should really try to find that door. Let's see if Novie will talk to you. Sometimes she talks a blue streak and some days she doesn't so don't be upset if she doesn't, and it's a little early for her."

I shook my head. Rosy asked me what she was talking about. Still half asleep I answered.

"Yeah, since we have moved here Novia has taken to speaking in French. She's pretty good at it too."

"Thanks Dad; way to clear things up. Does someone want to fill us in?"

I joined Sissy and Jack at the counter where they were preparing breakfast leaving the explanation up to Ava. I took over the beating of the eggs for an omelette. Rosy joined us a few minutes later and asked me when this "French allegation" had started.

"A month or so ago Vienna informed me that Tanny had told her that Novia was talking French and she couldn't understand her. Vienna assured her that it was just baby talk, but Tanny said it wasn't and that Novie wasn't a baby, Sammie was. When Vienna and Lili came home to us from Verde El Mar, Lili was fifteen months old and was talking pretty good. Tanny spent a lot of time with her and takes credit for helping her learn English. If you recall, Lili had quite a few Spanish words in her vocabulary. So, now here is Novia, and Tanny is trying to teach her not understanding that her sister isn't even a year old yet. I have no explanation as to where she got this French thing. She insists that Novia calls Vienna Maman which is French for Mama. I haven't heard it."

"What about Zander?"

"She is not worried about him because he is special, whatever she means by that I know not."

"Can you imagine a day without Tanny in it?"

"Never." Then I reminded myself that I might soon be doing just that.

Rosy asked what she could do to help. I told her that she could dish up some porridge for the kids. "Tanny and Lili like theirs with a little milk and maple syrup, Zander doesn't care because he will toss most of it anyway, and the little French girl likes cut up peaches in hers."

She hit me with the tea towel. It was just like old times at the castle.

I had made reservations at the best restaurant in town for Ava and Nash's anniversary for five P.M. That way they could all visit Vienna afterwards. She had been moved to a private room last night. Sissy's daughter Joanie had arrived on Sunday, so she and Zoe would look after the kids until I got back. Vienna was overjoyed to see Rosy and Evan and gave them heck for coming because it was winter and Christmas. She also blamed Ava for calling them. Ava thought it best to let her think that. Jack and I had entertained the girls in the daytime playing games and sledding down the hill in the back yard while everyone else was at the hospital.

Ava and Nash kept us entertained at dinner relating some of their more harrowing accounts from their adventures in the wild Canadian north last year after the plane crash. Vienna and I had been morosely sure we would never see our daughter again, but miracles of miracles, she survived and she and her new husband arrived home on February the 4th. That was also the day Evan found Vienna lying on the path to the mausoleum bleeding from a placenta abruption. He and Johnny got her to the hospital and the twins were born. I had been neglectful of watching over her again… three times now…three times too many.

After dinner Jack and Nash came back to the Palace with me. We sent Zoe and Joannie off to attend a party at one of Zoe's friends' house and played Rumoli around the kitchen table with the girls. Tanny understood the game while Lili just walked around the table relieving us of our chips. The twins and Sammie were all napping in the spare bedroom close by. Not long afterwards we heard the front door open. Ava called out to us not to panic because it was just them. They walked in toweling their hair. Apparently, it was snowing again. I asked if Vienna wasn't up for company and then realized Evan wasn't with them. Rosy said it was because he had kicked them out.

"Sure he did." I said laughing.

"She's not kidding Dad." Ava explained defending her sister. "We all visited with her for twenty minutes or so, and then he said that we ladies could leave as he wanted a private audience with Lady Vienna. Mom laughed and told him not to make her laugh as it hurt. He walked us to the door and said he'd see us later."

"Unbeknownst to me, he also had a letter from Johnny. I think those three have some secrets that none of us are privy to." Rosy declared.

Remembering Vienna's tearful farewell to Johnny when we left Scotland last summer had brought back some uncomfortable conversations that we'd had regarding their relationship over the years, and now it had come back full force again. I was ashamed that I had been jealous of their closeness, and now that ugliness had risen again wondering what Johnny had said in his letter and that I would never know. Rosy said that Johnny was going to call her on Christmas day. Great; everyone but me would be talking to my wife tomorrow. I swallowed my pride.

"Those three do have a bond that none of us will ever understand. I know Evan and Johnny have reiterated the events of that ill-fated night when Vienna almost died over and over again. I think more for their benefit than any of ours. That night changed everything for them, especially Evan being alerted to your mother's danger by your deceased mother. It was providence that both he and Johnny had been working late. Does Evan still talk about it Rosy?"

"No, not to me, but he visits the mausoleum regularly. I have actually seen him and Johnny going down the path together. Witnessing Maveryn's spectre that night has had a lasting effect on them both."

"Yes, that makes sense for Evan, but Johnny did not see her."

"Amma thinks he did. She told me that one night he awoke in a sweat saying that Maveryn had told him that Vienna was hurting. She asked him if she had come to him in a dream. He told her that Maveryn was at the hangar waiting for him. He went back to sleep and didn't remember any of it the next morning when she told him about his nocturnal dream."

"Do you remember when this was?" I asked curiously.

"I think it was shortly after you moved here."

I nodded thinking it may have been when Vienna had hurt her feet running away after we had the argument the day Jorja had come calling. I patted Rosy's hand. "I think that maybe dreams have a way of transcending across the waves, and especially those that have their beginnings in that mystical place known as Avanloch."

"That's very philosophical of you Dad."

"I've had my share of dreams under those skies, so nothing surprises me. Now you gals get your shillings out and join us in a rousing game of Rumoli. Is Evan going to phone for a ride?"

Rosy said he'd probably call a cab.

An hour later we had packed up the game and were enjoying hot chocolate and Vienna's Christmas cake when Evan arrived. Without a word he poured himself a cup of brew, cut a large chunk of cake and sat down asking what was going on.

Rosy laughed. "I think you had better go first and tell us what that tete-a-tete between you and Mama was all about."

He teased her. "It's kind of private Honey."

"Evan!"

"Okay, okay. I just wanted to talk to her alone and find out what the hell was going on with her. Seeing she wouldn't talk to any of you about Rainey or her abduction I thought maybe she would tell me. Actually, I was pretty sure she would."

"Well, are you going to keep us in suspense, or are you going to enlighten us?"

"Impatient aren't you Deary? Okay, I said that I had understood that she was going to divorce Rainey because he had cheated on her, and she didn't love him anymore. She said that just because someone disappoints you doesn't mean you don't love them anymore." He smiled at me. "She read Johnny's letter and put it under her pillow. I asked what he had said. She scolded me and said that was between him and her, and did I want to know what had happened. I said that of course I did, and she told me more than I wanted to know, and yet I'm sure she omitted the worst. She was unemotional as she relayed the events of last Friday as if they had happened to someone else. I asked her if I could tell the rest of the family. She said I could not. That's it."

"You're going to tell us right?" Ava beseeched.

"Nope, it's not my story to tell." Evan said as he got up to get another slice of cake. "Oh, you all know that she is coming home for Christmas don't you?"

"Very funny; she is still bedridden and her doctors wouldn't let her."

"I thought you knew your mother better than that Ava, and she is not bedridden. She walked me to the door, albeit that it was only four steps, and I had to walk her back and help her into bed. Anyhow, you and Rosy are in charge of her wardrobe and she wants it early tomorrow morning."

"Only you Evan; only you could get her to talk. Glad you're here Buddy." I said thankfully.

CHAPTER 7

CHRISTMAS

I tucked the girls into bed after reading The Night Before Christmas twice, and listening to their prayers. Tanny said that my reading was almost as good as Vienna's. I thanked her, kissed them both and went downstairs to the library to write a note to my wife.

I was the first one up Christmas morning, turned the coffee on and retreated to the library. I reread what I had written last night, ripped it up, picked up the pen and tried to find the right words several times over. I finally decided to get on with the day, slipped the short letter into an envelope and sealed it hoping that I wouldn't open it. I had settled on this:

Vienna, I know you don't want to hear from me, but I am hoping that you will give me a minute and grant me one last favor. My parents do not know the whole story of your hospitalization, or that we will be separating as I haven't the heart to ruin their Christmas. They are looking forward to spending the holiday with all the family so I could not ask them not to come. All I am asking is that you don't throw me to the wolves in front of them. I will stay out of your way as much as I can. I will leave with them on Boxing Day so you won't have to see me when you come home again. If you can do this for me I will be eternally grateful.

As Always, Rainey

I slipped the envelope into a pocket and went out to join the family in the living room. Ava asked me where I had been as the girls were waiting on me before they opened a few presents. We had decided last night after hearing that Vienna was coming for dinner that we would postpone the Christmas morning ritual of opening presents until she was here. I made sure that Lili and Tanny opened things that I remembered Vienna and I wrapping that would keep them occupied for the day. After a quick breakfast Ava and Rosy dragged me upstairs to help pick out an outfit for their mother. I told them I wouldn't be much help. I sat on the edge of the bed watching in amusement as they pulled dress after dress off the hangers and tossed them all aside.

"You're not helping Dad." Ava chided.

"I'll give you a little hint of what not to choose. Everything to the left of the grey coat is from Miss Mary's closet, so they are off limits. I can't see anything wrong with the ones you have discarded except the black ones."

"Why can't we choose one from Miss Mary's clothes?"

"She said they are all too tight as she still has baby weight. Hold on a minute, I'll be right back with reinforcements." I left paying no attention to their objections. I came back with Tanny and Lili in tow. I sat Lili down on the floor and passed her a drawer full of Vienna's everyday jewellery and told her to pick out something for her mother. Tanny was disagreeing with her older sisters about a dress they had chosen. It was the green paisley I had bought her.

"Mama loves this dress. You bought it for her didn't you Dad?" Rosy asked.

Tanny answered for me. "He did. I was there when she unwrapped the box it came in."

"What did she say; she liked it didn't she?"

"Close your ears Rainey." Tanny suggested. "Mom said, "Oh, what was he thinking? His heart is in the right place unlike his eyes. I'll wear it anyway because I love him."

"You can't possibly remember her saying that Tanny." Rosy laughed.

"I've never seen her in it again so I think Tanny knows what she is talking about. What do you think she would like to wear today?" I asked Vienna's lady- in-waiting daughter.

Tanny went to the back of the closet and pulled out a long sleeveless light blue dress. I believe it was what Vienna would call a shift.

"Mommy likes this dress because she says it hides her rolls and is comfy. She needs a sweater because she gets cold. She just had surgery you know so she just needs underpants and a slip, and a little sock that will fit in her slipper shoes, nothing tight. Is that good because I have to get back to help Sissy? Lili what did you pick out? Oh, pop beads…I don't know."

"I do; she always wears them when Lili gives them to her so she will know who picked them out. Are you ladies happy with the choices? Good, you better get it all together and get yourselves dressed. It's Christmas you know." I could fake being jovial because I had most of my girls with me. I gave Ava the envelope and asked if she would give it to her mother. She looked at me dubiously. I told her it was all good.

I showered and dressed in my usual light colored chinos and white shirt. I thought it best that I didn't wear one of the colorful shirts that Vienna had bought me. I checked on the kitchen staff to see if they needed anything before I left to pick up my parents. We had decided to have dinner in the kitchen because its large table along with the dining room table could accommodate our large family. Lara and Coop were joining us which meant eighteen would be sitting down to Christmas dinner. Vienna would be happy as it would be just like any meal at Avanloch.

The doorbell chimed just as I was putting on my snow boots. I opened the door to greet a young man with a wrapped bouquet of cherry blossoms in his hand. Damn, I had forgotten about asking the florist if she could find me any. Apparently, she had. I pulled out a twenty dollar bill and passed it to the young man thanking him for making the delivery on a holiday. I went back down the hall and asked the kith and kin what I should do with the stems.

"Where in the world did these come from?" Ava asked.

"I ordered them. They are the reason your mother got abducted."

She took them from me, laid them on the table, put her arms around me and told me to sit down. Everyone started talking at once. Evan put a halt to the questions by asking me to explain that ridiculous idea. I did. Of course there was understanding and no blame laid, but that still left the question of what to do with the blossoms as they would most definitely upset Vienna. Evan said to leave it to him and get going to pick up my parents. I trusted that he would trash them.

An hour and a half later I opened the door and ushered my parents into the entrance hall. Ava, Rosy, Tanny and Lili were waiting with arms open. They led them into the living room where everyone else was waiting. Tanny held back and told me that Vienna was home. Hesitantly I walked with her to see my wife for the first time after the debacle at the hospital four days ago.

There was no mistaking the sweet scent of cherry blossoms. Even the woodsy smell from the cedar boughs and fir tree could not mask it. The sprigs lined the mantel. I would deal with Evan later. Someone handed me an alcohol-free glass of eggnog. I could have used the rum. My eyes wandered. I tried focusing them on Mom and Dad as they made a big fuss over the babies and Vienna, but they had a mind of their own and forced me to steal a glance at my wife. She looked my way at precisely the same time, and an elusive smile crossed her face. I did not read anything into it. She was sitting on the large sofa with Tanny and Lili who politely vacated their seats to made room for my parents. Sissy sat Novia on my Mom's lap. Zander was nestled in Rosy's arms while Sammie slept in his bassinet. I took a seat close to the door and gave Ava and Rosy the nod to commence with the gift ritual. Jack was the acting Santa. We had been worried that Lili and the twins might object to the costume, but they appeared to be quite enchanted by it. Tanny knew that it was her uncle under the beard but kept the secret. Novia escaped from my Mom and made her way over to the girls sitting on the floor beside Jack. He scooped her up. She immediately started yanking on his beard and had a little temper tantrum when Ava tried to pry her away. This was very unusual behavior for Novia. Although it was amusing to us adults, I figured I had better rescue her from Ava before her screaming woke Zander and Sammie and upset her mother. I managed to do so by bribing her with a brightly wrapped box that had her name on it. I sat on the floor with her and helped her open it knowing that inside was a musical toy that portrayed animal sounds that Vienna and I had picked out for her. It did the trick and she settled back to being the little lady that she was.

An hour later Jack made his exit with his Ho -Ho -Ho and wishing us all a Merry Christmas. The girls left to get dinner on the table while Dad, Evan and I cleaned up all the wrappings and ribbons. Shortly after Ava came in and announced that dinner was ready. She asked Nash to help Vienna get into the wheelchair.

"He has his hands full with Sammie, so Rainey can help me. He's an old hand at getting me into and out of chairs, and everything else I get myself into." Vienna said surprising us all.

I wasn't sure what she meant by the last remark but was pretty sure there was a hidden meaning behind it. I approached her, put my arms around her and gently eased her forward on the sofa. She wrapped her arms around my neck as I stood her up and pivoted her into the chair. I asked her if she was hurting. She said she wasn't and thanked me. I wheeled her into the kitchen and sat her at her usual spot at the head of the table. She looked around. Her eyes said that she wasn't happy. Everyone took their seats including me. The girls had sat me and Lili between my parents at the far end of the table. Evan and Rosy had the chairs on each side of Vienna.

"I'm sorry, but this isn't right." She said.

Ava asked her what she meant.

I rose, picked Lili up and walked to the other end of the table. "You're in Lili's seat Evan, and Rosy, you're in Novia's place. Tanny you are going to have to scoot down one as you know that you're in my seat and Zander's highchair has to fit in between us. Everyone, please make the adjustment."

"Oh, musical chairs, this family is so much fun! I'm so glad I'm part of it." Joannie exclaimed.

"I told them Rainey, but they said it would be all right." Tanny explained.

"She's right; we should have listened to her. The seating arrangement is my fault Sis. I just thought you might want a break from the kids which was silly because you haven't even seen the twins for days. I'm sorry." Sissy apologised.

"It wasn't just her Mom; Rosy and I agreed." Ava defended her aunt.

"I should be the one apologising. This day was made possible by all of you. You have done all the decorating, planning, and cooking along with looking after the children. I will never be able to thank you enough. Sissy, you and Jack have been Godsends, and Evan and Rosy, you came all the way from Scotland, and Ava and Nash have been at my beck and call for months, my best friend Lara and Coop are here, the kids are all healthy, and Joannie, we are so happy that you could join us and be part of our family. Zoe, you take up the challenge every time I falter. I love you all. I am forgetting the father of my children, but he knows... but, enough for now. Please excuse my rudeness and let's enjoy the feast."

"Amen, our sentiments as well Lady Vienna. I believe that constitutes as Grace. Rainey has trusted me to carve the bird. I hope I live up to his expertise. Now, who wants a drumstick? Speak up; there's only two you know." Evan teased cheerfully.

How I had been so lucky to have this whole family in my life was never anything I had dreamt about in my years apart from Vienna. Everything was possible because of her, and I would always be grateful for the few years I had with her and this family, but it was all coming to an end, so I'd make the most of the hours I had left, and be as jovial as I could be.

The conversation was very lively. Mom wanted to know what was going on at Avanloch, why Lara and Coop weren't with their boys. According to Evan nothing exciting was happening at the castle because the instigator of all things out of the ordinary was no longer living there, so it was rather boring. In fact, they hadn't even heard from Rosy's mother. There was no patter of little feet running up and down the halls and stairs. It was very quiet.

"Believe me, Maveryn's there Evan. Sometimes a little peace and quiet can be rewarding, don't you think? And Mom," Vienna addressed my Mom. "Coop and Lara are off tomorrow to spend New Years' on Vancouver Island with the boys and their families."

Of course Tanny had to add her two bits worth. "I told Evan and Rosy that they should get some babies. Don't you think that's a good idea Grandma? And, if they want some excitement, they should investigate that key."

Evan laughed and Mom asked what key was that? Before anyone could answer Tanny filled her in. "Mommy found a big black key in the Harem Room after someone pushed her, and she fell down. She said Rainey did it, but he said he didn't. The key has strange markings on it and probably opens some secret room. We'd be investigating wouldn't we if we were still there wouldn't we Mommy? Hey, how come you're not eating?"

I looked at Vienna's plate. It looked like she had just been moving the food around. Sissy asked if she could get her something else that would sit better with her. Vienna said that she just hadn't got her appetite back yet. I excused myself saying I'd be right back. I went to the fridge and pulled out a bag of frozen strawberries, ice cream, milk, and a tub of plain yogurt and went into the pantry. I threw it all into the blender with some protein mix and pureed it all until it was the consistency of a milk shake. I poured a good portion into a tall glass, found a straw and took it out and set it in front of my wife. I relieved her of the plate and said the dog could have it. Her voice broke a little as she thanked me. Tanny reminded me that we didn't have a dog anymore. Lili asked if she could have some.

"It just so happens that there is enough left for you and your sister."

"Do you mean me Rainey?" Tanny asked.

"Well, you're her sister aren't you?"

"I thought maybe you meant Novia."

"I meant you. Come and help me."

"I think maybe Novia might like a little too if there is enough." Vienna suggested.

"I'll make sure there is. Sorry, I know apricot is your favorite, but we were out."

"The twins have apricots." Sissy smirked.

"Yeah, they also have pumpkin…" Ava chimed.

Vienna groaned, "Oh no, not pumpkin!"

"Yup, seems as though Sissy has a penchant for pumpkin and Dad and I found out what the end results are. Their wardrobe might be missing an outfit."

It was good to hear so much laughter. Sissy said that speaking of pumpkin it was time to clear the table for dessert. In no time the dishwasher was loaded, the coffee was perking, and dessert plates were set out. My job was to wash three little faces and their hands and pick up the utensils and anything else they had thrown on the floor. Tanny came back from the pantry with a plate of Christmas cut-out cookies and put them down in front of me.

"Did you forget something Dad?"

"Like what?" I asked.

"Like putting the ice cream back in the fridge?"

"Shoot; did I? I'll clean it up."

"I already did. You know I am used to cleaning up after you and Mommy."

"I beg your pardon little girl; what are you referring to?"

"Yes," Vienna said, "I'd like to know too."

"Well, not Rainey so much, but you leave your clothes and shoes, and jewelry all over the place. I don't mind, but I don't think I was hired to do that."

I wanted to laugh along with the rest of the table, but I thought a little discipline might be in order. "For one thing Tanny; you were not hired to work for us. You are our special chosen child. You know that, and no one has ever told you to clean up after us. I think perhaps you owe your mother an apology, but I will thank you for everything you do, especially keeping an eye on Lili and the twins. Perhaps we should relieve you of that chore." I was saying "we" like there was still a "we".

"What would I do then? I think I would be bored, and I'm sorry Mommy. I love you and I know you are going to need my help more than ever now that you don't have Amma and Johnny to help you anymore and Zoe is very busy with school, but we have Sissy and Jack."

"Come here my sweet. Give your old mom a hug. You are growing up so fast I can't believe it. I will try to be a little neater, and if I need more help I guess we will just hire someone."

"You don't need anyone else because that's my job. I'm sorry that I complained. Sissy, you and Jack are still going to be here aren't you, and Daddy is nearly always home, so it's okay."

I let Sissy answer as I swallowed another lump in my throat.

"You bet we are! Now, let's get on with dessert. Nellie McNamara made these delicious looking pies for us. I think I will have a piece of each one. How far did Jack have to go for the ice cream anyway?"

"I hope he didn't lock himself in the freezer. I'd better go check." I offered.

"Oh, he's probably just off having a cigarette."

"I could use one too." Vienna said surprising everyone.

"You don't smoke Mommy." Tanny reminded her.

Jack arrived with the bucket of vanilla ice cream and took his place next to Sissy to be the scooper. She smelled his breath, and asked him what took him so long. He said he'd tell her later.

"Ooh, an underground secret." She chuckled.

Vienna managed a few bites of blueberries and ice cream before she said that she was tired and needed a little lie down.

"Lara and I will help you Mom. It's been a long day and you are probably tired from sitting in that chair. Nash will warm the car up." Ava said soothingly.

"There is no need Nash because I am not going back to the hospital. I just need someone to make up the bed for me in the library."

"You mean that you just need a little rest before you return to the hospital don't you?"

"No Ava, I mean what I said. I am not going back to the hospital. I am home and I'm staying. I want to be here with all of you and not in some stuffy, stale smelling institution. I will recover much faster at home."

"Lara, did you know about her plans?" Ava asked.

"No, I certainly did not and I am quite sure her doctors didn't okay it. Vienna honey, I don't think you have thought this through. You are still on all kinds of medications, and it's not like we can run down to the pharmacy and get them."

"I have been thinking of nothing else for three days. Do you all have any idea how sick I am of hospitals? I spent a month in one last year, but it was because the twins had to be there so that was okay, but they are here, and this is where I want to be. Don't worry about the meds because I have enough for two days. You don't believe me... look in my bag; it's with my coat."

No one said anything as Lara fetched the bag. She opened it in front of us and laid a plastic bag on the table that held five vials. Lara inspected each one, said they looked official and asked Vienna who had authorized the medications.

"Can you not see that Dr. Fraser prescribed them, or do you think that I bribed someone to steal them and forge his signature?"

"Mom, that's not even funny. Lara, do the pills all look legitimate?" Rosy asked.

"Yes, they are all from the hospital pharmacy, but no one in their right mind would supply you with this amount."

"I want to be in the room when you tell that to Dr. Steven and his wife. Zoe, will you and Joannie help me into the library please?"

It was time for me to step in. "I think Vienna has made up her mind girls, and it appears as if she has the blessing of her doctors, and whether it's wise or not is not for us to determine. Nash, Jack, do you think you are up to another lift up to her bed?" I stood up and looked down at her. "You will not take up residence in the library. I have slept in that bed and it is a back breaker. You will be much better off in your own room. I am not in the least bit in favor of you not returning to the hospital, but your mind is made up, so we will abide by your wishes and hope for the best." I could hear Johnny saying in my head, "What Vienna wants, Vienna gets."

I'm not one hundred per cent sure, but I think she thanked me.

"I have a better idea." Coop said. "There are enough of us to take her up the stairs right in the wheelchair. That way there is no risk of hurting her while we are lifting her, and she will only have to be transferred once. What say, we give it a try?"

The boys agreed. Ava and Rosy said they would ready the bed. Lara said she would give them a few minutes and then go and check on her and see what pills she was due to take. She shook her head as she walked by me. "I don't know Rain; I just don't know."

Zoe and Joannie offered to do the clean-up. I told them that I'd prefer they look after the children. That left my parents, Sissy and me. My mother was on me immediately as to why I didn't object to Vienna's outrageous plans.

"You're the only one she would listen to. Did you know of her plans before hand?" She asked.

"Nope, hadn't a clue. She hasn't been talking to me for days so I would be the last to know."

"What are you talking about; did you have a fight? If you did then you had better high-tail it up stairs and beg her to forgive you. My God, she's been in a horrible accident, and you're acting nonchalant about the whole thing. What is going on with you Rainey?"

"Now is not the time Mom. Everything will be clear to you shortly. Why don't you and Dad leave the cleaning to Sissy and me and go spend time with the kids?" I guess it sounded like I was dismissing her as she huffed and turned and walked away. Dad raised his eyebrows. I went after her and told her I was sorry for the insolence.

"Something's wrong with you and her isn't it? I don't want to interfere, but whatever it is you must fix it." She said woefully.

I kissed her on the cheek and said I'd talk to her and Dad later. I filled a bucket with water, grabbed a mop and proceeded to wash the floor in the pantry where the ice cream had made a mess. The boys returned to help with the clean-up. Evan said that the lift had been a piece of cake. Jack informed me that we had an intruder with four feet in the basement. Somehow a window had been broken and a cat had come in out of the weather. I asked him if he could see that it had food and water as it was probably a stray, but today was not the day to be calling the SPCA. I needed a drink, but opted for coffee instead and went into the living room to join in the fun that was in evidence by the ruckus coming from there. They were playing a game called Duck, Duck, Goose. Tanny called me to come and sit beside her. I had just gotten the gist of the game when Ava came in and said that Vienna wanted to see me.

I knocked lightly on the bedroom door. "Ava said you wanted to see me?"

"I do; can you come in?"

"I can. What can I do for you?"

"I need to talk to you Rainey."

"I know we need to talk, but today is not the day. This is supposed to be a happy day, so could we not spoil what's left of it by talking about divorce? Tomorrow will be time enough. If it will ease your mind until then I will not keep you in limbo. I have already made preparations for you to have a full time housekeeper and cook, a part time nanny and caregiver. This would have kicked in a week or so after you were discharged, but seeing you've decided not to go back to the hospital that will have to be pushed up. Anything else you want can be arranged whether I am here or not. Will that put your mind at ease? I don't want you to worry about anything. After all, what happened was my fault, so it's the least I can do." I said turning around to leave.

"I don't want to talk about divorce. I want to apologise for the way I have been treating you."

"You don't owe me an apology."

"I do. You said you might not be here; where are you going?"

"I haven't given it much thought yet, but I suppose back to the coast."

"I mean right now…where are you going right now?"

"Downstairs to rejoin everyone. Before I go I want to thank you for being civil to me in front of my parents. I'm sure it wasn't easy."

"It wasn't hard as I love them just as I love you. I just didn't know how to react to you after everything I had said to you. I hurt you and I am sorry. You're wrong though as it was my fault."

She had just said she loved me. I wondered if she even knew that she had said it. "Nothing was your fault Vienna, so never think that."

"I opened the door to her. You can leave now, or you can sit down…"

I sat down and listened apprehensively to her traumatic account.

"You had phoned to say that you would be home in ten minutes. A few minutes later the doorbell rang. I was in the kitchen with the girls and the twins making treats for the birds and squirrels. Lili ran down the hall jubilantly calling "Daddy, Daddy, Daddy." I had just picked Zander up out of the high chair as he was fussing. I had him on my hip as I went to see who was at the door. Lili was waiting for me to open it. I suggested we see who it was first and pulled the curtain back on the side window. There was a little girl standing on the top step. She was dressed is some sort of uniform that I didn't recognise. She was holding a basket with little boxes in it. I said to Lili that she was probably selling chocolates or cookies and that we should buy some from her. Just as I started to open the door Lili stamped her feet saying it wasn't you and ran back up the hall. Zander distracted me by slipping to the floor just as I was opening the door. I looked down at him. When I looked back up she was standing there. The little girl was nowhere to be seen. At first I thought that it might have been her daughter, but she was more Tanny's size so I dismissed that idea. I told her that she couldn't be here and she best leave. She said, "Good morning Vienna. Is this Rainey's little boy?" I said that he was yours and mine. I bent down to pick him up, but she beat me to it. I asked her to give him back. She laughed and said that we were all going for a little ride. I told her we weren't going anywhere with her and tried to grab Zander away from her. She backed up and pulled a large knife out of her coat pocket and pointed it at his head. I pleaded with her to give him to me. She told me to get a coat and not to yell for help if I valued my son's life. I grabbed your coat and followed her outside not bothering to shut the door. She gave me the car keys and said I was driving and to remember that she had Zander's life in her hands. I told her to wrap the seat belt around him. She said I was a worry wart and that you would be upset with her if anything happened to his only son. I asked her why she was holding a knife on him then. She said it was to keep me under control because she would never hurt your favorite. I was hoping that Ava or Nash would be looking out the window. It was sleeting and the roads were slippery. I was driving a car that didn't have very good traction and twice I almost put it in a ditch. I suppose I should have, but I had to be careful because she had Zander. She had me drive back and forth down half a dozen streets two or three times. Finally she told me to drive out to the old cannery. We did a few loops around it before she directed me to a little house on the banks of the bluff. I think it may have been the caretaker's cottage at one time. After several times of driving around and around she told me to stop, passed me a key and told me to unlock the door, go inside and sit down in the chair at the table and put my hands into the cuffs that were on the arms."

I was appalled. "Hand cuffs?"

"They were made of leather and attached to the chair. She put Zander in a cuddle lounger that was on the table, came over to me and made sure that the cuffs were snug. I asked her what she was going to do with us. She said I'd see soon enough, but she had a few things to do before you came so I had better have a little sleep. I told her I wasn't sleepy. She said she would help with that, opened a drawer and pulled a loaded needle out. I tried to…"

"Oh God, she drugged you?"

"That was the least of what she had planned for me. For some reason she wanted me unconscious to do whatever she had to do. I don't think I was out for very long but I really don't know. At first I thought that I was hallucinating because the surroundings had changed. I was in another room and in a different chair. It was like a captain's chair that rocked. My arms were attached to it with some grey tape. At that point I wasn't aware that my feet were also bound. She was standing over me. She had brought me to by slapping my face. She said, "There's my girl. You know this isn't personal, but it must be done if Rainey is going to be free of you. Before I send you to the netherworld I feel compelled to tell you a few things that you might not be aware of." I wanted to ask her where Zander was but my mouth was filled with what tasted like cotton, and my eyes wouldn't stay open. She said that she supposed that I'd like some water, but I wouldn't be around that long so why bother. It was then that I heard a movement to my left. It was Zander. He was still harnessed in the cuddle seat. He had a soother in his mouth. You know how I hate those things Rainey. Then she said that she could see I had put a lot of weight on and that you hated it when I was skinny like when I came home from my two year rendezvous with Anton. You said that Anton must have been riding me hard. She told me not to look so upset because she had taken care of you while I was off fornicating in sunny Spain."

I was pretty sure I was going to be sick. "I don't want to hear anymore of her blatant lies." I pushed my chair back fully intending to leave so she wouldn't have to relive the nightmare again. She had been rather unemotional up to then, but there was no holding her back now.

"You think this is fun for me? Well it isn't, and it wasn't! I lived through her torture and tormenting, so I think you could be man enough to hear what your ex had to divulge. I didn't want to listen to anything she had to say either, but I didn't have any choice, but you do, so you can leave." She turned away from me.

It was the first time I heard real emotion in her voice as she wiped a solitary tear away.

"I'm sorry Vienna." I put my hand on her shoulder. Apparently that was all she needed because she turned back and tears filled her eyes.

"How did she know about Spain and Anton? How did she know that you didn't like me when I was thin Rainey?"

"Honest to God, I don't know. Your disappearance as well as the discovery of you being found alive was reported in all the newspapers so she must have read about it, and of course my name was linked to it all, so I surmise that she did some investigating."

"That doesn't explain how she knew the personal stuff does it?"

"Please tell me that you don't think I told her?"

"How about you hear the rest, and then you can tell me what I should think or believe?"

"If you feel you have the stamina to relive the ordeal again then I will listen, but if you want to stop at any time I will understand that it is just too much for you to re-experience."

"What do you think I did every day and night while I was alone in the hospital? At first I just wanted you to suffer like I did, but now I want you to understand why I was so horrible to you, and the only way I can do that is by having you hear the whole story. I'm sorry if it upsets you."

I placed my hand over hers. "You will not upset me, but what she did to you will. It is all on her, not you. I will try to sit quietly, but I can't promise that I won't be emotional."

She took a deep breath. "Where did I leave off…oh yes, my affair with Anton. She did not mention anything about me faking amnesia, or that I went by the name Katarina. She just wanted me to know that you tracked her down when you got to Vancouver. She said she had moved and had a job at some advertising agency. You looked for her at her old job and some bouncer there gave you her new address. You apologised for losing touch with her."

I hoped my facial expression showed her that I objected strenuously to Jorja's fabrication.

"So, you were in the clear because I was most assuredly dead, and it was just a matter of time before you would be able to claim your inheritance. Apparently, you would be rich beyond yours and her wildest dreams. I tried to tell her that you didn't care about money, but my mouth felt like it was filled with a hundred cotton balls, so I couldn't get any words out. She said you renewed your love affair with her, and that you had an insatiable appetite for her. She had known about your marriage to Louise and your two sons, but you had never mentioned my name, and she had only found out about me when someone told her about it just before you contacted her. Anyhow, I spoiled it all by turning up alive so you were back to stage one of plotting my demise. She said she could see by the look on my face that I was mortified. "Oh Vienna, you are so naïve. That visit I paid you last fall…it was all staged. Rainey was in on it." She laughed. "And the paternity test was rigged. You can alter anything if you have the right connections. Rainey is definitely Patricia Ann's father. He was with me when she was born. He has no need for anymore girls,so that is why he instructed me to make sure I got Zander who's his favorite."

I couldn't stay silent any longer. "Did that not ring any bells with you?"

"Of course it did. Even though I was still feeling the effects of whatever she had given me I was fully aware of everything she was saying. She made a mistake there didn't she because even though you deny it, Liliana is your favorite?"

"Yes, everyone thinks so, but you know that I love all our children equally."

"If you say so. Apparently, I spoiled all your plans again because I got pregnant *again* and you felt obliged to stay with me for a while longer. Then you finally convinced me to move back to Bridge Falls. She was waiting for you here, and the plans to get rid of me once and for all were completed. She described your torrid love making in such detail that I thought I was going to be sick. She said you couldn't get enough of her. I heard every nauseating word while I was trying to come up with some plan to escape. I knew I wasn't going to be rescued because no one even knew I had been abducted. I'd have to appeal to her motherly instincts if she had any. Could I bargain with her? Could I sacrifice Zander to her for the other children if she let me go? She could have him and you, gladly. There was one problem; I still couldn't speak."

"I'm so sorry Vienna. God, I am so sorry that you had to pay for my mistake." I felt the tears stinging my eyes. "I should never have believed that she would disappear after the maternity test proved I was not her daughter's father."

"It was fake remember? What have you left out about your relationship with her? Did you know she was obsessed with you? Did she find you after you walked out on her, or is that just part of this sick scenario?"

"Damn it Vienna, you know it's all lies! I never heard from her or saw her again until I came home and found you and our daughter having tea with her. I should have dealt with her then."

"What would you have done? It doesn't matter because despite her attempts on my life I am still standing. She couldn't make up her mind on how to slaughter me. She had been standing about ten feet away from me. The knife was sitting on a little table next to her. She opened a drawer and pulled out a hand gun which she said was her first choice, but it might be too loud and alert someone. She thought that if she used the knife she would get blood all over herself and she wouldn't like that, so maybe an overdose of the Lorazapan. Yes, that would probably be best. It would be easy to administer, and maybe my death could be passed off as a suicide."

"Jesus Christ Vienna." I uttered.

"Don't be anxious; the best is yet to come. Just then Zander's crying turned into screaming. She picked up the knife and started towards him. I had been rocking ever so slightly back and forth all the while. She had to walk by me. I waited for the right second, pushed myself backwards and with as much force as I could muster, screamed and threw myself and the chair at her. It was then that I found out that my feet were also bound. What was left of the rickety rocker was resting on top of me, but I was free of the tape that had been bonding my arms to the chair. She tried pushing me off her, but my rage was no match for her. I grabbed her by the collar on her blouse and rammed her head into the floor, over and over until she lost consciousness I know I cursed her with every profanity I had ever heard and probably made up a few of my own. She still had a pulse so I grabbed her by her long bleached blonde locks and sent her to hell. I righted myself and managed to free myself from the chair. I wondered where all the blood was coming from. If her head was bleeding it shouldn't be on me. Was I the one bleeding? I straightened up as much as I could and saw the knife protruding from my abdomen. I can see I am distressing you, but it's almost over. Can you hang on a few more minutes? I really need you to witness everything I had to endure so you can understand fully why I admonished you."

"Oh, I understand, and I did even before your telling of the assault. I am sickened by the whole thing as you have painted a very ugly scene, but I didn't live through it so it is your reliving it that is concerning me. This can never happen again Vienna."

"Are you suggesting that she may not be prosecuted and may come after me again?"

I tried to take her hand, but she pulled away. "I'm sorry; I didn't mean it that way. She's never getting out of prison; **never**! She should be in Landsford now undergoing psychiatric evaluation. It's my belief that she will spend the rest of her life in a mental institution."

"Well, that's reassuring coming from you because you'll be the one deciding her fate won't you? She wants you bad enough so she will find a way to escape no matter where she is, just mark my words." She said caustically.

"As I live and breathe, that will never happen. I will make sure of that."

"Sure, or maybe you will just run off with her."

"That was uncalled for. I thought we were making some progress here."

"Let me get the knife out of me, and then we will see where we go from there. When I was sitting in the rocker trying to drown out her suggestive sexual innuendoes of you and her, I was pretty sure that I could see a sink behind her, so I supposed that it was a bathroom. I knew that when I pulled the knife out I might very well pass out and I might even bleed uncontrollably, but what choice did I have; I had to get my baby home. She must have been living in that house for some time because the bathroom was very well stocked. Besides her toiletries, there was even a man's razor and shaving cream, and there was a man's white shirt hanging on a rack..."

She stopped talking long enough for me to get the picture which sickened me further.

"I guess she knew about your white shirt mania. Anyhow, if I am to believe that you didn't have an affair with her then I guess it was all there for my benefit."

"You know it was." I hoped my words hadn't fallen on deaf ears.

"So, I sat on the toilet, held a towel close to the knife and yanked it out. I may have screamed, but I didn't black out. I sat for a minute, got my breath, threw the bloodied towel on the floor and replaced it with two more. I tied them with a sash that was hanging on the back of the door. I found my coat; actually, it was your coat, put Zander inside of it and made my way home. A woman stopped and asked if I would like a ride. I said no and kept walking until the policeman picked me up. He wanted to take me to the hospital, but I told him that I had to get Zander home. Two minutes later you arrived. You know the rest."

"I do, and that is why I can positively say that nothing like this will ever happen to you again."

"You can't guarantee that Rainey; no one can."

"I can because I will be out of your life. I am the reason for every disaster that ever befell you, so you will be safe with me gone."

"So, you are leaving me and the children to fend for ourselves when another one of your jilted lovers comes to call?"

"That is absurd Vienna. Just because there was one deranged woman doesn't mean that there are more out there. No one ever loved me that much, and I certainly never loved anyone else."

"So, you finally admit that you loved Jorja? Well, isn't that just the icing on the cake?"

"You know damn well that isn't what I meant! I have **never** loved anyone but you. We have had this conversation before and..."

"And what Rainey; you're leaving, so let's get everything out in the open before you go. Do you think that I have been so blinded by my love for you that I believe that you never told Priscilla or Zeta or Louise, or any other unnamed woman that shared your bed that you loved them in the heat of passion? Have you been lying to me all along?"

"You already told me I was lying when I told you I loved you, so that is nothing new. If I have told you once then I have told you a thousand times that you are the only one I have ever loved. My leaving is different from you wanting a divorce because I am doing it to protect you, and you are doing it because you don't trust or believe in me."

"I told you that I don't want a divorce, and I do believe and trust you. I know I accused you of being unfaithful, of planning my abduction with Jorja, and I threatened to kill you. I need to tell you that I know none of that was true…well, I was angry enough to hurt you, but I know you didn't cheat on me. I'm sorry it took me so long to come to my senses, but you can't forgive me can you?"

"Whatever you said or did does not require an apology. A deranged woman kidnapped you from your own home and held you and Zander hostage. She filled your head with unimaginable things while holding a knife on you. She brain washed you. You were traumatised. I do not hold you responsible for anything you said to me. The unfortunate thing about it all is that not even in a tiny part of your altered mind did you trust or love me enough to talk to me. I can live with that, but not with the chance that I might be the cause of yet another disaster in your life. Three times is enough Vienna."

"So, you are still taking responsibility for my crossing the street in Nazeth without you and the aftermath that befell me, and my sneaking out of the house while I was under your house arrest that caused me to hemorrhage and almost miscarry. That is all me Rainey; all me. As I said before I opened the door for Jorja. How were you to know that she had become unhinged?"

It was the first time she referred to Jorja by name in her account of the abduction. "Yes, I am taking responsibility for it all. You will always be my sweetheart, and I am not too sure how I am going to live without you, but living without you because you died because of me is not acceptable. I have seen that you will want for nothing, and if you want a bodyguard, I will see to that also…"

She interrupted me again. "You can just take your egotistical conscience and shove it! Remember my death could have made your girlfriend and you rich, so I need nothing from you, not even a goodbye kiss because it just might be the kiss of death. I am done with the likes of you, and I will not give you the satisfaction of leaving me because I am throwing you out! Now get out of here before I have the men who really love me do that!"

I wanted to tell her that I was at the top of that list, but she had turned her head and her breathing had become labored, so I figured I had done enough damage already. I walked to the door, stopped, glanced back, whispered, "I love you Vienna." and left.

I walked into the living room as if I hadn't just ended my life, told Lara that Vienna wanted to see her, joined in on the conversation and waited for the shoe to drop when Lara returned. Fifteen minutes later she smiled at me and said that Vienna was out for the night. My soon to be ex-wife had spared me the embarrassment of explaining my departure for the night. I knew not why. I accompanied my parents to the spare bedroom and informed them that we were leaving early the next morning before the rest of the household was up. My mother shut the door in my face. It was going to be a fun drive to Hawthorne tomorrow.

We were on the road by 5:30 a.m. The house was silent. It had been a long day and night for everyone so I was not surprised. Jack and Sissy usually arrived before anyone was up so I didn't expect it would be any different today. I had spent the night in the library tossing and turning on the sofa bed. I had hoped that I would fall asleep because it would keep me from going up the stairs and climbing into bed with my wife and begging for her forgiveness. I guess I did sleep because I awoke with a memory of a knife wielding Jorja coming at me, or was it Vienna with scissors in her hand?

My mother climbed in the back seat and was silent all the way to the ranch. My father only spoke once and that was to say that I'd better have a damn good explanation for my actions. I told him that they would have the whole story once we were home. Half an hour later we pulled into the yard. I asked them if they would wait in the living room while I put a pot of coffee on. Mom had still not uttered a word. Well, she would have plenty to say in a few minutes. I waited for the coffee to perk and set the steaming cups in front of them on the coffee table. They were sitting side by side on the chesterfield. I pulled up a chair facing them.

"You are going to be very disappointed with me after you hear what I have to say, and if you want me to leave I will. I only ask that you bear with me until I am through. I will start by informing you that Vienna was not injured in a car accident like I led you to believe." I gave them all the facts which included my sordid affair with Jorja which was the cause of Vienna's tortuous abduction, and why I felt I had no other recourse but to leave her for her own safety. Dad asked me if I was expecting more of the same from previous lovers. I said, "No, but never in my wildest dreams did I think that what happened was even a possibility, so I have to err on the side of caution for the safety of Vienna and the children."

"So, the exemplary son we thought we had raised and loved doesn't exist because this man here before us has spent the best part of his life cavorting with whores, and in so doing has endangered the life of the sweetest woman in the world and all of our grandchildren… is that what you are saying? Because if it is then I think there is no room here for you under our roof."

My mother had finally spoken. I told her she was right and I'd take my leave. I got up and told them I was sorry. My father interceded.

"Just a moment Son; Patricia, you know you don't mean that."

She spoke with tears in her eyes. "Your dad is right. I just need time to sort this all out, but in the mean time you still have a home here. No one should lose two homes in one day. I will reserve judgement until I talk to Vienna."

I thanked her and asked her to give Vienna a few more days to heal. I went upstairs, showered and collapsed on my old bed. I hadn't even packed a suitcase. Luckily, I had one last change of clothes in the closet. I had nowhere to go so laid my drained body down on the bed. So, this was the way it was going to end, and how ironic that I was going to lose her again at Christmas just as I had twenty some odd years ago. Remembering how she had accused me of infidelity for no apparent reason a year and a half ago there was no way she could ever forgive me this time even though she said she believed me. To her, the truth was all too real and alive in a crazed and vengeful woman. No, my days with Vienna were over and that meant that my life was over too. I fell asleep reliving the days of wine and roses that quickly turned into the unspeakable nightmares of the last week. I awoke a few hours later in a stupor, got up, revised myself with cold water and told myself that there was one person who may not hate me yet. I needed to see my best friend. I didn't think my parents expected me to leave a note. It was 12 noon. I met Ruth who was leaving to visit her mother. We exchanged pleasantries for a few minute before Jimmy came to the door and called me in.

He shook my hand. "Didn't expect to see you today Buddy. What can I get you; coffee I guess because you're driving."

"A lot of unexpected things have happened Jimbo. I left Vienna this morning."

"Oh Christ; she really threw you out? I thought for sure that she would relinquish."

"I don't think you heard me right; I was the one who walked out on her."

"What the hell are you saying?"

The telephone rang. Jimmy said that it was probably Yates, so the machine could get it. Just before the answering machine kicked in we heard a woman's voice.

"Hi Jimmy; I was hoping you were home, but you're not. Maybe I will call back later."

He picked up the phone and turned the intercom on.

"Hey Honey, I'm here. Sorry, I was just setting the coffee pot. How are you feeling?" He asked giving me the eye.

"Have you seen Rainey?"

"Just briefly…"

"Did he tell you that he left me?"

"What do you mean when you say that he left you? Did he agree to a divorce without contesting it? That's what you wanted, right?"

"When I was out of my mind with suspicion and jealousy and traumatised, it was, but I know better now. I know he didn't cheat on me or have anything to do with her plans to kill me. I told him Jimmy, I told him I was sorry for not believing him and that I loved him and didn't want a divorce. He accepted my apology, knew I loved him, but I didn't trust him so it wasn't enough. I hurt him; I really hurt him Jimmy. I guess he has finally had enough of my tantrums. I don't blame him for wanting to get away from me, but how can he leave his children? They love and worship him Jimmy."

He gave me a dirty look.

"I know they do, and he feels the same way about them. Something is terribly wrong here Vienna. This is not the Rainey I know. There must be something else going on."

"He says it's for my protection, but that doesn't wash because if he was concerned for my safety he'd stay and fend for me. No, he is done with me, and Jorja gave him a way out."

I started to walk towards Jimmy indicating that she was wrong. He pushed me back.

"I don't believe that for one minute, and surely you don't either?"

"Well, he didn't say that he'd be in touch or anything, or that we could talk in a day or two. No, he's gone, probably back to the coast. He wants me to take his name off of everything and that he'll sign the house over to me so I can sell it, and he'll make sure that I am looked after financially. Isn't that just the craziest thing you have ever heard?"

"I know it's too soon, but will you put the Palace on the market and go back to Scotland?"

"Why would I do that? This is my home. Rainey and I had so many plans. Did you know that he was planning on building a house for us in Hawthorne on the hill above his parents? I guess he wasn't serious because no plans ever materialized. Anyhow, I will stay here because who knows, maybe, just maybe he'll come back. Maybe I was just a warm body to him, but he can replace me with any tart on any street corner, but the kids… how can he replace them? Oh, I guess he can."

I was only slightly amused by her reference to a warm body.

"Just how long do you think you would wait for him?" Jimmy asked inquisitively.

"Well, I waited twenty years for him once, so I guess another twenty. Anyhow, if you see him will you tell him that I love him?"

I motioned for Jimmy to hand me the phone. He had one last thing to say to her. "Why don't you tell him yourself?" He told me to make it right.

"Hi Honey." I said

"Rainey…are you there; are you at Jimmy's?"

"I am, and I heard every word you said, and unlike last night, I heard them with my heart. You said you'd wait for me for twenty years…how about twenty minutes?"

"What do you mean?'

"It means I'm coming home if you will have me. Don't cry Honey… Vienna, Vienna…"

"Is that you Daddy?"

"Where did your mother go Red?"

"She's right here. I just walked into the bedroom and found her holding the phone and crying. She's having some sort of spasm. What did you say to her?"

"I told her I was coming home. Look after her; I'm on my way."

Jimmy grabbed his keys. "I'm driving. What the fuck is the matter with you? What the hell were you thinking?" He cuffed me on the back of my head.

"Thanks, I needed that."

"What you need is a bloody head shrinker."

I thought he'd lecture me all the way to Bridge but instead he gave me a rundown on Yates and his new love life. We pulled into the Palace a few minutes past one. Jimmy followed me into the house. It was unusually quiet. H wandered down the hall to look for signs of life. I bounded up the stairs and heard voices coming from our bedroom. I walked in to see everyone standing around Vienna who was sitting up in bed. They turned when they heard me.

"What's going on here? You okay Honey?"

She nodded and smiled, but tears were running down her face.

"Okay then, everyone out. I need some alone time with my wife."

"Daddy, what did you say to excite Mama so much that she hyperventilated?" Ava questioned.

"Didn't she tell you?" I asked looking at Vienna who shook her head.

"Tell us what? What's going on between the two of you? Mom, did you ask Daddy to leave?"

"No Red, she did not. Now go; I'll explain later. By the way, Jimmy is waiting for someone to make him a cup of coffee."

"Oh goodie, Uncle Jimmy's here! Come on everyone, let's leave them alone." Ava said nudging them to the door.

"Hold up a minute; where are the kids?" I wanted to know.

Jack said that Sissy had taken them all next door to visit with Mrs. McNamara. Evan gave my shoulder a hard squeeze as he took his leave. He closed the door behind him.

"Hi Gorgeous; are those tears because I'm home, or are they tears because I'm back and you're not sure if you want me here?"

She took a deep breath and patted her chest as a new onslaught of tears ran down her face. I tried erasing them with my thumbs. I asked her if she was hurting. She nodded.

"Okay, enough of this my pretty; you're ruining your makeup."

"Please don't make me laugh."

"I'll get you a face cloth and you can wash your face, and then we will talk, and you can tell me that you love me."

"I do love you Rainey Quinn." She said through tears.

I kissed her softly and whispered tenderly. "And, I love you Vienna Lafontaine."

"Then you are not going to leave me again?"

"No, not even if you ask me to."

"I can't lose you again Rainey."

"You didn't, and you're not going to ever."

"It will be my fault if I do because my fanatical behavior may finally be too much for you. I don't know what to do about it. Maybe I need to have my head shrunk."

I laughed lightly. "Jimmy said the exact same thing to me, so I guess we will go together. I never want to go anywhere without you again. You have no idea how hard it was for me to stay away from you last week. I wanted to barge into your room in the hospital and demand you listen to me, but I respected your wishes so I didn't. The days dragged on and I pretty much knew it was over when you never asked to see me, and then you came home, and my heart soared when I saw you."

"Yet, you still left me when I asked you to stay."

"I didn't get very far did I?"

"It was far enough and long enough. Thank God you were at Jimmy's. If anyone could talk you into coming back to me, it was him."

"Last night I heard your horror story, but I couldn't fathom that it had happened to you because it wasn't you telling the nightmare. Your voice was subdued and unemotional. To be perfectly honest, I didn't think you cared one way or the other if I stayed or left. But, today it was you I heard on the phone, and I knew that I had made a mistake. If I hadn't already made up my mind I'm sure Jimmy would have done it for me. Now, who or what changed your mind? Was it Evan or Johnny?"

"You know about the note Johnny sent with Evan?"

"Yes, someone mentioned it. I suppose he cursed me out."

"On the contrary; it's in my carry-all, and if you bring it here, you can read it."

"That's between you and Johnny and I would never invade your privacy."

"I want you to read it. Now be a good boy and fetch my satchel." She insisted.

She pulled it out of her bag and passed it to me. It was written in a Christmas card.

My Dear Vienna, I know that Amma has already sent out our greeting cards. But we were just informed of your recent accident. So sorry to hear, and we hope it is not too serious as Rosy wasn't sure herself. Whatever happened we know that Rainey will see you through it. Say "hi" to the big lug. We miss you both. This place is so dull without you. Hopefully, we'll get through on the phone tomorrow. In the meantime, just concentrate on getting well. Love you.

Amma and Johnny

I put it back in the envelope and told her I'd place it on the string in the living room with all the others cards. I told her that there was one from the Sister Anita at the convent in Andorra. She asked what she had said. I told her I hadn't opened it. She seemed surprised that I hadn't and said she'd look at it tomorrow. Then I asked her if Johnny had phoned. She said he did but she had been sleeping so Ava took the call. She said that maybe we could both call later, and talk to the Duffys' also.

"Sounds like a plan to me. Have you eaten anything yet?"

"Not really; nothing tastes and it doesn't go down smoothly."

"I'll see what I can do about that in a few minutes." I said looking over her prescription bottles. "Do you know what they are all for?"

"The one you are holding is the anti-biotic, and I have already had it today. There is one for high blood pressure, pain, a sleep aid which also acts as an anti-depressant, and Gravol for the nausea. I've had all of them except the morphine. I am switching to extra strength Tylenol tomorrow."

"Are you sure you're ready for that?"

"Yes; I hardly have any pain. Now I want to go somewhere."

"Okay, where do you want to go?"

"Over there." She pointed to the recliner in front of the windows.

I helped her sit up on the edge of the bed being very cautious because I wasn't at all sure if she was as pain free as she said she was. Next thing I knew she was standing up with her arms around me. I scolded her for being so impatient. She said she just wanted to hold me. We stood for a few minutes with our arms around each other just rocking back and forth, and kissing.

"Come on, I'll dance you over to the chair." I proposed.

"Don't forget to unhook my catheter bag. You know I'm going to be indisposed for a while again don't you?" She asked timidly.

I sat her in the recliner and titled it back until she was comfortable. "How long do you think?"

"Just a day or two; I'm hoping to get this thing out tomorrow."

I laughed thinking that she thought the expected four to six week healing from the surgery was going to happen overnight. "Oh good, I think I can last that long before going down town and checking out some of those warm bodies on the street corners then." I joked winking at her.

"Oh Rainey, I didn't meant to say that. It just slipped out." She apologised.

"Sure it did. Before I go and make you a shake I have something to show you." I went into the closet and reached up on the top shelf and took down the tube, opened it, and showed it to her.

"Oh, is it done, is this our house?" She exclaimed clapping her hands. "It is."

"When did you finish it?"

"A while ago. I was going to give it to you on Christmas morning, but... well, here it is now."

"We weren't going to exchange gifts so I have nothing for you." She sniffled.

"You gave me my life back, *again*." I kissed her. "Tomorrow I will position it on the drafting table so you can see it better. Rest now while I go and deal with your subjects downstairs."

"Hurry back. They don't have to know everything Rainey."

I met Jimmy on the stairway. I asked him where he thought he was going. He said to see his girlfriend. I thanked him for the lift and said I'd see him in a week or so. Tanny and Lili were in the living room coloring. I asked them if they wanted to go and keep their mother company while

I made her something to eat. They were up with a hoot and a holler and up the steps before I even made it into the kitchen. The girls were getting dinner ready. I said "Hi, don't let me disturb you; just going to make Vienna a shake. Where are the guys?"

"Evan wanted to see Jack's shop, so they are over there. They'll be back soon with a couple of pizzas. There are lots of leftovers, but the girls asked for pizza. Oh, and Jack went out this morning and found some frozen peaches, but no apricots." Sissy answered.

"Just as good."

Ava asked me if I was going to explain about my cryptic phone call. I told her there was nothing cryptic about it and she would get the particulars when the guys came back because I was only going to explain what had transpired between her mother and me once. As if on cue, the three of them walked in the back door with three pizzas. I acknowledged them, finished up with the peach shake, sat down and made myself a turkey sandwich explaining that I didn't have time for a full meal. I ate while I reiterated what had gone down with Vienna and I last night. I touched briefly on the ordeal of her kidnapping, her not wanting a divorce, but my decision to leave anyhow because she'd be safer without me. Hence the phone call saying I was coming home. "That's it folks; disaster averted, and all is well in the Quinn household again."

Part2

And the Beat Goes On

CHAPTER 1

DISSECTING THE WEEK THAT WAS

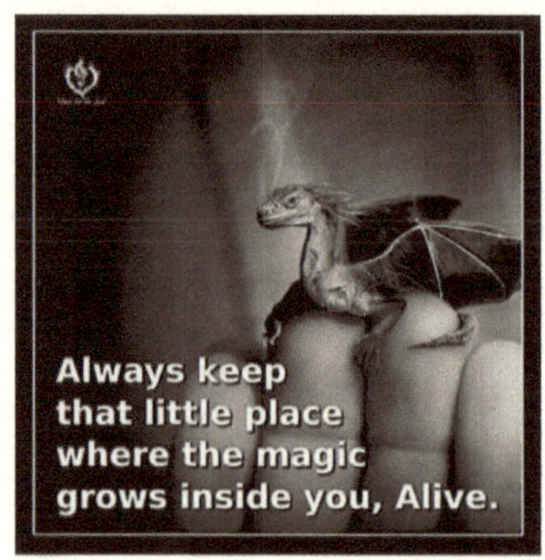

"Mommy, can you read us a bedtime story tonight?" Tanny requested.

"It's been a very long day, and as soon as your daddy gets back I'm afraid that I am going to have to go right to bed. Could you ask Zoe to read to you instead?"

"Zoe is with Joannie at Uncle Jack's watching scary movies. Sissy gave her the day off."

I laughed. "Oh she did, did she? Good for Sissy as Zoe works way too hard as so does everyone else since I have been in the hospital. I'll give you all a holiday when I get better."

"Can we go to Disneyland?" Tanny asked hopefully.

"What's this about Disneyland?" Rainey queried walking in with the twins in his arms.

"Mommy says we can all go on a holiday when she gets better, and Lili and me want to go to Disneyland. Is that okay?"

"We will talk about it another day okay? Visiting hours are over and your pizza is on the table so give your mom a kiss and vamoose."

Sissy had come in behind Rainey with my shake and pizza for Rainey. She set it down on my night table and came over and picked Lili up so her little arms could reach me. She said she'd be back to bathe the twins after supper. Rainey said he was going to do that. She told him that I needed her more than they did so he should get his priorities straight. He laughed, saluted her and told her to get out.

"Now my Lady, do you want the special little boy, or the little French girl?" He asked holding the twins before me.

"I told you not to make me laugh." I answered patting my chest. "Put them on the floor and give them the hatbox with all the bangles to play with while you feed your wife."

I ignored the pain in my right side as I sipped the delicious shake and watched Novia and Zander play. I thanked Rainey. He told me not to get too used to it. That brought a tear to my eye and I asked him if he was going to leave again. I saw that I had upset him and apologised as a new round of waterworks erupted. He took the shake from me.

"You know that is not what I meant, so what is going on here?"

"I'm so tired of this. I feel like I will never be healthy again. It's one thing after the other with me, and now on top of it all my hip is acting up again. I can't face another surgery, so I will just go on hurting for the rest of my days. I wouldn't blame you one bit if you did leave and never came back. You didn't sign up for a wife who is discombobulated all the time."

"Well, we can't have that can we? You're right though; I didn't sign up for what befell you because of my past indiscretions. What I did sign up for was to love you unconditionally for the rest of my life, and that included in sickness and in health. You are not now, or have ever been a burden to me, so lean on me. I want and need to know about every twitch, so don't exclude me from your pain. This marriage thing goes two ways you know. Give me a minute while I take these two ragamuffins across the hall to their cribs and then I'll get you into bed."

"I'll wait right here for you." I promised.

"That's my girl."

He stopped at my bed when he came back. I asked him what he was doing. He said he was just getting the bed ready. I told him that I needed to wash up first. He said I could do that in bed. He came over, scooped me up in his arms and deposited me gently into bed. I didn't object, but scolded him saying that I was too heavy and he wouldn't be much help if he hurt his back again.

"I've got news for you young lady; you are now a feather weight."

I humored him and said, "In my dreams."

"I'm serious Honey. That weight that you have been trying so hard to lose is gone, and I'm pretty sure a lot more. You haven't been able to keep anything down for almost a week, so it has taken its' toil on you in more ways than one. We need to get some solid food in you. You want to get your strength back don't you?"

"The shakes have lots of good things in them, and they have a special ingredient." I asserted.

"Yes, but love doesn't have enough nutrients. Tomorrow we will start experimenting. Now, let's have a look at that hip." He said pulling my gown up. "Yup, just as I thought; that padding you've had cushioning the hip is gone. God, I can't believe how much weight you've lost."

"It can't be that much Rainey; six or seven pounds maybe."

"Tomorrow we'll put you on the scale."

"Tomorrow, I'm going to have a bath and then I'm going to go downstairs."

"Tomorrow you can have a shower with me, and then we'll see about getting you downstairs."

"Are you going to wash my hair? Are you going to be my caretaker?"

"Yes, for as long as you need me to be. When you no longer need me you can fire me and resume life as the high spirited lady that you were before."

"I always need you Rainey. Can I tell you something?"

"Of course you can."

"I would have forgiven you even if you had of cheated on me."

"If I am to believe that then the moon is really made of green cheese." He kissed me and said he was going to go and help Sissy with the twins.

"What about *my* sponge bath?"

"You'll just have to wait my lady, or else I can summon one of your daughters. You need to come up with a plausible reason of why you just lied to me."

"I didn't lie. I don't want Ava or Rosy; I want you."

"Well, you are lucky then because I'm available." He winked at me. "Be back in five minutes."

I closed my eyes for what I thought was a few seconds, but apparently it was longer because when I opened them Rainey was standing over me with towels in his hand and a smile on his face. He said he thought that maybe I was out for the night. I assured him that I wasn't. He had filled the basin from my antique pitcher set with warm water. He positioned towels under me and over my suture dressing, and handed me a face cloth. I handed it back to him and told him that I was too weak to wash myself. He said that this was way beyond the call of duty but he'd struggle through it. I must say that it was indeed a most stimulating bath, but way too quick. He applied lotion to my back and massaged my hip. I sighed deeply.

"You are enjoying this way too much for a lady of your statue. The feet can wait until tomorrow as they haven't been walked on for a week. Now to find you a nice flannelette gown."

"Rainey!" I cautioned.

"Why do you have them if you never wear them?"

"I think they came with the house."

He slipped a soft satin gown over my head and pulled it down. I thanked him and said that this could be a nice bedtime routine. He laughed and said he didn't think so. He emptied the basin and took the towels into the hall where there was a laundry shoot. "Didn't we once have people to do this for us?"

"Yes, but we left them all back at the castle when you insisted we move."

"So, it was me who wanted to move eh?"

"Well, according to Jorja, you orchestrated it all."

"I am going to go and check on the kids and when I get back you are going to be honest with me and tell me everything that Jorja told you that you believe to be true. Do you understand?"

I had wounded him again. "I'm sorry Rainey; I don't know why I would say such a thing."

"You can explain why when I get back." He avowed as he walked out the door.

If I kept up this nonsensical harangue he was going to walk out the door again and it might be the last time. I had to take control of my emotions and my tongue. I was still admonishing myself when Lili and Tanny burst into the room. Rainey was right behind them.

"We came to say good night Mom." Tanny said giving me a kiss.

Rainey sat Lili on the bed. She put her little arms around me and said "Me love Mommy."

"I love you girls so very much. I've changed my mind; I want to read you a bed time story."

"It's okay Mom 'cause Evan and Rosy are going to read to us. We need to talk to them some more about getting their own girls anyhow."

I was about to ask Tanny what she meant when Rainey laughed and said he'd explain later. He sent them off to get into their pyjamas, opened a drawer and took out a clean tee and a pair of comfy pants and said he'd be right back after he had a quick wash. He came back shaving with the electric razor which he hated, as he walked towards me. He pulled up a chair.

"I guess this will do for tonight. I wasn't expecting to do any heavy necking anyhow." He grinned. "How are you feeling? Are you in pain; do you need a pill?"

I said I wasn't and I didn't need any medication.

"Are you tired, or do you have a few minutes for me?"

"I am rested, and I have all the time in the world for you."

"Good, then let's dissect what happened last week."

"Do we have to?"

"I have a few things to tell you that I don't think you are aware of. First thing is about the house that you were held captive in. What did you think of it?"

"I don't know what you mean."

"You were told to sit in the chair which had the cuffs strapped to it, but I am curious to know if you took notice of the kitchen. Did it look like someone was living there?"

"I didn't think anything Rainey. Almost immediately she went into a drawer on the table and pulled out the syringe and came at me still threating Zander with the knife. It all happened so fast, so no, wondering if someone was living there was the last thing on my mind at the time."

"I fully understand that. I know you were in what appears to be the living room when you came to, and that you could see the bathroom and bedroom from the chair that you were tied to. I realise that you weren't in any condition to take much notice of your surroundings, so I have done it for you."

"What do you mean?"

"The morning after I returned home after your ordeal in the hospital I had a dream that I was in a house I didn't recognise. Before I could figure out where I was I was awakened by someone poking me and telling me to wake up. I did, and saw Lili standing there with a sharp pencil in her hand. I asked why she had poked me. Tanny said Lili had thought I was dead, and why was I in her bed, so the dream became irrelevant. I didn't…"

"Wait a minute; why were you in Lili's bed?"

"I was upset when I got home from seeing you, so the first thing I did when I got home was to call Rosy. It was after one a.m. here so the day would be in full swing at Avanloch. After we talked I went upstairs to check in on the kids. Lili was in bed with Tanny, so I thought what the hell and crawled into her bed. Our bedroom was off limits, so that's why."

"I get the picture; sorry." I cringed envisioning what the room may have looked like. I put my hand on his and told him to continue adding that I thought it was Ava who had called Rosy.

"Yeah, we thought it best to let you believe that." He said grinning. "Later that morning I caught a conversation between Ava and Sissy about canning. Sissy had brought some of her wares over to share with us, and Ava was complementing her on her canning expertise. The word "canning" was rolling around in my head, but I didn't know why. Suddenly, it dawned on me that Les Arnold from the liquor store had mentioned that he had heard on the police scanner that something big had gone down on Canning Road. Sorry Dear, but after you threw me out I stopped at the liquor store fully intending to drink myself into oblivion, but coming out of the store I saw the ambulance at the house, so that nullified that. Anyhow, back to the story. I wondered if my dream about that house had anything to do with where you had been held captive. On a whim I drove out to Canning Road. My question was answered immediately as I could see three police cars across the field from the road. I went back after everyone had gone to bed and let myself into the house. So, you see my Dear, when you were describing that you had seen the shirt and the shaving kit in the bathroom I already knew about it all, and that is why I didn't register too much shock when you described it."

"I didn't notice anything different Rainey because you were grimacing throughout the whole thing. How did you get into the house; wasn't it locked, or cordoned off?"

"Use your imagination Hon. Do you want to hear what Sergeant Rolph discovered?"

"You know I do. Is he sharing information with you? He came to see me in the hospital you know? I didn't care for him one bit."

"You are going to have to talk to him one day you know, but we will talk about that another time. Evan and I lit into him when he came inquiring about you while you were still in surgery. He wouldn't share anything regarding Jorja, so we didn't share what we knew about her either. We did not get off to a very good start, so I was surprised when I confronted him the next day after I had visited the house that he was amiable. Of course he refused to answer any questions, but he changed his tune when I gave him the low down on Jorja's former profession. He got up and closed the door as soon as I mentioned the word prostitute, and that I had a distinct feeling that she may be engaged in the same activity here in Bridge. How else was she supporting herself? I asked who owned the car that you had been abducted in and the house that you had been held in. I stated that the car was missing. They had already had it towed to their compound where it was undergoing a thorough combing. The property and car were registered to the same person. His name is Mark Chester. I thanked him and started to leave. He asked me what I was going to do with the info. I told him I was going to pay this Mark a visit. He said he couldn't stop me but advised against it, and that he would save me the trouble because he had already tried to question Mr. Chester, but he was out of town on business until Christmas Eve. He had talked to Vera, Chester's wife who didn't know much about her husband's rental properties, but did know that Mark had rented the Canning House to a young woman two months back. She had not heard about what had gone down at the house, so Rolph had given her very limited details as there were two young children in the room. He had left saying he expected a call from her husband the moment he returned home."

"Are you thinking what I am?" I asked anticipating that he was.

"Yes; there were two girls. He said they were approximately three and seven years old. Would you recognise the girl whom you saw through the window if you saw her again?"

"Maybe, but I only saw her for a second. What's going to happen now?"

"Nothing I guess until Mark Chester gets home. Rolph should have already talked to him. He said he would not question him at headquarters until today."

"I suppose that is charitable of him because of the children, and it being Christmas. Are you expecting Sergeant Rolph to inform you of his findings?"

"He said he would keep me in the loop so I expect to hear from him sometime today."

"Did you see her Rainey?"

"No Love, I did not, nor did I care to. She was still in lock-up at the hospital on Tuesday, but was given the all clear Wednesday morning and returned to the jail until a Marshall came to escort her to Kingston."

"So, she is really gone? I'm still worried you know."

"Yes, I know you are, but you have nothing to fear." He said holding my chin and locking eyes with me. "I'm here, and I'm not going anywhere. She'll never see the light of day again."

"But, you did leave didn't you?"

"Did you really think I wasn't coming back? And, that reminds me; what was that remark you made about forgiving me even if I had of stepped over the line?"

"Well, we don't have to find out if I meant it do we, but I am sorry for any doubts I may had concerning your fidelity, drugged or not. It was a wretched week. Can you just crawl into bed and hold me, and put the week behind us?"

"You're wish is once again my desire my love. Just give me a minute to call Mom and tell her that I am back where I belong. I'm afraid she and Dad are both very disappointed in me."

"I'm sure it was a shock if you confessed all, but like me, they love you, and they will come to terms with it all. I'll make sure of that."

"Thanks Sweetie. I can't undo what's been done, but I can spend the rest of life making amends, and being a better husband, father and son."

"Don't you get all righteous on me now; I quite like you just the way you are."

He kissed me and picked up the phone.

It took me almost two hours to have a shower and get dressed the next morning. The scale said that I had lost sixteen pounds. Rosy and Ava wanted the men to carry me downstairs, but I insisted that I could walk, and I did with Rainey and Evan on each side of me holding unto me securely. Jack and Nash stood on guard at the bottom of the stairs just in case I faltered. I asked to be sat in the big yellow chair so that the girls could sit with me. Rainey made sure that Lili understood that she couldn't sit on my lap. Tanny told him not to worry as she would make sure that Lili behaved. Rainey left to check on the twins and to see what was cooking in the kitchen.

CHAPTER 2

ALICE, SISTER ANITA, JORJA MISS MARY, AND VIVIENNE

Tanny asked me if I could help her find Alice in her puzzle book.

"See Mommy, I've found the white rabbit, and the smiley cat, and the funny man with the hat full of numbers, and the mouse. I forget who these guys are," she said pointing to Tweedledee and Tweedledum, "but I can't find Alice."

"Well, let's have a look. It's nice that the opposite page shows you who you are supposed to be looking for." I explained that the numbers on the Mad Hatter's hat were representing what a hat cost back then, and a few other little tidbits about the book. Tanny reminded me that Alice was wearing a blue dress with a white apron. I told her that the apron was called a pinafore. I focused, but I did not find Alice.

"She's really hiding isn't she Mommy, just like your Alice."

I laughed a little. "I don't have an Alice, Honey."

"Not here, but the one that lives at the castle."

"I don't remember anyone living at the castle by that name Tanny."

"Maybe she was one of your ghosts. I think her last name was Grey."

"You have got me stumped. Why do you think I know someone called Alice Grey?"

Rainey had come back and asked what we were talking about. I explained that Tanny thought I had a friend at Avanloch and that her name was Alice Grey.

He asked jokingly if she was Avaleena's sister. I reminded him that Avaleena's name was not Grey and I doubted that her maiden name would have been Grey as she was Spanish and it didn't sound very Spanish at all. I told him that I had never heard the name Alice Grey before. Tanny piped up and said that Zoe knew. I asked Rainey to find her. He said that she was feeding Zander, but he'd take over for her. I told him I wanted him right here to hear what she had to say. He came back with Zoe and Zander and a jar of baby food. I explained what Tanny had told me and asked Zoe if she any insight into it.

She said that she had been attending to Liliana who had woken up one night crying when I came through the adjoining door asking her and Tanny, who was also awake, if we had seen Alice. I seemed very upset that I couldn't find her. They said they hadn't seen her, but I insisted that they must know, and then I said "Alice Grey is not a horse you know".

Tanny laughed. "Yeah that was funny."

"When was this Zoe, and what time was it?" I asked.

"It was after twelve and not that long after we arrived at Avanloch from Verde El Mar."

"I am a little surprised that you and Tanny remember that as it was a year and a half ago. Why have you never mentioned it before?"

"I thought that maybe you were sleep walking like Katarina used to do and was afraid that you might think that you were her and I didn't want to upset you."

"Did you think that I was Katarina?"

"No, you didn't have a candle like Kat did when she was sleep-walking, so I knew you were Vienna. I followed you to make sure you were all right. You went right back to bed and as I was leaving I heard you say, "I'm cold Rainey.""

I thanked her and told her to get on with her day, and that as far as I could remember I didn't know an Alice Grey. Lili started singing "Alisse, Alisse." Rainey said that this sparked a memory. I asked him what it was.

"After I had that dream about the Grey Lady when you were "away", I asked the family who she was. No one had ever heard of such a person, but there once was a horse named Lady Grey. Mary McDuff said she remembered the horse and that it was too wild and couldn't be tamed and was shipped off almost immediately. So, that might explain your comment about the horse, but not who Alice is."

"That horse was a gift to me from Jeremy not long after we were married. I'm the one who named her. She was a three year old dappled gray Arabian. Mary was right; the mare had a wild streak in her. It was my decision to send her off after she almost killed Johnny. I'm surprised he didn't mention it."

"Don't know why Honey. Let's put Alice to bed for now and get opening up these Christmas cards before breakfast." He answered as he collected all the cards and set them and a letter opener on the end table beside me calling Tanny to bring her puzzle book over to him.

"Let your ole dad have a look and see if he can find where Alice is hiding."

I wished him good luck and opened the envelope from Sister Anita. I extracted what appeared to be a greeting card. A long hand written letter fell out of the card. I glanced at it and didn't like what I saw half way down the page. I needed Rainey to be with me when I read it, so I'd wait until he was done with Tanny. I didn't have long to wait.

"You are so smart Daddy. Me and Mommy never seen her there." She kissed him on the cheek and brought the book over to me. "See Mommy, Alice is sitting under the tree and just peeking through the branches. Now I can go and see what's on the next page."

"I guess his eyesight is better than mine." I stated and asked Rainey to come and sit with me and hear what Sister Anita had to say.

December 11th
The Year of Our Lord 1984

My Dear Vienna,

I hope this blessed holiday finds you and your family well.

I will be eternally grateful for your return of the Infinity Bracelets. They are a gift that have revived St. Andrews' and the Parish. We here at the abbey thank you, the township thanks you, and mostly, the farm animals thank you for they now have new warm homes. The monetary funds from the museums and rectories in France and Spain who each displayed them over the past six months were substantial. A lovely lady by the name of Ramona Cardova brought their tragic story to life in an expose in world-wide newspapers which also brought in an abundance of pesetas. Have you access to this manuscript?

A Spanish businessman who had been intrigued with the bracelets and Katarina's and Anton's love story visited us and presented us with a remarkable copy of the bracelets that now rest in the museum in Andorra la Vella.

I stopped reading. Rainey looked at me questionably. I couldn't remember if I had ever told him that Anton had given me a reproduction of the bracelets as a Christmas present. Well, he was going to know now. I took a deep breath and continued.

He suggested that the real ones were much too valuable to be on display as the security in Andorra would be no match for criminals, and that there were still those who coveted them as their own. He was most interested in how they had been found. As per your wishes, the how, who or why was not revealed to him or anyone else. They remain a mystery as to the benefactor. Upon questioning he revealed to us that he had the duplicates crafted from a photograph that he was privy to for his wife. She was no longer with him, so he had no reason to keep them as they were only a sad reminder of her. I asked what he thought I should do with the originals. He said if it was up to him he would return them to the woman who had donated them as they had been a gift from her husband.

I shuttered. Rainey placed his hand on mine and told me it was okay.

I did not tell him that it was exactly what I was planning on doing. How he knew this about you I know not. Is it possible that you know this gentleman Vienna? His name, oddly enough is Antonia DeMarco. His deceased wife's name was Katarina. It is not for me to conclude that this is a coincidence as the Lord works in mysterious ways. So yes, the bracelets need to be on your wrist again; the wrist that they were meant for when Mr. Quinn discovered them.

They will be arriving on your doorstep any day. I do have one favor and that is if we run into financial distress again that maybe we could borrow them again. TeeHee.

With much reverence and affection I remain your humble servant,

Sister Anita, St. Andrew's

I let the letter drop to the floor, removed my arm from around Lili and covered my face with my hands. Rainey moved to the hassock in front of me, lowered Lili to the floor, and tried his best to comfort me.

"I don't want them Rainey. I don't want anything that he has touched." I sobbed.

Tanny rushed to my side just as Evan came in to announce that breakfast was on the table. She interrupted him. "Mommy's sad again Evan. That letter made her cry."

He asked what was going on. Rainey passed him the letter. "Let's just keep this between us for the time being; the rest can read it after breakfast. I have a few choice words for that reprobate, but let's put a positive spin on it. You did a noble thing when you returned the bracelets to the heir who just happened to be a nun and whose church was in dire need of refurbishes Vienna. They did their job and now they are coming back to you where they belong. Rain bought them for you as a Christmas gift long ago and now it's a new Christmas so it's fitting that they are being returned to you at this time."

"I don't think she wants them back Evan." Rainey said glumly.

"I don't believe that for one moment, but it's your call Lady Vienna. How about we go into breakfast and discuss it after you have had time to adjust?" Evan suggested picking Lili up and taking Tanny's hand.

Rainey asked me if I wanted to walk or did I need the walker. I opted for the walker, and said that maybe Evan was right, and that we would see what everyone else had to say after breakfast. I chose to have a bowl of cereal with fruit and one slice of toast over all the other offerings as it was the first solid food I'd had in a week, so I thought it best to keep it light. It was then that I learned that we had inhabitants in the basement.

Liliana said that she didn't want to sit beside Novia. Rainey asked her why and she said that Novie was mean. How an eleven month old child could be mean was baffling, and so I asked her what she meant by that. She didn't answer, but Tanny offered an explanation which was more baffling. She said that Novie had dropped one of the kittens, but it wasn't her fault because the kitten may have scratched her. It wasn't hurt because Novie was small and close to the ground. I asked her if the kitten belonged to Mrs. McNamara next door. Tanny said it was Jack's cat. Everyone was grinning as I asked him when he and Sissy had gotten a cat.

"Actually Vienna, it's your cat as she and her three kittens live in your basement. I discovered her on Christmas day when I went for the ice cream. Did you forget to tell her Rainey?"

"It completely slipped my mind. I didn't know about the kittens though. I would have remembered sooner or later though Hon." My husband said as a way of an apology to me. "Hopefully, the SPCA will be interested in a whole family."

"I checked Novia and did not find any scratch marks on her. I think the kitten just jumped out of her arms, but Lili thought otherwise, and I'm afraid she made Novia cry." Sissy said.

"When was this?"

"Jack didn't discover the kittens until yesterday. The mother had them tucked away beneath the furnace. He told us and we made them a nice comfy bed and later took the kids down to see them. The mother cat is very friendly. Tanny named her Mary."

"Did you name her after Mary McDuff Tanny?" I asked.

"No, after Jesus's mother."

"That is very sweet Tanny. What about the kittens; did you name them too?"

"No, because they have to go to a new home soon so they would just get new names."

"Maybe they don't have to go for a while Tanny. I think I might just know of a home for them. You've all seen them I take it. How did they get in and how old are the kittens?"

Jack said their eyes were open so about two or three weeks, and through a broken window which had gone undetected after the last wind storm which had brought large boughs from the maple trees down. Rainey wanted to know who the family was that wanted a litter of cats.

"Ours; I thought that we could keep them and maybe in the spring we could take them to the ranch to live where we can visit them until we move there. What do you think? Oh, I suppose I shouldn't have said anything before I discussed it with you, and got Tanny's hopes up." I said hesitantly.

"That's an absolutely wonderful idea! It will be great for the kids, and the ranch can always do with more mousers. What do you think of your mother's suggestion Tanny?"

"I think she's the best mom in the whole wide world. Do you want to see them Mommy?"

"I do, but I am going to have to wait a few more days I'm afraid."

"Don't be afraid Mommy because me and Daddy and Jack can bring them up here."

So, for half an hour I was distracted by the feline family. I entertained the idea that they should live upstairs, but decided it was best to leave them where they were for the time being. After the cat family was returned to the basement Rainey asked Zoe and Joannie if they could look after the kids for a while. That meant that it was time to pass Sister Anita's letter around.

I sat back and listened to everyone's take on it. Of course they all thought that the bracelets belonged to me, and should be returned to me. They didn't like the idea that Anton had anything to do with them, or had visited Sister Anita, and may have viewed them first hand. Jack had a most interesting question.

"I am the only one who has never seen this priceless piece of jewellery, and you all know what they look like, right? So, was Anton's replica of them so good that no one can tell the difference? If so, then how do we know that he didn't keep the originals for himself? Is it possible that he may have duped Sister Anita?"

That brought silence to the table. Ava asked me if I would be able to authenticate them.

I answered her honestly. "You were with me when Rainey gave them to me. You examined them just as I did; so would you recognise a copy if one was presented to you? No, I don't think you would, and neither would I even though I am the only one who saw the "Spanish ones." I was Katarina then, and they meant nothing to me. I just remember that I had an uneasy feeling when Anton gave them to me at Christmas. No, I do not think that I can tell if the ones that arrive are the real McCoy's."

"I'll know." Rainey stated.

"Really, you think you'll know?"

"No, I don't think; I'll know, and I'm stating outright that I will know without a doubt. The day I came home that Christmas and found you gone, not only was I broken, but I was angry. I went back to the farm, unpacked the suitcase with all the gifts I had bought for everyone. I found the box with the bracelets, cursed you, picked it up and threw it across the room. In the morning I retrieved it and found that the bracelets had fallen out of the jewellery box and a piece of it was lying on the floor. I won't divulge where it came from right now as I want all of you to see if you can discover it. I defy you to detect it, so I won't give you any clues. I have my doubts that the aged drawing of the bracelets that presumably Anton had a copy of depicted all the intricate designs and jewels on the bangles. It took me hours to discover where the broken piece had come from and I knew what I was looking for. It was very hard to detect even with a powerful magnifying glass. I thought I would have it repaired when I got back to Vancouver, but never did. I stored it all in my safety deposit box. I didn't even think about the broken piece when I finally was able to give them to the woman they were meant for." He smiled lovingly at me. "Sorry Honey; it was me who also broke the chain."

"I have spent the better part of two years wearing those bracelets. I have marveled over them and inspected them, and never did I find this blemish you are referring to. What did you do with the wayward piece?"

"It's still in the safe at the boy's house. When they get home from Switzerland I'll have them find the little piece and send it, and then we can have the bracelet repaired."

"I look forward to your challenge my dear, but first it has to get here. We may as well not speculate until then and we authenticate it."

"I think I can speak for everyone Mom in saying that we are all in anticipation of their arrival. I will be very disappointed if Evan and I miss the event, but it looks like we will. Jin will be here tomorrow and then we will be gone the next day." Rosy said disappointedly.

"I'd hate that too Red, but they may be at the post office already as I haven't checked the mail for days, so how about I go and check right now?" Rainey offered.

"I would imagine that they will come by registered mail, and it's early and a holiday, so the post office isn't even open so you'll have to wait until tomorrow. In the meantime, how about you share what Sergeant Rolph and you have discovered about my abduction Dear?"

He said he would be delighted. He started with explaining what he had done and what he had discovered at the "*house*" and his visit with the sergeant. He'd had a most enlightening conversation with Rolph earlier this morning. Mark Chester, the owner of the *house* had arrived at the station and was very obliging answering all the sergeants questions. He did not know about what had gone down at the *house,* and wanted to apologise to me personally. The sergeant said that he wasn't to come anywhere near me or my family. Mr. Cheater admitted to renting the *house* to Ms. Elliot and nothing more until he was confronted with his bank and rental records that his wife had supplied. Apparently his wife had been suspicious for months as he disappeared three or four times every week in the evenings without an explanation as to where he was going. When Sgt. Rolph had visited her and told her about my abduction she did some soul searching and investigating into her husband's secret life and found a hidden file cabinet in his garage that contained a ledger and two thousand dollars. Apparently, he had a list of clients of Jorja's and their monetary contributions of which he took a 40% cut. So, it looks like she was back at hooking and he was her pimp.

I took notice of Jack nodding silently at Rainey's disclosures, and wondered what he knew.

"You know just about everyone in town don't you Jack, so do you know this Mark Chester?"

"No, not personally, but I have heard his name tossed around lately."

Rainey wanted to know where he had heard it and what was being said. Jack said that he had heard the gossip at the coffee shop that Mark had been caught cheating on his wife with some little trollop who had just arrived in town.

"Coffee shop, as if you ever do that!" Sissy exclaimed.

"All right, you got me. It was at the liquor store. I walked in on a conversation between Les Arnold and a few other locals discussing Jorja's clients. How they knew her name or the names of her customers is beyond me. I didn't hang around when the name of a friend came up."

"I guess that friend was me, and you didn't want to be asked about your brother-in-law because I'm sure the whole town knows by now that I was once her customer and that she followed me here." Rainey said remorselessly.

"You're my brother-in-law? How the hell did that happen?" Jack joked.

I laughed along with everyone else, including my husband.

"Your name was never mentioned Rain, but if it had of come up in the banter I would not have given them the satisfaction that I knew anything. If you don't know by now, what is said, or happens in this house stays in this house. I've got your back Bro."

"Thanks, and I've got yours. To answer your question Jack, the reason we are brother-in-laws is because we were blessed with the love of two of the amazing LaFontaine sisters, and are fortunate to have married them. It doesn't get any more real than that."

I pulled myself up from the table. "It's getting a little too maudlin in here for me, and to tell you the truth, I've had enough talk about the exploits of Jorja to last me a lifetime. If you will please excuse me, I will retire to the other room and leave you to continue your postulations."

"We're done here Hon. I'll join you wherever you're going." Rainey got up and put his hand on my back guiding me into the walker.

"It's a beautiful day." Ava said. "All the sidewalks have been cleared, so I think we will bundle Sammie up and walk into town."

"Sounds good; Evan and I will join you. What about you and Jack, Sissy?" Rosy invited.

"I think we will go home because believe it or not, we do have our own house." Sissy said laughing. "The paint should be dry enough for a second coat, so enjoy your walk and your quiet time Vienna, and we will see you all tomorrow."

"We *will* see you tomorrow, but Rainey is ordering Chinese food for dinner, so we expect you back here at five o'clock sharp." I responded hoping it didn't sound like an order.

"If you want us here, we will be here Sis. I just thought you might just like some alone time with your family before Rosy and Evan leave."

Without warning I broke out in a flood of tears and fell back down on the kitchen chair. Rainey still had his arm around me so I didn't fall hard. Sissy had rushed to my side apologising for upsetting me. I tried telling her it was nothing she did, but it was all babble. I expected that Rainey would blame my outburst on all the events of last week, but he didn't.

"Sit down everyone. I know exactly what Vienna wants to say, and I share her sentiments. Sissy, you and Jack *are* our family, you know that, and we are going to need to see you more than ever once Rosalyn and Evan leave. You don't know this, but everyone sitting around the table at mealtime makes us feel like we brought a little of Avanloch with us. I haven't even admitted this to Vienna, but I miss that damn castle, and I know she does too. Someday we may be able to stand alone, but until then, just humor us. Now, get on with your day, and we are going to relieve Zoe and Joannie of the kids and let the urchins amuse us for a while."

I accepted all the hugs and love and let Rainey usher me out. He deposited me in the recliner, kissed me and asked how I knew he had a hankering for Chinese. I told him I loved him and said it was the least he could do, and to give me the special little boy who was pestering his twin, and to get dressed and go for a walk with the big kids. He said he'd rather stay with me and the little kids, thank-you very much.

Zander didn't even last two minutes before he was sliding down my leg unto the floor. He pulled himself up and took three steps before reverting to crawling again. He made his way over to his sisters laughing all the way. I turned in amazement and asked Rainey when our son had started walking. He said it was news to him. It wasn't only that, but Zander seemed to be stronger and more jubilant. I watched as he tried to pull himself up on the little chesterfield. Tanny reached around him and pulled him up by the seat of his pants. Lili put her arm around him and told him to be quiet as they were watching Lassie. Novia was sitting in one of the pint sized armchairs perfectly content to be alone. I reclined and closed my eyes half listening to Rainey and the chatter from the television. I awoke to utter silence. I must be dreaming. I blinked a few times and saw Ava sitting in the big yellow chair knitting. The clicking of the needles was the only sound in the room. "Where is everyone? I thought you all went for a walk?"

"We did. Nash is across the street with Sammie. I'm sure they are both napping. Evan and Rosy took the kids downstairs to visit with the kittens, and Rainey went to the post office despite you saying that it was closed, and I'm here watching over you."

"I don't need watching over Ava."

"Rainey says you do."

"Of course he does. We are so lucky to have such wonderful men to worry about us. I feel I am a little too hard on your father though."

"It's because of this thing with Jorja. We need to quit talking about her."

"It doesn't bother me Ava. It happened, and I am dealing with it."

"You will have dealt with it when you quit being jealous of the relationship she had with Dad."

"What?" I did not say anything further as Rainey walked into the room. I asked him to help me up as I needed to stretch my legs. He placed the walker in front of me, but I chose to hold on to him and walk back and forth up the hallway. I asked him if it was too cold for me to sit on the back porch. He said it wasn't and helped me into my winter coat and boots. I couldn't see why I needed the boots as surely there was no snow on the porch.

"Your feet were burnt and cut last fall, and recently they were frost bitten, so just covering all of the bases here in case something unforeseen occurs."

I told him he was very funny. I chose to stand at the railing and take in the scenery. The river had frozen over and there was a group of a dozen or so energetic people clearing the snow off a patch down the way for ice skating, I presumed. I asked Rainey if he remembered the first time he had been on this porch with me.

"You mean the day you conned me into helping you paint? Yes Dear, I remember it clearly."

"We had fun when we were young didn't we?"

"I'm glad you remember the good times because I caused you a good deal of grief."

"I've put that all aside, but Ava said something to me a few minutes ago that has got me thinking that maybe I haven't."

"What could she have possibly said about us back then?"

"It was more recent then that. She said that I would quit persecuting you when I quit being jealous of the relationship that you had with Jorja."

"That doesn't sound like something Ava would say."

"Never the less she did, and I think she is right. I keep throwing little barbs at you, and I am sure that she is not the only one who has noticed the sting in my voice."

"You're still dealing with the trauma from the abduction, the knifing and surgery, so I don't take too much of your insults seriously. Actually, I deserve a hell of a lot more."

"No, you don't. You have to stop babying me Rainey. I will try my best to hold my tongue, but *she* will probably remain a sore spot for me for a long, long time. I am not at all confident that this prison or institution that she's in can hold her. She'll find her way out somehow, someday and high-tail it right back here. Only death will stop her."

"She's not escaping Vienna. Come on, you need to sit down." He said pulling a wicker chair up and placing me in it. "I know there is no way that I am ever going to be able to convince you of that, so there is only one thing I can do. I am going to go out to Kingston or Landsford, wherever the prison is and check the facility out for myself. According to Sgt. Rolph it is the most secure facility in the country, but

I think for all our sakes I need to see it for myself. What would you say about that?"

"I don't like the idea that you'd be seeing her."

"You have to quit having negative feelings about everything Vienna. I have no desire to ever lay eyes on her again, and there is no reason for me to, but I would need to check out her quarters for security. What do you say?"

"I also don't like the idea that you'd be going away, but I do think it might help to ease my mind because I am convinced that the only other way to be certain is for her to die."

"Good; then it's done. Neither one of us is up to the gruesome task of eliminating her, so not another word on that."

"Speak for yourself. I would take great pleasure in pulling the trigger, or impaling her on a stake, and I would make damn sure that I finished the job this time!"

"This is taking your jealousy a little too far my darling." He said kissing me.

I beat on him a little and looked up to see two faces laughing and asking what trouble their brother-in-law had got himself into this time. It was Sissy and Jack. They had snow- skied over on the back trail.

My husband had the perfect answer. "Yeah, she's got murder on her mind again, so I let her take her frustrations out on me before they erupt. So Jack, I know you like the outdoors, but how do you feel about a road trip with me?"

"Depends on where you're going."

"Kingston Ontario, Landsford Prison, home of the notorious. I need to prove to Vienna that there is no escaping from there, and the only way I can do that is to check it out myself."

"Say no more Boss; I'm ready whenever."

"Thanks Jack. Sissy can you stay with Vienna while we are gone?"

"You know I will Rain. When are you going?"

"Thanks. I'll need to make arrangements and all, so next week some time hopefully. You okay with that Hon?"

"I shouldn't be so paranoid." I replied feeling guilty. "That's a long way for you to go."

"There is no harm in feeling wary, and if it will give you some peace, it will be worth it. It's not all that far; a quick trip to Potsdam and a few hours flight from there. Three days and we'll be home. Now, I have to order dinner, so how about we all head indoors?"

We found everyone else in the living room. Zander was sitting between Tanny and Lili who had their eyes glued to Tom and Jerry on the television. I think Zander was asleep. Novia was wandering around with an arm full of dolls. Evan and Nash vacated their chairs at the card table to Sissy and me and went to see what Rainey was up to in the kitchen. I didn't feel like playing cards, but didn't want to be a spoilsport so took over Evan's seat. Half an hour later I had to bail as the pain in my side had got the best of me. Ava went upstairs to get me a pill and I settled in on the recliner. I asked them not to tell Rainey as he worried too much and would want me to go to bed. I awoke to Evan's voice calling out that dinner was on the table. I came to slowly and said that I needed a minute. I was having a hard time reviving myself until I heard Evan asking where the little French girl was.

I shot up. "What?" Everyone started looking for her. Rainey was at the doorway saying she probably had fallen asleep somewhere. That somewhere was nowhere in the living room. Evan said they would have noticed her if she had wandered into the kitchen. I heard Rainey calling out to her from down the hall. I prayed that the gate to the upstairs had been locked. Then there was the sound of his voice; the voice that was reserved for the twins. A few minutes later he came in with her and sat her on my lap.

"She says she wants her Maman."

"Don't encourage her to call me that Rain. Oh, what do you have here?" I asked as she passed me a book. "Oh Honey, this isn't a book for you. Look, there are no pictures." I said flipping the pages. A faded piece of paper fell out. Rainey picked it up, read it, smiled, and passed it to me. It was a letter I had written when I was sixteen. I was embarrassed by what I had written, and tucked it into my bosom. I asked him if Novia had been in the library.

"Yup, she was sitting there talking to the woman on the cover. Kind of reminds me of you."

"You mean because she is wearing a similar green dress to one I own and is staring at a castle on the misty Scottish glen?"

"Look at her closely. Her eyes are bathed in sadness. I think she is leaving or running away. See, she has a satchel in one hand, and she is not in Scotland, but France. The lady is Vivienne, according to the title, your French sister, I presume."

"Have you been drinking again? Help me up and take that book away from her."

"You try. She wouldn't give it up to me."

"Don't be silly." I asked Novia for the book. She held it to her body and said. "Me Maman."

Evan came over and held his arms out. She went with him, but did not relinquish the book. By the time Rainey and I reached the kitchen Evan had Novia settled in her highchair between Rainey and me. The book was tucked in beside her. She was eating a buttered bun.

"I see you were successful in liberating her from the book."

Evan laughed. "She thinks the woman on the cover is you."

"She told you that did she?"

"Well, she keeps saying Maman, so I got the gist. What was on that mysterious piece of paper that made you blush?"

"I didn't blush."

"You kind of did Hon." Rainey teased.

"Come on Mom; don't keep us in suspense." Rosy encouraged me to confess.

I patted my chest. "If you all must know, it's a love letter I wrote to Rainey a long time ago. I suppose I must have hidden it in that book though I don't remember why."

"Oh my," Sissy moaned, "I'm the culprit. I found it between the mattress and bedframe in your room after you left home V. I didn't know whether to show it to mom and dad, and then Rainey phoned looking for you, so I hid it because I knew it would upset him because you had declared your love for him in the letter and you didn't want him to know where you were. I'm so sorry Rainey that I didn't give it to you"

My sister was crying, I was crying, all the girls were crying though I am sure Tanny and Lili had no idea why. Jack was trying to comfort Sissy with no success. Rainey squeezed my hand. He pushed his chair back, moved Zander's chair close to me so he could reach my sister. He put his arm around her.

"You were only thirteen then Sissy. You were beside yourself with worry because Vienna had left. I'm ashamed as to hard I pressured you for information on her. There is nothing to forgive you for. We've moved on from the past, and so should you. I don't love you any less for hiding this letter from me. Discovering it is a treasure I will cherish…that is if I can rescue it from your sister's bosom." He joked. "Was there a particular reason you chose that book to secrete it in Sissy?"

"I don't even know if I noticed the title."

"I wrote it after I had confessed my love to you. You were less than enthusiastic about my declaration and told me that I needed to forget you as you were no good for me. You took me home and said goodbye. I knew I'd never see you again." I confessed.

"I couldn't get you out of my mind no matter what I did, and thank God you agreed to see me again. I continued to make mistake after mistake, but you always forgave me and still do." Rainey said.

"Love is a crazy thing isn't it?" I said to the room and they all agreed.

I went to bed the same time as the twins. While Rainey settled them in bed with Ava's help, Rosalyn sat with me. She and Evan would be going home to Scotland the day after tomorrow. I was missing them already. We reminisced about life at Avanloch, and all the outlandish characters that had passed through the doors over the years. Rainey and Ava joined us as she was saying how boring it was without me.

He laughed. "Give it time Red. The former inhabitants are still taking note of the new mistress so I am sure one will be making an appearance any day and the castle will be filled with mischief once again."

"I hope not Dad. I'm pretty sure it was only Mama's magnetism that attracted them. I would not be a suitable entity for any departed souls. Sleep peacefully Mom; see you tomorrow." She kissed me and left with Ava.

I asked Rainey if he managed to pry the book away from Novia.

"It took a little coaxing, but I guess I convinced her that it would be safe up on the top of the dresser for the night. I held her and let her place it there where she could see it from her bed. I can't blame her for wanting to hold her mama all night."

"I don't think I look anything like the woman on the cover, so there must be another reason she is drawn to it. Perhaps we can replace it with a real picture of me?"

"We'll see what tomorrow brings. Are you all set for the night, pain pill and all?"

"I don't require anything, thank-you."

"The morphine is still working then?"

"I didn't have any morphine today; just Tylenol."

"I'm sure Ava told me she gave you some this afternoon. It doesn't matter as long as you aren't in any pain. Are you sure you don't mind me going downstairs for a while?"

"Check with Ava about the pill please. The morphine could become addictive, so I don't want, and I don't need it any longer. Maybe I could try Laudanum. What do you think? Could you procure me some? And no, I do not mind you doing what I can't. I'll just rest and maybe watch a little TV until you come to bed."

He kissed me and said he'd be back in an hour or so just after he took a trip back to 1600 to get the tincture of opium. "You say you haven't any pain, so I assume that you want to take it to enhance your creative imagination, or maybe calm your overactive mind?"

I laughed. "A little of both I guess. Why did you say 1600?"

"That was Avaleena's era wasn't it?"

"I thought her diary started off in the 1800's, but 1600 makes more sense, don't you think?"

"Honestly, I have never given it any thought. You don't need anything to stimulate your fantasies my dear, but speaking of that, I may as well tell you that the library is a mess. It seems your daughter went through a lot of books before she decided on the likeness of Vivienne."

A courier arrived just before lunch the next day. He was a young man named Lucas. He explained that he was a seminarian studying towards priesthood, and had been chosen by Sister Anita to deliver a package of great importance to me. Apparently, she was held in very high esteem and her request had been granted by the Theological Seminary in Andorra. We could not persuade him to join us for lunch as his driver, who had been hired in Potsdam, was waiting. His plane would be leaving that afternoon and he did not want to miss the flight. He stayed just long enough for the package to be opened. I had passed it to Rainey who examined the contents and said that we had a winner. Lucas left with our thanks and a thermos of hot chocolate and a box of treats that the girls assembled. He bowed to me, why I do not know, blessed us all, and left.

Rainey unclasped the chain that held the three bracelets together. He handed one to Ava, Rosy and me and told us to have fun finding where the missing lavender rose belonged. This was the first time that he had mentioned a lavender rose. I knew where they were on all the bracelets and so I examined them all, but could not find where one was missing. The girls couldn't either so we let everyone else see if they could detect it. Rainey sat back grinning like the Cheshire cat.

Half an hour later I said that he'd been duped. He said he hadn't and asked whoever had the second bracelet to pass it to him. Of course no one but me actually knew which one was the second bracelet. I enlightened them by saying that it had "Querido" on the inside. Jack reached across the table and gave it to Rainey who presented it to me.

"See where the little quartz roses mingle amongst the honeysuckle vine? Look very closely at the Q in Querido and you will see a very small indentation that is almost undetectable. The insides on all of the bracelets are so sculpted that the wearer cannot feel the impressions, but if you run your finger over the Q, you can feel a slight roughness or depression. Can you feel it?"

I did as he suggested. "Yes, and it is so miniscule that I am surprised that you even found it."

"I told you how I labored over it. For some reason it was important to me even though I feared at the time that you were lost to me forever."

"Well, I am found and I now have the bracelets back. Tell me that you no longer believe that they are cursed?"

"If they had of been in your possession last week I would have said "Yes", but they weren't, so no, I don't think they are cursed anymore." Rainey lamented.

"They are not, and just as I told Ava when she discovered them in her luggage last year that they were an inanimate object and were not responsible for the plane crash. She truly believed that they were cursed also. Thankfully I was able to talk her down, or we probably wouldn't be here with you all today. On the other hand, maybe they had a hand in bringing Ava and I together just as they did you and Rainey. Put them on Vienna and let them shine as they are home again, right where they belong, on a dearly loved person, and Querido!" Nash avowed

I let Rainey slide the bracelets on my left wrist. "I'm not surprised that you know the meaning of "Querido" Nash as it is obvious in your eyes when you look at my daughter. I love the bracelets but think that perhaps I will only wear them at home because now that they have been deemed priceless, I don't want to invite any treasure seekers."

"Good idea Mom, and don't put them in Lili's hat box of bangles." Ava suggested.

We all laughed, and so ended the Infinity Bracelets reappearance… at least for the time being.

Evan picked Jin up from the bus depot that evening, Saturday, December 29th. Sadly, we saw Rosalyn and Evan leave for home the next day. Jack and Sissy treated us to a New Year's dinner on the 31st, and the next day Joannie caught a flight home to Edmonton. Our family was now three people less. The house felt empty.

Rainey and Jack left for Landsford Prison on the third of January. Nash treated Sissy, Ava and me to a spa day, dinner and a movie on the fourth. He made dinner for the kids and entertained them while we enjoyed our pampered day. Rainey called me nine times while he was gone. Jack called Sissy twice. She commented on how much my husband loved me and missed me. I told her that he did, but didn't trust that something wouldn't happen to me while he was gone, so he just had to check in on me three times a day. I entertained the thought of not answering the phone next time he called. She pretended to slap me and asked if I wanted to give him a nervous breakdown. Of course I didn't, but we needed to get back to living our life the way it was before Jorja, and that meant not worrying about me every time I was out of his sight.

Rainey was very satisfied with Landsford. It was a maximum security institution for the criminally disturbed. He did not see Jorja, but was allowed to inspect her quarters and was satisfied to find out that she was under lock and key when not being supervised. He had made known to the officials of his concern of her history with men, and that she may very well entice the male staff for her freedom. He was assured this could not happen because of the protocol that was in place for all employees, both male and female, whether they be doctors, guards, care givers, janitors, kitchen staff or visitors. Everyone was under a supervisor and clock mechanism. Every internee wore a wristband. At the present time Jorja was still under psychiatric assessment. The charges that she had been admitted for was just as Sgt. Rolph had said; kidnapping, aggravated assault, a hostile threat to the public, and suspicion of a detrimental mental condition. Rainey said that his tour of the institution was very satisfactory. He declined to view Jorja in her daily routine. However, Jack did not. He explained how that had come about.

"I accompanied Rainey on the tour of the facility. There was nothing left except to visit the common rooms where the internees spent part of the day. Rainey had made it perfectly clear that he did not wish to see Jorja. It was suggested to him that seeing Ms. Elliot in her present state may alleviate any doubts that he was having about her rationality or ability to plot an escape. He was adamant about not seeing her, and it was then that I was asked if I would like to. We had come a long way, so I thought why go home with any doubts. I said that I had no connection to the woman whatsoever, but she had tormented Rainey's wife and family, so if I could give her some peace of mind regarding Ms. Elliot's condition then yes, I would do so. I was escorted to Observing Room 3. I sat with two attendants behind a one way mirror. I had no trouble picking Jorja out from amongst the other inmates. She was at a table with about a dozen others. They appeared to be playing cards. Denise, who was a nurse, said that they did that every day. They had yet to figure out what the actual purpose of the game was. When a certain card was put into play everyone would put their cards down, and the person holding this card which was the queen of spades, had to drink a glass of water, and then they would all get up and walk around the table and take a seat at a new spot and start all over again. This went on for a few hours. A tall large older man appeared to be the leader. They held hands when they paraded around the table and appeared to be singing. Denise said they were chanting."

I interrupted Jack. "Yes, I have heard their chant, and yes, there were twelve of them; Jorja was the thirteenth. They were all wearing cloaks weren't they?"

"How in the hell would you know how many there were Vienna?" Jack exclaimed.

Rainey said not to ask and told him to continue.

"That's about it. I was there to observe Jorja, and in my opinion, she certainly didn't pose any threat. She was almost in a comatose state. She had to be helped up most of the time. She was definitely the youngest, and I suppose, the most attractive. They were not wearing cloaks Vienna, and I cannot verify that there were thirteen of them. Now, do you want to explain how you would know about the chanting? Is that one of your psychic powers…"

"I saw it all in a dream Jack. It was just a dream. I'm sorry I inferred that I knew what was going on in that room. I wasn't there; you were, so I am sorry."

"There is nothing to be sorry for, and I am open to further discussion whenever."

"I think we will put it to rest. All that can be done has been done, and I thank you for accompanying Rainey to help alleviate my fears."

"It was my pleasure Vienna. I hope you have no more such dreams."

"I'm sure Rainey does also. I had the first dream the night before we left Avanloch, and the second one here a while back, so I guess the castle is not to blame. I did not remember it until Rainey told me that I'd had a nightmare. In both, I saw a blonde woman lying on the floor surrounded by a dozen hooded figures. Now I know for sure that it was Jorja."

"Sometimes you scare me Sis." My sister said shivering

"Sometimes I scare myself Sissy."

CHAPTER 3

GEORGIES DEAD

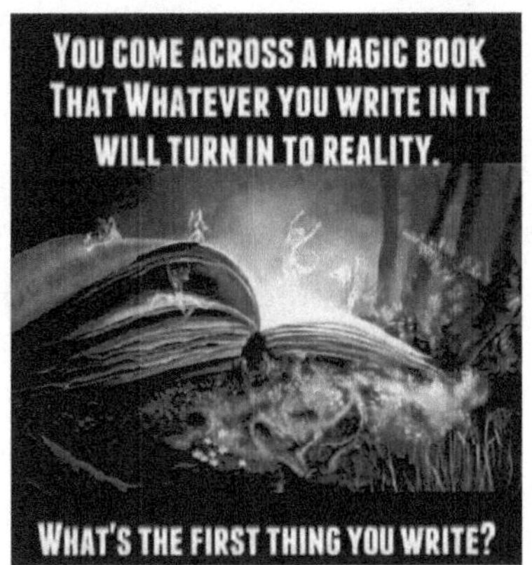

The first month of 1985 was most dreary and cold. Rainey had made my appointment with Dr. Barb for the 7th. I was scheduled to have the streptococcus pneumonia vaccine and an x-ray of my hip. The results of the x-ray showed that I had floating bone chips that had detached themselves from the hip joint. Dr. Steven asked if I'd had an accident that would account for the injury. I told him it was probably from the earthquake which had caused a brick building to fall on me. While I was envisioning a house falling on the wicked witch in Lansford prison Rainey explained the circumstances to him. He voiced his regret and apologized for not remembering the event as his wife had told him about it. He continued saying that I required an arthroscopy to diagnose these chips adequately and probably surgery to remove those "loose bodies". He said he would know more after the scope, but didn't think it would be a major surgery, but it did require anesthesia, but not a hospital stay.

He had no explanation as to why my pain from them disappeared when I was pregnant, but perhaps I was right and that the extra weight somehow cushioned them. I could tell that he was very sceptic with my reasoning though. He agreed with me that I needed a breather between surgeries. I was just to continue with the anti-inflammatory meds and heating pads or cold packs to alleviate discomfort for a few months, or as long as I could manage. He also suggested that I should avoid stairs and refrain from packing the children around on that hip. I told him that I could stop doing all that when I was dead and that I had heard that Laudanum was a great pain killer and was very helpful to women of my age, and could he prescribe some for me. He smiled and said that his wife had warned him about my eccentric sense of humor. I told him that my husband referred to it as sarcasm. I thanked him and used my need for a washroom as my excuse for leaving as he was writing a new prescription and was going on about exercises that would help me. Just as I was walking out the door I heard Rainey say that my way of dealing with the constant pain was to make light of it, but it was fun living with me as he never knew what wacky thing I was going to come up with next…case in point, the Laudanum.

He caught up with me and took my hand and asked me if I was okay.

"I am, and just thinking about more ways I can annoy you."

He said we would discuss it at home. His suggestion was that we should move our bedroom into the spare one downstairs so I wouldn't have to climb the stairs. I said that was a good idea and that we could put the twins into the dining room and we could cordon the kitchen off to make a new bedroom for Lili and Tanny. He said he had a better solution and that was to install a chair lift and he should have did so last fall. I told him that I would rather have an elevator. He threw his arms up and said, "Why me Lord, why me?"

February dawned with a promise of warmer weather. We celebrated the twin's first birthday a few days early. We chose February the 2nd as it was a Saturday and Tanny wanted to do the decorating. It was also the day Ava and Nash, and friends had been rescued from their forty seven day ordeal in the northern wilderness after their plane had crashed. Of course Novia and Zander had no idea why there were paper streamers and balloons all over the house, but delighted in helping Tanny and Lili tearing them all down and chasing the balloons. The kitchen floor required a major clean-up as half the three tiered chocolate cake had ended up under Zander's chair. I believe a good time was had by all.

I was icing cupcakes on Valentine's Day when the phone rang. Rainey was somewhere entertaining the children keeping them out of my hair, so I answered. It was Cal Stokey from Landsford Prison and Rehabilitation Centre. I wondered momentarily why Rainey had never referred to it as a rehab prison. I put the knife down, asked Mr. Stokey to give me a second to find my husband, and went in search of him. I turned the phone intercom on. I found Rainey in the library. He had laid a large sheet of white paper on the floor for Lili and the twins to draw on. He raised his eyebrows when I told him who was on the phone.

"Mr. Stokey, Rainey Quinn here. I trust all is well?"

"I am not too sure what your reaction will be to what I am about to tell you, but you asked me to keep you informed on anything regarding Ms. Jorja Elliot, so I think this definitely falls in that category. Ms. Elliot was found deceased this morning."

I covered my mouth to hide my astonishment.

"I see. May I inquire as to the circumstances?" Rainey asked unemotionally warning me with his hand to keep quiet.

"She was found early this morning by the staff in the common room. The group that she congregates with were found to be unusually rowdy by the team that monitors them. Upon investigating their peculiar dance and sing-song they discovered her lying in a heap on the floor. The alarm was sounded and she was pronounced dead by the medical staff. According to them there is no apparent cause, and it has been suggested that she may have succumbed to a massive heart attack. A lockdown was initiated immediately and the coroner has been informed. I am not at liberty for further discussions at this time. I am sure you can appreciate that."

"Yes, of course. When my colleague, Jack Jennings attended the common room he made note that Ms. Elliot was at a table with twelve others. Is it not unusual to have thirteen in a group?"

"You are perfectly correct Mr. Quinn; it is unusual. Our residents are usually in groups of four, six or twelve, but an exception was made for Ms. Elliot as she didn't fit in anywhere else. Is it your belief that her being the thirteenth member of the group is somehow responsible for her demise? I'm pretty sure that it was not, but we all have our superstitions don't we? It may take some time before we have the coroner's result, but I don't believe the number thirteen will factor into the findings." Mr. Stokey replied somewhat amused by Rainey's questions.

Rainey made light of the response. "My wife is somewhat of an expert on superstitions, and the number thirteen fits right into that, and I am sure she will have questions." He winked at me. "I thank you for your call Sir, and will be most interested in learning the coroner's findings. I hope you can, and will keep me informed."

"Ms. Elliot's assault on your family is the reason I have taken the liberty to discuss this with you as it is a most unusual circumstance. As I said before, the results may take some time. Though death is never a reason to celebrate, I hope this news may bring some peace of mind to your family. Good day Mr. Quinn."

I wiped my hands on my apron. "Well, that's that then."

Rainey said we should talk about it. I said that I had cupcakes to ice.

Lili ran after me. "Me ice too Mommy."

Rainey entered the kitchen as I was lifting her up onto the counter. "What did the doctor tell you about lifting?"

"Screw the doctor. Jorja's dead; the nightmare is over, case closed. You left the twins alone to eat the crayons I presume?" I snapped.

"I'll just leave you to have another one of your conniption fits then." He said walking away.

I opened the flip tops on three jars of sprinkles and told Lili to go crazy.

Five minutes later Jack rapped on the back door, came in and asked where I wanted the casserole. I said the pantry was good. Lili said, "Georgies dead."

He turned and said, "What?"

"Georgies dead." Lili said again. "Want a sparkle Uncle Jack?"

"In a minute Honey…"

"Did he do it Jack…tell me he didn't?" I beseeched.

He wrapped me in his arms. "I don't know what has happened, but if I'm making any sense out of Lili's statement, and you're asking me if Rainey is responsible then the answer is no."

"I'm afraid Jack." I sobbed just as Rainey entered the kitchen with a twin in each arm.

"What's going on here?" He demanded.

Jack let go of me and lowered Lili to the floor. "Let's go find a movie to watch. You need to talk to your wife Rain; she thinks you killed Jorja. Here, give me those rag-a-muffins."

I just stood there unmoving like I was glued to the floor. Rainey handed the twins off to Jack, thanked him and came over to me. "Let's get you off your feet."

He led me into the guest bedroom and sat me down. "You don't really believe that I had anything to do with her death do you?"

"You always said you'd do anything to make sure she could never hurt us again."

"And, how do you think I pulled this off?"

"I think you hired someone to do it; maybe someone from the prison. I know you have the money to do so."

"I didn't, and I don't have that kind of money, but I know someone who does." He said lifting my chin up and smiling into my eyes.

I let his suggestion set in for a few seconds. "You mean me?"

"Yeah, you're the one with all the money, and you wanted her dead, so..."

"I tried that and it didn't work remember? I have no idea how one would go about implementing an assassination, especially one in a secure prison, but you have the brains to do so, and you do have access to my millions, so I'm a little suspect. If you had anything to do with her demise you will be found out and you'll go to jail for the rest of your life, so tell me if you did so we can make plans to abscond back to Scotland?"

"Thanks for thinking that I could execute such a formidable task, but I did not. I had no hand in it unless wishing it to be so counts. Her death was just as much a surprise to me as it was to you, but if I had of, you can bet that I wouldn't have left a paper trail. Now how about you tell me why you blurted it out to Jack instead of coming to me with your doubts?"

"I didn't; Lili did."

"Christ! What time is it? I'd better grab Tanny before Lili gabs to her. Do you think Lili knew what she was saying?"

"No, I doubt it. She was just repeating what she heard me say. We have to be more careful around little ears Rain. Oh, here's Ava."

"What's going on? Jack says you need to tell me something."

Rainey asked Ava to pass me the walker as my hip was bothering me because I had been standing too long. It wasn't, but I went along with his excuse. He asked where Nash was.

"He's waiting for Sammie to wake up. It's almost four so should I put the casseroles in the oven Mom? I hope you made macaroni and cheese. I see Sissy made scalloped potatoes. I made Grandma's goulash as usual."

"I'm going to relieve Jack of the kids. Your dad has something to tell you. Do you think you can finish icing the cupcakes for me?"

"Sure, what's up Dad?"

"Let's wait until after dinner. Don't frown little girl; it's all good."

Rainey managed to corral Zoe and Tanny as soon as they walked in the door. They sat with me and we talked until Lara and Coop arrived with the baked ham. We were almost through with dinner when Sissy asked me if I remembered George Rayburn because he had brought in a pair of boots for repair and asked about me.

"Georgies dead." Lili said.

Rainey and I looked at each other and shook our heads.

"That's a very odd thing for Lili to say…Mom, why are you and Rainey looking like that? Does it have anything to do with what you're going to tell us?" Ava questioned.

"Georgies dead…say it three times." Rainey coaxed.

"Why, is this some sort of a game? Oh, okay Georgies dead, Georgies dead, Georges dead…oh my God, she's saying Jorja… Is Jorja's dead? Is that it?"

I put my hand gently on Lili's mouth to get her to stop singing Georiges dead. "That's enough Lili; eat your ham and potatoes, or there's no cupcake for you."

Her little eyes filled up with tears. "I eat Mommy."

"I'm sorry Sweetie. Mommy didn't mean it. Here," I blubbered taking her dish away "you've had enough; how about if Daddy gets you a cupcake?"

The table was silent. I had just stuck a knife in my own heart by injuring my daughter. Rainey was quick to get up and put his arms around me.

"I don't think any of us know the real toil these last weeks have had on this courageous woman; the woman I am proud to call my wife and the mother of my children." He said kissing me. "We've had a rather trying day, but it's all good I promise you. Finish your dinner while I take Lili to pick out the biggest cupcake, and I then I will enlighten you all."

He sat Lili down on my lap with two cupcakes. "Me bring you one Mommy." I hugged her amidst a new barrage of tears.

"I think it best if I leave you all to finish up as I don't seem to have any control over my emotions right now."

"You've been holding too much in Vienna. You are not just dealing with the aftermath of December, but now the renewed pain from your hip. You need to lean on us more. We all understand, and frankly, I don't know how you do everything that you do. Tears don't come easy to us men, but believe me when I say that we choke a lot back. We'll see how stalwart I'll be when Ava, Sammie and I have to leave you all behind in just a few more weeks." Nash said as he came and put his arms around me. "We all love you."

Jack stood with his glass in his hands. "Amen Nash; to you, Lady Vienna."

"Way to go guys; you've just made *all* the girls cry…"

"Well, maybe we will stop when you tell us *the story* Daddy. First, let's have dessert. I'll get the ice cream and Nash can pass Lili's sparkly cakes around." Ava suggested. "Can the twins have sprinkles Mom?"

"Just the tiny ones that dissolve quickly. Lili did such a good job didn't she? And, again I will say that it's because of all of you that I am somewhat able to cope with everything. You light up my life." I threw them all kisses. Lili smiled up at me and asked sweetly if she could have another cake. I told her she could and then Tanny would put on a movie of her choice. I didn't want her or Tanny sitting through Rainey's rendition of the phone call. I didn't care to myself, but I would.

There were many questions after Rainey finished recapping his conversation with Mr. Stokey. Of course he didn't have all the answers.

Ava asked me why I wasn't more elated to have Jorja out of my life for good. Rainey answered for me.

"As I said before, your mother and I had a little go- round. She thinks that I had a hand in Jorja's death. I thought she believed me when I told her I didn't, but maybe I'm wrong…

"And, maybe you are right, and maybe you still think *it was me* who hired an assassin?"

"Oh, you two! Like as if either of you could, or would do such a thing." Ava exclaimed.

"I guess we will just keep you guessing until after the autopsy." Rainey joked. "The subject is closed to speculation tonight, but so far Jack's supposition is the winner, and it corresponds with Vienna's dreams. Anyone feel like a rousing game of poker?"

"Did you dream of her death Mama?" Ava probed.

"What did your dad just say Ava Lane?"

"Sorry; I'll zip it for now."

"Good, now come and help me with your siblings while the rest clean up."

I set the alarm for 6 a.m. on March the 7th. It woke Rainey as I knew it would. He asked groggily what had set the alarm off. I said that I did as I had to be at the hospital in an hour. He bolted straight up and asked what was wrong.

"Nothing; I'm having the arthroscopic procedure this morning."

"When did you decide to have it, and why am I just hearing about it now?"

"I saw Dr. Steven on Tuesday and had my blood work done yesterday. I didn't tell you because you'd be hovering over me and thinking that it was too soon. Ava and Nash will be leaving in another month, and you'll be starting to lay the ground work for the new house and be gone all day, so I thought I'd better get it done while I still had help."

"Firstly, I think I have the right to hover over you as much as I want. Secondly, you are my number one priority, not the house. And lastly, I'm going with you whether you want me to or not. Zoe can skip school and look after the kids."

"Zoe has an exam today, so no to that. You may drive me to the hospital, and you may pick me up afterwards, and that's that. It's not major surgery, and I'll be home before noon."

"Thank-you for your consideration." He replied sarcastically.

"I'm going to be a little incapacitated, so I am going to need you to be at my beck and call for a while again, so you will have lots of time to pamper me. Are you okay with that?" I kissed him, told him I loved him and to get dressed. He said it didn't appear as if he had any other choice and it was a damn good thing he'd had the chair lift installed and the toilet seats raised wasn't it?

I didn't want to alarm him, so I didn't tell him that if all didn't go according to plan and Dr. Steven couldn't remove the chips while I was under a local anesthesia I'd have to be put right out and it would then become major surgery. Why add hot coals to an already simmering fire?

However, as promised, I was home before noon. Dr. Steven was pleased with how well it had all gone. He presented me with a brochure of things I could and couldn't do and a time line for everything. He gave Rainey a prescription for a pain medication just in case I had not been able to track down any Laudanum. I didn't even have the energy to laugh. I was fitted with crutches, helped into a wheelchair and escorted to the car with two nurses to assist Rainey. At home I was met outside by Nash and Jack and my old wheelchair. Ava was in the living room waiting with the kids. I was disappointed that I required help to stand and sit. I was in a lot more pain than I had anticipated. The recliner had been fitted with a comfy quilt and pillows to be placed where I needed them. I let Rainey and Lili fuss over me for a few minutes before I sent them off to lunch with the rest. By the time they returned the pain shot I'd had at the hospital had kicked in. I told Rainey to squeeze Lili in beside me and to bring me her favorite book to read while he put the twins down for a nap. He settled her in beside me and asked if I would be all right if he went outside to help Nash with the snow removal. Ava had taken Sammie home for his nap so I would be all alone, but to call him on the walkie-talkie when I needed help. I assured him that I would be fine. Lili seemed to be perfectly happy spending one on one time with me until Jack appeared. She squealed out his name and shimmied off the chair. I was definitely replaceable.

I asked him why he wasn't at work as he picked Lili up. He said he had closed the shop up early as he had other things to do. I asked him if that meant us. He said yes, and Sissy was baking bread and needed him to do some shopping so he had stopped by to see if Lili wanted to go with him. That was a very silly question.

"Me go Uncle Jack Mommy." Lili announced. It was a statement, not a question.

I told her to put her boots on while Uncle Jack did a favor for me. I asked him to retrieve a book for me from upstairs. He returned with "Vivienne" and asked me if I was reading it. I said I was, to dress Lili warm, and to let Rainey know that all was well with me. A few minutes later I felt a tugging on my leg. It was Novia. I hadn't noticed, but I guess Rainey hadn't put the rail up on the playpen when he'd put her and Zander down for their naps. She motioned to the book on my lap and said, "Mine Maman."

I took the jacket cover off and gave it to her. She held it to her little body and said something I couldn't understand, but it sounded like "Merci Maman." Well, that couldn't be, so it must have been just "Me see." I didn't even know she had learnt the word "mine."

I discussed it with Rainey when he came in. He assured me that he had definitely put the rail up, so he guessed our little French girl had figured out how to take that rail down just like she had her crib. He agreed with me that she couldn't possibly know the word "merci", but maybe Zoe had been talking to her in French. I doubted it, but would ask her. He wanted to know why I had the book and why I had given her the cover.

"She obviously likes the woman on the cover better than the picture of me you laminated for her. I'm reading the book because it takes place in the 1700's and I wanted to see what life was like in France compared to Avaleena's in Scotland."

"You know that it's fiction don't you?"

"I need to take myself into another world and live someone else's life for a while until I get mine back. I love you and the kids, but sometimes it's just not enough. I'm sorry I'm so glum."

"It's temporary Sweetie; only temporary, but our love isn't, so you need to build on that. Spring is on its way and with it you will be renewed, and I'll be with you every step of the way."

Jack arrived back with Liliana and a shopping bag full of books. He had taken her to the library where they were having a sale of children's books. She had chosen ten; one each for Zander and Novia, two for Tanny, five for herself, and one for me. Mine was entitled "A Duck in Every Pond." I thanked her and said we'd read it together later. I did not question why she had picked a book with ducks on it, but Jack enlightened me. Apparently, she had said that Mama and Papa like ducks. That was a little unnerving to think that she remembered Anton and me taking her to the duck ponds in Verde El Mar. She had never mentioned him before. She wouldn't have been much older than a year…was it possible, or had I told her about it? And, her saying Papa was a little unnerving. Rainey's eyes were questioning. Luckily, the telephone rang. Jack said he'd be on his way home as Rainey answered the call.

"Hold on Jack; I think you'll want to hear this. Go ahead Mr. Stokey. Just to let you know that my wife Vienna, and Jack Jennings are listening in as they are most interested in the results of the autopsy also."

"The results are very troublesome, and at this time, unexplainable. Ms. Jorja Elliot's cause of death has been determined as drowning."

"Drowning? That hardly seems plausible. You told us the last time we talked that she had been found on the floor in the common room, so how could she have drowned?"

"You are asking a question that I cannot answer Mr. Quinn. It is out of my hands as it has been deemed highly suspicion, and is under a major investigation. I hesitate to comment any further as it would just be speculation."

"Mr. Stokey, Vienna Quinn here; may I ask a question Sir?"

"You may, but I may not be able to answer it."

"I understand. It is a simple question; were all the inmates at Jorja's table wearing hooded cloaks, and were they chanting "Alleluia, the wicked witch is dead?"

He hesitated for a second and then laughed slightly. "That is a very strange question, but no they were dressed in the prison attire as always, and I believe their chanting was indecipherable."

"I am going to offer you my opinion as to what caused her demise and you may do with it want you want. Mr. Jennings had been invited to the viewing room the day my husband and he were at the prison, and he reported that Jorja appeared to be very weak and had to be helped to play the game and needed help when it was her turn to drink the water. Have you considered the possibility that she was over medicated and the group was fed up with her antics and took advantage of her weakened state and force-fed her water until she succumbed?"

Rainey was looking at me as if I had lost my mind, but Jack was nodding in agreement.

"I must say you have some imagination Mrs. Quinn." Mr. Stokey replied.

"I come by it honestly as I have lived in a haunted castle most of my life, and believe me, I know witches, both benevolent and malevolent. Jorja Elliot was the latter, and she died from a form of water boarding. Anyone who knows anything about witches knows that water can burn or melt the wicked ones. In her case, it asphyxiated her. I would dig deeper into the past of her associates at the table if you want to conclude this whodunit Mr. Stokey."

"I believe you have been reading too many fairy tales Mrs. Quinn, but thanks for the insight. As I said the matter is out of my hands, but your theory will make for good coffee table conversation. Rest easy Mrs. Quinn."

"Thank you for your call Mr. Stokey." Rainey said rescuing the phone from my clenched hands. "We will look forward to the verdict, and one last thing; I would take into consideration what my wife said. Believe me; she knows things that she shouldn't." Rainey said surprising me with his confirmation. "Good afternoon Sir."

Jack smiled at me. "I can visualise the group holding her and plying her with water as they march around the table, but witches and warlocks…that's far-fetched even for you isn't it?"

"Well, I have not had the pleasure of meeting a warlock to my knowledge yet, but I imagine they are not much different to their counterparts, except maybe stronger, and more dangerous."

"And, hopefully you never will my dear." Rainey chuckled.

"Jack, has Rainey told you about his experience with the witches of Eastbrook?"

"No, he has not. What's the story there Rain?"

"To paraphrase my wife, that's a story for another day. Don't wait for the account with baited breath because it is not note- worthy at all."

"Okay then. How does beef stew and freshly baked bread sound to you guys?" Jack asked.

I was terribly clumsy with the crutches. It took me forever to get from point A to point B. I couldn't understand why I had been given them when I was much more comfortable and steady using the walker. How this little surgery could be worse than the major spleen removal one was perplexing. I spent hours every day just observing Lili and the twins. I found I couldn't remember Lili's first year, so comparing the twin's development with hers was unproductive. I had more memories of Ava's first years and that was twenty some odd years ago. I had Zoe bring me the diary that I had kept when I was Katarina. Rainey was in Hawthorne visiting his parents so it was a good time for me to read it as he would surely be against my going back to Verde El Mar. I was almost through reading it when he returned. I didn't even try to hide it from him. He bent down and kissed me and asked me what I was reading. He frowned when I told him.

"I needed to refresh my memory of Lili's first year because I found I had forgotten a lot. In doing so I found that my life as Kat wasn't so terribly bad. I read it as me looking in on someone else's life. It did not upset me when I read what she had written about Anton. It had nothing to do with me except the notations regarding Liliana. I keep comparing Novia to her and I didn't find many differences except for their personalities. I was thinking that Novia's intellect was exceedingly high, but now I realize she's exactly where she should be for her age. Zander is a little slower, but that's to be expected, right? You should read Kat's diary."

"I will if you want me to, but I really don't need to. I know everything I need to about her and that is that she was a very remarkable woman, just like you. I'm sure there will always be a little of her in you, and I am good with that. We need to find you something constructive to do while you are convalescing besides comparing the children's behaviors. They will be who they are and all we can do is to encourage them to be the best they can be and to follow their dreams."

"Me thinks you are too wise for *your* age oh mystical Yogi."

He laughed. "Yeah, that's me all right."

CHAPTER 4

THROUGH THE YEARS

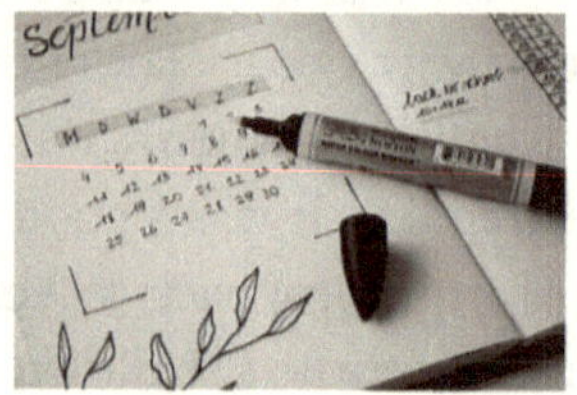

1985

Ava and Nash and our grandson left for their home in Akemantack in the Canadian north on April 4th. It was a very tearful day, but they would be back in seven months. Spring came early so Rainey was able to lay the ground work for the new house almost a month ahead of time. He planned for us to be moved in within a year. He was up every day at dawn and home just after dusk. I'd feed the children early and wait and have dinner alone with him after he'd spent an hour or so with Tanny and Lili before they went to bed. The twins were usually in bed so he would just peek in on them. The routine seemed to be working until the days became longer and he wouldn't make it home until dark. Tanny and Lili would be in bed and asleep. By the time he'd have supper he was too tired for me. We were all missing him, and I was exhausted trying to keep up the house without his help. The kids were my priority. Too bad they weren't his.

Jack and Sissy still checked in regularly, but they had a business to run so I didn't bother them with petty little chores. Zoe and Tanny helped with household chores but I still couldn't keep up. Jack found me teetering on a step stool attempting to replace a light bulb in the kitchen one day. He had stopped in to see if I needed anything before he joined Rainey in Hawthorne. He gave me hell and asked if I was trying to kill myself, and why hadn't I got Rain to do it. I laughed as he helped me down, but the laughter turned to tears and I blurted out that Rainey was never home. I had a little breakdown then and told him things that I should have been telling my husband. I sent him off apologising for my outbursts making him promise not to tell my husband. That worked well because an hour later the front door chimed. As usual Lili ran down the hall singing for her father.

"It's not Daddy Sweetie; let's see who it is?" I was still leery about opening the door so peeked out the window first. Rainey was standing there grinning from ear to ear. I opened the door and asked him why he was here and why didn't he use his key. Lili was already in his arms.

"My family lives here Ma'am, but they may not recognise me in the daylight so I thought I'd better ring to find out if I'm welcome."

Tanny had come up behind me. "Oh Daddy, you are so funny."

"I don't feel funny Honey, just sad." He said looking sorrowfully at me.

"Come in; no need to take off your shoes. The housekeeper hasn't come in a month of Sundays, and I'm not expecting her anytime soon so not to worry about the floors. On more thing; the lady of the house does not like to be called ma'am."

"Understood; I think I have a solution to the housekeeping problem."

I led the way to the kitchen where the twins were in their high chairs up to their elbows in peas and applesauce. "Housekeeping is the least of my problems."

He removed their bibs and attempted to wash their faces and hands with a wet towel that Tanny passed him. "What *is* your biggest problem my Lady?"

My answer was simple. "You."

I told Tanny to take her sister upstairs and get her ready for their lunch and movie date with Sissy. I asked Rainey if I could make him lunch. He said he'd had an early meal at the ranch, but offered to make me something. I said I was fine and started to clean up the messy floor under the twin's chairs. He asked me to sit down so we could talk.

"Sorry, you're too late, I am all talked out. Bring your half into the living room. It's time for their nap." I answered picking up Novia.

He followed me with Zander and placed him in the playpen. "How long have I been gone?"

"Almost two months."

"Well, it stops now. No more long days away from you and the kids anymore, and I'll even take Sundays off from now on starting with the rest of today. The first thing we have to do though is to get you some help. You rebuffed the idea before about hiring a housekeeper, but with me gone all day I think the time has come to hire one. We also need to hire someone to do the yard. It's in pretty bad shape."

"How nice of you to notice." I answered caustically.

"It's my house too you know."

"Which brings me to the question… what happens to it when we move to Hawthorne?"

"Let's not get ahead of ourselves Vienna. It's the here and now I am concerned about."

"When did you come to this revelation? Was it before or after Jack's visit today?"

"I admit; he opened my eyes. I'm sorry I let things come to such a state of disrepair. It's nothing that we can't remedy though is it?"

"Are you including our relationship in that list?"

"It's the number one thing. I realise that you think I have been neglecting you, but it's not so. I think about you all the time. I'm sorry that I have been so tired when I get home, but I am going to remedy that if I'm right when I say that I think you've been missing me too?"

"I miss you more than you can imagine." I admitted solemnly.

He pulled me into his arms. "Let's fix this then. What do you think about us packing up the kids this Friday when Tanny gets home from school and spending the weekend at the ranch? There is lots of room for us at the house and Mom and Dad would be delighted to have you. Zoe has a job on the weekends so she could stay here, or with Sissy and Jack."

I liked the idea because I would be able to see my husband whenever I wanted to, but I wasn't sure that it wouldn't be too much for his parents. I was proven wrong as Tanny was a big help to Patsy in the kitchen, and along with Lili they accompanied Paul every morning to feed the chickens and pigs. The horses and cows were on their own in the pastures. This was going to be my life soon whether I liked it or not, so I had better get on board. At no time did I recall Rainey asking me if I wanted to take over the ranch when his parents retired, but apparently it was his dream. I'd had mine in Scotland for over twenty years, but this was no Avanloch. Patsy kept a garden, and there were lawns and flowers, but nothing like my rose garden. I could plant a new one couldn't I? The land had been dug up all around the perimeter of the new house. It was drab and dusty. I couldn't imagine a garden. Where was the girl who had visualised and built an Eden at the castle? I got to see more of my husband so anything was possible. By summer we had pretty much moved into his parent's house.

Zoe had gone with Jack and Sissy to Edmonton in June for Joannie's graduation. She returned to Bridge Falls with them. She and Zoe had jobs at a local fast food restaurant, and they would stay between Jack's and Sissy's and the Palace. I had felt guilty about leaving her alone, so that solved that. She had her own car so she could come up to the farm whenever she wanted. Zoe wouldn't finish her schooling for another year. After that she and Joannie had plans to backpack and cycle through Europe ending up in Spain. Hopefully by then Rainey would have succeeded in tracking down Zoe's birth records or a relative. He'd put his research on hold when construction of the house had begun. He had asked me if I thought Somner might take up the task seeing he lived close to the orphanage that she had been in for years. It was an excellent idea and we posed the idea to Somner in a phone call. He surprised us by saying that he was had been working on it already. He and Lelani had been visiting orphanages as they had decided to adopt a child or two and had made inquiries into Zoe's quest. So far there were no leads as the orphanage Anton hired Zoe from no longer existed, but the children from it had been transferred to others throughout Spain. He was in the process of tracking down some of the previous workforce. He'd hoped that he would be able to surprise us with a lead. Rainey filled him on the particulars and told him that we'd reimburse him for all expenses. Somner wouldn't hear of it and told him that he could never repay the debt he owed me and my family for keeping my true identity from them, and that the almighty dollar did not enter into his desire to help Zoe. If he was successful perhaps he would have some self-vindication. It had taken me sometime to forgive him, but Rainey had convinced me that I needed to do so for my state of mind. Now I might just be indebted to him if he could welcome Zoe back to Spain with news of her lineage.

Nash and Ava and Sammie arrived on October the seventeenth. I'd had to go back to the Palace after Labor Day for the start of the new school year. Tanny was in grade two and I had enrolled Lili in a play group for three days a week. She did not like it. We didn't make her go, but told her that she could change her mind at any time. Her excuse was that she needed to look after Novia and Zander. That was a laugh because most of the time she completely ignored them, but tolerated Sammie because he was still a baby. He was walking, and babbling so he fit right in with the twins. At Christmas he surprised us all by calling me Ana. I thought that was a much better name for Grandma. Rainey became known as Pappy a few months later.

Nash had gone right to work with Rainey on the new house. I had become a day widow again, but it was much more tolerable because Ava was with me. The house now had a rough floor and the supporting walls were up. The inside could wait because it was a rush to get the roof on before the snows came. Besides Nash, Jack, Jimmy and Yates, every able body in Hawthorne came out to assist with the laying of the roof. We celebrated the 'roof shout' as it was called, with a huge party at the Grange. As usual, the women put on an autumn feast. It was comparable to the harvest festival at Avanloch. I guess it wouldn't be long before I would be known as one of the Hawthorne women.

I wasn't much of a social butterfly, and I never thought Rainey was, but he was that night. I sat quietly with the twins while he mingled with the crowd. Tanny and Lili were clowning around with Jack and Jimmy and all the other children on the dance floor. I watched my husband as he made his way around the room. He always had a drink in his hand. I hoped he wasn't taking any orders for his expertise in house constructions. He had hired a band from Bridge. They were basically a rock and roll band, but shifted to slow, mellow tunes to accommodate the older folks. An attractive young woman I had never seen before appeared and approached my husband. I guessed that she had asked him for a dance because he put his drink down and waltzed her out onto the floor to an old Elvis love song right in front of me. Suddenly, I was back at Avanloch watching my husband swing the Duchess of Cambria around. Where could I hide myself? There was no Miss Mary's room, or Maveryn at the crypt, and no Avaleena's secret chamber. I couldn't stay here and watch the man who had been too tired for me all week find renewed energy with a pretty blonde woman half my age. He hadn't once asked me if I'd like to dance. I grabbed my purse hoping that I had a set of car keys in it, awkwardly placed Novia under one arm and Zander under the other. I heard someone calling my name as I made a bee-line for the door. I think it was Rainey's mother. I couldn't remember where we had parked. The twins were too heavy so I had to put them down. I gripped their little hands and pulled them along as I searched for the car in the dark. I was six steps away from it when he called out to me.

"Where are you going in such a hurry Vienna?"

I didn't answer. Somehow I managed to hold on to the twins as I fished the keys from the bottom of my purse. I punched the fob just as he reached me. He rescued Zander from me.

"Why didn't you answer me? Is something wrong with one of them?"

"Thanks for asking if I'm all right."

"You look perfectly fine to me."

"Of course I do through those inebriated eyes of yours." I opened the back door and placed Novia in her car seat.

"I'm not drunk. Are you going to tell me why you are leaving? Are you going home?"

"Home…where is home? Is it here, or is it there? I've only had one home in my life and it's certainly not here in this God-forsaken country! Give me Zander!"

"I think not. I'm not letting you drive in the condition you're in."

"My condition is just fine; I'm not the one who's been drinking. I may not have a home or a husband at the time, but I'm a damn good mother and I am perfectly capable of looking after my children."

"You do realise that you left two of your children on the dance floor don't you?"

"Jack is looking after them as he has been more of a father to them than you for the past year. Now give me my son and you can go back to your party and dancing with your new little skank."

"That's what it's all about isn't it? You can't stand to see me looking at another woman can you? Well, I will have you know that she's a Notary Republic and has written up all our policies."

"Oh, so this isn't your first meeting with her…how lovely that I wasn't included in anything to do with the house that you supposedly built for me."

"There is no talking to you when you're like this, so go on then, go, and thanks for ruining an almost perfect day." He placed Zander in his seat, turned, and walked away.

I knew that Lili and Tanny would be looked after, so I put the car in drive and headed for Bridge Falls. It was nine forty five when I parked in front of the Palace. I carried Novia in first and left her sleeping on the living room couch, went back for Zander and got them both upstairs and into bed. I didn't bother taking their party clothes off. I was sitting at the kitchen table drinking a cup of coffee when Ava found me an hour later.

"Mom, I thought you were staying at the farm tonight. Why didn't you? Gramma said that you just up and left. Daddy said that you were mad at him…are you? What's he done now?"

"I'm not sure what your father is up to because he doesn't confide in me anymore. To be perfectly honest I think he is tired of me, but hasn't figured out what to do about it. That house has taken over his life and he has no time for me or the kids. I can't say for sure, but there may be a third party involved."

"Oh Mommy, there is no one but you. I know about his obsession with getting the house finished. Nash and I have told him to slow down, but he just can't seem to do so. He'll be home more now that the roof is on. You don't have anything to worry about, so just hang in there."

The front door slammed. He came bounding down the hallway.

"You've just taken another ten years off my life Lady! Why didn't you tell me you were coming here? Do you know how worried I was when I got to the ranch house and your car wasn't in the drive? You hate driving, and especially at night, so why did you come here, or answer the phone?" He demanded.

Ava got up, kissed me and then her father. "You two need to talk. I'll see you in the morning."

I told him there was fresh coffee.

"I don't need any. For your information I am not inebriated. I only had one bottle of beer and what you probably thought was whiskey in my glass was ginger ale. After you left I had two cups of coffee, said my good-byes and left with Tanny and Lili expecting to find you at Mom's and Dad's. I panicked when your car wasn't in the drive. I had to wait until Mom and Dad got home because I couldn't leave the girls alone. Why didn't you answer the phone? You had to know that I'd be worried about you." His voice and body language told me he was somewhere between wrath and tears.

"Why would I think that? You told me to go, and you didn't seem to care about what I was feeling. You ignored me all night long. Not once did you ask me to dance. You used to dance with only me, so visions of you and the Lady Lauren dancing at Avanloch came hauntingly back when you took another woman in your arms. And, by the way, the phone did not ring; I would have answered it."

He came over and sat down beside me. "What's become of me Vienna to not notice that you were upset? But, it's more than just tonight isn't it?"

"I think you are all used up Rainey. Every ounce of you has gone into the building of that house. Your idea for me and the kids to go and stay with your parents worked for a while, but it wasn't the solution to mending what was wrong between you and me. I think I have outlived your love for me."

"If you are saying that I don't love you anymore then you are completely off base. The way I feel about you has never changed and it never will. It still grows stronger day after day, but you're talking about our sex life aren't you?"

"There's not very much for us to talk about in that matter is there? Feelings change, people change, love dwindles…"

"My feelings or love for you has never dwindled, but I have. To be more precise, my body has. I should have talked to you about it, but I was embarrassed. I realise now that I was just plain stupid. You would have listened and you would have understood, and I hope that you will now. I finally went and saw a doctor last week."

He stopped talking waiting for my reaction which was probably not what he was expecting.

"Don't tell me; don't you dare tell me that you're dying!" I cried.

"It's not that bad Sweetie. Come here; you're shaking."

I managed to stammer. "You're never sick; you never go to a doctor so it has to be bad."

He took my hands in his. "It isn't Honey. I thought that it might be prostate cancer because I had all the signs. The biggest one was that I had lost my libido and that had never happened before with you so that was debilitating."

"Or with any of your other relationships I suppose."

"Vienna!" He scolded. "Do you want to bring up my past again? If you do then this conversation is over." He started to get up.

"No, I'm sorry. I was afraid that I was to blame and that you just didn't want to be with me anymore, and then I saw you with her tonight…Oh God, here I am feeling sorry for myself and you have a real problem and I am scared that I am going to lose you. I could fight for you if there was another woman, and I might be able to win you back, but if you were to die…"

"You're jumping to conclusions without hearing me out. I'm going to get you a glass of water, and then you are just going to have to calm down, or I am going to get you one of your anti-anxiety pills and we'll wait until you quit vibrating, or we'll postpone it to tomorrow."

I took a few sips of water and promised I'd be good.

"You are good Honey, and at everything you do, especially putting up with me. I'm at fault because I let it go so long. I guess I just thought it would all go away and that I just had a bug or something."

"What did you think was going to go away?"

"I guess it started with an upset stomach that never got any better. I had a bottle of antacids that I kept in the car because I didn't want you to see me taking so many. They helped a little, but the pain started to intensify when I peed. The clincher was my lack of sexual stimulation. I could only blame it on fatigue for so long so I made the appointment with Dr. Kuenene."

"He's an Oncologist from South Africa isn't he? Why didn't you go to Dr. Barb?"

"I couldn't even tell you about my personal problems, so do you think I would have been comfortable discussing them with her? Dr. Kuenene is an Oncologist, but he's also a family doctor. You'll like him."

"I'm going to meet him?"

"Yes, on Tuesday at my next appointment. I want you with me."

"How long have you been seeing him? You haven't even told me what's wrong with you?"

"It's bladder stones Vienna; I have bladder stones. That's all, just stones."

"That's all; isn't that enough? How long have you been in this pain Rainey…how long?"

"I guess it all started in June, but didn't get bad until the end of July."

"That's over four months, and I never noticed anything. What kind of a wife am I anyway?"

"The very best a man could ever have. I quit having my usual drink in the evening and stuck to a beer with the guys before I came home. That apparently was a good thing and helped me urinate more. I wasn't eating as much, especially red meat and you asked me why. I passed it off as watching my cholesterol as I was getting older."

"How did you manage to keep working?"

"Mornings were the best because I hadn't eaten yet. I managed to work through the pain because it would come and go. The day I was bent over in pain and couldn't climb down the ladder was the day I knew I had to seek help."

"Which was when?"

"I had my first appointment in mid- August."

"That was two months ago and I am just finding out now. Do you know how that makes me feel, and then to add to your troubles I go and accuse you of infidelity again. What is wrong with me Rainey? You couldn't confide in me and I didn't trust you again…I've made this all about me, and I am thoroughly disgusted with myself. No, don't try and placate me! You've always been my hero and I'm the villain, so don't you dare try and take the blame for anything."

"I love this feisty side of you. I don't think I can make it upstairs so how about we just go and lie down in that bedroom?" He proposed nodding to the spare bedroom.

"Are you in too much pain to climb the stairs? You can use the lift you know."

"I just need you to come and lay with me and be my wife. It's been a long time, so please let's not lose these moments."

"Are you sure?" I asked not too sure of what I was asking.

"Oh yes Baby; I have never been more certain of anything in my life before."

I didn't care *if* it was only for a moment; my husband wanted me, and my whole body had been aching for his touch so I let him lead me down the path to heavenly bliss. It was midnight.

I edged my way out of bed hoping I wouldn't wake him. I slipped into my nightie and was about to leave when he asked me where I was going.

"The twins could wake up at any time so I need to be close." I answered.

"I'm coming with you. Do I have to get dressed?"

"No you don't my darling; we'll just toss your clothes in the laundry room."

"I may as well just put them in the washer." He said following me.

"Good luck with that." I said opening the door. "There's already a load in the washer, one in the dryer and two loads on the floor, so just throw them anywhere."

He shut the door. "What were we saying last night about a housekeeper?"

"Your wife said she didn't want a strange woman in her house."

"Why not; Avanloch was full of them?"

"This was a different life, and I'm still trying to adjust. Ava is all settled in now so she will help. On the other hand, maybe a couple of strong young men would fit the bill. What do you think?"

"You've already got Jack, Nash and Jimmy, so I think not. I should have a few female friends don't you think; a nice little plump house maid maybe?"

"You're treading on sacred ground you know, or have you already forgotten about my jealous streak?" I started up the stairs, turned and told him to go ahead of me.

"I have not. Just trying to inject a little humor into the discussion, and I kind of like the view from behind."

"And that is the only ass that you better ever look at until the day you die."

He smacked my derriere. "You're a little harsh aren't you Mommy?"

"My house, my rules."

"It seems to me that my name is also on the deed."

"Oh no Sweetie, remember you asked me to take your name off everything when you walked out on me at Christmas, so I did; sorry."

"I see we are back playing games. If I wasn't so tired…"

The twins were still sleeping soundly so we crossed the hall and climbed into bed. I asked Rainey if he was in any pain, and how did he manage the long day yesterday.

"I didn't eat until the buffet and then I only ate sparsely. I had taken to wearing a back brace and it seemed to keep some. I drank a half a bottle of Maalox on my way home, and by the way we are out of Tums."

"Did any of that help?"

"Very little, but the doctor put me on potassium citrate to see if they would dissolve the stones and I'm thinking it might be working."

"How was it decided that you didn't have prostate cancer? Are the symptoms similar?"

"Yes, sort of. Blood and urine tests showed sufficient indication of stones, and a bladder x-ray confirmed it. We'll see what happens on Tuesday."

"Okay, that is enough information to take in at four in the morning. Shall we try and get a little more sleep." He told me he loved me dearly and was sorry for yelling at me.

I awoke to the tantalizing aroma of coffee. I glanced at the clock. It was eight a.m. Rainey was still asleep and the twins and girls must all be too. It took me a few minutes to wake myself up and realise that Tanny and Lili were in Hawthorne. I didn't remember setting the coffee pot last night. Ava was at the kitchen table waiting for me. I asked her why she was here so early.

"Good morning to you too. Why do you think I'm here? When I left last night Daddy was yelling at you and he never yells…"

I gave her a quick hug, poured myself a cup of coffee and sat down beside her. "He had every right to be angry with me, but we straightened that all out, so there is no need to worry about us. You and Nash both thought that your dad was not his usual robust self, and that is true, he wasn't. No one knows that any better than me. The last few months have been hell on steroids. His obsession with that house was going to be the death of him. He had promised that we'd be all moved in by spring, and come hell or high water it was going to be so. I could not talk him down. He would come home every night looking like death warmed over. He'd have a bite to eat and go straight to bed, and be gone at dawn the next day. His appetite had dwindled, but I thought Patsy was keeping him fed during the day, so I didn't worry. Once the roof was on surely he would slow down. Then I discovered he was consuming Tums like they were a major food source. I had never known him to have indigestion, but there was a reason for that, and last night, he finally told me. Your dad has bladder stones."

"Oh no Mom, he must be in so much pain. That's serious, but not as serious as other things, so why wouldn't he tell you? Obviously he has seen a doctor. What's the diagnosis; does he have to have surgery? I can't see how Tums could help him."

"I'm sure they didn't Honey. I am going with him to his doctor's appointment tomorrow."

The baby monitor squeaked. I guess the twins were finally awake.

"Vienna… I need you; can you come…"

I was up and running as a dull thud silenced the monitor. Ava was right behind me. We found him laying half-way into the bed clutching his stomach. The monitor was lying on the floor. He told us that he had awakened in pain, but made it to the bathroom where the pain became excruciating. He'd managed to get to the monitor with great difficulty. Ava said he may have passed a stone. I told him I was going to call for an ambulance. He didn't object to going to the hospital, but didn't want to go by ambulance as he could make it to the car with our help. Ava phoned Nash, walked out of the room with the portable in her hands saying she was going to check on the twins while I got her father ready. I knew she was dialing 911.

Ava and I sat with Rainey in emerg until Dr. Kunene arrived. He came and talked with us afterwards. The potassium citrate had not worked as he had hoped it would. He believed that Rainey had exasperated his bladder by not being able to empty it completely. Heavy lifting, anxiety and stress hadn't helped any. He was awaiting blood and urine cultures, but told us to expect that he'd be performing a Cystolitholapaxy before the days end. He said he had given Rainey something for the pain and was admitting him for observation. He left us with a pamphlet that would explain the procedure. I was glad to have Ava with me. I sent her home after she had a quick visit with her father. I sat with Rain until the doctor returned informing us that the tests were what he had expected. There was blood in the urine and the bladder was inflamed due to an infection caused by urine retention. He wanted Rainey to rest for the rest of the day and had scheduled surgery for seven p.m. It was usually a day surgery, but because it was to take place in the evening he wanted Rainey to spend the night in the hospital. I was fine with that.

I went home at his insistence around four. He needed rest and sleep anyhow and he wasn't doing so while I was hovering. He told me I had to quit blaming myself for what happened between us last night because it had nothing to do with his condition as that was all on him.

I nodded, kissed him and said I'd see him in a few hours.

Sissy and Jack were in the kitchen. Zander and Novia were in their highchairs eating strawberries. "I see you are cooking for us again."

"We have to eat too Sis, and we have been missing the family gatherings. You and the kids were away most of the summer and Rainey was pretty much non- existent…"

"You are right about that. Even when he was home, he really wasn't because he couldn't stop building that house. It was always front and centre in his mind. And then he got sick, but he was too pigheaded to admit that it was more than indigestion or to talk to me about it. Did he ever say anything to you Jack when you'd go up on Sundays?"

"I'd see him popping Tums, but like you said, he blamed it on indigestion. My suggesting that the carpenters he'd hired knew what they were doing and didn't always require his help or supervision only met with resistance and denial. I think he was close to telling me to mind my own business so I quit interfering before I lost my best friend. Hopefully, that has all come to end, and even though he'll be convalescing, he'll get some much needed rest. Now, what can I do for you?"

"I think that bottle of Crown Royal will become flat before its owner will be able to imbibe again, so if you will join me in a little nip before dinner I think it might just fit the bill, and I'll bum one of those from you." I said pointing to his pack of cigarettes in his pocket.

"When was the last time you smoked, or had liquor for the matter?" My sister asked.

"Sometime in the early sixties I guess. I'll be outside Jack."

I grabbed a heavy sweater from the coat rack and went out on the back porch to wait for him. A few minutes later he passed me a glass full of ice and Pepsi which had a tablespoon of whiskey in it. I was sure there wasn't any more than that in it. He lit two cigarettes and passed me one. "I hate Players' you know."

He laughed. "Yeah, I remember."

"Did you ever imagine that we would be sitting here partaking in a drink and talking twenty five years ago?"

"To be perfectly honest with you Vienna, I never thought that I would ever see you again after you and Rainey got married." He confessed.

"Well, I think the best thing I ever did was to get kidnapped because you met my sister and while you were commiserating you fell in love." I raised my glass. "So, good for me."

"Rainey is right; you do have a warped sense of humor. Thankfully, the tale has a happy ending for both of us. I have found my soul mate and I get to share the rest of my life with my best friends and their herd of lovable children."

"You are a second father to them Jack. They truly love you as I do. You really are a Jack of all trades. That you and Rainey are best friends is a miracle all on its own."

I spent an hour with my husband after his surgery. He was a little groggy, but said he felt better already and had very little pain. Nash brought him home the next morning to a house filled with balloons. Lili had insisted that Daddy needed a party because he had been sick and that he should have a cake too. I got on that right after I got my breath back after the balloon blowing ordeal. What I didn't do to appease a cantankerous child. Her father would be home for a week or so recuperating, so he could deal with her temper tantrums. After all, he was the reason she was the way she was. I told her that she couldn't jump on her dad because he was still hurting. She promised me that she wouldn't hurt her Daddy and she wouldn't let the twins or Sammie near him because they were wild. Talk about calling the kettle black.

Rainey chose to relax stretched out on the chesterfield. We chatted for a while and left Lili curled up with him reading him a story about the three bears. Ava had a hair appointment so Nash and I corralled the other three and retreated to the kitchen. Lili reminded me that I had a cake to ice with sprinkles.

The little ones were content in their high chairs with cheerios and banana chunks. Nash set to work shredding the chicken from last night's supper for me while I assembled the rest of the ingredients for the soup. He said he was glad that we had a little time to spend alone as he wanted to run something by me. I asked him what was on his mind. His answer shocked me. He said he was contemplating leaving the north and moving south and wanted to know what I thought about it. He had not discussed it with Ava yet because he was sure she wouldn't agree because it had been his way of life for so long. He loved what he did but had to think about Ava and the children.

"Children…is there another on the way?" I asked hopefully.

"Not yet, but soon I hope."

"Have you discussed your plans with Rainey?"

"No, because I know he would be all for it if it meant he could see his daughter every day."

"Does that mean you want to relocate here to Bridge Falls?"

"Or Hawthorne."

"What would you do Nash? I don't think there is a need for a wilderness guide in these parts?"

"I haven't got that far yet Vienna. I just want to do what's right for my family. I never thought I'd find a girl like Ava. That plane crash was the best thing that ever happened to me."

I laughed. "Yes, she says the same thing. She is happy where she is because she is with you, so I am pretty sure she will be happy wherever as long as you are together. We will say no more on this until you have talked to her, and she's not to know that you came to me first, all right?"

"She would be all right with it, but I'll play it by ear. You two are so much alike that sometimes it's uncanny."

"Oh, I hope she hasn't inherited any of my jealous tendencies. Did you know that Rainey thought she was me when he first set eyes on her that fateful winter day in Hawthorne?"

"I do, and you have nothing or anyone to be envious of. The one thing I am sure about beside my love for Ava is his love for you. That was heartbreakingly so last winter."

"I've been envious of his addiction with that damn house. He's spent more time with it than he has with me and the kids. I've dubbed it "Obsession.""

He smiled. "The worst is over Vienna. You've got your husband back and you can count on Ava and me to keep him in check."

I didn't tell him what I was really afraid of, nor did I tell him that I wished they would never go back to Akemantack.

The day was almost over. Dinner and the clean-up were done. Ava and Nash had left with a sleeping Sammie. Twins were bathed and ready for bed. Zoe was out with Joannie. I left Tanny doing her homework at Rainey's desk in the dining room. I left cookies and milk for her and took the twins in to say goodnight to their father. Lili was still sitting with him in his recliner. I told her that it was time to think about going to bed. She said she was staying with her daddy. I gave Rainey the look. He nodded.

I decided to let him deal with her and went back into the kitchen. The telephone rang.

"Hello, Mrs. Quinn?" A female voice asked on the other end.

"Yes, this is Vienna Quinn. May I help you?" I asked warily.

"My name is Pamela Clarke. I'm a notary republic and have been working with your husband on his policies. I was shaken when I heard that he had emergency surgery and am wondering if he is okay if you don't mind my inquiring."

"Why don't you ask him yourself Ms. Clarke? My daughter will take him the phone."

I think she thanked me as I passed the phone to Tanny, but I didn't much care.

Tanny came back and said that Lili wasn't going to bed. She kissed me and said good night. I gave myself a few minutes just in case Rainey was still on the phone before I went in to get Lili. She defied me. Rainey tried sweet talking her. I was in no mood. I pulled her away from him not saying a word. She yelled and hit on me all the way up the stairs. Tanny met us at the top and told her to be quiet because she was going to wake the twins and to stop hitting me. I unwound her from my arms and placed her in her bed and tucked the blankets tightly around her.

"I'm not in my pyjamas." She cried.

"You can sleep in your dress."

"I don't want to. I want Daddy."

"Daddy is sick and you hurt Mommy. You're a bad, bad girl, and I'm mad at you." Tanny said sharply. "Quit crying and go to sleep or I'm going to go sleep in the twin's room."

"I'm not bad Tanny."

"Yes you are."

I closed the door leaving them banter back and forth, went downstairs, took a load of laundry out of the dryer and put another one in. I retreated into the kitchen, put the kettle on and sat down and folded the towels. When the kettle whistled I made a cup of herbal tea and took it into Rainey. He hadn't felt like eating all day so I asked him if he wanted to try something yet.

"Thanks, but no. I was wondering when you were going to come and talk to me."

"What do you want to talk about; our belligerent daughter I suppose?"

"I'm sorry for what she did to you, and I will deal with her tomorrow. I think we had better talk about the phone call."

"What's there to talk about? Your friend phoned and wanted to know how you were, and I assumed that you told her, so what more is there to say?"

"She's just an acquaintance Vienna. I wouldn't categorize her as a friend, but I can tell that you think she is something more and her call has upset you."

"I am not upset. You've pointed out so many times before that I have male friends so you are entitled to have a female one, so good for you, you have a new friend. Drink your tea while I finish up with the laundry and then I'll help you up to bed."

"I don't think I said anything of the sort unless it was in fun. Never the less, as I said, she is just a business acquaintance. Are you coming to bed with me?"

"Eventually."

"Do you mean tonight, or not? You know we are still very early in our marriage and we have miles to go because we are going to be together forever. I am going to do and say things that you won't like, and I won't always agree with some of the things you say and do either because that is how life and relationships go. It's long past time for you to lose this jealousy streak of yours because it is nonsensical. I will say it one more time and then we will be done with it. Pamela Clarke is an associate and that is all. She will be bringing the papers by one day for you to sign so I hope you will be cordial?" He formed the request as a question.

"Oh, is the house in my name? She referred to it as yours, and I will be just as cordial as I damn well please. If I am nonsensical you can live with it, or use it as an argument against me in the divorce proceedings." I kissed him and told him to drink up again and not to mess with me or I was going to beat on him the same way his daughter had beaten on me.

"I would welcome a physical beating about now as your pounding on me might knock the silliness out of you."

"I will leave that to another day when you fall out of favour with me again but are able to defend yourself. I'm sure that day isn't too far away as I am sure your obsession with that house has not left you. By the way, "Obsession" is what I have dubbed it."

"Too late my dear as I have already named it "Cherry Blossom Manor". It's on paper so it is official. Are you okay with that?"

"I am. We will have to plant a tree then."

"Way ahead of you as two dozen will be arriving in the spring."

Lili came down the next morning hiding behind her sister's skirt. Tanny said that Lili had something she wanted to say to me. I asked her what it was. She said she was sorry. I said that I couldn't hear her so she would have to come closer. She nervously approached me.

"I'm sorry Mommy."

I asked her what she was sorry about.

"Because I hit you."

"I accept your apology. We will talk about your behavior later with your father. Now give me a kiss and you can go upstairs and see if he is ready to get up. Make sure he sits in the chair to come downstairs."

"I will Mommy I promise." She sang running down the hall.

Nash's parents came for Christmas. The house was full again and I was happy. Evie and Monty, Ava's and Nash's friends from their wilderness adventure paid them a surprise visit in March. They had arrived with two photograph albums filled with photos of said adventure. We spent hours marveling over them. Ava had kept a diary which I had read, but the photos added so much more to those two months of their adventurous plight.

1986

Sadly we had to say au revoir to our daughter and family again in April. They left us with the news that there would be an addition to their family in October. We were thrilled to welcome another grandchild. Rainey had made good on his promise to slow down in regards to his work on the Hawthorne house. His body had healed and he was chomping at the bit to get back to work, so I thought I best make my revisions to the house known to him before it was too late. Having taken advantage of Ava's two years of graphic art I informed him of what I wanted. He was surprised that I didn't want the kitchen that he had planned. I wanted a country kitchen, somewhat like his mom's. I wanted a window seat, a pantry like the one at the Palace and a nook that would seat the kids, and I wanted it completely open to the entrance lobby. I was sure that he had modelled this so called lobby after the grand entrance at Avanloch as it would lead to all the other rooms and the staircase. Those doors would remain open as I envisioned the room to be the family room where the kids could call their own There they would always be in my view when I was in the kitchen. It would be furnished with comfortable furniture that could take a beating, The proposed rounded stairway was fine, but I wanted the bottom four stairs to fan out in a half circle. Rainey thought that it was brilliant and he hoped his finances would be able to handle it.

"Is this not my house also? You're macho plan to pay for it all does not hold water. Is not our marriage a joint venture? Whatever I have is yours and you know it. You have carte blanche to finish the house exactly as you desire. Let me make this perfectly clear. I will be purchasing all the furnishings and appliances. Seeing that you had planned on me having a thoroughly sterile stainless steel kitchen, I don't trust that you don't envision the rest of the rooms the same way. This is to be a home, not a show house."

"I have never thought of it as anything but a home. I know you are not a thoroughly modern woman, but I thought you'd welcome a bright shiny kitchen. Sorry, I was completely wrong. I am very impressed with your drawings which just goes to prove that you have more hidden talents that I know nothing about."

I laughed. "Sorry to disillusion you once more, but it was your daughter's doing, not mine."

"I didn't know that the little French girl had graduated from crayons to inking."

"Very funny Sweetheart. Now, let's go through this mansion one room at a time to make sure that everything meets with my approval."

"So it is said, so it will be my dear."

We began moving into Cherry Blossom Manor in August as soon as the interior was deemed finished. Furniture began arriving and room by room came together as planned. There were five bedrooms upstairs and one downstairs. The twins would continue to share a room for the time being. Tanny and Lili chose to do the same. Zoe and Tanny would be taking the bus into school in Bridge in September so there would be adjustments that we were all going to have to make. There would be days when Zoe would drive because of her after school projects.

I wanted us to be out of the Palace before Ava and Nash arrived as it was to be their home from now on while they were here. They would sell the other house, and I imagined that the Palace would be empty for six or seven months of the year. Zoe and Joannie would probably make good use of it as would we when the need be.

Calla Lily Vienne made her entrance into the world on October the twelve. Her eyes were as blue as the deep blue sea, just like her mother Ava's and Pappy Rainey's.

!987

Colleen Maveryn Govern was born on August 24th. Rainey and I made the journey to Scotland for the arrival of Rosalyn and Evan's first daughter. Colleen entered the world boasting a head of red curly hair just like her mothers. In time I was sure her eyes would be green also.

Rainey and I had left the children with Sissy and Jack who were second parents to them so we had no hesitation about leaving them. They had graciously moved into the Manor for the ten days that we would be gone. The twins were three and a half then. Of course, Tanny and Lili were overjoyed, and Zoe was still home to help keep peace. She had graduated in June, and she and Joannie would be leaving in September for their adventures abroad.

It was wonderful to be back at Avanloch again with our family which included Johnny and Amma and the McDuffs. Rainey and I managed to sneak in a half day's ride to Widow's Hummock on the horses we'd had to leave behind three years ago and a visit with Meggie. The ten days sped by quickly. I was saddened to be leaving Rosy and Evan and baby Shannon. I probably wouldn't be back for a few years, but this was no longer my home, and I could come back any time I wanted to. All I had to do was close my eyes.

1988 sped by. We were one family member less now that Zoe was gone. The last we had heard from her and Joannie was that they were on their way to Spain. Hopefully Somner would have some good news for her when she arrived.

1989

We took the plunge and rented a large motor home, packed up the kids and made the long trek to Akemantack. It was our first real vacation with the kids. We visited with Nash's parents in Quesnel and spent two days in Barkerville, and two weeks with Nash and Ava and the grandchildren at their rustic yet thoroughly modern home and lodge. It was named Hackmatack for the Tamarack forests that surrounded the area. They had a nice little farm there and Nash was still guiding and had started teaching survival classes in the schools. Ava was perfectly content to be Nash's wife and mother to Sammie and Calla. She had taken several correspondence courses in nursing, but didn't have any plans to further it as a career. She did volunteer at the hospital in Spring Valley periodically and was Akemantack's answer to a medical doctor.

We enjoyed our visit immensely. The children did not want to leave. Sammie and Zander had bonded. There was much crying and carrying on when we left. It was only a few months before Sammie would be returning to Bridge anyway and then I guessed we would go through the same thing all over again when they had to part in the spring.

Our plans had been to go home and rest for two weeks before we left for Scotland. Rosalyn was due to give birth in late August, and we wanted to be with her and Evan. We got word that Rosy had gone into pre-mature labor the day before we left Akemantack, so we missed Beth's arrival into the world. It was a hurried trip back to Hawthorne and a short two day rest before we were on the road again. Evan had insisted that he send the plane, but regretted that he couldn't accompany Gin, but that Arron, the co-pilot was fully qualified. We didn't argue because it didn't require us booking flights and travelling elsewhere to make connections. Rainey insisted that I see Dr. Barb before the trip. I could not convince him that I needn't as she had given me a clean bill of health before the trip up north. My vaccines were up to date and my antibiotics were still valid. It was easier for me to appease him than argue.

The night before we were to leave I came out from our downstairs bedroom to find Novia sitting at the bottom of the stairs. It was after nine so she should have been in bed fast asleep. I asked her what was wrong fearing that she was ill. She patted something under her night coat and said that she had broken her, and that she couldn't take her to the castle now. She didn't have her new doll in her lap so I asked her who she was talking about. She said, "V."

That caught me by surprise. As far as I knew my children didn't know that V was what I called myself when I was young. They had never questioned it even when Sissy called me that. I asked her who V was.

"You know her Mommy." She stated uncovering the book cover titled "Vivienne".

I had no idea that she still had it. "Oh, I see that her dress is torn. How did it happen?"

"Zaney, but he didn't mean to."

"I'm sorry, but you know what, I can fix it. How about you come into the kitchen with me and we put V all back together?"

I wiped the tears from her eyes, gathered her into my arms and set her down on the table while I got the tape. Rainey came in and asked what was going on. Novia showed him the picture and said that Mommy was going to make her all better. He said he had an idea and to give him a moment. He returned just as I had V's dress mended. He had a small plastic envelope in his hand. He placed the book jacket in it.

"Look," he said, "she's safe in there, and there's even a little handle on it so you can pack her around with you if you like. Now, how about I give you a ride upstairs and tuck you into bed?"

She kissed him and crawled up on his back. He asked her if she had a kiss for me. She did and she said she loved me, and that V could go to see her castle now.

Rainey returned and asked me why Novia had called the lady on the cover V. I said I had no idea, but guessed that Tanny had named her that a long time ago because Novia couldn't say Vivienne when she was young. He said that sounded like something Tanny would do and asked me where she had been keeping the cover because he hadn't seen it since we had moved. I had no answer as I didn't have a clue myself.

"We have to pay more attention to her Rainey. She may be only five, but she is so unassuming that we have just left her to be. She only has to be told something once for it to be understood. We haven't worried about Zander because she speaks for him and has always understood what he wants. I've let her infancy slip by. Where did the years go? She'll be gone to school this fall, and I'll be all alone. I have to make up for the years that I lost with her, and I am going to start by finding the perfect green dress for her just like the one Vivienne is wearing just as soon as I can. I'm putting you on notice that she is *my* baby. You have Liliana and Zander, so leave Novia's pampering in my hands."

He laughed. "Good luck with that. All my girls need their daddy; especially this one standing right here. And, stop thinking that you have neglected Novia because you have not. She wouldn't be the little lady she is today if you hadn't nurtured her. Now let's put you and me to bed because apparently we are going to some fancy castle tomorrow."

Rosy was already home with little Elizabeth Elaina when we arrived. Elaina was Evan's mother's name. She had been lost to him as had the rest of the family for most of his life, but Rosy insisted on the name. Through the years I had hoped that Evan would confide in Rainey and me the circumstances of the separation, but he hadn't, so we respected his right to keep it to himself. I believed that Rosy knew, but never questioned her on it. We were all the family he had ever known so we were good with that.

We arrived at Avanloch late in the evening. Our new grand baby and Colleen were asleep so we only had a quick peek at them. Our troupe went straight to bed after a quick hello. True to my prediction, Colleen eyes had turned a stunning green just like her mother's. Beth, as she was already being called, favored her father and had dark brown eyes like his.

I planned on spending all day with my granddaughters, but my own daughter had other plans for me. I had checked in on the kids before I went downstairs the next morning. Novia was the only one awake. I helped her get dressed and took her with me. She had Vivienne with her. Rainey had gone somewhere with Johnny so there was just Amma, Evan and me as Rosy was feeding Beth. Evan asked Novia what she was holding in her arms so tightly. She showed him.

"Is that Vivienne? I remember her very well. It was nice of you to bring her to visit us."

I explained that Novia called her V and thought that this might be her castle so I supposed that I had better give her the tour. Evan said I would do no such thing as that was his job. He took her little hand and away they went down the hall. He winked at us as they left and said that he'd been missing the little French girl. I reminded him that he had his own daughters now. He said that a man could never have too many girls. I told him he sounded just like Rainey.

We all cried buckets of tears when we left three weeks later. I promised we'd be back soon. I was leaving them and Avanloch once more, but someday I would return never to leave again.

My father passed away in November of 1990. He was 91. We had a nice quiet ceremony for him at the family home in Arizona. The children needed to get back to school so Rainey and Jack left a few days later. Sissy and I spent a week with Mom and Addy and her family. We thought Mom might want to come back to Bridge Falls with us for a while, but she didn't, but did promise to visit in the spring. She even hinted that she may go to England one day to visit her sister. I was pretty sure that would never happen.

The years just seemed to speed by. There was always something going on with the kids. In 1993, Tanny was fifteen and in grade ten, Lili was eleven and the twins were nine. They were all involved in 4-H one way or the other, except for Novia. She did take swimming lessons, but had no interest in any other sport or 4-H. She preferred to stay at home and read. She was always writing in her notebooks. Quite often she would opt to stay with Rainey's Mom and Dad instead of going to Bridge with us for an outing even when we spent the night at the Palace. I was pretty much on my own with the kids when haying season arrived every year.

Although I was busy catering to the kids and their life, I felt as if I had none of my own. If Rainey wasn't working on the farm he was in the basement working on something. He'd completed the last room which was the rec room and had then built a little snug where he had set up his desks. Yes, he was back doing architectural work for other people. I was feeling like a widow again. We weren't going on dates anymore and half the time we weren't even sleeping in the same room. He'd still be working when I'd be ready for bed. Is this what a middle aged marriage crisis looked like? We'd only been together for twelve years, so how could it be middle-aged? Where had all the magic gone? Maybe it was just me. I hadn't been home to Avanloch in four years. There was a yearning in me to go, but I wanted to go alone and I just didn't see how I could do that.

It was an overcast day in late May when Rainey came in and said he had to go into Bridge to pick up some parts for one of the tractors and did I want to go for a ride. He hadn't asked me to do anything or go anywhere with him in months, so of course I said yes. Maybe I would even tell him how I had been feeling. I had kept quiet because I was pretty sure that he would say that I was just being silly, that of course he loved me, and that nothing was wrong.

We were about halfway to Bridge when I asked him if he had to get right back because his dad was waiting for the parts.

"Not necessarily; do you have something in mind?"

"I thought we might go for lunch. You're not too dirty."

He laughed. "I guess I should have changed. Is it hot in here?" He asked waving his hand in front of his face. He opened the window and said something that I couldn't understand.

The car suddenly lurched to the left. I yelled at him. He was slumped back in his seat. I grabbed the steering wheel and kicked his foot off the gas pedal as the car went careening into a ditch on the opposite side of the road. It had barely come to a halt before I had jumped on Rainey and brought both my fists down on his chest as hard as I could.

His eyes opened wide. "Jesus Christ Vienna! Why'd you do that? Are you trying to kill me?"

I couldn't talk. I kept looking at him making sure he was breathing. Someone was yelling. I managed to get the door open and climb out keeping my eyes on him. He undid his seatbelt and was starting to move.

"Don't you dare move!" I ordered. "You just had a heart attack!"

"What are you talking about?"

A young couple ran down the bank asking if we needed help. I told them to flag down a transport trick and call 911. They had a satellite phone so I asked to use it after they made the call. He picked it up on the second ring.

"I need you Jack. I'm at mile 14 on the Hill."

The young man was talking to Rainey and telling him to remain still until the ambulance arrived because he'd had a heart attack. He denied that he had, but something was wrong with me. I assured him that I was good right before I had an attack of vertigo. The young lady talked me into siting down. Jack found me there with my head between my legs. I managed to tell him what had happened and to look after Rainey. The ambulance arrived a few minutes later. Rainey was still refusing to admit that anything had happened to him and was refusing to go to the hospital. He did not win that argument. He was very upset with me, so I thought it best to ride with Jack into town. Sissy came and sat with us and agreed with Jack that I need to be checked out also.

There was nothing wrong with me except a small increase in blood pressure which was the exact opposite of Rainey's. He did not have a heart attack according to the electrocardiogram. He'd had a syncopal episode due to a sudden temporary drop in blood pressure. He had no memory of feeling warm and disoriented before he'd blacked out. Apparently, he would have snapped out of it momentarily. I needn't have pounded on his chest, but my instincts to do so were commended. He did not admit to having any pain beforehand, and he said that he definitely wasn't overworked or stressed. The doctor wanted him to spend the night in the hospital for observation. That met with great resistance. I asked to have a few minutes alone with my husband before they admitted him.

"I know you are in denial, and I understand that because I have been in denial myself for a very long time. I no longer have the fairy-tale marriage that I used to, but I have put up with your workaholic behaviors and neglect again because I love you, and in my heart I have hoped it would come to pass. Obviously, I did not win, and we will see what the next step will be when you recover because I am not happy living this way. You are going to spend a couple of days in the hospital whether you like it or not. I am sorry I bruised your ribs, but I would do it again in a heartbeat. I'm going home now."

"Don't go Vienna. You know I love you, and I am sorry if you have been feeling neglected, but I've been feeling that way myself. I honestly thought you wanted me to keep my distance. I suppose I let my ego get in the way. Tell me what I can do to fix us."

"You can figure it out for yourself, or not. A woman needs more than a peck on the cheek and a quick "I love you" before she heads off to bed alone, but if that is all you have to offer, and all the promises you made were just temporary, then that's the way it is. You should know by now that I need more, but if I made you feel unloved then shame on me. Again, I am sorry for what I did. Have a good rest. And, oh yeah, I never did like that car anyway so it can stay in the ditch."

I gave him the quick peck, said I love you, and left. He called for me to come back, but I kept going. I wasn't proud of myself for blaming him for the state of our marriage while he was hurting, but I had, so there. I wasn't home for very long before a taxi drove into the yard. I cursed and went out to help my husband into the house.

I settled him into our downstairs bedroom and gave him a glass of water. I told him to drink all of it because it was important for him to stay hydrated.

"I told you not to leave me didn't I?" He said.

"I had to get home before the kids did. I thought you'd have the sense to obey the doctors."

"Balderdash; you didn't play fair and you know it! Blaming me for the lull in our marriage while I was down was very indelicate of you my lady. When was the last time you went riding with me, or came down to see what I was up to in the basement? When was the last time you joined me in the shower, or even sat on my lap? Did you ever think that maybe I felt unloved? We've had our ups and downs before, but we always talk it out and admit how we went wrong. Do you know how afraid I am that one of these times it's not going to be repairable? Don't let it be this time Vienna. I'll give you a mile if you give me an inch."

"This marriage *is* fifty/fifty Rainey. I guess I forgot that for a minute."

"Has it only been a minute? I thought maybe it was months. I'm feeling like it was months since we even shared a bed. Am I wrong?"

"It feels like that, but I think it was actually only a few hours ago."

"You mean since you put the car in the ditch, and sat on the bed beside me in the hospital? By the way, thanks for saving my life. Now I get to fight another day for my sweetheart's hand."

"You're welcome, and you don't have to fight."

"Oh I will; you can bet on that. On the other hand, maybe you need a nice quiet vacation away from me?"

"I don't want a vacation away from you, but you need to tell me what you want."

"I want you and me back the way we were before whatever it was that drove us apart. We can't just kiss and make up every time after we have a disagreement. We have to get to the crux of the problem and I am pretty sure that the fault lies firmly in my lap."

"I know you like to win, but you don't get to take all the credit this time. It takes two you know. Now, what can I do for you?"

"I see this as you having two choices; one, you can go upstairs and pack your bags for Scotland, as I am sure that is where you would go, and I would be good with that, or you can climb into bed with me and break the rest of my ribs. I'd be better with that."

"Is there a third option; one where I climb into bed, but don't break any more ribs?"

"Yeah sure, I'll concede."

"You always do."

"Ain't that the truth?"

"I'll concede to that." I held his hand as I slipped next to him on top of the bed. "This is as far as it goes today."

He laughed. "Honey, I can barely move or even breathe with this corset they wrapped me in. I have no idea how you women can wear them."

"As if I have ever worn a corset…I think it needs to be tight, but I can loosen it for you if you like seeing you are at rest."

"I'm good for now. What are we going to tell the kids?"

"The truth of course."

"You mean that their mother tried to kill me?"

"I'll soften it a little."

"I love you Vienna LaFontaine."

"And, I am very glad that you are still alive for me to love Rainey Quinn."

He then told me about his plans to enlarge the sunroom, and did I agree with him that it was time that we put in a swimming pool? I agreed realizing that he was never going to stop building. As soon as the kids arrived home from school I took them in to see their father and together we told them about the accident and how his ribs had been bruised. Novia was trying hard not to cry so I suggested that she get her book and read him one of the stories that she had written.

She climbed onto the bed clutching her book and opened it.

"Is this a picture of your fairy garden?" Rainey asked her.

"Mommy helped me with the camera and put it in my book."

"Does your fairy live in it?"

"I think so, but she never lets me see her. I just hear her."

"What does she say Honey?"

"She just says tee hee. That's how she laughs, and she is very sneaky."

Rainey laughed and asked her if she had a name.

"I know it, but she doesn't like me saying it or telling anyone what it is."

"Okay. I hear you wrote a story about her. Can I hear it?"

"It's not really a story because it happened for real. One day I was out in my garden and I thought that I should put out some gifts for the fairies. I got a container and in the container I put a shiny bracelet, a pair of butterfly earrings and 2 of my chocolates that I had got at Easter. During that week everything was gone except the earrings. The container was gone too."

"Why do you think she didn't take the earrings?"

"Maybe she didn't like them."

"That is probably right. Can I hear more of your stories?"

She kissed Rainey and said he could but it was her turn to set the table so not right now.

The next afternoon he was feeling much better. I helped him get settled in his recliner in the living room, gave him the newspaper and started for the kitchen to get an early start on dinner. Tanny liked to help me with the preparation and cooking, but I thought I'd give her a day off. I looked out the kitchen window and saw Rainey's mother packing grocery bags into the house.

"Oh Patricia Ann, you shouldn't be doing that." I said out loud. Why had I said that; her middle name was not Ann. Oh damn; I went back into the living room.

"Rainey, I have something to tell you. Something happened eight years ago and in light of what we talked about yesterday I think it's time I told you."

"How important can it be if it was that long ago, and why wouldn't you have told me then?"

"It was in the spring when you weren't coming home until dark and were too tired to even talk, so I handled it myself. My conscience has gotten the better of me I guess. This seems like a good time to confess because you won't yell at me because it might hurt you. I will say that I am sorry in advance for taking advantage of your condition."

"When have I ever yelled at you?"

"When I went home to Bridge Falls after the party in Hawthorne and just the other day when I jumped on you and broke your ribs."

"My ribs are only bruised, and I am sorry for yelling at you. I believe I have already apologized for that and the other instance. I understand why you felt you couldn't talk to me back then, but why now, and what exactly have you been keeping from me?"

"You received a letter from a lawyer in Vancouver."

"That sounds ominous. What did he want?"

"He was Jorja's lawyer; she had named you as executer of her will."

"What?"

"You heard me correctly. I still have the letter if you want to see it."

"Christ, are we ever going to be free of her? What could she have that warranted naming me as her executor?"

"Her daughter. She had no properties to speak off, but she had stimulated that upon her death, you would know what to do about Patricia Ann."

Rainey sighed. "Did she say that I was her daughter's father?"

"No; just that you'd know what to do."

"I take it that you answered?"

"I stated that I was your wife and was answering for you. I said that Jorja was a remote acquaintance of yours and that you had no idea why she would have named you as her executor, and you had no idea what was expected of you regarding her daughter. However, since it had been brought to your attention that she was still in foster care, it would be advantageous to her if she was released to the proper authorities for immediate adoption. Hopefully, this will take place immediately as no child deserves to be in foster care. There are many deserving couples waiting to give a child a forever home but for some reason have been denied. If she is not adopted within six months it will be then and only then that I will intercede."

"Why in the world would you say that?"

"Because I want her to have a real home and I didn't want you to come off as being a heartless bastard. She is not responsible for what her mother did, and shouldn't have to pay for it by being passed from home to home as a foster child. She is Liliana's age, so think of her as being in Patricia's place. Anyhow, that's how I handled it. I ended by asking to be informed of any procedures, but my involvement as executor was to remain anonymous. I signed my name and forged your signature and sent it off."

"That was six months ago, so have we heard back?" Rainey asked dubiously.

"Yes; she was adopted by a young couple almost immediately."

"I am assuming that you know their names?"

"I do not. As far as I am concerned the matter is over and done with. Tell me if I should have consulted you."

"I probably would have told you to burn the letter as it did not concern me, so as usual you did the right thing and I thank you for being the voice of reason. You forged my signature eh?"

"I did, but I could have gotten Lili or one of the twins to scribble it. It behoves me as to how neat your printing and handwriting is so delicate and precise on your blueprints, but when it comes to signing anything it is almost inelligible."

He laughed. "I should work on that. Right now I will settle for a kiss and a cup of coffee from the most caring and generous woman in the world."

I obliged him and hoped that Patricia Ann would never come back to haunt me.

1994

A devastating wild fire destroyed Nash's and Ava's home and resort. We received a most distressing call from our daughter the morning of July 10th telling us what had happened. Nash had taken her and the kids to a friend's place in Spring Valley the night before and then had gone back to Akemantack to help fight the fire that was surrounding the little village. He wanted Ava and the kids to come home to us, but she didn't want to leave him alone as he was heartbroken. Rainey convinced her that it was the best thing for her to do as it would free Nash from worrying about them. She wasn't sure that she could secure passage out because of the fires, and she didn't know if passenger planes were even allowed in. Rainey said she didn't have to worry about that as he was coming to get them. He contacted an acquaintance from college who was a pilot for Air North that had a base in Warick, a town three hours away to the west. Luckily, his friend Dwight was available and he was more than happy to be helping an old buddy for such a cause. Rainey was going to make the trip to Warick, but Dwight insisted that he'd meet him at the Bridge Falls airport at seven a.m. the next day and they would take flight from there. The round trip should take approximately 8 to 10 hours depending on protocol at the airport in Spring Valley. He called us back and said that the plans were all set and the weather forecast was for a sunny day. He'd have our daughter and grandchildren home by days end tomorrow.

Ava was an emotional wreck worrying about Nash. He called her everyday but it didn't diminish her anxieties about their future. She believed that his passion for the north and the lodge would have a devastating effect on his mental health. Her solution was they would rebuild just as soon as possible. I asked her if they had ever discussed moving out of Akemantack.

"Never!" She answered surprised that I would even ask such a question.

"I am going to tell you about a conversation I had with your husband before Calla was born. He was contemplating moving you and Sammie to a more urban centre, possibly Bridge Falls, but he feared you would object because he'd be leaving the life he loved behind. So, it was on his mind way back then. Now Sammie and Calla are eleven and nine and their schooling is somewhat of a hazard isn't it? You drive them into Spring Valley every day when weather permits and when winter comes, you home school them. Can you see yourself doing this for another ten years? And, what about their social life, and yours for the matter?"

"I will do whatever I have to. Nash will want to rebuild and I will be with him all the way."

She did not want to discuss the matter anymore so I backed out. She was missing her husband, and was thinking about nothing but his well-being both physically and mentally. Every morning she would make plans to go into Bridge and spruce up the Palace so it would be ready when Nash arrived, but that plan fell through every day and she would end up with her dad and grandfather in the hay field or in the workshop. It was a blessed relief when Nash made it home two weeks later. Our plans for the kids to stay with us while they had a week to themselves in Bridge did not work out as they still came up to the ranch every day. Nash was not used to being cooped up indoors and there was always something to do here so until he found a job he said we'd have to put up with him. He had no intention of rebuilding up north.

Rainey's Mom and Dad would join us for dinner three or four times a week. Patsy and Paul were both in their late sixties and were in good health, but unbeknownst to us they had been planning to retire from the ranch. They had become quite involved in the senior citizen association in Bridge and had been contemplating moving so they wouldn't have to be on the road so much. Apparently, Patsy was having trouble climbing the stairs at the ranch house and Paul's eyesight was failing. Rainey knew that they had both slowed down, but the news of their plans caught him completely by surprise one evening at the dinner table.

"This life was not the one that you chose Son, yet here you are." Paul said. "It has been our greatest pleasure to have you and Vienna and the kids here with us for the last ten years. Leaving you alone to manage the ranch has not been an easy decision and we had pretty much decided that we couldn't do it, and then Ava and Nash arrive on the scene."

Paul turned his attention to them. "Patsy and I have a proposition for you kids. Feel free to refuse, but we hope you will give it some consideration. A senior's housing development isn't quite up our alley as of yet, but there is this house we love in town and you are here every day to help Rainey with the chores, so we are wondering if you'd be interested in trading houses…"

Ava was on her feet and hugging her grandparents. "I love your house and the farm and I'm pretty sure that this is where Nash wants to be… am I right Nash?"

Our son-in-law was grinning from ear to ear. "Yeah, you are Honey. It's a sweet deal, but I'm not sure that your Dad would like us as partners, or if your Mom would be happy with us living right next door, and then there's Sammie and Calla… how do you think they would like living so close to their cousins?"

"I see where there could be problems because the kids aren't used to living in the sticks, and Sammie and Zander don't get along, and Lili and Novia don't do anything with Calla, and we all know that Ava and I don't see eye to eye, and just because Rainey says he doesn't know how he managed before Nash came…yeah, it probably won't work out." I pretended to be doubtful.

"And, what about you Dad; what do you think?" Ava asked trying not to laugh.

"Oh me; do I get a say? Mom, Dad, are you sure this is what you want?"

"It is Rainey. Paul and I have been contemplating it for some time now but didn't know how to approach the subject with you, and then like I said, Nash and Ava arrive and we've come up with this plan. It seems to be an answer for us if it is to you and them."

"I'd be trading my parents living next door for my daughter and son-in-law and grandkids, and it seems to be what you want, so yeah, I'm on board. Now, I'll let you in on a little secret. Vienna and I were wondering what we could do to entice Nash and Ava to stay on here, and that maybe a new house would do the trick…"

That was news to me, but I went along with it. The next weeks were spent moving all into their new homes. It was a dream come true for me.

One day in November of 1995 Zander came home from school complaining of a sore throat and fatigue. After two days in bed and having no desire to get up or even eat we loaded him into the car and drove him to the hospital. He was diagnosed with mononucleosis. Luckily, none of the other kids contracted it though they had been in close contact with him. Rainey wanted to take full control of Zander's care because he was worried that I would come down with it because I had a compromised immune system. That was not a point of contention as I had been in contact with him during the incubation period. If his symptoms worsened he would need to be put on a corticosteroid, so we monitored him night and day, one of us sleeping in his room every night. He was one sick boy. Tylenol seemed to help with his body aches and warm herbal teas and honey soothed his sore throat. I asked Rosalyn to ask Meggie to make one of her special concoctions and send it special delivery. The throat ease tea and an aromatic balm arrived in the middle of December. Zander said the tea tasted like horse manure, but the ointment felt good and eased his muscle stiffness somewhat. I agreed with him regarding the taste of the tea. He was able to make it downstairs with Rainey's and Sammie's help for a couple of hours on Christmas Day. We presented him with a Shepherd/Collie cross two month old puppy. Sammie and Novia had been taking turns sleeping in Zander's room on the weekends for some time now, so they were in charge of caring for Rascal, the new addition. Those two kids and that puppy were instrumental in his recovery. Spring came and with it a renewed energy, but he was not well enough to return to school. He had no desire to even try to resume his studies as his concentration level was nil. By summer he was looking forward to starting grade six over again. He said that the one drawback of the whole episode was that Sammie and Novia would graduate one year before him. He had laughed when I said that with diligence he had six years to catch up. He said that he didn't even like school so that if he even made it to grade twelve it would be somewhat of a miracle.

1996, 1997.

Tanny graduated and applied to The Culinary School of British Columbia in Vancouver. She was accepted and her enrollment was to begin in February 1997. It was a one year course. She spent the summer and fall working in Bridge as a cook's assistant in a family restaurant. We'd bought her a car for graduation so she had transportation back and forth from Hawthorne, but spent her working days and nights with Paul and Patsy at the Palace. Rainey had his son Morgan find an apartment for her. The one he found was walking distance to the school and only two miles from him and his fiancé. They had been engaged for three years, but had no plans to marry. He worked for the city of Vancouver as an engineer. He was 30 years old. Mason was 29 and still lived in the house that Rainey had bought when he was newly married to Louise in the sixties. Mason had followed in his father's footsteps and was an architect in Rainey's firm, Quinn and Associates. He had no romantic interests. Rainey had a nice visit with them when he followed Tanny down to help get her settled.

Lili was 15 when Tanny went off to Vancouver. She was back to throwing tantrums and threatened to run away at least three times a week. Of course she was missing her sister, but her attitude upset the rest of us and was not acceptable. After four months of putting up with her threats I marched upstairs right behind her one day, pulled a suitcase out of the hall closet, set it on her bed and said. "You bring me the clothes and I'll pack them for you. Then I'll drive you to the bus station and buy you a one-way ticket wherever you want to go. I probably can get you four or five hundred dollars from your father's safe, but then you'll be on your own."

She started crying saying that I didn't love her and that Novia was my favorite, but her daddy would look after her no matter what. I asked her if we were packing or what. Rainey walked in and asked if he could help us. I explained what was happening. He said he'd see how much he had in the safe. She never threatened us again. I got my first grey hairs that year.

1998- 2001

Tanny graduated from culinary school. She had enrolled in a student exchange program and accepted a position in a restaurant in Sete, France. Of course that did not sit well with Lili, but Tanny told her that if things went well for her in France Lili could come and visit her there, but first she had to finish school.

That is exactly what happened. Tanny worked as an apprentice chef for a year and a half and then was named top chef. Lili's diploma wasn't even dry before she was on the plane to France.

So, we lost Lili to France in 2000, and in September 2001, Novia was off to the University of British Columbia, Rainey's old Alma matter. Sammie and she had left together. They said they would try dorm living, but if they didn't like it then we could find them housing. I knew Sammie would manage, but I worried about Novia fitting in. Zander was still struggling in school. If it wasn't for wood-working classes, he would have dropped out.

In 2002, our neighbor Claus Campion died and his daughter Izzy arrived.

Part 3

Hiraeth

n. (Welsh) A spiritual longing for a home which maybe never was. Nostalgia for ancient places to which we cannot return. It is the echo of the lost places of our soul's past and our grief for them. It is in the wind, and the rocks, and the waves. It is nowhere and it is everywhere.

CHAPTER 1

AVANLOCH IS CALLING

June 14th 2003

I put the final touches on the chocolate devil's food cake by showering it with walnuts and placing it in the cooler in the pantry. I wouldn't be here for Rainey's sixty third birthday which would be one month from today. I'd had a little guilty twinge earlier in the day and decided to make him one of his favorite cakes. He had modeled the pantry after the one at the Palace. It was more than ample, but it didn't have the homey touch to it yet. Never once had I ever told him that I didn't like this house that he had built, or living here in Hawthorne, just like I never told him that I hadn't even liked living at the Palace in Bridge. I took the steaks out and left them on the counter to unthaw and opened the back porch screen door.

"Come on you two; Izzy will be here soon." I called to Shasta and Miss Mary the 3rd. Rainey had surprised me with a little ball of white and black fluff on Valentine's Day five years ago. She was the rut of the litter and nobody seemed to want her. He was sure that I would, and he was right. There hadn't been a puppy in our house since the one we had got for Zander when he was sick. That was eight years ago, so this Corgi/ Collie cross was most welcomed. I had named her Shasta. Miss Mary the 3rd was an offspring from the original cat Miss Mary that had come to live with us at the Palace so many years ago. She had never had kittens of her own, but took to mothering Shasta. The two were inseparable except for the early morning hours when Shasta would tag along with Rainey and Rascal to romp and play with the other farm dogs while he did chores. I added fresh ice cubes to the pitcher of iced tea, grabbed two glasses and went out to wait for Izzy on the front veranda. Miss Mary curled up on her chair next to me and Shasta sat patiently wagging her tail. As soon as Izzy would round the corner she would ring the bell on her bike and I'd give the command to Shasta that she could go. She'd run to the end of the fence and race along with Izzy until they reached the gate, receive her treat and settle in back at my feet.

Izzy had made her entrance into my life one year ago. I was met by a bright yellow sports car entering the driveway as I was coming back from a visit with Ava. The driver got out and asked me if I was Rainey's wife or daughter. How old did she think he was anyhow? I'd had two unpleasant inquiries from strangers about my husband's whereabouts before, so I was leery of another. Most recent was my meeting with Pamela Clarke. I was washing my hands at the kitchen sink shorty after we had moved into the house. I looked out the window and saw her as she was getting out of her car showing her long legs off to my husband who was greeting her. Her skirt was hiked up to her yahoo. I knew who she was immediately. I laughed as I saw my reflection in the window. I was a little dishevelled as I had just come in from digging and planting in the garden. I ran my grubby hands through my hair letting it loose from its pony tail. Blue jeans and a smock and dirty feet…yup, this is what a real woman looks like. I sat down with a cup of coffee and waited for Rainey to bring her in. The back door opened. Shasta ran in and sat at my feet expecting a pat and a treat.

"Sorry Honey; she got away before I could grab her and wipe her feet."

"I don't think she could get me any dirtier. Who is your friend, and why did you bring her in the back door?"

"I'm kind of greasy. Anyhow, this is Pamela Clarke, our notary. She has a few things for you to sign."

"Hello; it's nice to finally meet you." I held out my hand. "Sorry, I'm a little earthy."

"Yes," she said giving my fingers a quick pass, "I was beginning to wonder also. Rainey says you are a master gardener."

"As usual his flattering description is inaccurate, but he's my husband, so he is required to say nice things about me. Can I warm up a cup of coffee for you, or would you prefer cold tea?"

"Thank-you, but no, I won't take up anymore of your time. If you can just sign and initial a few things for me, I'll be out of your way."

I took the pen from her. "Normally, I would read the documents through, but seeing Rain has already signed I see no reason to. You haven't disinherited me or anything, have you Honey?"

"Very funny." He answered.

He walked her to her car, returned and said he was going back to work. "Thanks for not impaling her too severely on your barbed tongue."

"You're welcome, but don't bring her into my house ever again."

"I won't and if I have reason to meet up with her again I'll make sure it's in some back alley."

"Thank-you as that is where all gutter cats belong."

He put a cup of coffee in the microwave and stood watching the clock tick by. "Oh, by the way, she can't make it to our house warming party."

"You had the nerve to invite her?"

"No, Ava did, but I uninvited her."

"You know you shouldn't stand in front of the microwave." I stated and then for some unknown reason I started laughing.

He came over and kissed me on the neck. "Sometimes I just want to wring this neck of yours, but thankfully for both of us I'd rather kiss it. Is date night still on?"

"It is. This was fun; when do you want to do it again?"

"I guess when I look at, or talk to another woman."

At that time I did not know that Izzy would be that woman, or that I'd have no qualms regarding her friendship with my husband.

For some reason I had thought that she was ten or so years younger than Rainey, but at first sight I realized that she was probably younger than me. Rainey hadn't seen her since she was a teenager because according to him he was always away when she'd come to visit her dad. He hadn't been the one who contacted her after her father had died, but he had given the lawyer his phone number with instructions for her to contact him as he had the keys to her father's house. She didn't call; she just showed up. She told me who she was and that Rainey was supposed to have keys for her.

I told her that I was Vienna, Rainey's wife as I eyed her up. She was a few inches taller than me. She was trim, lightly tanned and sported a mass of light brown curls, and a freckled face. She was cutely attractive.

"You don't look much older than you did forty years ago." She said smiling.

"I beg your pardon…"

"I don't guess you don't remember me as you only had eyes for my boyfriend."

Rainey had never told me that he'd had a romantic relationship for her so I was taken aback.

She laughed. "Oh, it's not what you're thinking. It was only wishful thinking on my part. To him I was just the pesky little girl who lived up the road. I was six years younger than him so by the time I was a teenager he was already in college, and in love with you. Whoever thought that he'd be with the same girl forty some years later? You must be some gal Vienna."

"You don't know our story do you?"

"If it's a juicy one I am all ears."

"Are you anxious to get to the farm, or do you have a few hours?"

"I have all the time in the world."

I took her arm. "Let's go have a cup of tea then. But first you have to tell me how we met as I do not remember ever seeing you before."

"I was barely sixteen and leaving home. It was at a party at Jimmy Douglas's home. Tell me; is he married, and how about Yates and Zane?"

"Zane moved to the coast many years ago, Jimmy married June Carr, and Yates is divorced and here when he's not working up north. They are very much a part of our lives."

Rainey found us chatting and laughing at the kitchen table when he came in for lunch. He asked who my friend was. Izzy scolded him.

"Rainey Quinn, do you not remember the annoying freckled-faced girl who lived up the lane?"

"I'll be a monkey's uncle! I never expected that you would actually show up. Get over here if you don't mind a hug from an old man."

It was a long hug, but I didn't mind. There was no stirring of my jealous gene.

"I see you have met my wife." He said giving me a quick peck on my cheek before sitting down. "What are you drinking?"

"Tea." Izzy answered winking.

Rainey picked up my cup and took a whiff of it. "Yeah, it's her brand of tea all right."

"I guess I had better get you something to eat." I said.

"I could use a glass of that tea and last night's chicken will do."

"It's pretty strong tea; don't you have to go back to work?"

"I think I'll take the rest of the day off and party with you girls, what do you say?"

A few hours later that day Rainey left with her to reacquaint her with her old home. He was surprised when I declined to go with them, and asked me when he got home why I had let him go off alone with a strange woman. My answer had been that I liked her and that I trusted him.

"Suppose if she turns out to be the one woman I could take a romantic interest in, where would your trust be then?" He'd asked with a twinkle in his eye.

"Don't be silly; she's not your kind. Now set the table because I have invited Jimmy and Yates to dinner. I didn't tell them Izzy was here so it'll be a surprise."

"She really hadn't run in our circles you know, but her dad and their dads had been friends so it was a neighborly thing to invite them. The dining room table I'm thinking."

"Then you'd be wrong as this is not a formal dinner. Use the yellow and blue dishes please."

"What constitutes a formal dinner and how come we never get to eat in the dining room? And just out or curiosity, how many sets of dishes do you have?"

"We are not at Avanloch where snobbish people come to check out the China, and I have fewer dishes than you have sets of tools, so a moot point."

Izzy was just what the doctor ordered. She was carefree, jovial and she made me laugh I never batted an eyelash when she flirted openly with my husband. He took it all good naturedly, but wondered where my jealous streak had gone. I had been afraid that she'd put the farm up for sale and move back to Mexico where she managed a hotel in Cancun. Two days after Claus's funeral she did return to Cancun, gave her two week resignation notice, packed up her belongings and returned to Hawthorne to take up ranching. By the end of summer we knew everything there was to know about each other. Hardly a day went by when we didn't talk or visit. She was very independent and learned the lay of the land quickly with Nash's and Rainey's help. Yates popped in whenever he was home. I hoped their friendship would develop into more someday. That was a year ago, and I was no longer content.

I poured the iced tea. Izzy took two cigarettes out of the package, lit one, and passed it to me.

"What's wrong Miss V; you seem despondent."

"Rosalyn called yesterday after you left."

"Is everything all right back at the castle?"

"She wants me to come over."

"So, are you going? What does Rain say?"

"I'm thinking about going, but I don't see how I can leave him alone because he can't go with me because of haying."

"He'll hardly be alone. Zander will be here and Ava and Nash and kids are just down the hill, and I'll see that he wants for nothing." She said grinning.

"Yeah, that's what I'm afraid of." I laughed half-heartedly. "Anyway, I haven't decided one way or the other, so I'm not ready to approach the subject with him yet."

"Oh, I think you've decided already, but are just afraid of how he'll react."

"There are strange things happening at the castle and Rosy needs me. I put all of it in motion many years ago, so whatever is going on, I need to be there for my daughter. I'll call Novia tomorrow and see if she wants to go. Oh, that's silly; of course she will. Maybe Nash and Ava will allow Calla to come also. But, I'm not ready to discuss it with Rainey. He's been too bummed out with the rain, but once the fields dry out, he'll be in a better mood."

"I have never seen him in a bad mood, so I don't even know what you are talking about. He's the consummate of what every man should be, and the man that every woman dreams about."

"You can't have my husband." I stated.

"I love him, but I love you more. There is not another woman on planet earth that could ever take your place with him. She would be completely off her rocker if she even thought she could."

"Jorja thought she could."

"Case in point. If any such vermin come calling you can count on me to see them off the property. You know he can deny you nothing and he will understand your need to go, so quit stressing and have the conversation with him today."

"There is another reason I want to go, but I can never tell him."

"What is it?"

"Sometimes I hate it here. I hate the house and I hate my boring life."

"You have the love of a devoted man and a life that every woman dreams about, so I don't understand what more you could possibly want."

"I don't know myself."

"Have you told Rainey?"

"He can never know."

"I thought you told him everything?"

"Would you want the man you love that you hated everything that you pretended to love?"

"That wouldn't include him would it?"

"You know I love him more than life itself and that he is my whole world, so why would you even ask such a silly question?"

"I just want you to think about what you have said and if you are so unhappy living here then you tell him before it becomes a problem you can't fix. Unhappiness breeds resentment."

"I am not that unhappy and maybe hate is too strong a word. A trip to Scotland without him will put me in a better state of mind. I will miss him terribly and when I get home I will appreciate him and everything I have a little bit more."

"Then don't put discussing it with him off for another minute. Promise me you'll do it today." She said as she got up to leave. She kissed my cheek and said. "Good luck."

I smiled, but I didn't promise.

CHAPTER 2

RAINEY

June 18th 2003

Rosy had sent the plane for Vienna and the girls. Novia and Calla had already boarded and were waving out the window two rows back of the cockpit. I shook hands with the two new pilots wishing that Gin hadn't retired. Rosy had guaranteed me that Edward and Peter were first-rate and that she and Evan, Ash and Gray had flown with them dozens of times over the past two years. I was apprehensive.

Vienna and I stood on the tarmac looking at each other. She was smiling; I wasn't. For six days I had been pleading with her to postpone her trip to Scotland until I could go with her. It was futile as her mind was already made up. I had been caught completely off- guard when she had announced that she was going to Scotland.

If the weather had of been in our favor we would have already been half-way through the first haying; but it wasn't. The rains had begun in early June, and all we could do was sit and wait for dry weather. Finally the skies cleared, and the fields dried. It was Wednesday, June 12, and Nash and I would be up bright and early to tackle the first of seven fields tomorrow. Our team of workers including Zander and Samie would be arriving on the weekend. Nash and I made one final check of all the equipment and satisfied that we were set to go called it a day around 5 P.M. The dogs met me and followed me into the house as usual. I shed my coveralls and work boots at the back porch as usual. I called out to Vienna that I was home as usual. She didn't answer. The kitchen was dark. There was nothing cooking on the stove. I opened the refrigerator thinking that we must be going to have cold cuts for dinner. Nope. The dogs passed me and went in search of their mistress. I followed them and found my wife sitting in the living room in the rocking chair noticing that she was wearing a dress I hadn't seen before. I bent down to kiss her remarking that she looked pretty. I asked her if I smelt smoke. She didn't answer me. Figuring that something was wrong I asked her if she was feeling all right. She said she was but had I forgot that we were having dinner with Jimmy and Ruth. I was pretty sure they weren't coming here as the table wasn't set and there was nothing cooking, and we had just been at their house three nights ago.

"I didn't realize we had been invited back so soon." I said questioningly.

"What do you mean so soon?" She asked.

"We were just there three nights ago Hon."

"What…isn't it Sunday?"

"No, it's Wednesday."

She put her hand up to her mouth. "Oh no, I've done it again! I've had so much on my mind what with getting Zander's room ready, baking for the haying crew, and packing…I'm sorry Rain, I just lost track of time. Oh dear, there is no supper!"

"It's okay Babe; how about we go into Bridge for dinner? Maybe we can even catch a movie; what do you say, and what are you packing up now?"

She got up and told me that I had better get myself into the shower, and she would go upstairs and finish packing seeing she was so far behind. I asked her again what she was packing.

She turned and smiled at me at the bottom of the stairs. "Clothes of course! I don't have much left at the castle you know. Have you forgotten? You talk about me having a bad memory." She laughed and ran up the stairs.

I showered quickly wondering if I was losing my mind because why would I consent to a trip when haying season was just beginning. I found Vienna sitting in Novia's room leafing through an old photograph album. There was not a suitcase in sight. I sat down and reminisced with her for a while before she suggested that I wear the new pale blue shirt she had bought for me.

I asked her if it was in our upstairs bedroom or downstairs one. She said it was next door. Almost timidly I told her that a trip to visit Rosy was out of the question right now. Her answer was not what I expected at all.

"I know that silly old goose. I would never ask you to abandon Nash during haying season. I won't be alone as Calla and Novia are coming with me."

"You're going without me?" I asked dazed.

She came over and kissed me. "I love you too, and I'm going to miss you something terrible, but it's just for the summer, so stop frowning."

"Summer…the whole summer?" I stammered.

"Rainey Quinn, why are you acting as if this is the first time you are hearing this?"

"Because it is; this is all news to me."

"Rainey, I would never plan a holiday without discussing it with you. You've been so busy; I think you have just forgotten."

"My wife leaving me for the whole summer and planning the trip with our daughter and granddaughter is not something I would forget. One of us is losing their mind, and…"

"Of course it's me," She exclaimed interrupting me, "because I have lost my mind before so it must be happening again!"

"I'm sorry, that's not what I meant at all. Can we talk sensibly about this?"

"We can, on the drive to Bridge…that is, if you still want to take me out."

"I do. I'll go and put a shirt on."

I knew damn well she had not told me of her trip. I wouldn't push her too much until after I talked to Ava. Surely Ava would know because Calla was supposedly going too.

I couldn't find the shirt she had asked me to wear. I was buttoning up my usual white one when she walked in. She asked me if I didn't like the new one. I told her I couldn't find it. She walked over to the bathroom door and took the hangar off the hook which held the shirt. She proceeded to unbutton the white one and helped me on with the blue one not saying a word.

She stood back admiring me. "There, there's my handsome husband. What do you think?"

"It's blue". I answered.

She laughed. She took my hand and we walked down the stairs together, put the dogs out, and climbed into her new Chrysler. She hardly ever drove, but I had bought it for her anyway. She started talking immediately.

"You are right Rainey; I never told you I was going to Scotland. Rosy called me several weeks ago, and I decided to go then. It seems that in her spare time, which she relayed to me that she seems to have a lot of this past year, has got her digging deeper into Avaleena's diary."

"Why, after all this time would she be doing that?"

"Just as I said; she had the time. If you remember correctly, there were still a few unanswered questions regarding Avaleena's and Robert Bruce's future, and then there was Gracie Darling and Quinn. I pretty much stopped translating the diary after Corinthia had given birth and made her get away, and I discovered that her last name was Novia. There were still many pages to be deciphered, but I never got to them, but Rosy has made some headway. Do you want to hear?"

"It is not much of an interest to me as I thought we left that all behind when we left Scotland, but if it gives me an insight as to why you are going then yes, I'll listen."

"Do you remember me telling you that Johnny's uncle had died, the one he lived with outside of the village? Anyhow, he had a will, and everything went to Johnny including chronicles of the O'Shea family that date back to the eleven hundreds. Do you remember me mentioning that Quinn's uncle or great uncle was a Templar Knight?"

"I do not."

"Well, Avaleena mentioned them in her diary. She said that because Quinn had connections to that fearless warrior sect, they would hide and protect him and Gracie Darling from Stewart."

"Correct me if I am wrong, but didn't all that take place somewhere in the 1850's? As far as I remember the Templars were all annihilated by one means or the other and wiped off the face of the earth in the thirteen hundreds, so those numbers don't jive."

"You are right, they don't. According to Avaleena's diary Stewart's mistress gave birth to Robert Bruce and Vienne in 1851 or 1852, and the Knights were supposedly all arrested and terminated on Friday the thirteenth, 1307. But, do you really think that none escaped? They were 30,000 strong…anyway, according to the O'Shea chronicles, there is evidence that some escaped to Ireland, and there had always been a sect in Scotland. I think you know that, and maybe one came right here to Domne. Now, another thing, which I also think I might have missed in Avaleena's diary, is that Domne was spelled DOMME, and it was so named because that is the name of the prison where the Knights were executed…Domme, France. So, that suggests that maybe an escapee came to the Village we know as Domne or Doome, and named it Domme or New Domme, and started setting up housekeeping."

Vienna seemed very sure of herself, but of course I was sceptic. Hell, I was an out and out agnostic. How did we get on this ridiculous subject anyhow? Oh yeah, it somehow tied into why my beautiful wife was going to Scotland without me.

"So you are caught up in this fallacy along with Rosy, and you think that by going to Scotland…well, Avanloch, you can aid her in deciphering the O'Shea chronicles that mention the Templars… is that it Vienna? Are you bored here on the ranch and think you will find some excitement and purpose back there?"

"I won't lie to you; I am somewhat bored. The story does intrigue me and especially the fact that Rosy has come across the name "Quinn" and Gracie Darling in Johnny's uncle's records. Doesn't that interest you? And, maybe I just want to visit my family."

"I can't say that it does interest me, but none of this explains why it took you so long to tell me of your plans?"

"I knew you would react just as you have, so I was postponing it for as long as I could. I'm sorry; I should have trusted that you'd be okay with it."

"Well, I am not okay with it, but it's what you want and I have never been able to deny you anything, so go if you must. I'll try and get along without you, but I won't be happy."

"Thank-you Darling; I'll miss you dreadfully. Just in case something unearthly happens you know my wishes for my remains right?"

"Don't talk like that Vienna!"

"Things happen; do you remember or not?"

"Yes, cremated and put to rest for eternity in the McAllister crypt." I answered dismally.

She called me the minute the plane touched down and informed me that all was well and that I needn't go shopping for an urn just yet. I told her to thank the pilots for me. She said she missed me already. For almost two weeks the phone would ring at eight p.m. and she'd be on the other end, and I would hear the same thing. She, Rosy and Amma were having fun with the girls and nothing very interesting was happening. She loved and missed me and we'd talk tomorrow.

One evening I thought I'd surprise her and call her before she called me. It was seven P.M. July 4th. I didn't get through on her cell so I dialed the house phone. Evan answered and I got a whole new perspective from him.

He greeted me with a question. "Hey Rain; you lonesome yet?"

"You know it Brother. I haven't heard from Vienna yet so thought I'd beat her to the punch."

He laughed "Well, you're an hour too soon Buddy."

"Oh, is she on a shopping trip or out riding?"

"You know she doesn't get up before noon don't you?"

"Sure, sure; now tell me something I'll believe."

"Has she ever called you before eight p.m. your time before?"

"No, but I'm usually still haying or having supper, so we are synchronised to that time."

"I take it then that she hasn't told you about hers and the other gal's nightly routine?"

"I'm almost afraid to ask. Please tell me that they aren't up to some sort of mischief with the games they are playing like that witch board again. I can't see Mary McDuff allowing it."

"I wish it was as simple as the Ouija. Mary had her eighty eighth birthday last week and has no idea what the girls think they can accomplish by keeping vigil until the wee hours every night. Amma hasn't gone home since the break-in at the Manor, and my own wife hasn't slept in the same bed as me since it all began."

"I think you had better quit beating around the bush and tell me what's going on, and that Novia and Calla aren't involved?'

"Wish I could, but I can't. Colleen and Beth are caught up in it all too. It started before Vienna arrived though, and to be perfectly honest Rain, I think Rose begged her mother to come because she knew she was way over her head."

"Over her head in what Evan?"

"In what she thinks she has discovered in Johnny's uncle's papers; at least that was how it started. Not just her; but Amma too. They think they have uncovered evidence of the O'Shea's involvement with Avaleena, and the subsequent disappearance of her man servant Quinn and Gracie Darling."

"Yes, Vienna did mention something of the like, but I don't see how that has anything to do with the here and now. You mentioned a break-in at Brackenshire Manor; what was taken?"

"Nothing that can be accounted for as yet, but Amma and Rose are certain that the intruder had to be looking for something of importance in Uncle Walt's papers. They had spent weeks deciphering and laying everything out in chronological order in the library and walked in one morning a few weeks ago to find everything strewn around, drawers dumped and books tossed from the shelves. They felt a presence and didn't stick around to find out what it was. Johnny and I investigated and concluded that it was just a mischief maker, but of course the girls were having none of that. They have moved everything up here into our library. Where the idea came from that they were in danger by a force unseen has us stumped, but Amma refuses to go home."

"So, they are not buying the idea that a prankster is the culprit and believe that an unknown force is at work?"

"Honestly, I have no idea what they were thinking, but then the elevator fiasco happened and a whole new suspicion took over. Now they feel if they don't keep vigil all night they'll miss something, or that the unknown something will surprise them."

"It sounds like mass hysteria to me. Are they keeping vigil with baseball bats and vials of protection that Meggie Magan concocted for them?"

"Bats for sure, but no vials that I know of. I don't think Vienna has even seen Meggie yet."

"Well, that's odd. What is Johnny's take on it all?"

"We both thought that Rose and Amma were making a mountain out of a molehill with the break-in so we let them have their fun, but now with the elevator thing, its' gone way beyond fun. It is so uncharacteristic of the both of them and our joshing with them has met with stern disapproval and evasion."

"I think you had better take me back to the elevator thing and what transpired after the workers walked off the job. All I know is what Vienna told me, and when you hear something third or fourth hand, the truth loses some of its' validity. It sounds like all this paranoia began with Johnny's reclusive uncle's passing didn't it? I never met the man, but remember Johnny saying that he barely stepped out of the house, and that the devil would have to be chasing him before he ever set foot in Avanloch again. I guessed that he'd had an unpleasant visit to the castle previously, and that wouldn't surprise me one bit."

"He did attend Johnny's and Amma's wedding as it was outdoors, but left immediately afterwards. As far as I can conclude that was the last time he was ever here, and keeps to himself. Johnny checked in on him at least once a month. The only other person he sees is a distant neighbor, Corky Doyle, and some other guy that Johnny doesn't know. Corky is the one who found Walt's body."

"I understand that Johnny took it pretty hard."

"I guess they were a lot closer than any of us knew. Anyhow, he left reams and reams of papers, documents and journals that date back to the thirteen hundreds. Johnny collected some of them and took them home thinking he would get to them in the winter, but Amma got interested in them and she enticed Rose into helping her decipher them. That should have kept the two some-what bored gals busy for months, and Rose was also back into Avaleena's diary so that was something else, but then the two nut cases, Pit and Pete say they were held hostage in the elevator by a ghoul, and as I said, here we are."

"This is the first I am hearing about this, but do remember Vienna mentioning that Rosy had mentioned she had found more information on Gracie Darling and this Quinn character. I didn't pay much attention to it because as far as I was concerned it had all been dealt with, but now I realise my wife was bored also, and now here she is back at Avanloch. I'm thinking you have a lot on your hands what with running the estate and dealing with a household of emotional women, and I'm wondering if you could use a couple of impartial ears and eyes?"

"If you're saying that you are coming then I'm saying I'm sending the plane."

"It's not doing me any good a thousand miles away worrying when I can be doing the same thing in the midst of it all with the people I love. I'll take a commercial flight into Edinburgh or Waverly and rent a car as soon as I find help for Nash."

"She'll be calling you soon."

"Tell her I called to let her know that I was taking the boys fishing to Mirror Lake for a couple of days and I'll call her when we get back. There is no cell signal up there so she won't be able to reach me. That should placate her. I trust you'll keep this surprise to yourself?"

"You can count on me. There may be a surprise here for you too. Looking forward to seeing you Rain; safe travels."

CHAPTER 3

VIENNA'S DILEMMAS

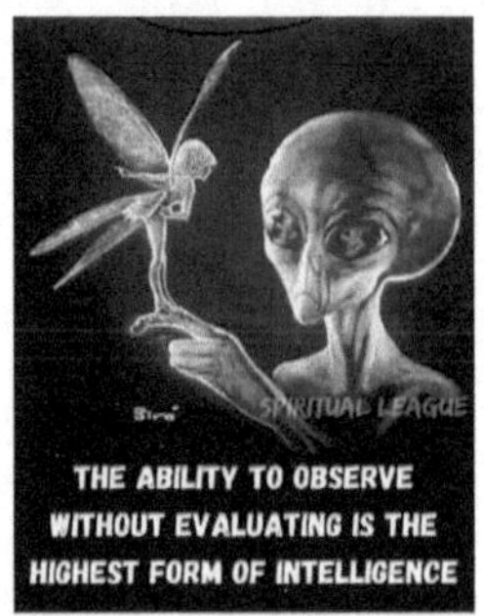

I splashed water on my face and ran my hands through my hair. I was as awake as I could be until I had coffee. It was all quiet in the rooms next door so I assumed everyone was still sleeping. I took the back stairs as usual and stopped at the bottom thinking I heard familiar laughter coming from the kitchen. Obviously, I was still asleep.

Evan, Johnny and Mrs. D were sitting at their usual spots at the table. "I really am sleep deprived I guess because I thought I heard Rainey laughing." I announced.

The three of them were grinning as I saw a movement by the coffee station.

"You mean me?" Rainey said turning.

"Oh, you're here!" I cried running into his open arms.

"Hi Gorgeous." His cheerful voice was music to my ears, but it changed to dismay almost immediately. He let go of me rather forcefully and looked at me questioningly. "What's this?"

I turned and saw Lili shuffling down the hallway. "Oh Daddy…" She lamented.

He was over to her in an instant comforting her in his arms. He patted her enlarged stomach.

"What's going on here, and how come I am just finding out about it now?"

"I didn't want you to see me like this and I knew you would come if you knew."

"Of course I would have, and I'm here now, so how about we go find somewhere comfortable to sit and you can tell me everything?"

"I want Mommy to come."

Rainey looked back at me. "Are you coming Mommy?"

"I think maybe that you two need some time alone right now." I suggested.

"Please Mommy…"

Evan and Johnny were looking at me with eyes that said "We told you to tell him." I took a deep breath and followed my husband and daughter down the hallway. I stood at the doorway of the parlor and watched Rainey lower Liliana onto the divan. He beckoned me to join them. I sat down in an armchair beside Lili.

"Don't be mad at Mommy, Daddy, I made her promise not to tell you."

"Why?"

"Because I didn't want you to be ashamed of me."

"I could never be ashamed of you Sweetie; why would you think that?"

"Because I'm not married."

Rainey made an attempt to laugh. "And, that is completely unheard of…do you think your old dad is a prude?"

"No, but I've always been your little girl, and I didn't want you to be disappointed in me."

"I'll never be disappointed with you, and you'll always be my little girl, but it looks like I am going to have a brand new one now doesn't it?"

"I think it is going to be a boy Daddy."

"So you've inherited your mother's intuition have you? Tell me that you are keeping the baby, and what does the father have to say?"

"Of course I am! The father is out of the picture. He doesn't even know."

Rainey gave me a look that broke my heart. "So, you became pregnant all on your own, and you are saying that the father doesn't have a right to know…is that what you are saying?"

"He chose his parent's business over me as if that is even a career."

I couldn't sink any deeper into the chair.

"I've heard this story before little girl and it doesn't wash. I take it that Rusty is the father and that you no longer love him?"

"He is, and I do love him, but I would just be a complication…"

Rainey's voice broke. "I think you need to have a talk with your mother."

"I know Daddy. Everyone knows how Ava came to be born without you knowing, but my circumstances are different."

"How is that Lili?"

"He has sanctimonious parents; they call him William Junior."

He laughed boldly. "Oh, is that all? Enough for now; we'll talk more later. Now, when is this new addition to the family due, and how long have you known Vienna?"

Lili answered for me. "I called her the day before she left Hawthorne. No one knew before that except Tanny. The baby is due on the tenth."

"Why did you come here to Scotland?"

"I was scared to be alone because Tanny had to work so much, and Mommy said she'd come and get me."

"So, you went to France?" My husband asked me irritably.

"No, Tanny brought her to London by boat and I met her and we came by train here."

"Okay, good to know that I wasn't important enough to be informed."

"It's not Mommy's fault Daddy. She wanted to tell you, but I wanted to wait until the baby was born. I didn't want you to see me all bloated and clumsy like a mule. Please don't be mad at her." Lili pleaded tears running down her face.

Rainey hugged her. "I happen to think that pregnant women are beautiful, and you are no exception and even more so seeing you're my daughter. Now, three days from now is your expected delivery date, so I take it all the preparations are in order; hospital and doctor aware?"

"I'm having the baby here Daddy."

He looked at me. "Whose idea was that?"

"I want to deliver here just like Mama did with Ava."

"Well, it's a damn good thing that I am here then isn't it? Tomorrow we are going to Waverly and await it out in the suite, and there is no further discussion, understand?"

"Okay if you think that is best Daddy."

"It is. Now let's go get you some breakfast."

I got up quickly and said that I'd wait for him upstairs. I expected to be thoroughly chastised. I knew every word that Rainey was going to bombard me with, and it all came down to the same old thing...I didn't trust him enough to confide in him. Had I just committed the ultimate sin? Was this going to be the final straw? I didn't want to go back through the kitchen and see the disapproving faces, so I took the grand hallway stairs. I stood at the first landing and watched father and daughter, arm in arm laughing as they made their way down the corridor

I was standing at the balustrade beside the Three Fates statue on my patio when Rainey joined me. He gently placed his hand on my back and asked if he could pour me a cup of coffee. Even after all these years I still felt a shiver run down my spine by his touch. I thanked him and asked him how much trouble I was in.

"You've missed all of this haven't you?" He asked waving his hands over the vista.

"I suppose I have." I answered wistfully.

"Come and sit with me. I'm still a little weary from the trip."

"How long have you been here?"

"About ten minutes before you came down."

"When did you decide to come?"

"A few days ago after I talked with Evan."

"He sent the plane for you?"

"No, I flew commercial."

"So, I guess there was no fishing trip?"

"Actually, I consider being here a fishing trip as I have no idea what is going on, and what has you and the rest of the ladies in such a frenzy."

"I wouldn't say that we are frenzied."

"We'll talk about that later. As for you being in trouble with me regarding Lili, you are not. She asked you to keep her pregnancy a secret from me for reasons that I don't understand, so I can't fault you for that. I am crestfallen that you didn't confide in me and trust that I would handle her with kid gloves, but what's done is done, and I'll try not to press you about your decision again, or anything else you chose to do."

"I do trust you Rainey and I would have told you, but I couldn't betray *her* trust."

"I understand that you felt you were in a catch-22, so I will relieve you of that burden once and for all."

"What do you mean?" I asked nervously.

"I don't want you to feel guilty about Lili's wish, or about leaving me, which I knew you did, so I will give you the freedom to do whatever you want without worrying about what I will think. It's fairly obvious that this is where you want to be, so I'll relent and try not to whine about your decisions."

"I don't want freedom from you, and I am only here because Rosy asked me to come."

"You don't have to justify your reasons Honey. I admit that I was thrown off my game by finding out that you hate the house back in Hawthorne and everything else about your mundane life back there."

"Where would you get such ridiculous ideas?" I exclaimed in disbelief.

"A little birdie that you confide in told me. I used to be that someone so it was very hard for me to hear how you feel about our home and life on the ranch from a stranger."

"So, she caught me in a mood and I said things I didn't really mean, and she couldn't wait to blab it to you. What other things has she been whispering in your ear?"

"Well, it was you who suggested that she look after me while you were away, and we all know I can't be without a woman in my bed don't we?"

"Izzy wouldn't do that to me."

"Oh, but I would eh? Well, no worries because thoughts of another woman never enter my mind. You might be pleased to know that she has a new friend. His name is Black and they seem to be enraptured with each other. You remember what that is like, don't you?"

"Rainey…" I stammered looking for the right words.

He stood up and patted my head. "Lili does a much better job of cutting your hair now. I like it and the color suits you. Now, how about you run your fingers through it, wash your face, and get dressed and join us downstairs? I've suggested a round-table and you should join us seeing you are one of the main characters in this ghost-hunt." He winked and said he loved me as he walked out.

I followed him to the door and watched as he linked arms with Novia and Calla who had burst into the hall shouting, Daddy and Pappy.

"Here's my girls." He said kissing them.

"Black who?" I yelled after him.

"Smith." He yelled back.

"Smith," I said out loud to no one, "Black Smith, is that his name, or is Izzy's friend a blacksmith? That's just crazy; who cares anyway?"

I closed and locked the French doors and set the alarm in the bedroom, and made my way to Miss Mary's room. I discarded my housecoat and looked at myself in the full length mirror. I heard laughter behind me. "Rainey doesn't like it when you're so thin Vienna." I threw an invisible rock at the mocking illusory Jorja. Six dresses later I found one that didn't hang on me. I topped it off with a long black sweater. There, I didn't look so bad.

"Thank-you for gracing us with your presence Lady Vienna." Rainey greeted me.

I bowed to him. "It's my pleasure Sir."

He grinned and everyone else chuckled. Rosy, Amma and the girls had all made it downstairs. I took a chair next to Lili who was seated by the kitchen window. I took her hand and announced that they could begin the inquisition. I assumed that it was Rainey who had assembled the bulletin board from the den. Marking pen in hand he asked when the first haunting had taken place. Rosy opened the diary she had been keeping and was just about to speak when the telephone rang. Amma answered and announced it was Tanny.

"Hello Sweetie. I suppose you want to check in on Lili. I'll put you on speaker so you can talk to everyone and they can talk to you."

"Thanks Amma. You all right Lil?"

"I am; Daddy's here." Lili answered.

"You relinquished and called him then?"

"No, I didn't. Did you?"

"How about if I answer that?" Rainey said. "How are you Tanny?"

"I'm good Daddy. Were you lonesome without Mom?"

"That goes without saying, but half of my family is also here, so I was concerned for their safety. Do you know that Avanloch is experiencing some unusual phenomena again?"

"I do, and the funny thing is that Mommy wasn't even there when it all started."

Everyone laughed a little. "Very funny little girl. You'll be happy to hear that we are taking Lili into Waverly tomorrow. Your father insisted and Lili didn't object." I informed her.

"Good, I'm glad. Is my little French sister there?"

"I'm right here Tanny." Novia answered.

"When are you coming to see me?"

"I'm waiting for the increase in my allowance. It usually comes about this time every year, so I am hoping. If all pans out, I'll see you in late August. Zander and Sammie want to come with me, and of course, we want to go to Spain to see Zoe." Novia mischievously said smiling sweetly at me and Rainey.

"Times are tough, and I had to take time off work to come here, so I doubt there will be any addition to you children's coffers this year." Rainey joked. "What do you say Mom?"

"You're the boss Dear." I replied trying to sound serious.

"Guess I'll be seeing you and the boys soon Novia. Evan, are you there?"

"I am. What can I do for you Tanny?"

"Any news on the key?"

Evan laughed. "What key would that be?"

"You know perfectly well what key I am talking about. I saw it in a dream and it unlocked a mysterious door in the elevator, so you need to take it seriously. Oh, my geese are here; gotta go. I'll call you tonight Lil. Love you all."

We all echoed the sentiment. "Tanny and that damn key!" I exclaimed shaking my head.

Johnny asked if we would excuse him for a few minutes. Amma asked him where he was going as he left. He said he'd be right back.

"What's this about geese?" Rainey asked.

"They are really ducks. I don't know why she calls them geese. A farmer delivers a dozen ducks to the café once a week and Tanny makes her version of Duck a l'Orange. It is a very popular dish. It is very aromatic in the kitchen when it's cooking." Lili explained.

Rainey said we may as well get on with things. He asked Rosy if she knew the precise date that work on installing the elevator began. She opened up the journal once again.

"Pete and Pit arrived on May the 20th to size up the assignment and returned on May 31ˢᵗ with all the equipment and started work on the first of June which was a Saturday. We offered to lodge them here, but they refused saying they had kin this side of Waverly. Myself, I believe they were too skittish to sleep in the ghostly castle."

"Did they say so Rose?" Rainey asked.

"No, but their behavior said otherwise."

"So, the stories regarding previous ghostly inhabitants are still running amuck?"

"Of course they are; not just here, but in every castle. Many have been turned into inns because costs have sky rocketed and they need outside finances to keep them operable. What's to captivate an audience if there aren't rumors about ghostly hauntings? Most of them are true anyhow. We are very lucky because we have the mill and backing from McAllister Enterprises."

"Right you are Red. Go on please."

"Apparently, it takes four to six days to install an elevator into a two storey structure with two workers, but seeing we have three storeys, it would take longer. We hadn't planned for the elevator to include the cellars, but that was what they had estimated for in the plans, so that was an extra two or three days. If they encountered any problems, it might take up to four weeks. Everything seemed to go according to plan with just a few setbacks, but with Johnny and Evan assisting, the installation was complete on the 12th. We took turns riding with them to the top floor, and were satisfied. Then they insisted on one more solo trip. The time between floors is about 40 seconds. Fifteen minutes went by and no Pete and Pit. No alarm went off and we could not here anything; no motor running or anyone shouting. Evan and Johnny took the old lift up the two flights. They heard and saw nothing. Two minutes after they returned, down came the new elevator and two very distraught, pasty looking men emerged yelling at us at the top of their lungs. If there were any ghouls sleeping they would have surely been awakened by the commotion those two made believe me!"

Rainey gave her a hug. "I can imagine Honey. Can one of you walk me through it?"

"Evan's calmer than I am, so I'll let him finish."

"I will tone the language down as there are ladies present. Apparently, Pit is related to Johnny in some half-assed way, so he attacked Johnny the minute he stepped out of the elevator. This is the accusation as best as I can recall."

"Johnny O'Shea, you bleep, bleep son of a bitch! You knew damn well that this monstrosity of a fortress was haunted, but you lied outright and fed us a line of bull and waited until the job was completed before you fed us to the ghouls!" He yelled and sprung at Johnny with such force that they fell to the floor. "I managed to untangle them before anyone got hurt. That's about right isn't it girls?"

"Evan's being too modest Rainey. He had Pit in a choke hold and wouldn't let him up until he released Johnny. Pit continued to curse us all out. He spit and said that he had did Johnny a f…in favor into undertaking the f…in job because of Uncle Walt, and this was the thanks he got. Well, just wait until you get the bill you f…in moron!" Amma asserted hotly.

Evan continued. "Johnny laughed at Pit and called him a stupid ass if he believed that he or anyone had control over the ghosts in the castle. Pit was on him again, and again I had to restrain him. Meanwhile ole Pete is still shivering in his boots. Rose tried to convince him to sit down and tell us what had transpired because we were all in the dark. He refused and stood with one foot out the door. He told her that she best get her family out before it was too late because they weren't going to stay in the walls forever. Pit laughed and accused us again of double crossing them. Rose had enough of him and told him that he was right and that the castle was full of ghosts and that they weren't friendly and that we waited until curious, gullible victims like him visited and then we released the hoard, so he better get out of her house while he still could."

"Good for you Red!" Rainey acclaimed. "So, that's it; no more of what they saw or heard?"

"Johnny and I escorted the two of them outside and demanded an explanation if they wanted the substantial bonus that we were prepared to offer. Of course I had to tell them that Rosy was just kidding. Don't think they believed me though, but I cared less. So, their story was that the elevator just stopped dead. The doors would not open. They had no idea if it was between floors or in the middle of nowhere. The emergency call button and the floor numbers were pushed, but to no avail. Ten seconds or so passed before they felt a slight rocking and thought the elevator was going to start up again but instead they had the sensation that the walls were closing in on them. I imagine it was because they were panicking. Then they heard whistling. They talked themselves into believing that they were close to a floor and someone would hear them if they yelled, and so they did at the top of their lungs. They knocked on the walls and the walls knocked back so again they were sure that someone could hear them. Then they heard a voice warning them to get out before they were discovered. It was a woman's voice. She kept repeating for them to leave because the Liard was close and no amount of gold was worth their lives. They heard what sounded like chopping and a door bursting open and screaming just as the elevator started up. They think it took almost a minute to reach the first floor which I estimate puts the stalled elevator somewhere between the second and top floor. That's about it. Johnny suggested that it was their own screams they heard and the voices were those of the kids. That brought another round of contempt from Pit. Johnny told them to get off the property and that we'd forward their belongings and told them to be sure and change their underwear as the stink was overwhelming." Evan ended the narrative, but not before he added one final tidbit. "The girls were out with the grooms Al and Roger on a riding adventure to Widow's Peak, so there was no one else in the house except him, Rose, Amma and Johnny and the McDuffs. The help and Cora, the cook, all had the day off."

Rainey said it sounded like hysteria. I did not agree with him. Johnny returned and laid a small wooden box on the table. Amma asked him what was in it.

He looked directly at me. "It's all come full circle now."

I shivered. Lili squeezed my hand and said she thought her water broke.

CHAPTER 4

LILIANA

Lili sobbed and apologised. "I'm sorry Rosy, I ruined the chair, oh look at the mess I made! It just happened so fast."

"You did nothing of the sort Sweetie, so don't even think about that old chair. Are you having contractions?" Rosy said rushing to her sister's side.

"Just little twinges. Is it time?"

"Maybe; what do you think Mama?" Rosy asked.

The girls hardly ever called me Mama anymore. It was usually just Mom or Ana. Before I could answer Rainey said we weren't taking any chances and asked Evan to get the car. I assured Lili that everything was normal, and to take some deep breaths. All the young girls were huddling together eyes fixed on Lili looking concerned.

I thought it best to give them something to do. "Novia, take Calla, Colleen and Beth and go upstairs and get Lili a new dress and under things and anything else you can think of okay?"

"And, get your mother a pair of shoes." Rainey added.

"Don't worry about anything Mama. Amma and I will get you a change of clothes and your overnight case. We'll follow behind you just as soon as we settle the girls down. Johnny, you will stay with them won't you?"

"That goes without saying Rosy. Don't worry; I'll keep them busy and out of mischief."

"You don't mind if I go with Ava, do you?" Amma asked.

"Of course I don't Honey." He replied informing us that their girls had told them that there wasn't going to be any more grandchildren for them. "Hell, six are enough anyway, but Lili's will be like a seventh as we've become very fond of her. The girls and I can bring all the baby furniture down and spruce it up for the new arrival."

Rainey thanked him and agreed that six was enough, but we'd probably have sixteen or more by time our brood was through. He told Rosy to drive his rental car to Waverly and passed her the keys. I shooed everyone out so I could get Lili changed. Rainey and I walked her out to the car each with an arm around her and each other. He squeezed my hand at her back. I returned the squeeze, but for some reason felt the need to apologise.

"Everything that Izzy said was taken out of context. I'm sorry that you believed it to be so."

"Are you two fighting and who is Izzy?" Lili asked concerned.

"We are not fighting Sweetie. Sometimes we just have little disagreements, but they always iron themselves out. Izzy moved into the neighborhood to take over her father's farm after he passed last year. She and your mom have become good friends." Rainey answered.

"As if you have a neighborhood Dad; farms are miles apart. You okay Mommy?"

"I'm not the one about to have a baby, so don't worry about me and your dad Lili. He and I are just as much in love today as we have always been." I assured her.

Evan insisted on driving as he knew that Rainey's concentration was elsewhere. Lili had only minor tics on the hour long drive. If it turned out to be false labor we'd take up residence at the suite until she was ready to deliver. I had been in attendance for both of Ava's deliveries and for one of Rosy's so I should be an old hand at it, but some reason I was very apprehensive. Maybe it was more to do with what was in the box that Johnny had produced, or in what he meant when he said that it had come full circle. What was it, what had come full circle?"

Two minutes after we arrived at the front desk of the hospital a candy stripper appeared with a wheelchair. I left Rainey dealing with the admitting paperwork as I continued on with Lili to the second floor. We were met by a nurse who took Lili under her wing and readied her for the doctor. Half an hour later Rainey joined us and another half passed before the doctor showed up.

"Well, who do we have here?" She asked Lili enthusiastically.

"I'm Lili Quinn."

"I'm Dr. Iris Henning. Everyone around here calls me Sheila so I am good with that. I like to dispense with the formalities right away. We are going to become good friends over the next few hours so we may as well be on a first name basis. Have you been seeing another GYN?" She announced all the time conducting a gentle exam of Lili's extremities.

"I saw one in France a couple of times." Lili answered.

The doctor stepped back. "France?"

"Yes, I live there with my sister, but Mommy was coming to Avanloch so I came here. I was going to have my baby there with the neighbor women, but Daddy came and insisted I come to the hospital."

"By neighbor women I take it you mean self-proclaimed mid wives? Doesn't matter as you are here now, and we are going to look after you." She looked at me and Rainey. "I take it that you are Lili's parents."

"We are; Vienna and Rainey Quinn." My husband said holding out his hand.

She shook it and said it was a pleasure. "Mrs. Quinn…Vienna is it? Your name is ringing a bell with me, but as of yet I don't know what it is. Lili said she came to Avanloch to have her baby because you were there; are you living at the castle?"

"I came over with another daughter and granddaughter a few weeks ago for the summer. Rainey only came yesterday."

"May I ask from where you came?"

Lili squealed and clutched her stomach.

"Getting a little bit stronger; that's good." The doctor called Sheila said rubbing Lili's shoulders. I think it's time we did a thorough exam now. Will you excuse us mom and dad? I will be with you shortly." She spoke into her pager. "I'm ready for you and Janet."

The last thing I heard before we closed the door was, "Are you related to Evan Govern?"

I asked Rainey if he thought she knew Evan.

"Could be; maybe they even knew each other down under."

"What makes you think she's from Australia? It's a very big country so chances of them knowing each other from there are scarce."

"It was just a supposition Honey, but she likes to be called Sheila even though her name is Iris and her accent is much like Evan's."

"Evan doesn't have an accent." I asserted rather harshly.

Rainey laughed. "Really; you don't hear it? I suppose Rosy and the McDuffs don't have one either, and you know you still have a faint Scottish lilt yourself."

"Now you are just being silly."

"I think I'll mosey on down to the cafeteria and grab a coffee. Can I get you something?"

"No, I'm jittery enough already. If I'm not here when you get back you'll know where I am."

I started pacing. Maybe I had time to go outside and have a cigarette before Rainey got back. I asked myself just how long did I think it took to go to the cafeteria and back. The door to Lili's room opened just as Rainey returned. Dr. Henning emerged. She was smiling.

"Let's have a seat. You have nothing to worry about folks. Everything with your daughter is just as it should be. Her cervix is as close to 6cm as it can be, so I estimate that the full 10 cm should be achieved within 5- 7 hours for the start of active labor. Her contractions are still quite mild, but have increased in intensity since I first saw her. I think this baby is in a hurry to be born. Lili is a delightful girl. I am very pleased that you have entrusted her to me. We have had quite the conversation during the examination. I was most curious as why she was at Avanloch Castle and I now know that it is a family estate. I told you Mrs. Quinn that your name sounded familiar and now thanks to my nurse Janet, I realize why. Your name must be on half a dozen plaques throughout the hospital for contributions that you have made throughout the years, and your picture is displayed several times also. I think the Quinn name through me off, but Lili explained that all away. I have yet to take your son-in-law up on the offer to tour the castle, but I am very much looking forward to it. I don't suppose I have to plaudit his aptitudes to you, do I? He has this way of taking charge all the while calming the situation. He is a remarkable man. I do hope that we will be able to form a partnership soon as this district certainly needs it."

I'm sure Rainey could see that I was seething and quickly intervened.

"We are at a loss here Dr. Henning. Though we certainly agree that Evan is an outstanding man and we are very proud to call him our son-in-law, we have no idea just what partnership you are referring to."

"Please call me Sheila. So sorry for the misunderstanding and assumption that you may know about our plans. We here at the hospital and surrounding clinics are indebted to him for his quick response to calls to rescue those who are in medical distress in perilous situations in the outlying districts. I have accompanied him several times when called upon by first responders. Our Search and Rescue crew may already be engaged and not available, and that is when Evan has been called, or he has been engaged to assist. Sometimes SAR doesn't need to be engaged as it is just a simple pick-up, but it may be a woman in labor and that is when a nurse and I have accompanied him. To avoid all the red tape, we need to form a legal alliance. I'm sure he never mentioned it because he is too modest. We're both from Australia you know."

"There is always so much going on at the castle and seeing that I have just arrived I am not caught up on everything yet. Have you met Evan's wife and our daughter, Rosalyn yet?"

"No, I have not had the pleasure."

"She will be here shortly, and I am sure would love to meet her husband's would-be partner."

Her pager sounded. "I will look forward to it. Go be with Liliana. Catch you in an hour or so."

"It sounds interesting, and she has a good rapport with Lili, don't you think?" Rainey asked hoping that I would agree. I did not.

"I don't like her." I stated ardently.

"Dare I ask why?"

"Because she is after out daughter's husband."

"Oh, just as Ava's doctor was after *your* husband?"

"Exactly." I turned my back to him and opened the door to Lili's room.

"Please don't start anything Vienna. Tell Lili I'll be in shortly. I'm going to find Evan and see if he will join me for a pint."

I didn't bother reminding him that it wasn't even half noon.

Rosalyn and Amma popped in to do a quick check on Lili before they went shopping for foodstuffs for the apartment. At two Rainey arrived back and said that Evan was out in the family room and wanted to speak to me. I supposed that he had told Evan about my suppositions about the doctor. It was something else entirely. He said that he was going back home for the night and would return in the morning with the helicopter. I asked why.

"I'm going to fly Rain to London. He wants to track Lili's beau down and inform him that he is about to become a father. I want you to know that I agree with him."

"I do too Evan. I don't want my daughter to make the same mistake that I did. Why is it that you are pitching this to me and not Rainey? He thinks I will object doesn't he?"

"I think he believes that you will think he is doing this to avenge your decision to keep Ava's birth from him. That is far from the truth Vienna, and you know that, but he is very wary and will call the whole thing off if you disagree."

"I love you and I will see you in the morning." I kissed him and sent him on his way. He returned the sentiment and the kiss and told me to pass it on to Lili. A vision of him picking Lili up almost twenty years ago and swinging her like an airplane over his head made me smile.

"What are you two up to in here?" I inquired melodiously of my husband and daughter when I rejoined them.

"Not much Mom; just trying to have a baby. What did Evan want?"

"He wanted my permission to take your dad on a heli ride around the valley tomorrow. I told him that it was a good idea as your dad would probably be in our hair fussing too much over you and the baby."

"I don't mind if you fuss over me Daddy." Lili murmured as she gave in to a contraction.

"That's it Honey, go with it. Now breathe and settle back. Rainey, get her a fresh cold cloth and she needs some fresh ice chips."

"What about you; what can I bring you?"

"Maybe an iced tea, and then you should go and have something to eat."

He kissed Lili and then me whispering 'thank-you' in my ear.

The day wore on. Lili was up and down like a yo-yo. Sometimes she felt better walking only to want to lie down a few minutes later. By seven p.m. she was exhausted and babbling about one thing or the other, but she never mentioned Rusty. In between one of her ramblings I asked her if she had thought anymore about baby names.

"Jeremiah." She said dubiously.

"Oh, that's a nice name for a little boy."

"Jeremiah's a bull frog; you know that Mother."

Before I had time to ask her what she meant she added that if it was a girl, she'd call her Joy.

I laughed a little. "Have you been listening to my old records Lili?"

"They are all so sad about lost love and cheating and then I found the three dogs and I felt like dancing. Do you still dance with Daddy, Mommy?"

"Not for a long time Sweetie, but as soon as Jeremiah is born we'll dance in celebration."

Dr. Henning checked in a few minutes later and said that it was time to get Lili into the delivery room. Jeremiah made his entrance at seven forty five. He weighed 6 pounds 7 ounces. The first thing Lili said when he was returned to her all fresh and bundled up was, "Look Mommy, he's got Daddy's and my eyes."

"Of course he does. Let's see what he thinks about his Pappy."

I ditched my cap and mask and paper gown in the garbage and went to the family room where the girls and Rainey were anxiously waiting. One by one they visited Lili and Jeremiah for a few minutes each. I stayed with my daughter and new grand baby until almost nine when Lili fell asleep. Baby J was sleeping peacefully in a tiny crib beside her. I made sure the night nurse had my cell number and started for the apartment. I made it outside to a bench before my legs gave way. I dug into my bag for a cigarette, but decided to call Rainey instead.

"Is everything all right Babe?" He answered.

"Can you come and get me?"

"I'm on my way."

He ran across the street when he saw me. "What are you doing out here?"

"Waiting for you. I'm afraid I didn't trust my legs to get me across the street."

"Well, that's what I'm here for. You're exhausted aren't you? Where are your shoes?"

"They hurt my feet. I think I threw them down the laundry shoot."

He laughed. "Let's get you to the apartment and to bed. You need to eat first as I fear you didn't have anything substantial today. The girls have made a nice light meal for you."

"I had some ice chips."

"Who is it that says you have a warped sense of humor?"

"You, I think, or Jack or Jimmy, or Evan."

Just as the elevator door closed behind us I said that I was worried about tomorrow. He asked if I meant his going to London to find Rusty. I said, "No; it's for what Johnny is going to say."

I opened the apartment door before he could ask me why. I sat down to a nice creamed vegetable soup and crudities, and a peach tapioca dessert. I explained how Lili had come upon the name Jeremiah. I left them laughing as I excused myself saying I was going to bed. Rosy said she had laid a nightie out on the bed for me and hung the clothes in the closet. I thanked her, picked up my bag and went into the bedroom. As I was closing the door I heard Rainey tell Rosy to buy me a decent pair of shoes tomorrow. I yanked my dress off and wondered what had possessed Rosy to bring me such a mini nightie. I pulled a comfy chair up to the open window and relaxed with my first cigarette of the day. Rainey came in when I was half through it carrying a fire extinguisher.

"And, you talk about my twisted sense of humor. I'm not going to burn the place down you know." I said butting out.

"It's not for that, although it is a non-smoking hotel, but for what I fear is burning inside of you. I don't mind if you smoke you know. If it helps you to relax then who am I to complain as you put up with my drinking? Do you care to enlighten me as to your remark about fearing what Johnny has to say?"

"Not tonight." I answered climbing into bed. "You hate how I smell, and I don't begrudge you a beer now and then. It's the hard stuff that I object to. Anyhow, I'm too tired to debate."

"Did you wash your feet?"

"I did not. You don't have to sleep with me you know."

"I didn't come half way around the world to not sleep with my wife, dirty feet and all unless she doesn't want me to."

I lifted the coverlet. He undressed, redressed in a pair of light night wear and crawled into bed with me. He reached for me and I snuggled into his chest.

"I love you Pappy." I murmured.

"I love you too Ana. Sweet dreams; I'll see you in the morning."

I heard muffled voices coming from the other room when I awoke the next morning. I jumped out of bed and picked up my dress from the floor where I had thrown it and everything else last night. I could hear Tanny scolding me for being so messy. The dress was creased and soiled so I threw it back on the floor, put my sweater on over my short gown and went out to say good morning to my family. I plopped myself down on Rainey's lap and thanked him for last night.

"I guess this is where you and I make our-selves scarce Amma." Rosy teased.

Rainey laughed. "It's not what you think Red. Your mother was asleep two seconds after her head hit the pillow."

I took a few sips of the coffee that Amma had passed me. "It was the best sleep that I have had in weeks. How did you girls sleep?"

They agreed with me. Rainey said it was because we weren't back at the castle hunting invisible spooks all night and it was time that we ended the fixation that had been planted in our heads by two hysterical men. He asked if we had ever entertained the idea that they were just putting us on.

"Why would they do that Dad?" Rosy asked. "I saw their faces and you can't mask the fear I saw in their eyes. Anyhow, we have not passed any of our suspicions onto the girls, but have included them in our searches, and sort of made a game out of it. Colleen and Beth know about the secreted rooms and all, but Novia and Calla don't, so they are all having fun telling them the history as are we. Evan and Johnny think we are nuts, and I am sure that Evan made it sound more than it is over the phone, but I think he just wanted you here, so exaggerated the danger to entice you, and here you are, so we are all happy!"

"Yes, and I am happy to be here, but I'm keeping an eye on you all. It's pretty obvious that you believe that Pit and Pete did hear voices in the elevator, but I am not too sure that they did. I think that they have an agenda, and I intend to find out what it is."

"How are you going to do that?" I asked.

He gave my bare thigh a little tap. "You just leave that to me. Now go and get dressed if you want to come with me to see Lili before Evan gets here."

"I don't have anything to wear."

"Did you not like anything that I brought you Mom?" Rosy asked.

"Sorry, I forgot. I'm sure there will be something I like. Do I have time for a shower Rainey?"

He told me I had ten minutes. I checked the closet first. There was a pair of tan slacks and a peach colored blouse, a long blue and white dress and a yellow short one which I did not recognise. I showered quickly, styled my wet hair with my fingers, put lipstick on, dressed and considered myself presentable. The girls had already left to go shopping for a car seat and anything else they figured Lili and baby would need. Rainey said he liked my dress. I told him it wasn't mine. He asked if it was Miss Mary's. I said "No." He shrugged his shoulders and told me to sit down while he put some uncomfortable sandals on my feet. Evan arrived so I sent them off to have a quick visit with Lili while I went to a little shop down the block. I wished them good luck with finding Jeramiah's father. Rainey told me to make sure I ate something. Half an hour later I walked into Lili's room. I kissed her and my new grandbaby. He was asleep in her arms. She told me she liked my dress and that yellow looked good on me.

"It's not my dress." I stated.

"Miss Mary's?"

"It's Katarina's."

"Mom…how could that be?"

"I think that Zoe must have packed it when I asked her to get some things together the day your dad came for us in Spain. I suppose I hung it in the closet at Avanloch planning on getting rid of it, but it's obvious that I didn't. It's been at the back of the closet for twenty some years, and Rosy just happened to come upon it."

"So, you recognised it? Is that the only thing Rosy brought for you?"

"I can't say for sure that I recognised it, but see here on the pocket is a red carnation. That is Spain's national flower, and there are also two pink water lilies on the back just above the zipper. Lilies are a popular insignia in Verde El Mar. I'm not sure why I chose it over the other dress."

"Is that why you called me Liliana; was it after the lilies? Did you ever tell me before?"

"You know I had amnesia when you were born, so it has never been clear to me as to why I named you Liliana. Maybe it was after my mother. Of course I didn't remember her then, but maybe subconsciously I did. Anyhow, I like the name and you're stuck with it."

"I like my name, no matter why you named me Mama. I don't have any memories of Verde El Mar or Anton except for one where I am in a pool with ducks."

"You would only have been fourteen months old so I don't understand how you could remember that. Perhaps you just remember me talking about it. The pond was very shallow so you weren't in any danger. You were on your haunches bent over feeding the ducks and you tipped headfirst into the water. Anton grabbed you and you came up sputtering. Uncle Jack took you shopping when you were almost three and you came home with a book for me with ducks on it. You told Jack I liked ducks. Do you remember that?"

"No, I don't. Oh, Jeremiah is awake. You know I may not keep that name for him. He doesn't want to suckle Mom. Am I doing something wrong?"

"Jeremiah will do for now. You aren't doing anything wrong Sweetie. He will when he is ready. Just be patient and relax and he will too."

I sat down and reached into my bag and pulled out a ball of yarn and knitting needles. Lili asked me what I was doing. I told her I was going to make a blanket for Jeremiah. She asked me when I had learned to knit. She remembered Sissy trying to teach me but I wasn't interested in learning. I told her that Katarina knew how.

"Mom, what are you saying…"

There was fear in my daughter's voice. I put my hand on hers. "If you're thinking that I am Kat, I am not, but I have made friends with her. I hardly ever think about her, but the dress must have sparked something in me and then I saw the yarn and the needles and I just picked them up, and look, I can knit!"

"Oh, I don't know what Daddy is going to say."

"Don't worry because he already knows."

"Knows what?"

"He knows I have memories of her now and then. We talk about it and then I put her away for another day."

"I can't imagine what that is like. Do you think the baby and I can come and live with you at Avanloch for a little while?"

"I expected that you would and you don't have to ask. I don't see you going back to France any time soon. We should talk about Rusty don't you think?"

"What's to talk about? He chose his parents over me." She lamented.

"I won't push you on the subject anymore today, but you know it'll come up again don't you? I think there is a lot more to your reasoning that you don't want to talk about. I don't want you living in regret like I did."

"He's not Daddy."

"Of course he's not. There are not many men out there that are as forgiving as your father, but I am sure Rusty has many endearing qualities or you wouldn't have fell for him."

She did not offer any more information, but asked me why the castle was called Avanloch.

"It was called King's Down originally. It was nearly destroyed during the Scottish Wars which raged from the eight hundreds to the eighteenth century. Don't quote me on that because I really don't know when they started or ended. All I know is that Scotland seemed to be always at war with one country or the other; mostly England I believe. It is not clear as to when the castle was constructed or if the McAllister' were the original title holders, but it appears that they were. However, they may have claimed it as a trophy after defeating the previous titleholders in a battle. That's just conjecture on my behalf. After the dust had cleared, Rosalyn's father Jeremy's great, great, or maybe add another great to that, grandfather returned to King's Down and began reconstruction of the castle. My understanding was that the inside was basically intact and that it was the outside that had been destroyed. That makes sense because if the interior had of been destroyed the secreted rooms would have been also. The original plans have never surfaced, but conjecture is that they had not been incorporated into the new plans, but who knows really? That McAllister passes and another one takes over and eventually Stewart is the new Laird. He marries Avaleena whose father was a nobleman from Spain, and he renames it Avanloch in her honor. It was a round- about way to explain it, but that is all I know and have been able to figure out. The dates have always been suspect to me, but according to Avaleena's diary, Stewart's son was born on August the 13th 1852. He named him Robert."

"Why do you think the dates are wrong and why did the Loch come from? Isn't a loch connected to the sea? I mean the only water around Avanloch is the little river, and there isn't even a moat."

I laughed a little. "I don't really know; but by my calculations the point in time is out by at least a hundred years. I have calculated that Jeremy's two great grandfathers may have died young, say forty something, and I know his Dad and granddad were both in their seventies, and Jeremy was almost sixty, so that puts the date of Avaleena's diary to around 1752 or earlier, not 1852. Perhaps someday I will revisit my doubts, but then again, I probably won't as I have not the time or inclination to do so as Avanloch is no longer my home, and what would it matter anyhow? As for moats; I don't think all castles had them or still do, but don't quote me on that either. Actually though, Avanloch did have a moat in the early years. I believe it stretched all the way to where the gates are now. You haven't been here since you were fourteen or fifteen so I don't think I have ever taken you to Widow's Peak, but I will just as soon as you are able to ride. From there you will see the North Atlantic Sea. McClaren Inlet's waters flow from there and it might be called a loch though I have never heard it referred to as such. I don't think I've ever thought about it. Anyhow, that is where Millerfloss River flows from. It once flowed into the moat that surrounded the castle, but was diverted when the moat was demolished. A loch is an arm of the sea which is surrounded by a large land locked area which is what Avanloch is I guess, so hence the reason why loch is in its name. Johnny or your Dad can probably explain it better. Does that answer your question for now?"

"It does and I got a history and geography lesson, so thank-you. You are very knowledgeable Mom, and I think you may be right about the dates. Could Avaleena have made a mistake?"

"I don't know how one could make an error of one hundred years. She was a very smart woman. Something just doesn't jive, but as I said, who cares anyhow? I had years to dwell into Avanloch's history Lili. It was quite a task to get any details out of Jeremy, or his sister Ash who had no interest whatsoever at all. It wasn't until Avaleena's diary was discovered that Ash took any notice. Jeremy was gone by then, so I have no idea what he knew, or what his take would have been. I'm sure that there may still many things to uncover, but that's up to Rosy now, and she may be on her way in light of what has surfaced in Johnny's uncles files."

"Do you think that Daddy will join us on a ride to Widow's Peak?"

"I am sure he will, but at this point I have no idea on how long he plans on staying here."

"Are you going back to Hawthorne when he goes?"

"I'm unsure about that right now too Sweetie."

"It's my fault isn't it? How can I make it right?"

A knock on the door saved me from having to explain again that she wasn't to blame for anything. Amma and Rosy had come to take me to lunch. I asked them if it had been an order from my husband. Rosy laughed and asked if I really thought that he could order her around. I answered that he would make it sound like a request and she would be happy if it pleased him because she was just like all his other girls and couldn't refuse anything he asked of any of them. She said I was right and that he had gently reminded them that I needed to eat, and as usual had offered his credit card.

We had a lovely lunch at one of Rosy's favorite cafes. Amma said that she liked my dress and was it new. I said it wasn't mine and told them how it must have belonged to Katarina. They appeared to be shocked at my revelation, but I told them it was nothing to worry about and my wearing her dress was not a problem as after all, we were one and the same person, sort of. Rosy ordered a white chocolate Cranachan, a favorite Scottish dessert of mine for us to share. Halfway through it I was stricken with a blinding painful headache. Rosy managed to get me back to the suite, undressed and get me into bed before I collapsed. Amma arrived back having stopped at a pharmacy to pick up ice bags. I swallowed two aspirins, positioned one ice bag behind my neck and the other on my head, and went with the pain remembering the debilitating headaches I used to get in Verdi El Mar. The next thing I remember was hearing a door close and Rainey whispering to me.

"Hey Gorgeous, are you going to sleep all day?"

"Oh Rainey," I moaned. "you're here. I had a headache like you wouldn't believe."

"Is it gone now?"

"Almost."

He placed his hand behind me and pulled out a dripping ice bag. "I think the bag has a hole in it. You should get up because you and the pillow are soaking wet."

"I don't want to get up."

"You want to stay in bed for the rest of the night?"

"Is it night? I can't tell because Rosy pulled the drapes."

"It's four thirty."

"Oh; where are the girls now?"

"They flew back with Evan."

"Did you find Rusty?"

"I did and he will be here tomorrow morning at ten."

"Did you tell him about Jeremiah?"

"I did, and he can't wait to meet him and reunite with Lili. He loves her Vienna."

I moved over in the bed. "And, I love her father."

"You want me to join you?" He asked smiling.

I nodded. He said he could probably oblige me and went in to wash up. Next thing I knew it was after six and Rainey was inviting me out to dinner because he was starving. He passed me the yellow dress. I told him that I would pass on the dress as I'd enough of Katarina for one day.

He said I'd have to explain myself, so I reiterated the story for the third time before we went to say goodnight to our daughter and new grand baby. We found the two of them cuddling on the bed. Rainey asked if he could hold him. He gazed at me and said. "I miss this."

I picked up my knitting. "Don't look at me with stars in your eyes. My baby making days ended on the path to the crypt."

"That's really harsh Mom."

"It's the truth just like all the other times tragedy struck when I disobeyed your father."

"None of it was your fault Mommy."

"She knows that but she likes to play the martyr Lili." Rainey sighed.

"I'll have more babies for you Daddy, so don't you worry." Lili promised.

"That's not going to do me much good now is it with you a continent away?"

"Mommy said I could come and live with you; didn't she tell you?"

"No, she didn't, but I like the idea."

"Look Daddy, Mommy can knit!"

Rainey just shook his head and rolled his eyes when I said that Kat had taught me.

"You two are okay aren't you?" Lili bemoaned.

"Yes, we are my little mother, so not to worry. It's been pretty boring and lonely at home without your mother, so I am very happy that I decided to come over and see what mischief she has gotten herself into. I admit finding you here was a shocker at first and I was a little upset with her because she hadn't told me, but all is forgiven, and that means I forgive you too. I love you Sweetie and this little blue eyed tyke." Rainey kissed them both gently and said he'd see them in the morning.

"We love you too Pappy, you and Ana." Lili said through tears.

Rainey was very emotional so I said my goodnights. "Sleep peacefully my darling because tomorrow is going to be a very busy day. Now I best get your father out of here before he succumbs to starvation

"I may have to stay another day, so I shouldn't get my hopes up."

"Get your hopes up my sweet for I am pretty sure we'll all be heading back to the castle of unimaginable delights and unbelievable revelations tomorrow." Rainey vowed.

We had a lovely dinner. I pretty much put an end to that when I asked Rainey if he minded if I waited outside for him while he paid the cheque. I picked up my wine glass, tapped his glass, drank it down and said, "I think I slept with Johnny."

I walked out, took my shoes off, lit a cigarette and started walking. I heard him behind me singing "You take the high road and I'll take the low road and I'll get to Scotland afore ye."

I turned and asked him if that was his way of telling me that I was going the wrong way.

"Yes, but don't worry, I'll straighten you out like I always do. Sit down here and I'll put your shoes on. You shouldn't be walking barefoot on this dirty walkway. Why'd you take them off?"

"They hurt my feet."

"Why didn't you wear the flats that Rosy bought for you?"

"They were too short for these pant legs."

He patted my head. "The wine has gone to your head. What possessed you to drink it so fast?"

"I thought it would give me courage to confess to you."

"Your so-called confession fell on deaf years for nothing of the sort happened."

"Well, something did. What else could I be harboring in this selected memory of mine?"

"A hundred other things and tomorrow we will find out what happened behind room 6's doors a hundred years ago, and then we'll deal with it just like we have always done with everything."

I slipped my arm through his and we strolled slowly back to the apartment. He asked if he could draw me a bath. I said no as I had been in the pool at Avanloch every day and a bath would just seem inadequate. I added that I had taught Beth how to swim.

"She has a huge pool at her beckon, so how is it that she never learned how to swim?"

"She said it was because her father tried to drown her when she was young."

Rainey laughed. "Yeah sure because that is something he would do. There must be more to it than that?"

"I think he slipped and she slid out of his arms."

"Well, that I can see."

"Colleen did something and she is afraid to tell Evan because she's afraid of what his reaction will be, and if he loses faith in her she will just die."

"What did she do?"

"She and Calla took the elevator for a joy ride."

"I don't know what you are trying to say."

"Everyone was told to stay clear of the new elevator after the fiasco with Pit and Pete, but Colleen wanted to prove that there story was a line of bogus. She asked Calla to go with her."

"I thought Johnny decommissioned it?"

"Obviously not."

"Is that the end of the story?

"It is not. They rode it up to the tower floor, disembarked and all was well until they heard whistling that sounded as if it was coming from inside the elevator. They panicked a little, but decided to call up the old lift as they were not getting back inside the new one. They returned and no one was the wiser."

"So, just how do you know this, and when did it take place?"

"A few days before you arrived. Calla made Colleen tell me. I said I would talk to Evan on her behalf. She asked me not to, but said I could tell you and you could decide what to do about it."

"It's not my house, and she is not my daughter, so I am not going be the decision maker, but I will offer to be with her when she confesses. Why would she want me to anyhow? We hardly know each other. And, this being afraid of Evan is ridiculous."

"I know it is, but she's still your granddaughter and a teenager, and teenagers can be weird."

"You don't have to remind me of that. We still have two of our own and Lili may as well be one. Did I ever tell you about this teenage girl who had a crush on me in the sixties, and wouldn't give up on me no matter what I said or did?"

"Yes, I remember her, and I am pretty sure she still has a crush on you."

"Talk about crazy eh? Do you happen to know if she has plans on returning home with me?"

"I think it's a definite possibility."

"Good; now let's talk about what you think is going on at the castle, and why you never mentioned anything to me during our phone conversations?"

"I didn't want you to worry. You knew that Rosalyn's and Amma's findings in the O'Shea's diaries interested me because there were mentions of Gracie Darling and Quinn and the Templar Knights just like there had been in Avaleena's diary. Initially, just having a visit with my daughter and family was enough, but going without you put a damper on that. The more that Rosy relayed to me about what she and Amma had deciphered the more intrigued I became. Rosy asked for my help and I came. The elevator thing had happened a day or so before I arrived, so that was something new for Amma and Rosalyn to contend with on top of the suspicions that Johnny's uncle was murdered, so of course I got swept up in that also, and..."

"Hold up there Lass...this is the first I am hearing about murder." Rainey interrupted curtly.

"Didn't Evan mention it to you?"

"He did not."

"That's probably because Johnny wants to keep his doubts hush-hush until he can find more evidence to support his suspicions."

"So, it's Johnny who believes this and not just Amma and Rosy? Is there a suspect?"

"Yes and no. He hasn't confided in me or anything. In fact I would say that he has been giving me the cold shoulder and avoiding me, and that is not the Johnny I know. It has to have something to do with whatever is in that damn box. It concerns me somehow, but I haven't a clue as to what it could be."

"I am sure that what may have happened forty years ago is not why he is avoiding you. This haunting and suspected murder took place before you arrived, so quit worrying your pretty little head over things you have no control over. You came here for a holiday and it has been anything but. My instincts tell me to get you and our girls out of here, but Rosy wouldn't come, and you would fight me all the way, so as usual I am overcome with a predicament that encompasses my reasoning's. I suppose I am also intrigued with Johnny's suppositions and the elevator mystery so tomorrow while you are waiting with Lili for Rusty I'm going to take a little trip out to Lansing and see what I can worm out of Pete and Pit."

"How do you plan on doing that?"

"Well, they don't know me so my inquiring about having an elevator installed in an old house I plan on buying won't be suspect. From there I am sure I can get them to divulge some of their frightening experiences like the rumor of their Avanloch haunting."

"Good luck with that Hon. You need to know one more thing and it may set your mind at ease. I have not felt or seen anything unusual, and I told Amma and Rosy that, but we could continue with the searching, but we could treat it as a game and an adventure for the girls' sake just like Rosy told you. They are enjoying our sleep- parties and felt part of what was going on which of course, I am not too sure what it is. It's been a long time since anything out of the ordinary has happened at Avanloch, so I am a little intrigued. I know Johnny and Evan are leery, but we would never do anything to endanger the girls."

"To say you are a little intrigued is putting it mildly don't you think? I'm wondering if Evan laid it on a little thick over the phone."

"I think maybe it's like Rosy said; he just wanted you here. I am very happy with whatever it was that brought you here. I was profoundly missing you."

"We both know that it was my missing you that brought me here, don't we?"

"I like to think it was, but I also think you were a little intrigued too and didn't want to miss out on the action. Did Evan talk to you on the trip to London?"

"Yes, he talked to me." He said laughing.

"I mean about what happened in Australia?"

"He did, and I understand he told you also."

"I was out in the rose garden deadheading one day last week when he came along and asked me if I would like to go for a walk with him down to the pond. We sat at the water's edge and fed the swans and the ducks. Out of the blue he said that he had been at a birthday party for his friend Halsey Millan when he was five years old. They had all seen the smoke arise from across the plain. It continued into the night. The next day he found out that it was his house that had burned to the ground and that there was no sign that his parents or sister had perished with it. Can you believe that no trace was ever found of them, and it remains as one of Western Australia's biggest unsolved mysteries even today? He said that at first there had been talk that his parents were facing bankruptcy and had set the fire themselves as to a way of collecting the insurance, but they hadn't materialised, so that ended that. Then there was the idea that they had been taken by an aboriginal tribe in the outback who believed that his mother was one of theirs. It was common knowledge that she was an ancestor of some obscure tribe of the Outback; the Noongars I think he called them.. They were a friendly tribe so that didn't make sense and of course there was the UFO abduction theory. Nash was too young to believe anything except that he had been abandoned. He was raised by the Millan family until he was fourteen. He left and wandered the arid outback for two years searching for some clue to the disappearance of his family. Eventually, he found his way to Perth where he found work and eventually became a bush pilot which enabled him to continue the search which he did until he came to London and in doing so came to work for McAllister Enterprises as a pilot. He had a hard and lonely life, but that is all behind him now he says as Rose and all of us are all the family he will ever need."

"Yeah, that was pretty much the way I heard it too. Australia's loss was our gain. And, by the way, he has no intention of ever entering into any partnership with Doctor Shelia."

We kissed and left it there for the night. I dreamt of Johnny rescuing me from the Black Russian who was trying to drown me in the Millerfloss River

Rainey left me at the hospital the next morning and went off to look at real estate and track down Pete and Pit. I babysat my grandson while Lili had a shower. At half ten a strapping young man sporting a mass of ginger curls appeared at the door holding a large bouquet of red roses. Lili and I both looked up at the stranger at the door. He was no stranger to her.

"Halo, a bheil failta orm?" He crooned all the while smiling at my daughter. I now knew why he was called Rusty as he had a head of ginger colored curls.

Halo was hello in Scottish, but whatever else he was trying to say was lost on me.

"Oh Rusty, what are you doing here? How did you know, how did you find me…it was my father wasn't it?" Lili blubbered.

"Yes, and thank God he found me before I took off for France to find you. I have been worried sick about you. I lost Tanny's phone number and your phone was dead, and for the love of me I couldn't remember the name of the café. But this, this…" He was by her side gazing at Jeremiah. "Why wouldn't you tell me Lili; why wouldn't you tell me?"

Okay good, he could speak English.

"I didn't think you would want to be burdened…"

"Don't say another word. Are you okay, is the baby okay? That's all that matters."

"I named him Jeremiah. Do you want to hold him?" Lili asked.

"Can I? Jeremiah Thompson; I love it!" He seemed to notice me for the first time and reached his hand out across the bed. "Rusty Thompson, Mrs. Quinn. Do you know that you have a beautiful daughter? Oh, of course you do, what am I saying?"

"I think you are just a little overwhelmed Rusty. It's a lot to take in. I am going to give you all some privacy so you can get caught up." I shook his hand and blew them a kiss as I left, but not before I heard Lili say that she was going to name him Jeremiah Quinn, and to cradle his head.

"I love it, Jeremiah Quinn Thompson! We can call him J.Q. or J.T."

Well, that settled that.

I went back across the street, made some sandwiches for our lunch, stuffed our dirty clothes into a sac and packed the rest into the suitcase. I had no idea how long Rainey would be so I made myself comfortable and called Ava, Sissy and Tanny to give them all an update on what was happening with Lili. Rainey arrived at twelve thirty. Over lunch he relayed what information he had managed to pry out of the brothers. I didn't know that Pit and Pete were brothers. Rainey said they weren't; only brothers in crime. The story was very interesting yet added more mystery to the elevator haunting episode.

At three o'clock we were on our way to Avanloch. The usual boring trip sped by quickly as Rusty's enthusiasm kept us entertained. He wanted to know everything about the castle and life in Canada. It appeared as if wherever Lili and JT were going he was going too. Lili seemed to be very pleased with his decisions to start a new life away from London and his family. He had no hard feelings though and hoped his parents would come out and meet their grandchild, but if they didn't then it would be their loss. I knew that he had been a street artist in Sete where he had met Lili and Tanny, but wondered if one could make a living doing such. Well, certainly not in Bridge or Hawthorne, so was curious as to how he planned to make a living for his family. It didn't matter to me, but I wondered if Rainey was wondering the same thing, and apparently he was because he asked Rusty if he had any aspirations for any future vocations besides managing a furniture store. Lili said that he was an amazing artist.

"Thank-you Lill, and although I love drawing and painting, the meager earnings won't keep JT in diapers so I am hoping there will be some work for me at the castle that will help pay our rent until I can figure things out."

"We understand that his has caught you completely by surprise, but no worries regarding your keep. There is always work to be done on the estate grounds, and an extra hand is always appreciated." Rainey assured him.

"How is your hand at portraits Rusty? I may just have a job for you if you are interested."

"I most definitely am Mrs. Quinn."

"First thing we need to get straight Son is that my wife is Vienna or Ana, and I am Rainey or Pappy, and there is no formality at Avanloch."

We arrived at Avanloch at four in the afternoon. Rusty told us that he had visited half a dozen castles in England and a couple in France, and as magnificent as some of them were they had seemed cold to him, but despite the brick and stone of Avanloch it seemed to have a warm feeling to it. I told him it was because it was not just a castle, but a home full of love.

Rainey had planned on driving up to the back door, but the front door opened and changed that. The adults hung back but the girls circled the car trying to get a look at the new arrivals. Rainey asked them if it was safe to get out. They laughed and told him to hurry. Lili handed JT to him and he proudly introduced him. I took Rusty's arm and presented him to the rest of the family. The others caught up and together we walked into the grand entrance which was adorned with welcome paraphernalia. We left Rusty in the girl's hands as he marveled at the ornamentation. Mrs. D was waiting in the kitchen and as usual was teary eyed as she hugged Lili and kissed JT who was still in Rainey's arms. She welcomed Rusty and told Rainey to get Lili into the family dining room as she needed to get off her feet and there was a comfy chair waiting for her. I followed along with Rusty who was still a little overwhelmed. I recognised the twin's two bassinettes in the corner. One was adorned with streamers and balloons and was filled with gifts while the other one was fitted with bedding for JT. Rainey laid JT in it and pulled it up a long side of Lili and Rusty. Rosy said they could tackle the gifts after dinner. She said a nice welcoming grace bringing tears to the eyes. A feast had been prepared for us and we made good work of it.

After a little break, Rusty and Lili with the help of all the girls opened the gifts. She cried at every one and especially the ones from strangers. They weren't strangers to me though as I knew them all. They were from the Village and surrounding small hamlets. They had put their skills to work in the construction of blankets, booties, bonnets and little outfits. How they all knew that there was a new life at the castle was not surprising. Lili wanted to thank everyone personally which was going to be a daunting task especially with the elevator and murder thing unsolved, but Colleen had a suggestion. She and the other girls had been scheming while we adults had been otherwise occupied. They wanted to have a "tea" like in the olden days just for fun, but now they could invite the village as a thank-you for their kindness.

"What a wonderful idea girls!' Rosy exclaimed. "It will take some time to do all the baking and to get the invitations out, but it's a marvelous plan. What do you think Mama?"

"It is indeed a lovely thought, and I am very proud of you girls for coming up with the idea. We'll all pitch in, but let's give Lili a few weeks to recuperate first okay? Oh, and one other thing, those olden days were not so long ago. I remember how I had dreaded them at first because I thought people just wanted to come and see what kind of a woman had a child but no husband, and then marries the king of the castle. I was sure they thought I was a fortune hunter. I was very wrong, and soon I started to enjoy the "teas" when I realised that they hadn't come to judge me, but to friend me. Of course, there are always those few that are just out and out snoops, but not to worry about them. I'll do my best to make it a fun experience for everyone."

"Ana, I didn't mean to be disrespectful when I said "olden" because you sure aren't old."

"Oh, I know you didn't Colleen, but I am getting up there." I laughed.

"You'll always be young at heart Mama." Rosy declared. "Now this is what we all agreed upon, but you and Daddy and Lili have to agree with it or we can change things up."

"Perhaps if you tell us what you are talking about we can give an opinion." I answered.

"Until things get back to normal around here Johnny is going to stay here with Amma and will move into Ash's rooms. Colleen and Beth want to continue staying with Novia and Calla in the rooms next to yours, so we thought that Lili and Jeremiah could have LizBeth's suite. That was before we knew about Rusty so it makes good sense don't you think? But, if you want them closer to you we can switch rooms up."

"What do I think? I think that you are amazing. You and Evan never even blinked an eyelash when I asked if I could bring Lili here, and you have made everything so easy for us, so thank-you, thank you, thank you. Now let's head upstairs and see if Lili and Rusty like their new digs."

"That goes double for me. And, special thanks for bedding JT next to you and Evan, Red. It's been a while, but I seem to remember that babies have a way of waking the household several times over in the midnight hours. I think Ana and I will be far enough away not to worry about that." Rainey said winking at Rosy making us all laugh.

"Yeah, I thought about that too, but considering how you need your beauty sleep, it was a no brainer." Evan said sweet-talking Rainey. "Come on, I'll help you up Pappy."

"I've got a couple of years on you, that's all, so don't get too cocky 'cause your day's a comin Son." Rainey ribbed.

"Quit horsing around you two. Rusty is going to wonder what he's got himself into." Rosy scolded humorously. "And Mom, this will always be your house, and it is because of you that we have such a beautiful place inside and out, so I just hope that Evan and I do it justice."

"Oh, you and Evan do and so much more. What do you think about it all Rusty?"

"I am overwhelmed by the warmth and kindness you have all shown me. I am but a stranger to you all, and yet I already know that I want to be a part of this family. When Lili's dad came to London to find me I was overwhelmed to find out that she had given birth to my chid, but I was also ecstatic. I couldn't wait to see them both, and I thought I'd bring them back to London until we could decide what to do. Even though I had a pretty good idea what her family was like through our many conversations about our childhoods, I still had no idea just what she was talking about. I see it now and I feel the love and I hope I can live up to your expectations."

"We have no expectations Rusty. If you love Lili like you say you do, actions will speak louder than words, so you have our blessings. How about if we get this new mother and babe upstairs for a much needed rest? You help Lili and I'll bring JT." Rainey suggested.

Half an hour later I made my way back downstairs. I left Rosy and Rainey explaining the layout of all the rooms on the second floor. JT was asleep in his crib and Lili was resting on the bed beside him. I stopped at the kitchen and grabbed my purse and headed for the door.

"Just where are you sneaking off to My Lady?"

"I'm just going for a walk." I replied.

"Do you always take your purse along for the walk?"

"Okay, you caught me." I tossed my bag aside after taking a cigarette and lighter out. "I'm off to smoke my last cig because I can't have the stench of smoke on me for Lili's and JT's sake."

"Is this a relatively new habit of yours?"

"No, not so new. Let's just say a revival of a sixties bad habit."

"I see. Would you like some company on your walk?"

"Surprisingly I would, and maybe you will enlighten me as to why you have been avoiding me since I arrived? Have I done or said something to meet with your disapproval?"

Johnny took my arm and steered me towards the path to Miller Floss crossing. He squeezed my hand. "I'm sorry Vienna. You must know that you could never do anything wrong in my eyes. No, I'm afraid that it is all on me. When Rosy told me you were coming I made up my mind that I would keep what I had discovered to myself. There was no way to involve you in what you didn't remember happening forty years ago. Then Tanny brought up that damn key again, and well…"

"What could that key, and I am thinking that it is the key that I found twenty years ago, have to do with anything?"

"Here, let's sit."

"I think I'd rather sit on the bank and put my feet in the water. It's unusually low isn't it?"

"It is, but we haven't had much rain. August storms should take care of that." He assured me and helped me down the bank. He lit my cigarette and took a drag.

"Does Amma know that you still have the urge?"

"Yeah, she does. She blames in on the new hired hand. I suppose Rainey knows?"

"He tolerates it, but I mainly keep it to myself. What's in the box Johnny? You looked right at me and said that it had come full circle. What did you mean by that? Something happened between us didn't it? I need to know before you expose it to everyone else. I've been anticipating something disturbing…"

"Stop right there Vienna! I'm afraid to ask what you think happened."

"I have had visions of you leaving my bedroom, but I have no memory of anything else, so why would you be in my room in the middle of the night unless…"

"Unless we had been in bed together…is that what you are trying to say?"

"I guess it is."

"Well, you can quit torturing yourself because nothing like that happened. I would never do that to Amma or you. God Vienna, it's been forty years! How many times did I tell you that we needed to talk? You always said that it had to remain just between you and me, and there was no reason to speak of it ever. I honestly thought you just wanted to put room 6 and Tatylyanna to rest for good and never wanted me to mention it again. This is all so bloody screwed up, and I'm to blame for letting it go on for so long, and I will understand if you can't forgive me."

"I don't think anything requires my forgiveness, but something disturbing must have transpired in room 6, so what was it? It's time I knew don't you think?"

"You honestly don't remember do you?"

"I don't remember anything about that room except that it was bitterly cold, and it has been that way for all these years. I doubt if I'll ever have a recall even after you reveal what took place. You have answered the question I most feared so I am good, and now we just have to figure out what it is that has you on edge."

"I've been wavering between two worlds off and on for years trying to understand if what I think took place that night actually did, or if it was really just a dream. If it was real then that meant that I had entered into another dimension, and the bonds of reality were shred. That wasn't in my realm back then so I decided to ignore it, but it was always somewhere in the recesses of my mind."

"I understand; you were in "the in-between place" weren't you?"

"You remember that story?"

"I do, and I have been there myself, so now something has brought you to some sort of realization hasn't it?"

"Yes, my uncle died, and I have come upon some evidence in his papers that may settle the matter once and for all. Believe me, I was…"

A voice caught us by surprise. "What are you two doing down there? You're not planning on making off with my wife are you O'Shea?"

Johnny helped me up. "Yup; you've caught us Rain; foiled again."

Damn, now I guess I was going to have to wait until tomorrow to find out what Johnny had been harboring for forty years. I asked Rainey what he and Rusty were up to.

"Just showing him the lay of the land. Amma's going to give us a tour of Brackenshire, and she's making us tea; want to join us?"

"Don't be silly. Thanks for accompanying me on the walk Johnny. Now off you go to collect your wife. See you back at the castle." I left them hearing Rusty ask Rainey why it was silly that he'd invited me to tea.

"You'll soon learn that my wife has a very distinct sense of humor which you'll never quite understand, but we love her anyway don't we John?" My husband quipped.

CHAPTER 5

THE IN-BETWEEN

The house was silent except for a murmur coming from the television in the media room. I took a pitcher of milk from the fridge, loaded a plate with a dozen freshly baked cookies, put them all on a tray and made my way to the lift. The door was open into the sitting room of LizBeth's suite. I found Liliana standing over JT's crib.

"Is he asleep?" I whispered.

"He is. Are you coming to keep me company?"

"It looks like you are ready for bed so I'll just stay for a minute."

"Oh no, this is just a lounging outfit Rosy gave me. It's too special to sleep in. I'm not tired at all. Daddy took Rusty on a walk around so I am feeling rather lonesome. I was hoping you would come by. What's on the cart?"

"I didn't know what was in your fridge so I brought a snack."

"Goodie; I'm always hungry. Will you tell us a story Mommy?"

I smiled amusingly. "You want me to tell you and JT a story?"

"Yes, it will be his very first fairy tale."

"May I listen too, please?" My oldest daughter asked from the doorway.

"You have caught me off guard girls, but I suppose I could. What story do you want to hear?"

"It doesn't matter as we love them all." Lili said making room for me beside her on the bed.

"Okay, I'll see what I can come up with. Pull up a chair Rosy and pour us a glass of milk. Give me a minute to put my thinking cap on. My memory isn't as good as it used to be you know, but I'm sure yours are, so feel free to jump in if I disremember. Is that even a word?"

"I think it is Mom, but you've always made up your own words to suit your unique stories, so we never question do we Lili?" Rosy asked her sister who agreed.

"You know what; I may have a new story. What do you think?"

"A new story; how wonderful!" Rosy exclaimed.

"Actually, it is somewhat of a true fairy tale. It is not really mine though; it's Johnny's."

"Our Johnny?"

"Yes Rosy; our Johnny. Perhaps you have even heard it before."

She laughed. "I doubt it Mom as he isn't that chatty, and I can't imagine him making up a fairy tale. He has said some pretty funny things after a few drinks though."

"Exactly, and that is how the story came out. I don't believe he made it up though. He and your father were celebrating something with a jug of whiskey around the campfire one evening shortly after our wedding here. It's been a long time, but I'll tell it as best as I can. You know that your Dad's ancestry is Irish, but he doesn't know much about their customs or anything. His father and grandfather were both born in Canada and the lineage is not a topic of conversation. Rainey has always been going to do a family tree, but so far he has never done so. Anyhow, Johnny had filled him in on some funny Irish folklore. They were having a snorting good time when Amma and I joined them. A few minutes later Johnny threw the remainder of his drink into the fire which sent a burst of flame into the air. He asked if we would like to hear an old tale that was regarded as a family legend that had been passed down from his clan for many a year. His mother told him the story the year before she died. He was eleven years old. It was told through his great, great grandmother Orla's eyes and Ella, her granddaughter. Now, close your eyes and be transported to another world.

The O'Shea Fairy Tale

"Come and tell me why you are so quiet child."

"I have made them the stone circles Grammama just like you told me, but they still do not come."

"That's because they are not here Ella."

"Where are they?"

"They are somewhere between dusk and dawn sunning by the corral sea, or sleeping in a verdant woodland, or frolicking in a luscious meadow, or maybe bathing in the babbling brook where the waters tumble down from a snowy mountain top. It is summer, and they are giddy and adventurous as they cavort from one place to another. They may never let you see them, but you may feel one brush by you in a gentle breeze, and if you are very, very lucky, you may hear them laughing. But, my dear Ella, none of this can happen if you don't believe, and you have to be able to transpose yourself to somewhere unseen. If you don't have the ability or desire to be spellbound you will never be able to enter their realm. But, if you are of a kindred spirit and believe that the visible and the invisible can become one, then you will have the gift of being able to mingle with fairies."

"Do you have the gift Grammama?"

"I have been in the presence of the sprites many times when I was a young lass. They seem to prefer the wee children. I am just an old soul to them now."

"Am I too old Grammama?"

"If you are truly of a mind to enter into the "in-between", then we must hasten to ready you."

"What is the in-between?"

"It is what your Celtic ancestors described as a place neither here nor there, not one thing or the other. It is a place of transition to another plane, another world, so to speak. If you can clear your mind from the humdrum of the day you may see and hear what your heart and mind want to. Are you ready?"

"Yes, yes; what do I have to do?"

"Do you have a place in mind that is peaceful and enchanting?"

"Once Dadia took me to a little brook beyond the green meadows It was very peaceful there. We crossed over a little bridge and I sat on a big mossy rock and listened to the birds singing while he fished. I want to go there, but it is very far away."

"It is not so far if you have a companion."

"But who would come with me?"

"The dragonflies; they will lead you."

"Oh Grammama, I cannot catch a dragonfly. They are way too fast."

"They are friends of the fairies here in Eire and are filled with spiritual energy, a sort of magic that can travel between dimensions."

"What are dimensions?"

"The spaces in-between the real and the mystical. I will walk with you to the edge of the meadow. You must not become disheartened as it will take many days for the winged ones to come. They need time to know that you are their friend. Every day they will accept you a little bit more if they can feel

your sincerity. Do not be loud and do not beg for them to appear. Listen not only with your ears, but with your heart. Some days you may fall asleep, but when you awake you may see a tiny footprint on a toadstool, or you may feel that one has passed your way as a warm breeze caresses you, or you may hear singing. Oh, I hope you hear singing! It will be a wonderful, joyous experience. I have much faith in your determination. What have you to offer them?"

"I have nothing."

"You do Ella. That poem you wrote, the song you sing every day, that picture you painted...they will love them all. Now, we must go as you need to be home by dusk and the day be half away already, and the dragonflies won't wait forever."

"Are they waiting just for me?"

"The whole world is waiting for you child."

I said, "You can open your eyes now." and watched for their reaction. It was what I expected.

"Mom, that can't be the end. Did Ella find the fairies?" Lili asked disappointedly.

"That's for you to decide. I think the story is a challenge to one's beliefs. Are you satisfied with the life and world that you live in, or do you believe that there is magic of your own choosing to be found? Do you dare to see what's possible beyond your imagination? I chose to believe that Ella gazed into the glimmering pond and saw pixies gazing back at her, and that she watched them splashing and laughing, and that when she turned to go home, a beautiful blue dragonfly sat waiting for her on a toadstool imprinted with tiny little footprints."

"I went to the brook with Ella because your voice took me there Mama." Rosy said.

"I did too. I saw everything that Grammama described because you drew the pictures in my mind beautifully as always Mommy." Lili applauded.

"Did you believe she was able to descend into another realm and fulfill her dream?"

"I do. I'm sorry Johnny's mom died when he was so young. I can't imagine growing up without you or Daddy. Do you think his mom had the enchantment, and what about Johnny; do you think he went looking for the pixies?"

I laughed. "You will have to ask him that yourself Lili, but don't expect an answer."

"I can't even believe that Johnny told this story." Rosy declared. .

"I may have embellished the original tale. I think I hear your dad talking to Amma."

"What are you doing out here all by yourself Amma?"

"I didn't want to interrupt…"

I called for her to come in and asked why she would think she was interrupting.

"I came to bring you your phone as it had wedged itself into a cushion seat, and I heard you mention Ella…I hope you won't be upset with me, but I surmised that you were about to tell Johnny's tale, so I sat down and listened."

"Oh, you silly goose; of course I am not upset with you. Are you with me for telling it?"

"I doubt that he'd even recognise it to be the same one he told. You have such a picturesque way with spinning yarns and turning words into pictures Vienna. I was enchanted, but I have another confession. I had your phone in my hand and I turned the record button on because my girls have never even heard the story. I doubt very much if Johnny will ever tell them. I will erase it if you would prefer and maybe it didn't even record."

"You will do no such thing, and if it didn't turn out, I'll do it all over for the girls, but first I will need to get Johnny's permission. I did embellish a lot you know."

"His telling of it was pretty simple so he will love how you made it come alive.'

"We will see, but we must not bother him about it because he is very troubled and we need to help him come to terms with whatever it is first."

"I'm thinking you know more than any of us what is troubling him besides the belief that his uncle was murdered?"

"I do not Amma, but hopefully we will all have the answers tomorrow."

Rainey and I met Evan and Johnny coming down the hall. They had left the girls watching a movie on the TV, and told us not to worry as Novia was in charge. Apparently, they had moved the TV from the remodeled room 6 and a couple of sofas into the girl's room as they didn't want them downstairs in the media room and they would feel they were safer next to us. I thought they were being paranoid, but didn't say anything. I left Rainey talking with them and quickly changed and was snuggled in bed by the time he came in. He said he was going to shave and did I want to join him. I told him that I did not.

"I thought you liked to watch me shave?"

"I have that down pat thank-you."

"Okay; I just thought you might want to keep me company as we haven't seen much of each other today. Are you going to tell me what you and Johnny talked about?"

"It's all good; nothing happened between us. Well, not what I thought anyhow. He was about to tell me something, but you and Rusty showed up so that ended that."

"Sorry. I guess we'll find out what's in the box tomorrow."

"Lili thinks the key is in it."

"Your key? Why would she think that?"

"Tanny told her, and just because I found the key doesn't mean that it's mine."

"It materialized out of nowhere, and you found it, so I believe it was meant for you to find."

"I have no idea why, and I doubt that the key will come into play with what's going on today."

Rainey went into the parlour and returned saying that the key was missing. Of course it was.

CHAPTER 6

THE KEYS

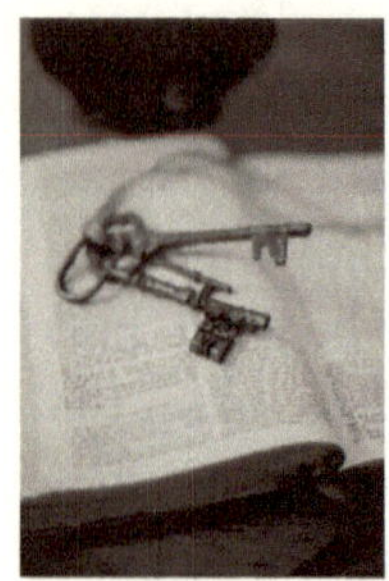

Evan presented me with my own special omelette, sans mushrooms, and told us to join Amma and Johnny and Mary in the other room. It appeared that he and Rosy were the cooks this morning. Rainey filled his plate with the other offerings that were on the warming trays. He made me toast because he knew that along with the butterflies in my stomach I wouldn't be able to tolerate anything more. I thanked Rosy and Evan with a kiss. Rosy poured me coffee from the large electric pot on the sideboard in the dining room. Evan set fluted glasses and pitchers of mimosas in ice buckets on the table and told us to help ourselves. Johnny said he needed a clear head so would pass for now. Rainey said he'd do the same. The rest of us agreed. I hoped there would be reason to raise a glass after the revelation. I placed my hand on Johnny's shoulder and gave it a squeeze, gave Amma a quick hug and sat down between Mary and Rainey. Evan shut the door into the kitchen. That was something that was never done, but he didn't want the kids disturbing us so he'd laid down the law to them last night and told them not to disturb us. Rusty had Lili were having breakfast upstairs. I hoped the worst would be over by the time everyone made it downstairs, and that we would finally know what was in the little red box that seemed to be the reason for Johnny's distress. It was nowhere to be seen at the moment. After everyone had satisfied their appetites, Evan and Rainey collected all the plates, utensils and condiments and put them in the dry sink to be dealt with later.

Johnny took a deep breath. "I want you all to know that I had decided to keep all of this to myself years ago. It only concerned Vienna and me, and she had no memory of it, so it was better to let sleeping dogs lie, and maybe I had just been dreaming after all. Then two things happened. First, my uncle died and some unusual findings in his belongings gave me reason to question if it had any bearing on what I had come to believe was a dream some thirty odd years ago. When Tanny mentioned "the key" on the phone the other day I seriously began to wonder if the findings and the keys were all related."

"Are you talking about the key that Vienna found years ago, and are there more, and what possible connection could it have to you and her?" Amma asked curiously.

I shuddered. Rainey took my hand at the same time as Johnny was taking Amma's.

"It's not what you are thinking Honey, but I understand that you might be feeling confused when I said that it only concerned Vienna and me. I just found out yesterday that she has been unsure of what happened between us for years. Let me be perfectly clear; **nothing** of an immoral nature transpired. It was something completely unimaginable. I used to regard the occult as a supernatural phenomenon that only occurred in an overactive mind, but that was before I came to work and live here. You all know that I lived with my Uncle Walt just down the road for many a year, but I had only seen Avanloch from a distance. I wondered what it was like to live in a castle, but never in my wildest dreams did I ever think I would come to work for and become part of the family that inhabited it. The day Amma and I were married Jeremy asked me if I would like to come and work here. I didn't have to think twice and accepted immediately. It was a great pleasure to work for Jeremy and Vienna who were married a week later." Johnny stopped talking and smiled at me. "You were known as Vela then and we became good friends. You never considered me as just a hired hand, and you trusted me to do what I thought was best for the estate. Now the darling little lassie who was the flower girl at Amma's and my wedding is the Lady of the house, and we love and respect her and Evan just as we did you."

"You and Amma *are* Avanloch Johnny, and we couldn't even begin to manage without you. Rose is a little too teary eyed to speak right now, but shares my sentiment." Evan acknowledged.

"Sorry for the sappiness, but I needed to acknowledge my gratitude. Things are about to change direction and get a little outlandish now. No hauntings or anything unusual happened that I was aware of until Joe, one of the hired hands was remodelling room 6, fell through the balustrade. He believed that he was pushed by an invisible force. So now I will take you back to the night Vienna and I entered room 6 with Jeremy and the ghost hunter, Allister. They had hopes of confronting Tatylyanna. I was sceptical that her life-force existed to say the least. Rainey, you, Evan and Rosalyn of course were not there, but you have all heard the story countless times over, so I think you will be able to picture the setting as I take you back there. As Vienna will concur; the room was bitterly cold. It was black except for a small pen light that Allister would turn on at his discretion."

Amma interrupted. "Excuse me Johnny, but I was not there. I had taken Rosy and Ava down to my mother's. I believe some of the household staff waited and took notice downstairs with Jannie, Duffy and Mary though."

"You're right as usual my dear; I stand corrected. I am sure there is an account of the time and day and year somewhere, but I'm thinking it was around 1970…what do you say Vienna?"

"I believe it was the summer of 1969 as the girls and I had just returned from a visit to Bridge Falls. The carpenter, as you said, insisted that he had been pushed. Jannie and I had one hell of a time convincing Jeremy that Taty was still in room 6. I'm pretty sure that your retelling of the night will not awaken any recessed memory of mine, but I'm aware that there is something about events of that night that are troubling to you, so it's time that I pay attention, so carry on please."

"There was someone else in the room that night… or entity, I suppose I should say."

"Yes of course, Tatylyanna." I blurted out as a chill enveloped me.

"There was another presence Vienna; it was Avaleena." Johnny said emotionally.

"How can that be? We didn't even know about her back then?"

Rainey suggested that I let Johnny continue and could ask questions later. I apologised.

"No reason to apologise Vienna and you are right, I didn't know who the apparition was until later that night which I will explain later. I can fully understand why you did not see her as at the same time she appeared, you were entranced by Taty's voice. Sorry, I don't know how else to describe it. So, here I was holding your mesmerised limp body wondering what the hell was going on, and then this spectre in grey is before me warning me to get you out of there."

I had the feeling that there was more to come. "She knew who we were then; did she call us by our names?"

"She did. She addressed me as Quinn."

Johnny stopped talking again. I didn't know if it was for effect or because it was unnerving. I think we all said "WHAT?" in unison.

"Her exact words to my memory are: "Quinn, take the keys and get Gracie Darling out of here before it's too late. Go at once to Alissgrea, go, go.""

"Alice Grey, Alice Grey…what could she have had to do with any of this?" I demanded.

Mrs. D patted my hand. "It's a place, not a person Dear."

I was confused. Rainey understood and asked how it was spelled. Mary said she was sure that it was A-l-i-s-s-g-r-e-a, and that it was a monastery and was alleged to have secretly housed expatriates in the seventeenth century. It had been destroyed when its' true identity had been exposed by whatever forces were in power back then, and that was all she knew.

"Thank-you Mary, I think you have answered a question for us." He smiled into my eyes. "I think you were saying "Alissgrea" the night you had your sleep walking ordeal, and not Alice Grey. The girls also heard it as you did. Do you agree that it is a possibility? It you do, it would mean that you do have a repressed memory of that evening. How do you feel about that?"

"I suppose that it's possible. How have you lived with this all this time Johnny?"

"I guess I talked myself into believing it never happened, and didn't dwell on it. The night Lady Maveryn came to Evan to warn him about your dire situation as you lay haemorrhaging on the path to the crypt, I decided that yeah, these things do happen, and I vowed I'd tell him about the happenings in room 6."

"I wish you had Johnny. What made you change your mind?"

"I'm not sure Evan, but then I would have also told you what happened later that night, and…I don't know. I guess I didn't want to risk you dismissing it as a hallucination, but now, with my uncle's death and discoveries, it's come full circle, and needs to be told. We both thought we had our feet planted firmly on the ground didn't we? And what about you Rain; did you ever come to terms with your encounters with the Grey Lady who was Avaleena when we came to know who she really was? Unlike Vienna, who embraced the echoes of the castle's inhabitants, we chose to pass it off as happenstance I suppose."

"You obviously have more to say John, so let's have it." Evan suggested.

"I'm thinking that it was probably around midnight when I decided that I needed to go and check on Vienna. Her reaction to hearing the tape of Taty talking through her did not seem to have upset her at all, but I believed otherwise. Amma was sound asleep so I didn't wake her. If she awoke she would know that I had gone for a walk like I usually did when I couldn't sleep. The castle doors were never locked back then as the dogs were trusted to keep vigil. They wagged their tails as I stepped around them on the back entrance and let myself in. I took my shoes off as I knew Mary was a light sleeper and I certainly didn't want to wake her. I thought I'd go up the grand stairway as it was less creaky. I arrived at Vienna's door, tapped lightly and asked her if she was all right. She didn't answer, so I tapped again and opened the door just enough to peek inside. It was pitch black except for a flickering lamp coming from across the room. I stepped inside and asked her if she was awake. I realised then that the light was coming from the west side of the room which was odd because Vienna's bed is against the south wall. I walked towards it and found her sitting up in a four poster bed that was enclosed in sheer netting. I had the presence of mind to know that something was wrong as the bed was in the wrong place and the light was coming from a gas light. I asked her again if she was all right. She said she was and that I should go because I had a very busy day tomorrow. She shut the lamp off and I made my way through the dark to the door and opened it. I turned as she said "Goodnight Johnny." There was enough light coming from the hallway that I could see that she was back where she was supposed to be; in the bed against the south wall. I shut the door, but was tempted to re-enter the room because I thought that maybe my eyes had deceived me. I thought better of it and went back down the stairs and scoured the walls in the reception room. There hung a portrait of the woman who had ordered Quinn to take Gracie Darling and the keys to Alissgrea. So, what's the word; do you all think I had a few moments of irrational episodes, not once but twice, or is it too outlandish to even render an opinion?"

Evan spoke first. "I believe you had an out of body experience in Vienna's room, but the encounter with Avaleena…hell, that was strange Brother!"

"Who am I to question John? Hell, apparently, I walked through a bookcase with the same woman who visited you in room 6. She's everywhere, and she may not be done with us yet. If there is a wrong to be righted, I guess we're all her pawns to set it right." Rainey said solemnly.

"What about you Amma; you've been unusually quiet throughout it all?" Johnny asked.

"I'm still trying to understand how or why you kept it to yourself, but I'm sure it all happened exactly the way you described it. Nothing good comes from keeping quiet. Vienna has lived for thirty some years wondering why you were in her room, and thinking the worst. You should have sat her down and talked it out Johnny."

"He didn't know what I thought Amma, so he is not to blame. And, I was like him; I put it in the far corners of my mind and left it there, so it did not eat away at me."

"How can you be sure that the uncertainty of that night isn't what caused your depression?"

"The reason for my melancholy is sitting right here beside me Amma, and no one is to blame for that but me. If I hadn't of been so pig headed and had talked to Johnny when he asked me if I wanted to talk about what had happened he would have told me about Avaleena's visit in room 6, and he wouldn't have had to live all this time wondering if he was mad, but I was so afraid of what I thought happened that I thought it would go away if I just ignored it."

"Mom, what did you think happened, and what's this about your sleep walking and looking for Alice Grey?" Rosy asked.

I explained the incident the way Tanny and Zoe had explained it to me, and seeing I didn't know any Alice Grey, maybe I had said Alissgrea which now made more sense. I wasn't sure how to answer her other question, but Johnny saved me the embarrassment.

"This is the first I've heard about Vienna's sleep walking also Rosy, but it might explain how she used to disappear on us years ago but had no remembrance of any such thing the next day. As for your other question, I just found out yesterday that she thought that we'd slept together."

Rosy came and put her arms around me. "Oh Mommy, that is so sad. I can't believe you have lived with that notion for thirty years. Did you know Daddy?"

"I always knew there was something between them, and I was jealous of their close relationship at first. I had no right to be jealous because I had been absent from her life for twenty years, but you know me. Anyhow, Johnny set me straight, and I soon learned that they had a special relationship that did not include sex. I did not discover Vienna's fears until a few days ago. She didn't know what the box had to do with anything, but thought Johnny's conscience couldn't keep the secret of what had happened between the two of them any longer. Thankfully, she was completely mistaken."

"As I said before, I filed that whole night in the recesses of my mind and left it there so I was not consciously in a state of uncertainty. When Rainey first suggested that I had a selective memory I was vaguely aware of that night, but put it away again. I'm pretty sure that this is the first time I am hearing the name Alissgrea, and am wondering what it could possibly have to do with your uncle Johnny?"

"That is the million dollar question isn't it? I guess I am going to have to make a trip to this Alissgrea place; what do you all think?" Johnny asked.

"It's not a place for you to be going to Johnny Boy." Mary stated.

"Why do you say that Mary?"

"It's like I be saying; it be in ruins and there be nothing there. The isle be bitter and cold."

"Isle; Alissgrea is on an island?"

"It be the island."

"Interesting; I guess my knowledge of the area is in arrears. I'll see if the computer can help.

"Let me do that for you John; but first you need to open that mysterious red box and show us what's inside." Rainey said.

"Yes, for God's sake, open that thing! You've been guarding it like it holds the Holy Grail, and it's driving me crazy." Amma bemoaned.

Johnny reached down and picked up the box from under that table. He told Amma to open it.

"How can I; it's locked."

He said it had never been locked, opened it and laid a key on the table.

"Oh my God; it's that stupid key!" Amma exclaimed.

"No, you're wrong my dear," Johnny said reaching into the box and placing a second key on the table, "*this one* is the stupid key."

"So now there are two?" She asked confused.

I think we all sighed. Evan examined the keys and said as far as he could see they were identical except one was labelled 22 and the other 44. He asked Johnny if key 22 was the one I had found and where did he get the other one.

"I discovered it in Uncle Walt's possessions and wondered if it was a match to the one Vienna had found. Now the only reason it caught my attention was because finding it brought back the night in room six when Avaleena had told me, or Quinn," Johnny quipped, "to take the **keys** and get Gracie Darling to Alissgrea. She had definitely said keys and not key, so there I was wondering what they meant, and so I retrieved the one from your parlor Vienna. Sorry for the intrusion but you weren't here yet, so I had no qualms."

"And, you shouldn't have. But, still the question remains, what do they open is twofold now, and what do they have to do with anything anyhow. I mean, are they somehow connected to your uncle's death or something here in the castle? I can't comprehend how one can have anything to do with the other."

"My questions exactly Vienna, and do the answers rest on the Island of Alissgrea?"

"My question is; why is Gracie always referred to as Gracie Darling and not just Gracie?" Roslyn asked.

"There is no answer to that Sweetie, unless it's in Avaleena's diary, but my remembrance is that she was always called that, so it is her name." I offered my thoughts.

Rainey stood up and poured us all a glass of the champagne mix. "Cheers to you Johnny and your reveal of a most disturbing affair. It's my belief that the events of that night would have remained with you forever if not for the discovery of the other key and data in your uncle's possessions. Drink up, and then we will see what we can discover about the isle of Alissgrea." He laughed. "I told Vienna last night that we should consider moving back as it was pretty dull back home compared to the unexpected and mysterious going-ons here. She called me silly, but I was serious."

"That would be wonderful! Why do you say the idea is silly Mom?"

I didn't have to answer Rosy as my phone was ringing. As usual I had no idea where it was. Amma passed it to me as Johnny asked her why she had my phone. She said that I was always losing it so she was safe-keeping it. I answered, and found Ava on the other end.

"This is a surprise as I thought you couldn't get through on my cell."

"I didn't want to call the land line so took a chance. Don't put me on speaker Mom."

"Okay; is everything all right?"

"Yes. I gather that you are not alone but it would be better if you were."

"Okay." I said getting up and indicating that I was going down the hall. I assured Rainey that all was well. He nodded and said that he and Johnny were off to the media room and told Evan that he should join them as he had something to run by him. Johnny said he had a few minutes before Armand showed up. I cursed silently upon hearing his name.

"Okay; I'm alone." I said as I walked into the parlor. "What's wrong Ava?"

"You tell me. I signed for a registered letter for you yesterday."

"Who is it from?"

"The return address is from Vancouver in the name of Patricia Ann Franklin."

"I don't know anyone by that name."

"Really Mom; you don't know any Patricia Ann?"

"I don't know why she would be writing me as she doesn't know who I am, and I have no idea how she would get my name and address. What does the letter say?"

"I didn't open it."

"Well, for God's sake, open it child!"

"Okay; hold on a moment. It's dated two months ago. She refers to you as Ms. LaFontaine and that is how the envelope was addressed; Ms. Vienna LaFontaine. Okay, here goes:

> Dear Ms. LaFontaine, I do not know who you are so have no idea why you would have set up a trust fund for me…

"Mother, what have you done?"

"Never mind; just read the damn letter!"

"Don't yell at me."

"Sorry Dear; I'm a little anxious and I will explain later."

"Okay; she goes on to say that she will not be accepting the funds as it sounds like blood money to her and that you are trying to ease your guilt for giving her away."

"What?"

"Well I don't know, so let me finish reading…"

> I see no other reason why a stranger would do such a thing, but I will not ease your conscience. I have known since I was a teenager that I was adopted. I was told that my father was unknown and that my mother had died. No other information was available to me. I was raised

by a loving family and decided a long time ago not to pursue having my adoption papers opened, and then on my twentieth birthday I get this surprise offering from you.

Are you my biological Mother? I see no other reason as to why you would set up a fund for me. I have deducted that the circumstances of my conception may have been traumatising to you, but I was a part of you and you chose to hide your shame by giving me away. It's obvious that you have money by setting up the trust. I hope it has eased your guilt, but as I said, I won't be taking your grandiose misplaced gift. There is one other probability though and that is that you are responsible for my biological mother's demise, and this is your way of making restitution thus labelling it blood money.

I toiled with not sending this, but decided that I needed to. Give your money to someone who you feel is deserving of it and who is not a blight on your reputation.

Goodbye Ms. LaFontaine.

"Oh my God Mom, that is so sad and ugly. Why did you do it, and does Daddy know?"

"No, your father does not know."

I heard a movement behind me and turned to find Rainey walking towards me. He asked what her father didn't know.

"I just told her that you hadn't decided when you were going home. Here, talk to your daughter." I passed him the phone and walked over to the window and stared outside not paying attention to what Rainey was saying until he spoke to me.

"Ava says you have something to tell me and then you are to call her back. So, what is it?"

"I've done something."

"Again?"

"Yes, and you won't like it. I set up a trust fund for someone and she has just turned twenty so she is able to access it now."

"That sounds like something you would do Vienna, so what's the problem? Sorry for intruding, but we were wondering what was keeping you. Rose was worrying that something was wrong with Ava." Evan said from the doorway where he and Rosy were standing.

"I just talked to Ava and everything is fine back home, so not to worry. You know as much as I do at this point as to whom my wife has set up a trust fund for that she thinks won't meet with my approval. I can assure you that my approval is not necessary, but you said that I won't like it, so do you want to enlighten us as to who the mystery person is Hon?" Rainey asked sweetly.

"It's Jorja's daughter; Patricia Ann." I said bluntly.

"Why would you do such a thing Vienna? Just when I think I've heard the last of her, here she is back in our life again. I have no words at the moment to voice my bewilderment." Rainey said and walked towards the door looking back at me with dismay.

"I am sure Mom has her reasons Dad; don't you think you owe it to her to explain?"

"I suppose I do Rosy. You have the floor Vienna."

"I would have told you eventually, but I couldn't at the time as it was shortly after we had promised each other that we would never keep anything from each other again. I had asked Jorja's lawyer to keep me informed as to Patricia Ann's adoption, and when I heard back from him that she had been adopted I decided to set the trust fund for her."

"I remember you telling me that she had been adopted, so why wouldn't you have mentioned the trust fund then? So much for promises eh?"

"I guess because I knew you would have the very reaction that you are having now. Anyhow, it's inconsequential because she is not accepting it as she thinks it's blood money because I was responsible for her biological mother's death, or that I am her real mother and abandoned her."

"Oh Mommy, that is horrible! How is this just coming to light now?" Rosy cried.

"She sent me a registered letter. Ava picked up the mail yesterday and it was there. You and Rainey can get the full accusation from her if you like."

"I think I have heard enough so I'll pass." Rainey said as he walked out the door.

Rosy and Evan embraced me and Evan said that his father-in-law needed a talking to. I told him not to waste his breath just as Rainey walked back in the door.

"Here's what we are going to do. No one gets off calling my wife a murderer or a liar, especially the daughter of the most despicable person I have ever known."

He took me in his arms. "Sorry Darling."

"Your apologising for something that was my fault in the first place is a moot point. Didn't we come to an understanding regarding apologies years ago?

"We did, and I am not apologising for not understanding the reasons you choose to keep the fund a secret, but for not having the compassion to see how this letter and accusations must have upset you. I know that you are the kindest and most loving person in the world, so none of her words apply to you. They are just guesstimates on her part, and we will set her straight on all of it when we get home. For now, we can get Ava to acknowledge the letter and tell her that we knew her biological mother and ask her if she would like to meet us so that we can any questions that she may have. What do you think?"

"Thank-you; that seems like the right thing to do, but we can't tell her the whole truth about Jorja, or how she ended up in prison, or how she died."

"No, of course not because that would imply that you may have had a hand in her demise."

"Why would you say such a thing Rainey?" Rosy demanded.

She never called him Rainey so I knew she was ticked. I laughed. "It's just a little joke we have between us Rosy. He thinks I may have orchestrated Jorja's death."

"That's absurd! How could you accuse her of such a thing?"

"She thinks I may have had her murdered too, so tit for tat." Rainey said winking at her.

"You two drive me crazy. I am rethinking my agreeing to you moving back here."

Evan took her arm. "Sure you are. You know you would like nothing better, but I have to agree, your parents' behavior can be confounding, but we wouldn't have it any other way. Janzen is probably here by now, so let's see what he's found out."

"Who's he." Rainey asked.

"He's a long- time friend of Johnny's who just happens to be a Scotland Yard Detective. You'll like him Dad; he's quite the character." Rosy said.

"Is he here in the friend department, or is it an official visit?"

"He's on assignment with Police Scotland who requested an agent to assist them into a criminal investigation in the area. He dropped in to see Johnny shortly after Uncle Walt's death. At that time Johnny believed that Walt had died of natural causes, but then he discovered evidence of a break-in, and then the one at the Manor, plus the cryptic documents, he suspected that his uncle may have been murdered. He relayed his findings to Janzen who agreed that it was a possibility and returned to survey the site. Walt's body has been exhumed and undergone another autopsy. He is here to reveal the results. Personally, I hope that nothing has been found that would indicate foul play, and that Johnny can lay his suspicions to rest." Evan explained.

"You and Johnny have torn walls down and searched the whole place from top to bottom, but have found nothing that would indicate that a crime took place, right?" Rainey asked.

"I'm of two minds Rain. I was all set to dismiss it as a natural death until we discovered the break-ins, and then Johnny's revelation this morning about the keys has got me wondering. Let's go and hear what the detective has found out shall we?"

I took Rainey's hand and we walked into the kitchen. I hoped Armand Janzen would not greet me as he usually did. Of course, I was wrong.

"There they are, the beautiful Ladies of the Manor! As always, it is a delight to see you Miss Rosalyn." He beamed as he greeted her. Then he focused his attention on me. "What, who is this Lady Vienna, another man has your hand? I am crestfallen."

I laughed slightly. "Yes, this man has my hand and my heart. This is my husband, Rainey Quinn. Rainey, this is Detective Armand Janzen."

"So, the truant husband has shown up. Sir, you are a fool to leave this lady alone in a country overrun with rakes such as I. Perhaps the time has come for me to state my intentions. I believe a duel is in order Sir. What would be your weapon of choice?"

I had never seen Rainey at a loss for words, and he didn't disappoint me with his comeback.

He extended his hand to Armand. "My daughter told me that I would like you Detective Janzen, but she forgot to inform me that you moonlight as a comedian."

Armand laughed heartedly taking my husband's hand and bowing ever so slightly. "Touché Monsieur, I concede to your flair in capturing this delicate lady's heart. I am a feared that she is lost to me this time for good."

"Quit clowning around Janzen!" Johnny ordered. "Let's get this show on the road. Rain, I'd like you to come with us if you don't mind?"

"Sure, whatever you want John, but where are we going?"

"Armand wants another look around at Walt's house, and I'd like your opinion as to your thoughts on there being a hidden room."

"No one is going anywhere until we hear the results of the autopsy!" Evan insisted.

Armand pulled an official looking document out of his shirt pocket, unfolded it and laid it on the table. "Have a gander folks; looks like Uncle Walt was the victim of a criminal offence; murder to be exact."

"Damn! A little more information would be beneficial. Johnny, you don't appear to be surprised?" Evan queried.

"He already informed Amma and me of the results while the rest of you were down the hall. It seems that Walt was the recipient of a lethal injection consisting of several opiate drugs which was not detected by the first autopsy. It was hidden from the naked eye at the base of the left ear. Sorry Evan that this has ended up on yours and Rose's doorstep. I guess it's in the hands of the crime squad now, and I will have to back away." Johnny said dejectedly.

"You and I have come too far with this to walk away, and what about all the hours Amma and Rose have devoted to deciphering the documents? No, there is more than just Uncle Walt's murder at stake here, and we are not through with our investigations yet, so take Armand

and Rain and get over to the house and see if there are any more clues to be found." Evan suggested.

"Thanks Bro. I trust you to hold down the fort here."

Rainey said he'd meet them outside after he had a word with me. The word was that I'd be doing some explaining to him when he got back. I told him that we would do it right now as I was going with him. I asked Evan if we could take the jeep. He walked us to the door, handed me the keys and said we could as long as I wasn't the one driving. He gave me a quick hug and told me to stay out of trouble and hoped a bad moon wasn't on the rise again. I punched him. Rainey asked me what that was all about. I said that Evan was just being facetious.

I waved to Johnny indicating that we would follow them. Rainey asked me how far Uncle Walt's cabin was. I said I knew it was in the Thistle area, but that was all I knew.

CHAPTER 7

THE THISTLE LEGACY

"Thistle, is that a village?"

"I have only been there once and that was a long time ago. There was only a church that doubled as a community centre and school, and a small general store there. I doubt that not much has changed in forty years. Hurry up or we'll lose Johnny."

"There's only one road so need to get excited. By the way, Evan and Johnny know about Colleen and the elevator. They've been waiting for her to fess up. I'm guessing you have something to confess to also and that is the real reason for your ride along?"

"I do not, but I didn't want you going off half-cocked and making a fool of yourself."

"It wouldn't be the first time would it? What do you think I was going to do?"

"In your own words; you're a lover not a fighter, so there is no danger in you engaging in fist-ta-cuffs, so you would have to do the attacking in words. There was suspicion and annoyance in your voice and eyes when

Armand greeted me so I need to assure you that it is all an act on his behalf. I am not entertained by any of his conjectures. He is a buffoon."

"I admit I was a bit surprised by his boldness, but I didn't think there was anything to be concerned with. Now I am wondering if he has had his eye on you for a while and has used his interest in Johnny's uncle's death as an excuse to see you. Just how many times has he been here in the last two weeks? Is it possible that he's one of your pursuers from your early years here, and if he is, how come this is the first I am hearing about him?" Rainey asked somewhat dubiously scanning my eyes for an acceptable answer.

"A lot of questions, but I do have all the answer and hopefully they will satisfy you. Apparently, he was in attendance at Johnny's and Amma's wedding. I do not remember meeting him then. He came to Jeremy's memorial though I do not know why as he didn't know him very well. He expressed his sympathy, but that was all. Supposedly he visited another time, but it was when I was in my dark place so I have no memory of it. A few weeks back he came to see Johnny. He did not know I was here or that Walt had died. He has been back twice that I know of, but it has nothing to do with me. He believed that Johnny's suspicions had validity, had Walt's body exhumed for a second autopsy and that is it. I have never mentioned him because it was of no consequence and did not factor into anything. If you recall, you said the same thing about Zeta's phone call to you while I was "away", or your business ventures with Pamela."

"It always comes back to me doesn't it?"

"Yup; now put it in your back pocket and admit that you were wrong for jumping to conclusions again."

"I will if you will."

"I have many times over. Slow down; did you miss that Johnny turned off here?"

"I guess I did."

"You always told me to keep both eyes on the road so you should do the same instead of studying me for a telltale sign of fibbing."

"Maybe I just like looking at you. Anyhow, I'll keep my eyes on the road and the scenery. How far does Thistle Road go?"

"I have no idea. I believe Uncle Walt's cabin is at the end of it though."

We came to a cross road five or six miles down the gravel road. A crooked worn sign pointed to Thistle Township. Rainey stopped and asked if I wanted to sightsee. I told him that we could see it all from here so after a few minutes we continued up the rugged road. Ten minutes later he asked me if I had brought any snacks as we might need sustenance if we got lost.

"Don't be funny. There is no place to go except straight ahead, and we'll be home by lunch.'

"Well, it wouldn't be the first time you led me on a road of deception would it?"

"What are you talking about?"

"Some forty odd years ago, you led me to believe that you were this innocent and shy little sprite who knew nothing about sex, but all along you were only interested in my body and baby making abilities, and now here I am, father of a dozen kids and we are on an abandoned road and I'm pretty sure you have mischief on your mind."

"Oh God, I'm married to a maniac! Stop the car and let me out before I die of laughter."

"Laugh as you may, but you can't fool a fooler."

"I think I can. Look, there's a house ahead. Well, it can't be Walt's as his is just a cabin, so I wonder whose it is. Oh, maybe it is as there's Johnny." We pulled up beside him. He asked us what took us so long. Rainey said we got lost.

Cork Dole, Walt's neighbor and friend had greeted Johnny and Armand upon their arrival. Apparently he checked on the house every day, and had surprised an intruder attempting a break-in the day before. He and the detective were off investigating the site where the burglar had tried to gain entrance. Johnny had the measuring paraphernalia all ready for Rainey as he was certain that there was a secreted room that he could not find, but that Rainey would detect that the inside and outside dimensions did not measure up. I gave myself a tour of the house starting with the living room. It was a mess. Remnants of wallboard and plaster lay in piles, the carpet had been pulled back, and the linoleum underneath had been lifted. Ceiling tiles had been dislodged and were hanging treacherously by threads. I decided it was dangerous to continue. I didn't find anything among the rubble that I thought was worth stealing aside from the antique furniture. I was sure that any papers of interest had already been rescued so didn't bother examining what was left. I didn't feel like traipsing after the boys as it was too hot outside so pulled up a chair beside the kitchen door, picked up an old newspaper, and sat down to wait for them. Rainey showed up half an hour later saying he was parched, turned the tap on and opened a cupboard to get a glass. I asked him what he had discovered outside.

"Nothing; Johnny's still not convinced though. Hey, did you see this?"

"No, I didn't want to run into any spiders so I didn't open any cupboards or drawers. What have you found?"

"A map, a very old map; come and see."

I peered over his shoulder. "Look, there's a date in the right corner… can you make it out?"

"I think it says 1679."

"What's underneath it?"

"What do you mean?"

I reached around him and lifted the other corner. "See, there is another map of sorts."

He pulled a pocket knife out of his pants and lifted the tacks out. He passed them and the old map to me. "Holy Christ; get Johnny!"

I had a quick glance and rushed out to find Johnny. I only had to shout for him once before he came running around the corner of the house and asked what was wrong. I said nothing except that we had found something he needed to see. He joined us in the kitchen. Rainey had laid the map down on top of the other parchment. Johnny didn't blink an eye.

"I see you've found the old map. I think it might be worth a quid or two; what'd you think? I guess it's best to get it out of here before some fortune hunter finds it."

Rainey lifted it up and exposed the other find. "How much do you think this one is worth?"

"What the hell…where did you find it?" Johnny stammered.

"It was under the map. I take it you haven't seen it before?"

"Not only haven't I seen it, but I didn't know such a thing existed. We'll need to have it authenticated and age dated of course, but it's no ones' business but ours for the time being. For now, I say get it home to the Aussie expert. Vienna, you roll it up because your hands are cleaner. This just might be the answer to all of our questions. I'll finish up here with Armand and Corky and see you back at the castle. God, what a find!" He exclaimed embracing us.

We found Rosalyn in the kitchen making cookies with the girls. Rainey grabbed two oatmeal raisin, said she was a life saver as he was starving, asked where the boss was and invited her to join us. Evan and Amma were in the formal dining room. The twelve foot table was covered in papers. Rainey asked if they could clear a small space for something we had found. He unrolled the map and laid it down asking Evan if he had seen it. He said he had.

I stepped forward and carefully stretched out the scroll I had been entrusted with which was entitled "The Thistle Holdings". Rainey placed paperweights on the corners and on the key point of interest, stepped back, and told Evan to have a gander. He scrutinised it for a minute or two and asked us where we had found it.

"It was under the old map of Scotland. Beside Rosslyn Chapel, are any of the others familiar to you? I take it they were once sites of Templar posts?" Rainey asked.

"I recognise five of these; Temple Midiothan, Templar's House in Turnif, Abherdeenshire, Darvel is in Ayrshire, Kiwinning Abbey and of course, Rosslyn Chapel. Rose and I have visited Rosslyn Chapel a few times and most recently just last year. We did a side trip to Midiothian. It is a village of one street south of Edinburgh. The once temple is now a civil parish. I have not heard of the others, and they may not even exist anymore, but I am still relatively new in my investigations into the origin of the Templars, but I do know that they had over 500 sites alone just in Scotland dating back to the1200's."

I stepped back as Rainey removed the paperweight that was concealing the Isle of Alissgrea.

"What do you think about this one?" He asked with a chuckle.

Evan didn't say anything for a minute. Then he looked at Rainey and me. "Are you f…in kidding me? Excuse my language ladies, but come on; how did you manage to make this look like it belongs with the rest?"

"Yeah, like we'd know how to do such a thing. It's just as we found it. Johnny had a look and told us to get it home to the expert on the Templar Knights."

"Well, I am hardly an expert, just one of thousands who find the medieval monks fascinating. It all started when I was about ten or twelve and came across a book in the travelling library that came by once a month to the outback. I don't remember the title, but it kept me interested all that summer. Now and then I would get my hands on other books that chronicled the warriors, but I lost interest when I got older. I didn't really take any interest in the subject again until that discovery of that key. It has sparked many amusing conversations between Tanny and me through the years as you all know, and now it appears as if it and its twin are related to an age old mystery. Several months ago Rose came home with a book for me titled The Da Vinci Code. It is a new offering from Dan Brown who wrote Angels and Demons, and my interest was activated once again. Are either of you familiar with his works?"

"I've heard of the Da Vinci Code, but have not read it. How has it sparked your interest again Evan?" I asked.

"Rosslyn Chapel plays a significant role in the novel. Anyhow, they are both good reads and I think you will enjoy them. Do you know that the order of the Thistle still exists today Rain? It does and is second only to in precedence in England to the order of the Garter. The Queen is the Sovereign of the Order and it is her personal gift to award someone who has contributed to national life to Knighthood. I imagine that Jeremy was a member of the Order, and perhaps you were too Vienna as being married to him entitled you to be."

"I was not. I have no idea if Jeremy was or not as he was very tight-lipped about his personal life. I imagine that all the ancestors that went before him were members as it appears as if it was the thing to do. Being married to a Lord can qualify you, but I had no interest in such a thing when I was Lady Vienna. Perhaps you and Rosalyn are interested?"

"You are still Lady Vienna Mama. Evan and I have no interest in the Lord and Lady titles either. I'm wondering though if women were allowed to become Templar Knights?"

"They were called Dames, but officially they had no place in the Order's Rule. Apparently they were forbidden to be recognised and rules were made to keep them away from the men as the monks were supposedly chaste and women were just temptation." Evan laughed. "But, there are records of a Templar nunnery in Austria, and I have come across several names of women in another book I read recently that prove they did exist, and were quite a force. Anyhow, I have veered off the Alissgrea finding on this parchment long enough. Are you all thinking that it requires further investigation?"

"What's that you're saying Boss?" Johnny boisterously voiced making his presence known.

"You missed all the rhetoric John Boy, but I was just asking everyone's opinion regarding this Alissgrea discovery on the Thistle map. I'm thinking we ought to investigate. What say we crank up the heli tomorrow and have a look see?"

"I'm with you on that. What do you say Rain?" Johnny asked.

"Someone has to mind the castle, so I'll let you two have the honors of discovery while I keep the woman folk company. I'm sure we'll find something interesting to do. Those two cookies didn't do much to satisfy my hunger so I think I'll mosey on down to the kitchen and see what I can drum up."

"I'm with you on that." Johnny echoed.

"You just stay put; lunch is made so give us a few minutes to get it on the table." Amma said.

I left with her and Rosy and was half way to the kitchen when something dawned on me. I turned around and went back to the dining room door. "Evan, do you think that Gracie Darling was a Dame in the Knight's organization? Is it possible that she holds the key to everything?"

He walked over to me and put his arm around my waist. "Let's go for a little walk."

"Hey, where do you think you're going with my wife?" Rainey called out humorously.

"Someone has to satisfy her curiosity." Evan quipped.

He led me into the library, pulled a book from a shelf and handed it to me. It was titled "Medieval Warrior Women."

"I think this might just hold the answer. I haven't had the time to read all of it, but have browsed it, and I'm thinking that it might give us an insight into some of the roles women played in the crusades. Could one be that they were trusted with priceless religious artefacts and could travel less conspicuously than the Knights could? Is one of these treasures hidden right here at Avanloch? Have we misjudged Gracie's role? Yes, I think we may have and that she may have been a Dame. Her role as Avaleena's maiden was a front to hide her and the treasure, and that Quinn may not have had an uncle who was a Templar, but was guarding her because she was."

"How long have you been thinking that?"

"About five minutes."

"Well, I have been thinking it for six, so I win."

He laughed. "Come on, let's go to lunch before that jealous husband of yours comes barreling down the hall to see what we are up to."

"I have a jealous husband; whatever gave you that idea?" I asked raising my eyebrows.

"Oh, just by the way he looked when Detective Armand greeted you."

I left Rainey downstairs with Johnny and Evan planning strategies that evening. I took one of Uncle Walt's journals to bed with me and was trying to wade my way through his ramblings. There was no rhyme or reason as to why he jumped from one thought to another writing it all down. Sometimes he reverted to Gaelic. He was of Irish descent, but had been in Scotland since he was a young man and had taken an interest in Gaelic so he could understand the history and culture of the land he called home.

"What are you so engrossed with there?" Rainey inquired as he climbed into bed with me.

"I'm just trying to make sense of it all. Uncle Walt had his own brand of shorthand. It's like trying to find your way through a corn maze while at the same time trying to connect the dots to a three century old mystery."

"You should put it away for the night as you've had enough to cope with for one day."

"If you mean what I did for Patricia Ann I knew what I had done, and I knew I would tell you someday. I certainly never thought it would come to light over here in the middle of a family who-done-it."

"I wasn't referring to the fund thing, but the amorous advances you had to deal with."

"It was nothing I couldn't handle, but there you were thinking that I had succumbed to his charms while you were still in Hawthorne."

"You'd think I'd be used to it by now wouldn't you with Jack and Jimmy always fawning all over you, not to mention your sons-in-law? You know it won't surprise me one bit if you and Jack hook up the minute I'm out of the picture."

I put the note book down and slid out of bed. "Excuse me for a second; I just remembered that I have to do something." I said as I made my way to the bathroom picking up the antique ewer.

"What are you going to do with that?" He called after me.

I filled the pitched up with cold under the tub faucet, lugged it back across the room and attempted to pour it over my husband's head. It was too heavy so the majority of it landed on the bed. He let a barrage of profanities as he sputtered and spewed asking me if I had lost my mind.

The pitcher broke into a hundred pieces as it fell to the floor. "I lost it forty years ago and I am done with your ridiculous innuendos! I Will be in my room down the hall, and if you ever want to see me again you had better come crawling on your hands and knees and beg for my forgiveness. If you can't lower yourself to do so, then pack your bags and get out of my castle!" I walked out slamming the door before he could utter another word.

Five minutes later I had changed into one of Miss Mary's satin nightgowns and was about to get into bed when the door opened. He stood there dripping wet.

"Jesus Christ Vienna; were you trying to drown me?"

"That only works on witches, so consider yourself lucky that you won't suffer Jorja's fate."

He walked by me into the bathroom, came back naked, towelling off, and climbed into bed.

"What do you think you're doing?" I demanded.

"I guess I'm sleeping here because mine's all wet. Now get in here so I can apologise, and then you can tell me again how you had nothing to do with Jorja's death."

"I'm not that easy. You can't fix everything with sex."

"I kind of have a way with you." He said smugly.

"You won't be having any way with me tonight. Seeing you want to continue irritating me in a most uncouth manner and won't leave, I will. I've had this ridiculous altercation with you some thirty odd years ago when you accused me of cavorting with Roberge. Now you have brought Sissy and Jack into your disgusting fantasy and can't see that you have crossed the line with me, so I'm out of here." I avowed as I opened the door.

"Did you forget there's a murderer on the loose?"

"The only murderer I see is the one in Miss Mary's bed. He just killed me with his innuendos."

"Are we in the place of no return Vienna? I thought that we had made a pact never to go there again? Can I amend what I said please?" He requested.

"I'm listening."

"I do not want you to be alone when I'm dead, and I know Jack would look after you. Of course Sissy would no longer be alive either, so can you see how I meant it? I was not suggesting anything tainted Honey."

I walked over to the dressing table and sat down. "Do you think I need looking after?"

"I wouldn't want to see you alone like you were before. That's all I meant Honey."

He came over and placed his hands on my shoulders and gently caressed them and kissed my neck. "You're very tense. I'm sorry that I'm the cause."

"I want to go home; Zander needs us." I lamented.

"Oh Honey, I miss him and our family back home too. Don't worry about him because he has Sammie, Ava, and Nash. Jack was taking the boys camping on the weekend, and just as soon as the situation here has been resolved, we'll all be on our way to France and Spain with them."

"I want it to be 1984 again when all our family was together at the Palace."

"Despite the trauma that Jorja inflicted on you, and you not talking to me, it was a fantastic time. Rose and Evan and the kids will pop over one day and we'll have a wondrous time again."

"Will Zoe and Tanny be there too?"

"Yeah, I think I can arrange that. Now let's get under the covers and I'll let you take your wrath out on me anyway you want." He promised.

"I'm still mad at you, you know?"

"Yup, I know."

I awoke the next morning to my husband shaking me gently. "I need you to get me something to wear Hon."

"Wrap a sheet around you and get something yourself."

"And, suppose if one of the girls wakes up and sees me?"

"So what?"

"I won't ask anything else from you for the rest of the day, and you can go back to bed if you like, but I want to be up to see Evan and Johnny off on their quest."

I got up and donned one of Miss Mary's robes. "You are such a pain in the neck you know." I said as I stepped into the hall.

"Looking for something to wear?" A familiar voice called out.

"Not for me, but for the spoiled man in there." I replied pointing behind me.

"That sounds intriguing." He said joining me with a grin and peering into the room.

"Your Mother-in-law tried to drown me last night Evan."

I shut the door.

Evan laughed. "Do I even want to know?"

"I'm sure you'll hear all about it." I kissed him on the cheek. "I'll see you downstairs, and the coffee better be sweet and strong."

CHAPTER 8

ALISSGREA

Johnny was on the phone when Rainey and I made our way downstairs. He and Evan had both tried to get some information regarding visitation to Alissgrea from the Department of Lands and the National Trust yesterday. They thought it might have been designated a heritage site and that there may be legalities about visitation. No one appeared able to answer their questions and had been referred to another department. Each time they had been put on hold for fifteen minutes before they had hung up. A last ditch effort this morning had been met with recordings stating the hours of operation. Obviously it was too early.

"Well, we tried, so screw the powers that be." Johnny said annoyingly.

"Armand hasn't called either so I guess we are on our own." Evan agreed. "Rose, you know what to do if we're not back by dark. Rain, I trust that you'll keep the girls out of mischief?"

"I have a busy day planned for us all, so nothing to worry about here. Don't take any chances with the landing. If it looks iffy, scrub the mission. Nothing is as important as your lives."

"I hear you Dad." Evan grinned.

"Don't get smart with me Kid." Rainey responded heartily. "Now get out of here you two."

"Take lots of pictures. What might not appear to be important to you at the moment might prove beneficial later when we sort through them." I suggested.

We walked them down to the hangar, had a group hug and stood back and watch the helicopter take flight. It was seven fifteen a.m. Friday, July 11th.

We had a busy morning with the girls playing badminton and lawn bowling. Rusty joined in the games while Lili sat cheering and keeping score with JT. The day became unbearably hot by noon so we went in to have lunch and then a swim. The four girls ate and went upstairs to change into their bathing suits while the rest of us cleaned up before suiting up. They had barely been gone two minutes when we heard piercing screams. Rainey was up and running up the back stairs at the first shriek. He had them somewhat calmed down by the time the rest of us arrived. They were all talking at the same time saying something about whistling. Rainey suggested we all go into the TV room and have a sit-down. Colleen reminded him that the sofas were in the bedrooms so we'd have to go there. Calla clung to me as did Beth to Rosy. Novia and Colleen held Rainey's hands as we walked down the hall. Rusty and Lili decided whatever the crisis was, we could handle it.

One by one they each relayed what happened. Their stories were all the same practically word for word. They had taken the lift up to the second floor. As soon as they stepped out they had heard what they thought was a peep like a bird would make. Then the peep became louder and they realised that it was whistling, and it was getting closer and closer. They screamed and they heard Rainey yelling and the whistling stopped. They all agreed that the whistling was coming from inside the wall of the other elevator. Amma and Rainey took the lift to the tower floor and searched all the rooms and closets and found nothing out of the ordinary. Against Rosy's and my qualms Rainey decided to check out the condemned elevator and the only way he could do that was to take it for a ride. Rosy insisted on accompanying him. They rode it up from the bottom floor to the top and down into the basement getting out on each floor and investigating. They saw and heard nothing. Rainey locked the elevator again. He tried to convince the girls that what they heard was just old pipes acting up. Colleen was having none of that.

"We all know that Pit and Pete say they heard whistling coming from inside the elevator walls, so we are confirming that they did not make it up because we all heard it too; right girls?"

Rainey smiled as the other three agreed with her. "Okay, you can't blame a guy for trying to explain it all away can you? I do not believe that there is anyone or anything hiding in the walls, but it *is* a castle and *it* has told many tales already, so I guess this is just another story waiting to be unscrambled, and maybe what has been going on is all connected, so what say we head into the dining room and look for clues in those stacks of papers?"

"I think we would all like to be a part of cracking the mystery that surrounds Johnny's uncle's demise Daddy, but just for the record, I think there is, or has been an intruder in the house, and that he can come and go as he pleases undetected." Novia stated perceptibly.

Colleen agreed and said that her mother and Amma were right all along. "We enjoyed playing detective with them and pretending that it was all a game all sleeping together and staying up all night, and then Ana came and she joined in the games, so it was more fun, then Lili had her baby and things changed. It's serious now, so let's get to work on deciphering those papers."

Rosy hugged all the girls and praised them for being so brave and observant. "I think we have a whole crew of Nancy Drew's here folks so let's put them to work as you so suggested Dad."

Amma and Rosy had organized all the documentations in a chronological order of what they thought was important. Each pile was labeled significant, unimportant, or undetermined. Novia picked up the last stack which was labeled "no opinion as not read." Rainey questioned whether she and Beth should be tackling something that Amma and Rosy hadn't examined yet.

"I think Amma and I need to reassess the "undetermined" papers again, so I think their young eyes will spot anything of significance Daddy." Rosy suggested.

"You are probably right, so go to it girls." Rainey said as he put up a fresh sheet of paper on the information board. "Here's what we are looking for: names, years, events, places, transactions. Anything you are not sure of just ask okay?"

Evan had made up a list of known Templars in both Scotland and Ireland. Two hours into our project we had amassed twenty or so names from Uncle Walt's papers that corresponded with his. As far as we knew they were public knowledge so it really didn't prove anything. Some of the names dated back to the eleven hundreds.

"I think we may have found something Daddy." Novia announced just as we were all ready to take a break. "It's a receipt of sorts. It's hard to make out the date, but it looks like 1679. It's made out to Godfrey Q Champagne and there's a squiggly signature that looks like Lord Robert Bruce. There is also what I think is a seal and although it is hard to make out, it could be McAllister."

"Oh my God, the McAllister seal from the signet ring. I found it amongst Jeremy's things after he died." Rosy exclaimed.

"Do you still have it?" Rainey asked as he collected the receipt from Novia.

"I think so."

"Well, go get it girl! Let's see what you've found Novey."

She had brought over a worn piece of vellum that resembled cardboard. It was wrapped in what looked like cellophane and laid it in front of her father.

"This is most interesting. Come and look Vienna."

It was definitely a receipt made out to Godfrey Q Champagne and signed by Lord Robert Bruce. It was for the lands south of Avanloch and Domme, west of Hansel and north to the Miller Floss, approximate 10,000 measure to be enclosed in Thistle Proper. It was granted as a gift and to remain in the realm of the reigning monarch of Avanloch. It was dated May 11, 1679.

"Looks like you were right about your assumptions that Avaleena's dairy was out by two hundred years." Rainey said. "I think it is quite possible that the 6 somehow became an 8."

"That might suggest that it was smeared as it was written in ink and on paper, something that was very expensive back then, but her family was wealthy so I imagine she brought reams of it with her. Blotting may have disfigured it, or maybe I copied it wrong. In recollection, I do remember having difficulty understanding some words as they were smeared. But, it would also mean that my father's records of his lineage are also erroneous because they correspond with the 1850's, and I don't see how that can be."

"Let's not dwell on that right now, but I think this receipt is irrefutable."

A chilling shriek came from the end of the table. Calla was sitting on the floor holding a dog-eared piece of paper. She dropped it and cried. "He killed them, he killed them, he killed all the little Dames. Dya and Asha and Alia, and now he is coming for Gracie Darling!"

I skirted the table, sat down beside her and took her in my arms. "It's okay Baby, it's okay. It happened a long, long time ago. You mustn't take it to heart."

"But me and Colleen know them Ana."

Rainey had joined us. We looked at each other, eyes questioning her declaration. He picked up the piece of paper and said that it had been burned.

"He told Alson to burn it. He said they were witches and he burned them on the stake Pappy."

"This had nothing to do with any of us Calla. Like Ana said; it was a long time ago. Now I think we have all had enough for one day. How about you and the girls all go with Ana and leave Amma and me to clean up?"

"Where is Colleen? She needs to know what happened to them."

"She's with Rosy." I said coaxing my granddaughter to come with me by saying we'd find her cousin and the two of them could commiserate for a few minutes, and then they were to put their encounter with the Dames away and go on to a new adventure.

I found Amma and Rainey alone in the dining room still discussing what the receipt and tattered paper that had upset Calla meant. Although an attempt had been made to destroy the letter the crux of it was intact. Whoever the recipient of the letter was addressed to was not clear. There was a partial name in the salutation that consisted of five letters "alson."

The rest had been burned off as had all the other corners of the document including the signature. It was written in a bold archaic font, but was perfectly understandable. The contents were exactly as Calla had recited to us; the "the monster" being King Edward the Second.

Rosy arrived out of breath with Colleen. "Sorry it took me so long, but I couldn't remember where I had put it. Here Dad; what do you think?"

"In a minute Honey. Right now we have a more problematic situation to contend with and it involves Colleen. Ana will explain."

"Oh my, what have you done now?" Rosy asked her daughter.

"Is it about the elevator Ana?" Colleen said ignoring her mother.

"No, it isn't, but don't fret about it because everyone knows. This is an entirely different matter. What do you know about Dya, Asha and Alia?"

"Who are they?" Rosy demanded.

"Let the girl speak Rose." Rainey recommended. "Can you tell us Colleen?"

"Did Calla tell you about the diary?"

"No, she told us about a letter that mentioned them." I said.

"I don't know anything about a letter, just the diary."

"Okay, I think Calla found it when you went with your mom to look for the signet ring."

"What is this about a diary?" Rosy demanded.

"I was going to tell you about it, but then Ana and Calla and Novia came and I forgot about it. Sorry Mommy."

"I don't know what you are sorry for as yet, so how about telling us who this diary belongs to and where you found it?"

"I dropped the box of papers that you and Amma had me bring in from the car, and it fell out. It was just a little book and I opened it and saw all this fancy writing. I had to go back and help you so I didn't have time to read it so I put it in my pocket. I didn't think such a little thing had to do with anything."

"Where is it now?" I asked.

"Upstairs in my room."

"Do all the girls know about it?"

"No, just Calla."

"So, you enlisted her to keep a secret just like you did in the elevator fiasco which we will talk about later." Rosy admonished.

I put my arm around my granddaughter who was crying. "We don't know what is in the diary Rosalyn, or if it even has any bearing on anything, so until we find out can you please have a little compassion for your daughter? She already told you that she was going to tell you about it, How about we go and collect it Colleen?"

The little book consisted of paper-thin pages that didn't appear to be velum or parchment. I suspected that it may be papyrus. The pages were strung together at the seams with a string-like thread. The cover page was decorated with embossed faded yellow fleurs-de-lis. It was approx imately four inches by four inches. I could see why Colleen had been attracted to it as it was indeed a delicate little keepsake. I carefully opened it to the first page. It was perfectly legible in some medieval serif, but so minute that I would need a magnifying glass to read. Colleen's eyes were younger and apparently could read it easily. We went back downstairs where Rainey, Amma and Rosy were waiting anxiously for us.

Colleen opened the journal saying that the first few pages had been ripped out. She read for us.

> "We waited until the dead of night before we made our way to the church to meet the new inductees, Dya, Asha and Alia. It is not clear to me why Sir Alson has sent them to me to train. Does he not know the danger of travelling, let alone the threats from the Irish and Scots to eliminate anyone they are suspect of? Children are no exceptions. Quinn and I will do what we can, to keep them and the treasures you have entrusted to me, but I afear it will not be enough."

I told her that was enough for now. It was obvious that it was Gracie Darling's journal. It was a gem that I'm sure no one had anticipated finding. I told the rest that Colleen and I were going to join the other girls that I had left with Gramma Mary and they could go ahead and decipher the rest of the journal and that I would catch up with them later. Rainey said they'd wait for me as he had other things to do with the rest of the info that we had gathered today. Amma stayed with him and Rosy accompanied Colleen and me. She apologised for her sharp tongue and hoped we would forgive her. We hugged and all was well with the three generations of emotional ladies once again. I told Colleen about the letter that Calla had found and told her not to get upset as it had happened hundreds of years ago. It was brutal, but unfortunately that was the way of the world back then. She sniffled a little and said that they were just three young girls learning how to defend themselves and country, and that the king was a monster.

Amma arrived a few minutes later and asked who was going to join her in the gardens as they needed vegetables for supper and fresh flowers for the tables, and maybe they could even pull a weed or two. It was a wonderful idea and the girls definitely needed to put the ugliness behind them. She told me that Rainey needed my help with something so I waited for him wondering what he was up to now. He said that he'd had an epiphany.

We took the lift to the second floor where he asked me to listen for anything unusual and to wait for him. He said he'd only be a few minutes and boarded the lift again and was gone before I could ask him where he was going. I heard the elevator stop and then I heard a clatter. It sounded like the dumb waiter but it had quit working years ago so it had to be something else. Then I heard the whistling. I shuttered. The lift landed and he stepped out holding what looked like a tape player in his hands. He asked me if I had heard the whistling.

"I certainly did and it unnerved me. Did it come from in that, and where did you find it?"

"It was inside the dumb waiter."

"How did you get it? It's been stuck between the second and third floor for twenty years."

"It ain't stuck anymore Hon. I opened the cupboard and pushed the switch up and voila!"

"So, what do you think?"

"I think someone who has access to the castle and knows its interior workings planted it for some ulterior motive that is yet to be uncovered. Hopefully Evan can shed some light on that when he gets home."

"I know that we all discussed and hoped that it was some sort of recording, but searches were unable to locate it. What made you think to look there?"

"Well, as you said, we had searched up and down and no sign of anything. Everyone knew the dumb waiter was kaput, so it was just an oversight that none of us checked out. I'm sure the recorder is activated remotely and we'll know more when the guys get back and we examine it. I pushed a button, but I don't want to be responsible for screwing up the insides or destroying fingerprints."

I left Rainey to secure the CD player in the dining room. He had decided to hear what Evan and Johnny had discovered before he presented his find. I decided to make myself useful and joined the crew in the garden. Half an hour later we heard the heli approaching. Rosy and the girls ran down the hill to wait for it to land while Amma and I took the overflowing baskets into the kitchen. She sorted and washed the veggies while I arranged the flowers into vases.

"Look Ana, Daddy brought us all a souvenir from the island." Beth carolled putting two rocks on the table. "Which one do you want?"

I laughed smiling at Evan. "Either one Honey; you chose for me. I will treasure mine as no one has ever given me such a gift before. What else did you find on Alissgrea pray tell."

"Nothing; absolutely nothing! Here's the camera, see for yourself."

Rainey took it saying he'd put the photos on the laptop so we could all see at the same time.

"What are you looking so smug about Johnny?" Amma asked her husband passing him a bowl of green beans to snap.

"No matter what the big boy says, it was an amazing flight. I saw dozens of islands of northern Scotland that I never knew existed. The views and heights were amazing. I swear we could see Russia from the top of a mountain in the St. Kilda Archipelago. Everything looked green and lush from above and then we came to the island of rocks, also known as Alissgrea. Why in God's creation there was a monastery there is unfathomable and yet there from the air we could see the ruins. After several passes Evan set the heli down in what appeared to be the one and only grassy mound. A herd of about thirty wild goats went scattering in every direction. There was no way off that desolate isle that we could see, so it must provide enough fodder for them to survive. There didn't appear to be any breach along the rugged rocky shoreline that would allow boats to dock safely, but yet we know they did. A lot has changed over the eight or so centuries, so I guess it is not unreasonable that the terrain has also. Here's Rain with the photos so I'll shut up."

"We need a running commentary so between you and Evan we are waiting with baited breath."

"Sarcasm or humor Vienna?"

Evan answered winking at me. "I'd say probably a little of both John."

There really was not much to see as like they said, it was a pile of rocks. Evan operated the clicker that took us from ruin to ruin guessing on each heap of toppled stone as to what it may have been; a workshop, sleeping quarters or bath house. The priory remains were easy to see as a few giant pillars remained standing amidst the rubble of stone. There was one octagon structure that remained virtually untouched. The guys assumed that it had once been some sort of worship chamber. Rainey said that he had seen one such formation in Greece, and that it was a communal wash centre and that all the collapsed cavities had been sinks. He had never told me that he had been to Greece, and I wondered why. Another chapter of his life I knew nothing about…

There was a semblance of a stone structure that appeared to be the makings of a Stonehenge. Of course it had been destroyed, but the way the stones were laid out didn't leave much to the imagination. The last photos were of two large broken tablets that had thirty three names etched onto them. Only seven were decipherable as the rest plus the dates had been chiselled out. There were traces of what might have once been crosses on the tablets which may have been a link to the Templars, but then it was a religious post, so that proved nothing.

"That's it kids. You can view on your time if you like, but I'm done for the day. Anything exciting happen here while we were gone?" Evan wanted to know.

"I have something to show you that I think will interest you. Vienna, do you want to fill Johnny and Evan in with what the girls found today?" Rainey asked me.

"We don't have to be here do we Pappy because we want to go swimming and you know everything that we know?" Colleen requested.

"I want you girls to hear this too because it will put an end to the fright you had earlier. I'll just be a minute and then you can go to the pool." Rainey answered.

"What's this then?" Evan demanded.

I explained about the girl's encounter with the whistling upstairs and how they had helped us decipher some of Uncle Walt's papers and had found the letter and the diary which we could discuss further after Rainey's revelation. All eyes were on him as he laid the recorder on the table and hit the play button that released the eerie whistling. The second button was the whistling plus laughter, and the third was both the whistling and the laughter plus threats from a chilling voice to get out. Rainey stopped it abruptly. I feared there was more but that was enough to pacify the girls, and it was.

They had shuddered when they heard the whistling again, but were appeased when they saw that it was all on tape. One by one they kissed Rainey and thanked him for finding the tape and said they were going swimming. I asked if they wanted me to go with them. They didn't. Beth said to call them when dinner was ready.

Evan was somewhat mortified, and more so when Rainey told him where he had found the tape deck. "That's on me then. I should have opened that damn little door!"

"I could have checked it out too Evan, but we all knew the dumb waiter was stuck, so my question is, when and how did it become mobile again?" Johnny probed.

"I haven't a clue. Just a sec; I think I mentioned it to Pit and Paul saying that they may encounter it in the shaft but not to worry about it because it didn't work anyhow. Damn."

"I hardly think that they are responsible for placing the tape player in the dumbwaiter, but they may have unstuck it. I suppose now is a good time to tell you that I paid a little visit to the boys when I was in Waverly. I pretended that I needed an elevator installed in an old house I was buying and had heard that they were experts. Anyhow, to make a long story short I asked if they had ever had any encounters with ghosts as I had heard that many buildings and especially castles had many tales of hauntings to tell. They were only too eager to share stories that they had heard, but only had one such experience themselves. Pit had shaken his head and clamed up as Paul relived what they had encountered here, which is almost word for word as you related it and what is on the tape. He said he'd never been a believer and was sure that the owners had deliberately manifested the eerie serenade they had been exposed to. Pit was not convinced that it was orchestrated by the family and admitted that it was one scary, creepy episode. I'm pretty sure we are looking for someone else, someone who could come and go and not be considered an intruder. They must have a hidden agenda, but how it coincides with a murder is not clear. Any ideas people?" Rainey probed.

"Good thinking with the brothers Rain. I agree with you that they are not involved. No, that falls on me, and I might just have an answer. Pass me a phone will you please Rose?"

He put the speaker on. "Hey Butch, is Carruthers around?"

"Haven't seen him since you fired him Boss."

"What do you mean by saying I fired him?" Evan looked at Johnny who shook his head.

"I mean just that; you fired him."

"That doesn't sound like something I would do. Did he say what my reasons were?"

"He just said that you had up and fired him. He gathered his belongings and hit the trail."

"When was this?"

"Hell, I don't know…a month or so I guess."

"Christ! I know I've been busy, but not to notice that an employee is missing is unacceptable. Did he leave a forwarding address?"

"Nope. He wasn't very likable Boss, so no loss."

"That doesn't make me feel any better. Here, John wants to talk to you."

"What about his locker Butch? Did he leave anything behind?"

"Never checked. I'll go right now if you want?"

"Wait for me, I'm on my way."

"Okay Boss."

"Let's hope we can get some fingerprints to compare with the ones at Walt's house. Give the detective a call Evan. This might just the break we've been looking for." Johnny said hopefully.

CHAPTER 9

THE GRANDFATHER CLOCK

"Wake up Rainey!" I pleaded shaking him.

"What; what's wrong?" He asked alarmingly.

"Nothing, but I need to ask you a question."

"Can't it wait until morning? What time is it anyhow?"

"It doesn't matter, but I won't be able to go back to sleep if I don't have an answer."

"Apparently I won't either, so what is it?"

"What did you and Johnny find at the end of the tunnel that led to the crypt?"

He sat up and stared at me. "What? Have you had another nightmare?"

"No, but there was a door wasn't there?"

"Yes, and you know that, so why the urgency to have it confirmed at three a.m.?"

"Because I saw it."

"So, you saw it in a dream, so what?"

"Were there any symbols on the door? Explain to me exactly what you saw please."

"The passageway ended at a door that's all. It did not have any symbols on it. Can we go back to sleep now?"

"I think you missed something."

"Okay, I'll bite; what did we miss?"

"I remember you telling me that the door opened right into the crypt; is that right?"

"It is, and we entered and found no means of another exit. That's it Babe."

"There were no steps or writings of any kind on the door then?"

"I seem to recall that there were two steps, but nothing but knots on the door."

"Were the knots miniscule or big enough to be keyholes?"

"What are you saying Vienna?"

"I think our two keys open that door."

"The door swung open, so no key of any sort was needed, and no, I don't believe that any of the knotholes resembled any kind of keyhole."

"I think you are wrong and that the black keys open another entrance and that that entrance leads to the outside, and that is how Quinn and Gracie Darling entered and left the castle without being discovered. The keys have nothing to do with Alissgrea. When Avaleena came to Johnny, akn as Quinn at the time, she was just telling him to get out of the castle. Why they needed to go to Alissgrea is the only mystery here." I took a deep breath and waited for my husband's reaction. It wasn't what I thought it would be.

"Outlandish as it sounds, I know better than to dismiss any of your visions." He patted me on the head. "Now, lie down and let's try to get a few hours of sleep before we collect the keys and traverse down the path of no exit. You always say that all roads lead to Rome, right?"

I kissed him and told him that I loved him and was sorry for waking him.

Three hours later I was at Ash's suite which was now occupied at the time by Amma and Johnny. I tapped lightly on the door not wanting to wake Amma. Johnny was always up early so I thought that he may already have gone out to do chores. He opened it immediately, stepped into the hall and asked what was up. I took his arm and asked him if he would like to come with me and Rainey for a little stroll. He was suspect of what I had on my mind so early in the morning.

"Let's go down the main stairs so we don't wake anyone. Rainey is making coffee. I had a dream last night and I hope you will be game to check it's validity out with us."

By the time we reached the bottom I had explained what I had dreamt. I asked him if he thought I was bonkers for wanting to check it out.

"If this was any other day in any other month in any other year, I would say yes, but I would be a fool to dismiss anything that may provide an answer to the mystery that surrounds us, and those damn keys are definitely at the center of it, so lead on my lady. I take it Rainey is on board?"

"Well, he is my husband, so has no choice."

He laughed. "Well I'm not, so I don't really have to be on board, do I?"

"You're my best friend, so you kind of do."

"I think I lost that title to Jimmy or Jack a long time ago."

"I'm in Scotland not Canada, so you own that title Johnny O'Shea."

Rainey handed us each a to-go cup that he had appropriated from Rosy's stash of airplane supplies. "This shouldn't take too long and we'll probably be back before anyone else is up, so we may as well save time by drinking as we walk. I guess it's safe to say that my charming wife's intriguing dream has caught your attention John?"

"I've always found that it's easier to go along with her ideas and schemes than to try and explain them away."

"I'm afraid that I'm still learning."

"If you two are finished analysing me let's get going. I left a note just in case." I said.

"Just in case what Hon?" Rainey asked.

"Who knows what lies beyond the door?"

"I can pretty much assure you that nothing unexpected does, but we can't have you wondering, so let's get a move on."

We stopped at the office where Johnny opened the safe and extracted the two keys. The door to the passageway to Avaleena's room was concealed in the formal reception room by a large antique credenza on wheels. The guys swung it away, removed the heavy bars that barricaded the door and unlocked it. An offense of cold air and stale air greeted us. Rainey flipped the switch which turned on the dim wall lights. It was a two minute walk to the turnoff to Avaleena's room and the backside of the Grandfather clock. We bypassed it and continued onwards for another few minutes. I had never been this far before. Suddenly, we were at the door that I had supposedly seen in my dream. I ran my hands over it. Rainey had been right; it was a very knotty door. Not one of them was big enough for any key to fit into; not even my jewellery box key.

"Well, that's that isn't it? Sorry for the wild goose hunt. Let's go back." I said disappointedly.

"Not so fast Hon; you may as well see the other side of the crypt while we are here." Rainey said as he opened the door. It swung open freely to reveal two steps that led into the back side of the mausoleum. Johnny's and Rainey's flashlights lit up a twelve by twelve windowless dark area. I set my coffee cup down on the ledge where a flap covered a small window. Rainey opened it and I looked into the backside of the burial chamber. Why anyone would want to view it from here was questionable. I shrugged my shoulders, grabbed my cup, put one foot on the top step unaware that the cup had sprung a leak. I slipped. Hands managed to grab my coattail and save me from landing hard on the bottom step. A flashlight went sailing over my head.

"You okay Hon?" My husband asked anxiously.

"The only thing that's hurt is my pride because I'm sitting in a pool of lukewarm coffee. Thanks for the save Sweetie." I got up, shook myself off and started back down the tunnel feeling disheartened.

Johnny said he had never heard such unbecoming colorful language from me before. Rainey laughed and said, "Believe me John; she knows all the words."

I said that yes I did, stopped suddenly and turned to face Rainey and Johnny.

"This passageway is on the first floor isn't it?" I asked though I knew the answer. "But, all the others are in the subbasement aren't they? How do you expect that they will all meet up? This one would have to drop down ten or twelve feet wouldn't it... that is if it ever did join up?"

"What are you getting at Vienna?"

"I'm not sure, but things don't jive." I turned around and continued on until we came to the Grandfather clock. I stopped dead again. "Ever since I discovered this clock I have been trying to find a plausible answer as to why one can pass through it into the Harem room, but not back from it into this passage. You've both thought it was a conundrum too haven't you?"

They both agreed, but it wasn't something they dwelled on.

"I'm going through." I announced.

"I'll pass and meet you in the kitchen." Rainey said.

"You need to meet me in the Harem room first please."

Johnny followed me through saying it was against his better judgement as he always felt like the clock had some hidden agenda. I laughed dubiously saying that maybe it did.

Rainey joined us a few minutes later. "Why did you want to come in here Vienna?"

"We have all wondered where this clock came from, but have never found any answers. It is a remarkable work of art and I think the consensus is that it was constructed right here by some talented craftsman for whom, or why, or what its purpose is we don't know, but I believe I may have an answer. It was Avaleena who showed me how to enter the clock, and although you don't like to admit it, she also showed you Rainey. I, in turn have passed the knowledge on to everyone else. I have always admired the intricate carvings of flowers and birds woven in among the waves and vines. These little doors have always intrigued me." I ran my hands over them. "I doubt that you ever opened them to find that inside were finials of laurel and roses surrounding a peculiar shaped orifice? I did, and I looked up the meaning of laurel and roses and found that the laurel plant was significant to the Romans and Greeks as it meant victory in battle and they wore crowns of the leaves woven into them. I'm sure you both knew that. Anyhow, I learned that the rose symbolises respect for the dead. I'm not sure why I told you all that because it has no bearing that I know of in regard to the aperture they are covering. May I have one of the keys please Johnny?"

He came and stood beside me and placed a key in my hand. I inserted it into the slit. A loud crackling sound followed instantaneously. Rainey grabbed me from behind and pulled me away.

"What have you done Vienna?" He demanded.

"I don't think she has done anything Rain but find the reason for this illusive clock. I'm imagining that it will be revealed when I insert the second key. Do we want to see what will happen, or do we want to go on wondering?"

"What are you musketeers up to now?" Evan inquired as he slid in quietly behind us.

Johnny explained what had transpired so far, but said that we weren't sure about the next move. Rainey gave him a minute to digest the information and then told him that it was his house so he should make the decision whether to insert the second key or not. Evan asked Rainey and Johnny what they thought would happen. They both agreed that the floor would open onto a deep hole and that the clock would fall into it breaking into a thousand pieces, but the opening may lead to the outside passageway that had so far alluded us.

"I'm pretty sure this is all you Vienna because no one else in the room thinks like you do. I'm interested as to when you came up with the idea that the keys and the clock were meant for each other, and what do *you* believe is going to occur when the other key is inserted?"

Before I could answer Rainey said he was right about no one else thinking like I do, but even he was amazed as to how I had come up with this idea.

"After the farce at the crypt I was really beginning to believe that those damn keys didn't open anything, and then I stopped at the Grandfather clock and a light went on. I now think that Rosy and Ava misinterpreted what Jeremy had told them about the three secreted rooms when they complained about being bored one cold winter night when they were young.. He didn't say that they were *all* on the first floor, but that only *one* was, and this is it. He knew they would never find it so he didn't worry which brings up the theory that he not only knew about the clocks' purpose, but everything else too. It's obvious that he didn't trust any if us to keep the McAllister's secrets."

"But you've outsmarted him haven't you?"

"Rainey's reasoning's found the other rooms so I can't take the credit for them Evan. I lived here for twenty years in complete ignorance of what went on below."

He laughed. "Until Avaleena came into your life you mean?"

"I guess, but I kept her a secret because I didn't want the girls and the household thinking that I had gone overboard though I guess I came pretty close."

"We would never have thought that Vienna." Johnny assured me.

It was my turn to laugh. "Well, you might think it now because I believe when that key is inserted Grandfather is going to slide over and create an entrance to the secret exit."

Evan said he agreed with me.

"So you think it's just going to slide over? Are you assuming that it's sitting on some sort of platform because if it isn't, it would rip up the floor and probably tip over? I think we had better investigate the situation a little more before we do something rash." Rainey advised.

"Do you want to tell him Vienna?" Evan smiled giving me the option.

"How long have you known?" I asked him.

"Amma informed me that the floor and carpet hadn't escaped the wrath of a torrential rainstorm last fall. I inspected it and called Johnny in to help. You remember what we found don't you John?"

"Yeah, a line of track that we supposed had been laid a century earlier for Jeremy's grandfather's obsession with trains. Are you saying that… Christ; say you're not?"

"I think I am. We decided to leave the track in as it was too big a job to remove it at the time, so we just repaired the damage to the floor as best we could. A good thing we didn't eh? I didn't think that it was anyway connected to the clock though. I have examined it from top to bottom and I suppose I may have popped open those little doors to see what was on the other side, but I didn't see anything that looked like keyholes until just now. That is all your intel Vienna."

"Whoever thought that when I found that first key years ago that it was going to lead to this discovery, and it wouldn't have except Johnny found its' twin in his uncle's things, so it led to all of us speculating what they opened. I did not remember the holes inside the clock and I did not put two and two together until I stood on the other side just a few minutes ago so it's still conjecture. Jeremy had told me all about his grandfather's folly with trains so I knew about the tracks, but never investigated because this room spooks me as you all know."

"What do you all say; should we insert the key?" Evan asked.

"It's quite possible that it might shake the whole downstairs so I think we should warn the rest of the family. Let's bare the track as best we can John." Rainey suggested.

"Right you are. Amma and Rose are in the kitchen so I'll buzz them and they can relay the message to the upstairs." Evan said as he walked over to the call centre. Rosy answered and said not to do anything until she and Amma joined us. After a brief explanation to them of what we'd come up with, Evan cautioned us to stay back as he started to insert the key.

"Wait!" Rosy cried. "You're expecting the clock to move and expose a deep hole aren't you? What will keep you from falling into it?"

"I'll just step aside Rose. There is nothing to worry about."

"Suppose if you can't move fast enough?"

"Johnny and I'll be right beside him Red, so we'll make sure he doesn't fall. Also, I am quite sure that it's going to be a slow movement, that is, if it moves at all." Rainey guesstimated hoping to calm her.

"Do I have the green light Honey?" Evan asked.

"Okay, but be careful, and you better be right Dad."

Amma and I clasped Rosy's hands and held our breaths as an all-encompassing grating sound filled the room when Evan inserted the key and turned it. He stepped aside easily before anything happened. We watched in amazement as the mighty clock shook slightly before moving slowly sideways. I asked what that grinding sound was. Rainey said that the clock was shifting gears and he imagined that the mechanism was probably rusty. I estimated that the clock moved six feet. It seemed to teeter ever so slightly just before it came to an abrupt halt.

"Come look girls, but don't get too close." Evan invited as he shone a flashlight into the void.

It was pretty much what one would expect to see in any hole except this one had steps that led down to a cave-like opening. The men were giddy.

"I'd say that we have our work cut out for us the rest of the day boys. What say we gather some equipment and get to exploring?" Evan proposed. "How would you gals like to send us off to the unknown on a full stomach?"

An hour later they were all geared up with picks and shovels, the walkie-talkies and proper lighting and ropes in their back packs. Amma, Rosy and I saw them traipse off down the hole and into the cavern. Evan looked back and said not to wait on supper and broke into song singing, "High ho, high ho, it's off to work we go…"

"This diversion is just what Evan and Johnny need. They have been so wrapped up in the bizarre going-ons around here that haven't been able to focus on anything else. Thank the stars that we have trusted employees, well most of them anyway, who can keep everything running sufficiently. You and Dad being here is just icing on the cake. We would never have found that tunnel if it wasn't for you Mom. We believed we had enough security to keep us safe and never worried about intruders because why would anyone wish us harm, but it appears as though we have been overly trusting. I never put too much stock in what Pit and Pete said they heard, but when the girls heard the whistling and laughing it became tangible and alarming. Where is my mother? Why isn't she here to protect us like she came to help you on the crypt path Mom?"

"Perhaps because no one is in grave danger Rosy. There may very well be no threat to any of you, so she is just watching. Have you been to visit her lately?"

"No; Evan doesn't want me out on my own."

"Well, you won't be alone if I am with you so perhaps we will take a little stroll later when the men get back. Everything that has happened is related to Johnny's uncle's murder so what say we get the girls fed before their hike and get back to work trying to connect those names to something relevant to the case, or on the other hand maybe we go out to the shooting range as I haven't fired a gun for two decades, and I should be prepared."

Rosy laughed and said we should invite Meggie Magan over to conduct a séance to see if we could conjure Uncle Walt up instead and wondered if there was still a priceless treasure hidden somewhere in the castle. Amma said she'd rather ask the Ouija board, or we could go weed the garden. After we had a good laugh, and made another breakfast and sent the girls off, we went into the dining room and gathered all the names that Evan and Johnny had copied off the headstones at Alissgrea as well as the ones from Uncle Walt's documents. There was another list of surnames that I thought might be relevant, and that was those of known Templar Knights in Scotland on record from the 1300's and beyond.

We did find several names that corresponded to the Alissgrea headstones, but Sinclair, Alexander and Abercromby were all common last names so it didn't really mean anything. I was curious about the Q in the name of Godfrey Q Champagne and wondered if it could be Quinn.

Our enthusiasm had waned to the point of boredom when Johnny poked his head in the door. He announced excitedly that it was all coming together. Amma ran after him. We heard her ask him where Evan and Rainey were and then a door closing. We awaited her return.

"Well, that was strange. I asked him where Evan and Rain were and he said he was going to go get them. Aren't they in the basement? He grabbed three bottles of beer from the fridge, told me to wish them good luck, went out the door, jumped in the jeep and took off down the drive. What do you think is going on?"

"I'm guessing that they've found a way out." I answered. "We'll just have to wait and see."

"I imagine they'll be starving when they get back, so I guess we may as well start the vegetables cooking and assemble the salad." Amma suggested.

Mary joined us and asked if we had time for a game of cards. We did and spent the next half hours having a rousing game of Whist.

"Did you hear that?" Rosy asked as she got up and went into the hall. "Where do you think you're all sneaking off to?"

The three explorers were half way up the back steps. Evan said they were going up to shower as they were filthy and rather smelly as they had just come from the graveyard.

CHAPTER 10

THE TUNNELS

Finally we were going to hear what happened on the boy's decent into the tunnels. They sat down with us at the kitchen table and argued over who was going to do the talking. After a few minutes of this I couldn't keep quiet anymore.

"You're acting like school boys so I guess we will treat you as such. Fess up or go to your rooms without supper!"

They laughed.

"Okay Mum, got you. Rainey, you tell them about the first two tunnels." Evan suggested.

"First I will assure you that there is no entrance into the castle. There were three different tunnels; the one that led in a southerly direction was completely destroyed. We were met by a cave-in a minute or so upon entering. The ceiling had caved in completely obliterating any passage. The tunnel that would have led into the castle was bricked off.

I believe it was the other side of the one that was discovered years ago. It is impossible to even guess as to how long it has been impassable, but my guess would be two hundred years or more. Evan will describe the third tunnel." Rainey said nodding to him.

"First thing I want you to know," Evan smiled looking at Rosy, "is that we were never in any danger. The individuals who dug this tunnel and the others too I guess, were master excavators. Whether it was accomplished by the labor of many, or merely a handful of bodies, it would have taken a colossal amount of time. The floor was solid packed loam as were the walls and ceiling. Every six feet or so, the roof and walls were reinforced with timbers. Johnny believed they were either pine or elm. There were half a dozen niches cut into the walls along the way. If they had once held anything is just conjecture. However, one did and it may be of particular interest to you Vienna. I had taken Beth's little Polaroid camera and snapped a picture which Rain has."

My husband pulled the photo out of his pocket and gave it to me. Carved into a large jagged stone were the initials GD & Q 1683. He said he would have brought it back but it weighed 25 pounds so was too heavy to pack, and it was history so should have been left for perpetuity.

"The date corresponds with the receipt from Robert Bruce that deeds the Thistle property to Godfrey Q Champagne. I'm thinking that Q is Quinn and that he and Robert had some sort of alliance, and he and Gracie Darling had a romantic relationship and perhaps they were even married. What do you think?"

"It is what I have believed ever since I met Gracie in Avaleena's diary. Her character was way too strong to just be her hand maiden. She and Quinn were at the castle before Robert was born, so I think she must have known who they were because Stewart was an enemy of the Templars. That stone validates it doesn't it? I'm anxious to see what else you all discovered in that tunnel."

"Okay," Evan continued, "we could see that the tunnel went straight east for what we believed was the length of the grand reception room and the driveway before it veered off to a southerly direction. The tunnel was about five feet wide so comfortable for one person. We donned out helmets, turned on our flashlights and proceeded down the path single filed. The corridor to the south was only about ten feet long before it veered off to the east again. We followed it for what seemed like miles until we came to a dead end. There was nowhere to go but up. A rickety wooden ladder indicated that we should do so. Johnny volunteered to climb the seven foot high ladder. He came down saying there was a huge manhole like cover at the top that was unmovable from inside. He said he knew where we were, told us to sit down and take a breather and he'd be back to get us out in ten minutes. We had no idea where we were but he seemed to know. We asked him where he was going and he said to the graveyard."

"The graveyard!" Amma exclaimed. "You mean the tunnel went under the road and all the way across the village?"

"Not that graveyard Amma; the other one." Johnny said.

"You mean the forbidden one?"

"It's not exactly forbidden now is it? It is just posted as Private Property with No Admittance and Danger to Unstable Ground signs."

"Well, you should know as you posted them all and put up the barbed fence." Amma added.

"How come you did that Johnny?" Rosy asked.

"It was one of the first things your father had me do when I started work here so that was a long time ago. I think Haworth the village custodian may have erected new signage."

"I don't remember even seeing any signs there." Rosy mumbled.

"When were you there?" I asked her.

"I don't know exactly, maybe when I was eleven or so."

"Was Ava with you?"

"Of course; we were always together."

"I don't think that I would have okayed it."

"We wouldn't have told you Mom because you would have said it was too dangerous."

"It appears as though you and Ava were adventurers at an early age. I don't see what is so dangerous about a stroll through a cemetery though." Rainey said.

"It wasn't Dad. The only thing scary was Mr. Rochester. He caught us there one time and threatened to tell Jeremy. He knew who we were and called us by name. We never went back after that."

"So, you were there more than once? Do you suppose Colleen and Beth have visited also?" I asked curiously.

"I doubt that they even know about it, but if they ask I'll take them there."

"I think not my dear. It is not a place for children. I have to say that there is something about it that unnerved me, but I don't know why. Maybe because some of the names that have come across our table could be buried there and may have died in a violent way."

"Were Quinn and Gracie darling buried there?"

"I never saw their names Vienna, but that doesn't mean they weren't there as there are a lot of damaged and destroyed headstones. Work of the village youth years ago I assume. Did you ever visit it in your early days here?"

"No, I had my own mausoleum on my doorstep. Perhaps you can enlighten us as to how Johnny managed to free you and Rainey from the tunnel?"

"That's your cue John Boy."

"I hadn't thought about that graveyard for many a year and drove right by it. It wasn't until I got to the Thistle turn off that I realised that I had missed it. I turned around and drove back slowly to where I figured it was. There was no place to park so I had to put the jeep in the ditch. I got out and found my way through the trees and bushes to the gate."

"Excuse me a second, but how do you get off putting the jeep in the ditch and don't receive a scolding from Evan like I do?" I teased.

My son-in-law grinned. "Probably because Johnny won't require a tow truck like you do, and I never scold you. I do like the playacting on your part though."

Rainey asked me how many times I had ditched the jeep since I'd been here.

"Only once that we know of." Johnny chirped.

"Quit teasing my mother." Rosy said coming to my rescue. "Get on with it please Johnny."

"I figured that the tunnel would come out somewhere in the middle of the graveyard so I fanned out from there tapping the headstones with a wrench that I had the sense to bring. It took a few minutes before they answered me with a distinctive tinny rap. I imagined it was knocking on the cover with one of the helmets and I was right. Anyhow we made vocal contact and I set to work moving the stone behind the tombstone. It didn't budge and so I thought I'd have to get the jeep and winch it. I found a large solid tree branch thinking I might be able to pry it off. That landed me on my keester. I felt a hand reach down to help me up.

"Need a hand there John?" A raspy voice asked.

"It was Haworth, the watchman. I chat with him once or twice a month when I encounter him on his rounds around the mill. He asked me if I was trying to get into the tunnel or trying to get someone out. I told him that Evan and his father-in-law were down there and how did he know that there was a tunnel. He said that we could have that conversation another day, but if I wanted to gain entrance to it he would show me how. Apparently, I was at the wrong end of the slab. I followed his lead and started pulling all the moss that had accumulated on the backside of the tomb. He estimated that it had been growing for decades. He was probably right as it was black and foul smelling. Once it was sufficiently cleared we could see that there were two hinges on the slab that had been hidden by the moss. Haworth grunted and said. "So, it is so." I asked him what he meant. He said we should rescue my friends and as he had said before we may have a conversation another day. We pried the hinges open and slid the slab back. I saw Evan sticking his head up and when I turned around Haworth was gone."

I wondered if he was the keeper of some long forgotten code of the Templars. I voiced my idea and was met with various opinions. Johnny said he might just have that conversation with the watchman someday. I was most interested but Rainey burst my bubble and said that we were done with all the capers and that as soon as the girls had their tea party we were out of here.

"I agree." Evan stated. "It's been interesting and fun, but I say it's time to put the past to bed and leave the investigating to Detective Armand. We have a little work to do on concealing the opening of the tunnel and moving the Grandfather back to his stance, and we're done."

"How do you expect to do that?" Rosy wanted to know.

"I have no idea."

"One more question. Johnny, why did you go to all that trouble to get Evan and Dad out of the tunnel when they could just have walked out the way they went in?"

"We wouldn't have completed the mission then would we have?"

CHAPTER 11

LABOR DAY WEEKEND

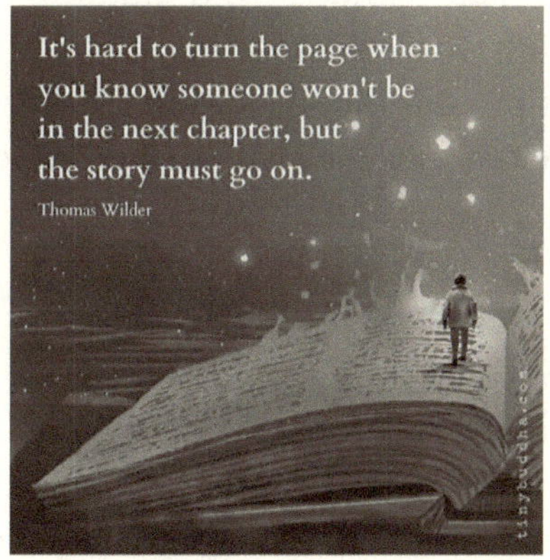

August 29th

Rainey and I collapsed in our chairs in the living room. He asked me if I thought Lili would settle in at the Palace, and were we finally done with her tantrums.

"I'd like to say that she's Rusty's problem now, but I fear she will always be our child to contend with, and whatever she wants I'm sure her Daddy will see that she gets it."

"Do you know what *I* need right now?"

"No, can't say that I do."

"I need my wife."

"Well, I am right here."

"Do you think you can muster up the energy to come see me?"

"I think I can." I said getting up and walking over to him. "Is this close enough?"

"I think not." He answered pulling me into his lap and kissing me. "Umm, that tastes like more. Do you want to make love or just fool around?"

"I think we could fool around and then make love my Lord."

"I like the way you think. Lead me on wench." He said taking my hand and leading me into the bedroom. "I want this to be a new start for us Vienna. Our life together has been anything but normal, and now that the castle's tribulations are behind us I say let's give normality a chance."

"I find it amusing that you think that we have seen the last of Avanloch and its past, and normality is not a word found in our dictionary, but it may be fun pretending that it does."

"First we have to put this bloody wedding Labor Day debacle behind us and then it will be fast forward my love, and "nevermore" will be done with us."

"From your lips to God's ears Darling."

3:30 a.m. August 29th 2003

"Did you hear that Rain?"

He didn't answer so I rolled over to nudge him. He wasn't in bed so he must have heard something too and went to investigate. I glanced at the clock. I turned on a lamp and found one of my dressing gowns on the floor. I put it on and opened the door into the hall. I stopped. I was upstairs and yet I knew I had gone to bed with Rainey in our downstairs bedroom. Had I been night prowling again? I would think about that later. The house was dark. I lit up the recessed lights in the stairs and made my way to the bedroom. I opened the door asking if he was in there.

He wasn't. I went back out towards the kitchen noticing that the basement door was open and the door to the porch where the dogs slept was closed. We never closed it as they were fine with just the gate latched. They were whining so I opened the door to pet them. They let out a yelp and headed for the French doors that opened onto the pool patio scratching at them. I figured that Rainey had gone out to the pool for a breath of air. I opened the doors and they took off in the opposite direction running around the corner of the house barking all the way to the road. This was most unusual behavior for them. They were trained to stop at the gate so I wasn't worried. There was no traffic up this way anyhow as the road dead- headed at Izzy's.

I went back in the house and called out for Rainey as I went downstairs. He was not down there, but I saw that the safe was open. I peered in seeing that it was empty. Curious.

"Mom, what are you doing, and why are the dogs out?" Zander asked from the top of the stairs.

"I can't find your dad."

Novia joined him. "What do you mean you can't find him?"

"I woke up after hearing a noise and he was gone. I'm going to get dressed and get the dogs before they wake Nash up."

"I'll get them; just give me a minute. Go stay with Mom Novie."

I flipped on the exterior lights. Five minutes later Nash was at the door asking what was wrong. I told him that Rainey had disappeared. He didn't seem to grasp what I was saying, so I explained in greater detail that Rainey wasn't in the house or the yard and the vehicles were all accounted for. He said that didn't sound like Rain. I agreed.

Ava arrived a few minutes later having met Zander in the front yard so knew her dad was missing. She asked me if I had tried to call him on his mobile.

"I didn't; I never even thought of it. What's wrong with me?"

"You're worried Mom, that's all. Here, I'll dial it."

I walked away from her as I heard ringing. I sat on the bed and answered Rainey's mobile. I called out to her that I had found it. She came in saying it was a long shot as she knew he didn't always carry it with him, or have it turned on. She said that Nash and Zander had gone to check out the barns and out buildings. She handed me her father's wallet and asked if anything was missing.

"His credit and bank cards are here and so is his ID, but he usually always has two or three hundred dollars so I guess he took the cash. He picked up my blouse and jeans off the floor last night and folded them and put them on that chair beside his things which are gone now. He was very amorous. Maybe that was his way of saying good-bye."

"Mom, that is just silly. Daddy adores you and you know it. He would never just leave. He was so restless when you went off to Scotland without him. Nash kept telling him to go but he said he didn't want to interfere with your holiday and he didn't blame you for wanting time away from him, and of course he couldn't abandon us at haying time. Soon as Evan said something fishy was going on at the castle, he was out of here like a lightning bolt. One thing I am sure of is that he did not leave here of his own volition!"

"I shouldn't have gone away without him. Maybe he is getting even with me and is off on a holiday without me."

"He would never do that Mom, plus he said he'd had enough of holidays to last a life time. He was very happy to be home. Is anything else missing?"

"No, except a wedding picture of us that he kept in his wallet."

Novia arrived at the door and said that Izzy was on the phone.

"What could she want at this time of the morning?"

"I don't know but she asked if Black was here?"

"Oh Lord," I said as Ava and I followed her into the kitchen, "don't let this be related." I picked up the phone. "What's wrong Izzy? No, what do you mean…okay. I think you had better come down here as Rainey is missing also. Do you have a car? Good, drive slowly."

"Is Black's truck gone?" Ava asked.

"No, she said that it's in the garage. Let's put on a pot of coffee as Nash will need it."

The back door opened and Sammie ushered a sleepy-eyed Calla in saying he was going to join his dad and Zander in the search to find Pappy. Calla said that he must have fallen down somewhere and couldn't get up. She said she hoped he hadn't broken a leg. Novia put her arm around her and suggested they go upstairs and go back to bed for a little while making me promise to wake them as soon as there was some news. I said I would. It was 5 a.m. I picked up the phone.

He answered on the second ring. I said, "Rainey's missing." He said he was on his way.

Izzy arrived confused and distraught. Ava explained about Rainey and asked her what she knew. She said that waking up and finding Black gone was surprising, but now that Rainey was also missing was frightening. Then she came up with the ridiculous idea that Rainey must have hijacked Black for an impromptu bachelor party. Ava said that was ludicrous. She had nothing more to add, grabbed a coffee and went outside to have a smoke. Jack and Sissy pulled in the drive meeting up with Nash and the boys whose search had proved futile. Zander and Sammie took the truck and were off to search down the road and all the roads around Hawthorne.

Jack had a few questions for Izzy and went to find her. He shook his head when he came back saying that she was scatter-brained. He and Nash left saying they were taking the jeep for an extensive search of the ranch and Izzy's place. The rest of us had nothing to do but sit and wait.

At 6 a.m. The boys returned with Jimmy whom they had found at his garage working on Black's truck. He comforted me and then took to the phone calling everyone he knew including Lara. She said that her and Coop would be here in half an hour. We decided not to call Rainey's parents yet. Rusty arrived for work. I sent him back to Bridge to get Lili. I feared she'd come up with some reason to blame me for her father's disappearance so the sooner I got it over with the better for everyone. Jack and Nash had no luck finding Rainey or any clues as to where he might have gone. They had searched every inch of the property including the line shack, the Shepherd's Hut, the hay storage barns, and every out building at Izzy's. Jack picked up the phone at 7:30.

"You gonna sleep all day Goose?"

"This better be damn news worthy Jennings or I'll have your hide!" The anonymous voice at the other end of the line threatened.

"Would a suspected kidnapping be of any interest to you?"

That was the first time anyone had said the kidnap word. I didn't like it at all.

"Not particularly, but who's the "suspected" victim?"

"Rainey Quinn." Jack answered grimly.

"You're screwing with me right?"

"Unfortunately I am not. He's been missing since sometime late last night and before you remind me about that archaic seventy four hour rule for a missing adult, you need to hear the circumstances first hand, so may I suggest you get your fat ass over here to the Quinn Ranch before the trail is further compromised. Over and out."

"Was that Sergeant Rolph that you talked so rudely to?" I asked.

"Don't worry Sis; Jack and he are bosom buddies since they ended up on the same baseball team. Believe me that was just a small banter as to what goes on between them." Sissy explained.

Jack chuckled. "He'll be here." He took my hand. "Now how about you and I take our coffee out on the back porch?"

"Go on Mom; we'll man the phones and bring you fresh coffee."

I went with Jack fulling knowing that he was going to question me about Izzy and Black. He let a cigarette for me. I told him that I had quit. He laughed.

"Tell me that you're not buying into this bachelor party crap that she's peddling?"

"I'm not because it is not something that Rainey would do for someone he doesn't even like. He only agreed to be Black's best man for Izzy's sake, but he was not happy doing so. I would rather believe that though over the idea that he's been kidnapped."

"The first thing Rolph will do will be to run a background check on Smith. It won't surprise me to learn that he is not who he says he is. You are taking this relatively well I must say. Are you on some magic drug?"

"I wish I was, but to tell you the truth I'm terrified. Neither of us had even unwound from our summer of strange events in Scotland and our European holiday, which believe me, was anything but a holiday thanks to Lili demanding to come with us with a two week old child. And, any minute she will be bursting in here blaming me for her father's disappearance."

"You try and stay calm and let me handle her."

As if on cue, the door opened and there she was. She threw her arms around me. "Oh Mommy, my sweet, sweet Mommy, I love you so much. Don't worry because I will look after you. We'll all look after her won't we Uncle Jack, and when Daddy gets back we'll forgive him for scaring us won't we?"

I imagined that Ava had a talk with her sister before allowing her to confront me. I told her I loved her too and that everything would be all right because her daddy would be home by dinner. We went into the kitchen and found Sissy and Jimmy making breakfast. Ava was holding JT. I relieved her of him and for the first time tears filled my eyes. Rainey loved him so much.

8:30 a.m.

Two police cars pulled into the drive. Nash and Jack went out to greet them. Ten minutes later Sergeant Rolph knocked on the door. Ava let him in. He thanked her, took his hat off and approached me.

"Mrs. Quinn, as always I am delighted to see you, but regret that it is under troubling circumstances. Hopefully, we will have the situation resolved quickly." He turned and spoke to Izzy. "I have just been informed that your fiancé is also missing Ms. Campion, so I will need to get some background information on Mr. Black. I will be obliged if you can assist me. Let's start with his description, occupation, and any other pertinent statistics you can think of…like family and former residences."

"Do you not remember meeting him on Canada Day in Bridge Sergeant?" Izzy asked.

"I talked to a lot of people that day so please refresh my memory. A photo would be helpful."

"I have one at home that I can get."

"I will send an officer if it is all right with you."

"Of course it is. I didn't lock the door in case he came back. The photo is of the two of us and is on the buffet in the dining room."

He thanked her, said he'd send Mr. Nash with the officer, spoke his orders into his communicator, and then asked me if we had a fax machine. I said we did and I escorted him into Rainey's office in the basement. I gave him the information and was about to leave when he asked me what I knew about Mr. Black.

"My family and I have been away on holiday for most of the summer, so I just met him a week ago. I basically know nothing about him. Rainey knows him better, but then, he isn't here…"

"I'm sorry that you are going through this Mrs. Quinn. I know we haven't seen much of each other over the years, but I think of you and Rainey often and have the utmost respect for him. Emotions are going to run in every direction and there will be speculation, so I am going to voice this so you are prepared for what may come. I know the answer, but I will ask it anyway. Is there any chance that the two of them have run off together?"

"You may call me Vienna, and you were right; you already knew the answer. A word of caution though; I wouldn't pose that question to your baseball buddy." I answered amusingly.

He laughed. "Thank-you for the warning and your candour Vienna. While I am waiting for the photo of Mr. Black I'll do an inquiry on him and see what pops up."

"You may consider Rainey's offices yours for as long as you need to and I'll try and keep everyone out of your hair."

"Thank-you, but that won't be necessary as I'll be chatting with everyone by days end. One never knows who holds a vital clue to the case until they are quizzed."

"I think I am remembering that Rainey told me that you had retired. I guess he was wrong."

"It's in the works, but no definite date yet."

Zander called out to me from the top of the stairs. "Mom, will you ask Sgt. Rolph a question for me?"

"Come on down Son, and you can ask it yourself." Rolph invited.

Zander was holding a paper bag. "I'm just wondering if you will be taking fingerprints of us and all the doors?"

"That is standard procedure Son. Sonia Carpenter, the area's fingerprint analyst is on her way from Potsdam and should be here before noon. She is excellent at her job and will not only be taking fingerprints, but footprints and palm prints also."

"How would you get Black's prints if he isn't here?"

"I'm thinking that you might have something for me in that bag?"

"The patio lock was broken and Black offered to fix it. He had to put a new one in and passed me the old one to put in the trash. I put it in this bag which came from the hardware store with the new one. I never did trash it."

"Was there a reason you didn't?"

"I forgot. Jack has doubts about Black's identity. He said his story is a crock of bull."

"Zander!" I scolded.

Rolph laughed. "That sounds like Jack. Did you tell him about what you had?"

"No, I just thought you might be interested. My prints will be on it too."

"No problem as we can rule yours out. So, let's see what you've got?"

Zander passed him the bag. He looked inside without extracting the lock and said that Ms. Carpenter would be able to get a good print from the surface. He thanked Zander for his insight just as Nash came down with the photo. Halfway up the stairs Zander turned back and told the Sergeant that he knew where there was a half smoked cigar of Black's if he needed to do a DNA.

By 12 noon everyone I knew and loved had arrived including Dr. Barb. I asked her if Ava had called her. She said no, Nash had. He had told her that Ava and I were not exhibiting the usual signs of anxiety and he was worried that we were both going to crash at once, and then there was Lili, so he wanted to be prepared if worst came to worst. I told her that so far there was no need to panic and that no news may be good news. I thanked her for coming. She left a little "something" if Ava and I needed something to help with anxiety and sleep.

Jimmy's wife June came and spent some time with me. Sissy and Lara went home with her to help with baking and preparation of meals to feed the crew here. Food was the last thing on my mind. Ava asked Novia and Calla if they would take Lili and JT down the hill to the farm house as it was too congested and noisy here. Amazingly, Lili agreed, but made me promise to call if I needed her, or if there was any news.

Sonia Carpenter arrived with her assistant Dale. Rolph consulted with them and then suggested we congregate in the living room while the experts did their thing in the kitchen and family rooms. Ava, Nash, Jack, Jimmy, Coop and Izzy and I joined the sergeant. I could tell by his body language that whatever he was going to tell us was not good. He looked directly at Izzy.

"I am sorry to inform you Ms. Campion that your fiancé is not whom you think he is. He has multiple identities; his registered birth name is Blackie Bruce Elliot."

I was sitting on one of the sofas between Jack and Jimmy. They were each holding one of my hands. I stiffened when I heard the name Elliot. Jack asked why it sounded familiar.

"It was Jorja's last name." I answered unemotionally.

"I'm sure it's a very common name Vienna, so it means nothing, right Lou?" Jack asked Rolph. It was the first time I'd heard the sergeant's first name. He was not agreeing with Jack.

"Don't say it, don't f…in say it!" Jack commanded.

"Sorry, but its's so. His siblings are listed as Jorja Jean, deceased, and Leslie Lavern, no info regarding status; deceased parents are Carl and Judy Elliot."

"The sister is dead." I said out loud.

"We have no evidence on that one way or the other Vienna."

"She's dead. It's obvious that Jorja convinced her twin sister into taking her place in prison and she's the one who was killed. Jorja lives and is making good on her promise to me."

Ava cried out. Nash suggested they take a break and go for a walk.

"I'm not going anywhere until Sergeant Rolph tells my mother that she's wrong!"

"There is no info stating that the sisters were twins Vienna. Furthermore, it is hardly likely that such a charade was carried out as the prison has the highest of security measures. You can attest to that can't you Jack?"

"I can, but I don't think that anything you or I say is going to convince Vienna that it was impossible for the two of them to switch places. I think a DNA test is advisable here."

"That may not prove anything as identical twins have a 95% genetic mutation, but fraternal twins can differ by 50%. It is most disturbing that such a thing could happen. I suppose the next step would be to contact the prison and the police force in Landsford and perhaps have her body exhumed. What was her promise to you Vienna?"

"She was cremated per my husband's instructions, so there is no body to exhume. She named him as her executor you know, and she promised me that she would never rest until she had Rainey back, and that she would move heaven and earth to do so."

"When was this?" Lou asked.

"When she tied me to a chair and held a knife to Zander's head. She said Zander was the only child that Rainey loved but the rest of my children were all disposable as was I."

Ava stood up and screamed. "I will kill that lying bitch with my own hands if I ever lay eyes on her!"

I walked over to her and took her in my arms. "I'm sorry my darling; I don't know why I said what I did. Of course she is not alive. Just hearing that she was Black's sister made me a little crazy. Knowing that they were cut from the same cloth is unnerving to say the least. I reacted badly and I apologise. Rainey loved all his children passionately; you know that Ava."

"I took no pleasure in divulging his lineage Vienna, but you needed to know." Lou apologised.

"I'm sure you didn't, but the facts are the facts and I am sure you have more to divulge about the man who deceived us all, and may have kidnapped Rainey, but we are forgetting what this revelation has done to Izzy. I'm so sorry my dear friend." I said tearfully as I embraced her.

"I am not shedding one tear over that con man, but I will cry a river for what he has done to you and your family. I only knew him for a few months, but you have had a lifetime loving the kindest man I have ever met, so I will swallow the bitter pill and see if I can shake anything from the tree of lies that he fed me that might put a light as to where he is holding up." Izzy vowed.

Jack asked if Rainey's disappearance was officially regarded as a kidnapping.

"Blackie's rap sheet lists many variable offences, but none are linked to any violence. He has spent some fifteen years conning unsuspected people out of their life savings. Most of his illegal ventures have involved pyramid schemes. They seem to attract those individuals who are looking for a quick get rich investment. He has spent a total of six years in prison for various convictions. I am not going to label this as a kidnapping just yet as our investigation is just beginning, but I fully expect that a ransom demand will be forthcoming so we will see what happens in the next few days. We'll be monitoring the land line and all your cells so a crew will show up in the next few hours to do the tapping. Although I suspect that Vienna will be the target, it's just possible that anyone of you may get the call, so let's be diligent friends. Vienna has graciously set me up in Rainey's office downstairs. My doors are always open."

There was a knock on the door just as we all sat down to the delicious fare that the girls had cooked. Nash opened the door and there stood Yates. He shook his head and said he didn't know what to say. I told him not to say anything but to get over and give me one of his bear hugs. He stopped at Ava first, hugged and kissed her.

"You know your Dad is like a brother to me, and you were almost my daughter in-law so I love you like my own."

"Just a minute there big boy…what's this about my wife?" Nash asked pretending ignorance regarding the short lived romance between Ava's and Yate's son, Cam.

"Ignore him Yates as he knows not what he says." Ava laughed.

"Yeah, I've found that out through the years. How are you my dear, dear forever friend? No answer expected." He embraced me like I was a China doll.

"Most all my family and friends are here, and now you've arrived, so the circle is almost complete, and when Rainey returns it will be all encompassing."

I hadn't meant to bring any tears to eyes, but apparently it didn't take much. Jimmy lightened the room by telling us that whenever June made lasagne Yates magically appeared at the door.

Sergeant Rolph was the lone officer left so we invited him to dine with us. He said he couldn't impose on our hospitality and humbly declined. However, Jack talked him into accepting the invitation. He left at eight p.m. saying he was still on full alert to any incoming information and would return in the morning. He had been an interesting dinner guest relating some of the most unusual and comical cases he had investigated. There was no mention of Jorja from anyone.

The rest of the gang departed a few hours later. I had insisted that Izzy spend the night. She accepted graciously. Nash and Jack had made sure that all the doors and windows were secure. In retrospect, Rainey and I should have done that last night.

Ava wanted to spend the night with me. I did not object as it was going be a sleepless night for both of us. I was hesitant for either of us to take the "help" that Dr. Barb had left on my night table. We were stripping the bed when something fell out and went clattering to the floor. Ava picked it up. It was Rainey's mobile.

"Oh, we forgot to have Daddy's phone bugged." She said.

"Maybe that's a good thing so let's keep it to ourselves. Put it on charge just in case."

"Just in case what Mom?"

"I don't know; it's just a hunch. I think I'll phone Clive Owen at Quinn Associates tomorrow."

"Do you think Daddy will get in touch with him if he can?"

"We have to be diligent and contact everyone your dad ever knew. First on that list are Morgan and Mason and Patsy and Paul."

"I'll head down to Bridge first thing tomorrow morning to tell Gram and Gramps."

"I'm going with you. Scan your dad's cell and see what contacts come up and then let's crawl into bed and find something on the telly to help us fall asleep."

"Okay, but first I have to make a call." She said dialing a number I knew all too well.

Rosalyn answered cheerfully. "Hey Sis, what's happening in Hawthorne?"

It was crying time again.

Day 2, August 30th

There was nothing to report except that this was supposed to be Izzy's wedding day.

Day 3, August 31st

Three old cronies of Blackie's had been found. Two were in jail and had been for three years. They had no idea what he had been up to since they had parted ways with him when he left them holding the bag in a bank robbery. The third was dead. The search for the sister and other associates continued. The phones were manned 24 hours a day. Why was there no ransom call? Why else would Rainey have been taken if it wasn't for money? Rumors ran wildly.

Day 4, September 1st: No news day.

Day 5, September 2nd: Rosy and Evan arrived. Evan demanded answers. There were none.

Day 6, September 3rd: Rolph arrived with an FBI friend from Spokane Washington. Kidnappings in Canada were out of their jurisdiction but they could offer assistance. Rainey's unusual disappearance was on their watch list, but they had nothing as of yet to report.

The days dragged on.

Day 10, September 7th

I had barely put my feet on the floor when the phone rang.

I picked it up and said hello. It was still ringing. It took me a second to realise that it was Rainey's phone ringing. I opened the drawer where I had stashed it.

"Rainey?" I answered hopefully.

"I wish it was Vienna, but it's Owen, and I have heard from him in a way."

"He's alive, oh thank God! Where is he?"

"That I don't know as he has asked for my help in what I believe is a ransom appeal."

"I need to record this Owen."

Ten minutes later I was dressed and in the kitchen to making coffee. It was 6:30 a.m. No one else was up. I called Ava, Jack and Jimmy, waited ten minutes, and then went upstairs to wake Evan and Rosy, and the kids. Of course they all thought that I must of heard from Rainey because I was so elated, but I kept mum because I wanted to wait until everyone arrived before I turned the recording on which I did the second Jack and Sissy arrived. I told them that Clive Owen was the one talking.

"I hope this will bring Rainey home Vienna. There was an envelope with my name on it in the overnight letter drop this morning. I don't usually go into the office so early, but I had awakened early and couldn't get back to sleep so I came in. I opened the envelope and extracted a hand written letter. It was a combination of printing and lettering that is used by architects and I recognised it as Rainey's unique style. I am reading it verbatim.

Owen, I need your help. This will be short and to the point. You may or may not have heard that I am missing. It's true and I have been instructed to pay my own ransom of two million dollars. My family cannot be involved and I beg of you not to involve the police as My life may depend on you keeping this just between you and me. I am asking that you and the associates will buy me out. I'm hoping that along with the sale of my shares it will be enough. Time is ticking as I have been given 48 hours to make this happen. This is not a joke Owen. Only you and I know my ID CODES. The funds are to be transferred to that account and forwarded to the address I am enclosing. Hoping, I remain your friend no matter. Rainey

"You will do no such thing Owen. There is no need to buy him out as the company is very important to him. I do not understand why his kidnapper didn't send me the ransom note as he knows the worth of the family and as you know, it is a hell of a lot more than two mill, but I suspect that this may just be a teaser as to what he really wants. Anyhow, I am paying what he has asked for. The funds will be in your hands within a few hours. I want and need to do this."

"I understand and thank you for removing this troublesome burden from me. Here is the info. you need and you can be assured I will not be contacting the police. I will be in touch with my bank and wait for your call when the transaction has been completed. My prayers are with you and your family and I await the news that Rain has made it home."

"I have the instructions written down so who wants to drive me to the bank?" I asked sweetly.

"Ava and I are going with you Mom. Can we please have a few minutes to celebrate?"

"Of course you can Rose, but the real celebration will be when your dad walks through that door unscathed and smiling."

There was no sleep for any of us. The funds had been transferred into the account that only Owen was privy to. There was nothing to do but wait.

September 8th, Day 11

It was a heartbreaking day as there was no word from Rainey.

September 12th, Day 15

We had to accept the facts and that he was not coming home. It was time for Rosy and Evan to go back home as their girls needed them, and it was time for Novia and Sammie to resume their studies at UBC.

Everyone else needed to carry on with their lives. Evan said that he and Rose wanted me to go home to Avanloch with them.

I was feeling very vulnerable. "I don't see how I could do that Evan."

Jack was sitting next to me. "I think that you should go Vienna."

I smiled. "Will you come with me Jack? You should come too Sissy, you and Ava. When was the last time you were home Ava?"

"I'd love to go Mom, but this is my home now and Nash and Calla need me."

"Sissy and I have to stay and look after things here Vienna." Jack said regrettably.

"And, I have to stay and look after my girls, and wait for Rainey." I avowed.

"And, we will all be here for you Mom." Ava promised.

September 14th, Day 17

The house was empty again except for Zander and Lili, Rusty and JT. I relinquished my bedroom upstairs to Lili and Rusty. There was no need for me to have two bedrooms anymore. I didn't sleep much anyway.

September 27th, Day 30

Jack and his son Jake, and a distinguished looking gent of about fifty showed up at the door. The man's name was Duke Spencer. He was a private investigator who worked out of Calgary Alberta. Jake was apprenticing with him as he had decided that was to be his vocation. They had come to offer their services in the search for Rainey. Duke was very familiar with the Vancouver area as he had once lived and worked there as a P.I. Ava hired them on the spot even though Duke insisted that it was pro-bono. She insisted upon paying expenses. I had no qualms as every exploration by the police force had come up blank.

Sergeant Rolph stopped by regularly and agreed that a P.I. might just turn something up as they weren't bound by the same rules as the force was.

October 14th Day 44

Jack found me outside on the back porch. It was 7 P.M. Yates and Izzy had just left. The two of them had become close. I was happy for them. Jack said he was worried about me.

"It's time you quit doing that."

"How can I when your daughter informed me that you get up every evening at eleven and go traipsing into the night?"

"Lili shouldn't be alarming you. It's not like I don a long black veil and walk the hills when the night winds wail and there certainly isn't a grave for me to visit. You are worrying about nothing Jack. I have always had a sleep disorder and it is just a little more intensified right now. It will sort itself out in time. Now let me walk you to your car as Sissy will be waiting for you."

October 29th 11 p.m. Day 59

I opened my eyes. Had I been dreaming? What was it I was trying to recall? It was unusual for me to have even fallen asleep before midnight. I closed my eyes and there it was plain as day.

She was mocking me. "I told you he loved me. You lose Vienna. He's mine for eternity." She turned her attention to a spirited steed rising out of the mist. On his back was a blue eyed dashing young man with a crooked smile. He was dressed all in black as was she. He rode towards her, picked her up, embraced her and they faded into the night. He'd gone over to the dark side. I knew not whether they were alive or dead, but I knew, I knew. They were together, but nobody would ever know but me. It was better they thought he was dead than know he was with her.

I picked up the phone. He answered on the first ring.

"I'm ready to come home now Evan."